COLOSSUS OF ARMS

MADELEINE LYCKA

Copyright © 2015. D. Madeleine Lycka.

All Rights Reserved.

1st Printing.

ISBN 978-0-9859758-4-5 (print edition)

For information: nightweavernovel@gmail.com

Darkest Queen Press, San Francisco

Many gracious thanks to Anne-Marie Corley, Melissa Corley, Dennis Lycka, and Kathy Badertscher.

Cover design by Carina B. Velasquez.
Editor, Alec Wagner.
Production assistance, Joe Crocenzi.

And my special thanks and love to Britta Seuren for all the indefinables. For everything.

:CONTENTS:

1, ARRIVAL

"**A**udio log: On day 735, we saw the Earth. At first notification, the planet was a small blue fleck, little more than a star. After a cycle, the planet had more than quadrupled in size, and it hung like a jewel on the crown of the sun, floating there, filled with muted colors of brownish-green and blue, appearing translucent with a powder blue outline. End log:" Jansee, the ship's flight engineer, was surprised by her uncharacteristically colorful language. She thought of deleting the log, but this wasn't the time to start being self-conscious. She decided to let it stand, for historical purposes. With some effort, she turned away from the ship's window. She needed to continue making progress on the long pre-arrival checklist, there were still so many things to do, but certainly she could spare a minute each day to report what she had seen.

"Audio log: By the third cycle, the planet was quite large, but most of it was eclipsed in black. We saw it as a down-turned crescent, a blue-and-white-swirled fingernail, and then the sun crested the horizon and sparked magnificent rays of sunlight in all directions like a spiky crown. Half a cycle later, we saw deep indigo waters and detailed flourishes of white clouds. None of us could sleep after seeing this. We were 24 hours from our planned arrival time. We'd been circling the Earth, staring at the flattened midnight blues of the ocean and the stacked, jagged-edged clouds that occasionally parted to reveal greens we had never seen before, as well as various shades of Earth — from the blond and red sands of the deserts to the black peaks of the Alps in Central Europe. End log:"

"Audio log: We've successfully entered the atmosphere. Within the hour, the ship will make a stop in an ancient quarry town, on a large peninsula that was once called Italy. We won't disembark or even land. We will extract and load a piece of marble for reasons that were not disclosed to us. End log:" Jansee straightened her uniform and made her way to the bridge, a circular room of adjustable tables with no chairs, where most of the numerous windows were darkened and being used to display various forms of live data.

Commander Torrance stood in the center of the room, her espresso brown skin in sharp contrast to the bright white of her uniform, her dark face set in concentration, two vertical lines between her squeezed eyebrows, her black hair twisted into pyramidal nubs that gave her head the look of an ornamented scepter. She greeted Jansee with intense eye contact and a nod, then said, "Pilot, confirm ship position is stable to continue with extraction plan."

Pilot Gantu answered, "Commander, position is locked and stable. Ready to proceed with next steps."

Once Jansee was standing at her station, Torrance said, "Isolate a 300,000 to 350,000 kilogram piece of the quarry wall."

Most of Jansee's black hair was buzzed short except for a few long strands that fell forward to frame each side of her face. She stood with her head hanging down, her chin nearly touching her chest as she studied the bank of monitors; her chocolate brown eyes, black in the purple light, darted from one screen to the next. She was wearing the same type of white uniform as the rest of the crew — a fitted, uncreasable one-piece that silhouetted her slender form. The monitors reflected a pattern of alternating blue and red grids onto her white face, making the soft, wide planes of her East Asian features look sharp and angular. Her pursed lips betrayed her concentration as she guided the laser-cutting operation with skilled hands that gripped the controllers on the console in front of her. "Switching to natural hand controls," she said, then with her right fingertip she drew four lines on the palm of her hand. "Execute."

The ship's laser made four successive cuts. The crew waited several seconds after the last cut, watching the smoke-like clouds of dust undulate upward. Then the massive piece of stone began to slide off of the rock face of the steep wall in slow motion, gaining speed as it slid six meters down the hill, crumbling the pointy bottom upon impact with the road before coming to rest in a pile of crushed smaller pieces and rock dust.

"Mass scan to get the true weight," the commander ordered.

"330,000 kilos, Commander. Eighteen percent over our rated cargo weight," Fazeef, Scientific Payload Commander, said in a flat baritone. Physically he was the same height as the women, and only slightly more muscular. As the only man in the crew, he felt he was under particular scrutiny. He felt the urge to add his opinion, that the rock was too big and presented too much of a risk, but those were not his decisions to make, so he kept quiet. He looked over at his twin sister, Gantu, and when she nodded, he knew that he had made the right decision to keep his opinion to himself.

"Acknowledged. But look at it — it's magnificent. We'll take the entire piece instead of cutting it again. We'll compensate during takeoff," Commander Torrance said.

The chalky white beauty now swung in the ship's cargo claw like a drop of milk about to drip from a tit. Derthan, Mission Specialist, watched the whole operation from her station, on full zzHD 3-D monitors, which exposed all the nuances in the rock and the defiant plants that somehow grew on this rocky earth; things she had never thought to dream of on Kepler-442B.

While Derthan observed the white and gray shades in the marble, she traced her fingertip along its darker veins on a monitor. The ship swayed up and down, and side to side, a nauseating state of flight called hover-slosh, a state of flexed acceleration that was the direct effect of three flight variables fluctuating violently. As the ship groaned and shimmied to one side, Derthan could hear Commander Torrance shouting across the bridge, "Stabilize! Sixty-five percent thrusters lower quadrant." The ship strained to slowly lift the precious cargo against the force of gravity that insisted the rock not be separated from its mother Earth.

"Vid log: So can I say takeoff was a little rough?" Jansee said as she winked into the vid cam closest to her.

"Jansee, stay focused," Derthan said. Since there were no security-related duties for her to attend to until they landed, she was free to comment and observe.

"The rock is cut and secured. And this *is* my way of being focused, I'm fully engaged in the mo…" Jansee said, her last word trampled by sounding alarms — a whooping note that bleated three times then faded before bleating again. Accompanying the whooping alarm were lime green LEDs that pulsed above doorways and along the floors leading to escape hatches. The monstrous rock was succeeding at pulling the ship back toward Earth.

"Full thrusters on all quadrants. Prepare for nitrous accelerators to fire on my command," Torrance said.

The nitrous accelerators were used primarily for unplanned, immediate escapes, but the ship wasn't escaping. The ship was sleek and understatedly powerful, the best in the fleet for long distances and planet-hopping, but she wasn't built to haul anything so weighty. The ship was struggling to gain altitude, huffing like a small tram full of pulverized Smithson rock coming out of a blasted terraforming site; it corkscrewed slightly, more widely at the nose, as it climbed a few hundred meters at a time.

"Steady now!" Commander Torrance barked. "One more nitrous release on... 3...2...1."

The ship sprang upward and Derthan felt the weight of her body pulled down into her feet. The titanium claw that held the stone groaned at a bass frequency that made her bones vibrate, then shifted to a drilling whine, beyond high-pitched. She clasped her hands over her ears during the painful few seconds of noise. She was ready to scream when the noise subsided. She checked the gauges on the fuel cells, nearly depleted, but once the ship gained another hundred meters of altitude, the intake processors would begin to cycle the nitrogen of the atmosphere into the system for replenishment. She knew they were successfully ascending. She leaned against her window trying to get the best view possible of the boot-shaped landmass surrounded by electric blue water as it extended down from the plump thigh of the European continent. The ship lurched to the right one last time, causing her head to knock against the glass. Derthan backed up two steps and rubbed her forehead, where already a small knot had risen. Rookie mistake.

"Ascent continues predictably. Altitude is 100 kilometers above sea level and climbing. Cargo is secure, Commander," Gantu said. She turned to look at her brother, Fazeef. His profile was lined in a brilliant yellow light that beamed in through the portside windows. Gantu made a purring sound in her throat, a sound they had used since childhood to call each other. When Fazeef turned to look at her, she noted the two tiny blazing yellow suns reflected on his black pupils. Fazeef smiled at her, then returned to watching his instrument panel. Gantu stood still and straight, her eyes patrolling the table of monitors in front of her, while her delicate hands rested on fingertips, a master pianist's graceful poise, ready for action. When her hands did move, they glided to adjust throttles, soothed accelerator dials and booster controls then always returned calmly back to the ready position.

Derthan looked out her station's window. She was fascinated by the golden, early summer light from the moment they spotted the green mountains of lower Europe. She wanted to live in that warming yellow light every day for the rest of her life. It filled a place in her that she hadn't known was empty, a revelation that she feared instantly, knowing something so simple as the color of light, a brief taste of the sun's increased proximity, might somehow affect the mission's objectives. The light faded quickly to a saturated navy blue as the ship climbed higher into the atmosphere. Changes to the light were dramatic at these speeds, as if a dimmer switch were being turned down.

"Increase speed to orbit velocity, and level out at 160 kilometers. I want this rock to be in free fall for this final haul," Commander Torrance said. For half a minute, no one spoke or moved, the low rumble of thrusters was the only sound, then the ship went silent too.

"All clear. Microgravity achieved. The rock is virtually floating," Gantu confirmed. Her voice was consummately female, middle range and clear with lower accents, every word enunciated crisply. The linguistic control of her tongue exemplified almost everything about her (and her twin brother Fazeef) — perfected Homo sapiens.

Derthan preferred to remain at her station on the far end of the bridge where she didn't have to look at Gantu and Fazeef, siblings of Egyptian descent, mirror images of each other. They stood on the bridge with a stillness that seeped from them into the immediate space around them. It didn't take much imagination to see them as reincarnations of Nefertiti and Ramses. Their general lack of conversation with the others shrouded them in mystery. Commander Torrance had seen their dossiers, picked them specifically for the mission due to their reputations as scientists, their keen observational skills and emotional intelligence, but that is all the crew knew about them. There were no other details. They were Immaculates — or e-macs in the short form — genetically lab perfected, sterile, and probably celibate (as most of their kind were). Their ancient beauty was unsettling. Looking at them or making direct eye contact made one feel so common, far inferior to the divine beauty and deep souls they seemed to possess.

"Set course for Republic of California, Trinity County, Weaverville," Commander Torrance said.

"Yes, Commander. Course set for coordinates 40.7367° N, 122.9361°W. And... under way," Gantu said, pointing her index finger and smoothly sliding it over the console to activate the command. "Beginning destination acquisition. Prepare for acceleration." Her voice echoed through the bridge, followed by a countdown from five by the ship's voice over the comms system.

"The rock continues to remain stabile," Fazeef added,

The ship's acceleration was notably intense, but smooth. "Speed approaching target of 28,000 kilometers per hour. Time to destination is 45 minutes," Gantu said.

"Commander, permission to leave the bridge?" Derthan asked.

Torrance turned her head sharply, focusing her intense stare on the junior crewwoman. Torrance's eyes were squinted and her lips slightly open as if she were about to say something, but had been interrupted.

Torrance looked angry, but the look could be interpreted as pure concentration, or annoyance at having been asked a question while focusing on something as important as a previously untested over-weighted takeoff. Derthan tried to reel in some of her created possibilities and just wait, as she held the commander's stare.

"Yes, dismissed," Torrance said.

Derthan could feel the eyes of the crew on her as she left, and confirmed it as she turned back to look. She wasn't sure why they all stared at her, but she guessed it came from the same apprehension that was building inside her, as their arrival on the new planet, after such a long journey, became imminent. She didn't think on it for too long. She wanted to shower and change before they arrived. A short walk to the end of the corridor, then a climb up an aluminum ladder to her quarters. Within minutes, every view was of water, infinite colors of dark blue, she knew Earth's second-largest ocean to be dipping and undulating as if it was being sloshed in a cup, but from this altitude it looked flat and calm, slightly textured like snake skin. Derthan had only seen videos of this much water. White caps flashed then died away back into the semi-flat blue expanse. When she blinked she saw blue. How could she choose personal hygiene over this blue splendor? Sometimes clouds overhead cast shadows, leaving blackened spots in their shapes on the water. Where the sun touched, with the right angle, the water looked silver, mesh-like, not round and smooth but metallic and stiff, a 3-D structure ready to be overlaid with some other material, not an undulating fluid of salted water. Derthan stared for another minute, but couldn't pull herself away, so she stripped her clothes off quickly where she stood, removed everything from hat to boots in under 15 seconds. She turned and sprinted toward the shower only to be flung sideways suddenly. She was weightless for four seconds as the ship lost altitude and an alarm sounded. As the ship stabilized, she landed on her hip, bounced twice as the rest of her body made full contact with the floor. She climbed to her feet and held onto the nearest railing, in case it happened again, but no other disturbances came. She showered with one hand, the other gripped a handle in the center of the shower wall, then dried herself the same way.

The remaining flight across the Atlantic Ocean was smooth. Beneath the ship, the water, which had looked so massive on the map was gone from sight in less than ten minutes, but still Derthan watched it from the comfort of her bunk as the sun torched the surfaces with oranges, and pinks, then the deepest indigoes before leaving the lands behind them in darkness. There was no time to sleep before they reached the East Coast of the United States, now called the United Northern Hemisphere since it had joined with Canada and Mexico to form a non-violent trading state that eliminated the pre-warming borders.

"Derthan, report to observation deck," the commander's voice came over the speaker above her bunk. Derthan sprung from her bed, slid down the rails of the ladder and jogged down the short corridor, picking up speed in the final corridor leading to the bridge, she vaulted herself using the handrails over the stairs to land with a gracefully light thud.

Torrance was known to go without sleep for up to 72 hours if the mission was sensitive enough, and since the crew had heard the first alert, 48 hours ago, of approaching final flight phase to Earth, she'd been awake. She rubbed her eyes as Derthan stood beside her. They looked down through the glass-paneled floor of the observation deck. Beneath them the treetops were a bulbous carpet still touched by daylight sun.

"Tell me what you see," the commander said, her voice low, rough from so much use after the long, silent journey.

When Derthan shared a new idea or experienced something exciting she could be manic, chattering so quickly her mouth could barely keep up with her mind. "Emerald, sage, lime, khaki, avocado, jade, olive, unripe bananas, the green highlights in your irises." Derthan tried to stop that last one, but it had already tumbled out of her mouth. She stared down at the trees below, wished she could recover the words she'd just spit out, hoped her gaffe would dissolve into the fascinating vision they were sharing.

"My eyes have no green highlights Derthan, they are brown," Commander Torrance said.

Derthan's worry was swept aside when she looked at Torrance and saw a tear running down her cheek. Derthan swallowed twice in a row, trying to keep down the lump of emotion in her throat. "We're home," Derthan said.

But she wasn't home. She'd never been on this planet.

2, DELIVERY

Inside the metal barn, the morning air was always ten degrees cooler, and stayed that way through the afternoon. Nix loved the cool and the quiet in equal measure. Here, she could lose herself in her work, not think about how her own heart had begun to resemble the cold stone around her, how her libido had been shut off like a welded faucet with the handle broken off.

Along the full length of one wall was a wooden workbench. The bench was meticulously arranged with Nix's tools: hundreds of rasps and files, pneumatic hammers, chisel sets, diamond-bladed ring saws, and some smaller diamond-tipped electric rotary tools. An overhead crane, once used to remove gas engines, was built into the steel framing of the building and had full horizontal range across the width of the building. Another hydraulic crane, its base a wheeled triangular frame with the profile of a hump-backed giant sat parked in a dark corner. The building was well ventilated by massive fans, big enough for a person to stand inside with arms upstretched or outstretched without touching the sides. The fans turned constantly and lazily. There were sliding doors on the east-facing side that hung on rollers from beams that crowned the building. The building with no permanent roof, functioned more like a hatchway in a boat — fitted with a stiff pull-back canvas that could be battened by two-by-sixes beneath the eves in the rainy season. Most often the roof was retracted to expose Nix's work area to the light of the naked sky. The years of sunlight left the interior surfaces faded and weathered, and Nix herself was no exception. Her face was a map of lines, the deep creases of a fair-skinned woman who had chosen to ignore the limitations of her skin and had paid the price with a browned, lived-in face that made her look older in years than she was.

Every tool was within reach, in a consistent, exact location on the long bench, laid out in an order that made sense only to her. She moved key tools closer to her work area as she moved through phases of a project. Anything she used less often – like vices and anvils that maintained other tools – was at the far end of the bench. This morning Nix would continue the finishing touches on the face and head of a figure of a woman who was bending to pick up a letter she had dropped on the floor while looking behind her at the same time. The image was some long lost memory that had surfaced from the flotsam of her unconscious and visited her dreams for two months before she finally gave in and started the work. For the past seven days, she had been sanding the stone, polishing it. The end of a project was always a relief, but messy. The air was thick with dust-fine white particles, and even with the mask covering her face, she could feel it in her eyes when she blinked, could taste it on her tongue or feel it as grit when she found herself grinding her teeth gently as she concentrated.

The days of her life were usually punctuated with the pounding metronome of the hammer hitting the chisel, but not for the past week. The never-ending hiss of the polishing sander was all that filled her ears, but today far off in the distance, behind the hissing sound she heard beating blades, the thud of a runner's heartbeat — a helicopter. The beastly thudding grew closer, interrupting her rhythm, since it pulsated faster than the sheeesh sheeesh of the sander.

"Fucking sons a bitches," she mumbled. Why would they be flying so close to her property? She did her best to ignore it and keep polishing — the more focused she could stay, the sooner she could be out of the mess of billowing, silty clouds. She shook her head and felt the grit between her teeth, she spit on the floor, then she pressed the sander hard against the stone, working the heavy machine with her shoulders, using her weight for leverage. When the earth shook beneath her, enough to sweep her away from the stone and nearly pull her to her knees, she dropped the heavy sander onto the floor and it spit up some concrete chips that clanged against one of the metal walls. Without her hand on the switch, the grinder slowed and stopped. She imagined a meteor had just landed in her yard. She stumbled outside to see what the sky had deigned to deliver.

Emerging from the metal barn, Nix put her right hand up to shade her eyes but hit the plastic shield of her facemask first, having forgotten that she was wearing the respirator mask. She pulled the mask up and off of her face, using it and her forearm to shield away the sunlight as she squinted against the midday bright blue summer sky. And then she saw the enormous piece of rock, shining and blinding as snow, taller by two stories than any of her outbuildings, embedded, though she couldn't tell how deeply, in her yard. She stepped closer, dropped her respirator mask to the ground. How could a gift like this fall from the sky? Maybe she was hallucinating. Hell, maybe she was dead. She just didn't know sometimes out here in the middle of nowhere. So what was this and what was it doing here? It had landed well, at least none of her other work was damaged, and she couldn't imagine a reason for how this — what appeared to be Carrera marble — could have gotten here. There was no skid trail. It looked like it had just fallen directly out of the sky and into her yard, ready to be carved. She pulled off her gloves and dropped them where she stood. She touched the stone with bare hands, smoothing her palms from side to side over it, tracing the blue-gray veins with her fingertips.

"Feels like Carrera. God damn, makes no sense," she said. Given over to stone lust, she continued to rub it with both hands; she hadn't felt anything this good in years. She flattened her palms against the stone — more precious to her than gold and more exciting to her than naked skin — a thing that in the post-warming seemed impossible to have come from the quarries of Carrera, Italy. She put her cheek against the stone and closed her eyes. "God, are you real?" Nix said. "I've waited for you, beautiful." She licked her lips then kissed the stone, the wetness releasing the stone's mineral aromas. "You even smell right."

Nix stood in the shadow of the great stone, and couldn't see what was perched at the edge of her yard. A great whooshing sound, a sound of released steam or pressurized gas came from somewhere near the forest. The pitch and force made Nix come around the side of the rock to look toward the trees. *What am I seeing?* The thing was impossible, such height, several stories higher than the rock, thin and sleek as a reed and looked like the hilt-less samurai sword of a titan, impossibly balanced on its tip. Nix stood stock-still. The polished silver skin was blinding when it caught the sun at the right angle, and yet it blended into the surroundings, almost invisible as it reflected everything around it. Looking at the sun reflected on the ship's skin, made green spots appear everywhere she looked. As she stared, a black rectangle appeared in the shiny silver skin at the point where the tip touched the ground, and beings, looking human in form, jumped out onto the ground. Each being looked first in her direction, though she wasn't sure that they saw her, then they looked back toward the opening, and another being would emerge. She counted five of them. They clapped their hands on each other's shoulders, and adjusted their glasses. They pulled their shoulders back, looked at each other one more time, nodded, then began to approach her.

Nix took a bottle of water from her cargo pants pocket and poured it over her face. She rubbed her eyes, poured more water until it felt like the dust was gone; but it changed nothing.

3, CONTACT

Torrance was the first to disembark from the ship. She watched as the rest of the crew jumped out, landed gracefully, then quickly stepped aside to allow the others to disembark. They smiled — big, beautiful smiles. They surveyed the area with some apprehension, though their monitors and scans had confirmed only one human and four large, non-carnivorous mammals in the immediate one-mile radius.

Jansee bent down onto one knee and ran her gloved hand over the grass, plucked some blades, then crushed them between her finger and thumb and inhaled the rich green aroma. "This feels like a memory to me..." she said, her words drifted off as Derthan landed, her boots crushing the grass down with a dull shush.

Derthan landed solidly and stepped to the side. She stood at attention, but shifted her weight from one leg to the other, as if she might just explode from the excitement that threatened to overtake her. Her head turned lightning fast from side to side, she was ready to get started with mission objectives, but everyone was taking their time, enjoying the moment as if they were Thomas Russell landing on Kepler-442B and claiming it for the future of humanity. Gantu landed next, stepped aside, then turned her face briefly up to the sun, and extended her hand toward her brother. Fazeef was the last to leap from the portal, going up several feet into the air before coming down with a heavy two-footed landing.

Once they were all out, Torrance said, "Sync up." They clasped each other's shoulders, making one connected circuit to calibrate their systems. All systems were functioning optimally. When they saw the confirmation readout on their retina screens, they patted each other's shoulders and arms in congratulations for their successful arrival. "Put your eye shields on; set to maximum darkness," Torrance said. They all removed wraparound eye shields from their suits, secured them and touched the side until the glasses tinted down to maximum darkness.

"Putting these glasses on is counterproductive," Derthan said. "Yes, it's part of protocol, but Earthians follow diurnal patterns. Their circadian systems are activated by a blue spectrum light of at least 1,000 lumens, the light on an overcast day, entering their retinas. The sky is blue, so we are well above the minimum activation level. We should forego the glasses and use the sun in the way the natives do to regulate our sleep patterns and adjust to a daylight pattern of activity while we're here."

"Agreed," Torrance said. "But we'll also follow protocol for the first 48 hours while we acclimate. Then we will discuss this topic again." *Have I made a mistake choosing such an impulsive security officer?* Torrance wondered, forcing a smile and looking each crewmember in the eyes as she straightened her jacket and her glasses, then set her shoulders back and inhaled so that her jacket would form nicely around her breasts. With the reassurance that all commanders have, she stepped forward first, striding confidently, then signaled with her raised left hand for them to follow in close formation.

The trees, majestic brown poles with feathery green branches, stood like sentinels around the perimeter of the yard. Tall, almost as tall as the ship, but alive and draped in shaggy green needles that were spaced so evenly that one was struck by the perfection nature could achieve. The wind made a hushed sound as it passed through the swaying needles, and all they could compare it to was someone whispering breathily into an ear. They walked a meter or two at a time, cautious and awestruck in equal measure. They made their way across the cleared area, their heads turned from side to side and up and down scanning the area, looking toward the trees on three sides, the mountains, the sky, and always the ground in front of them. Their retina screens displayed supplemental information in the form of pictures and text about what they were seeing — height and diameter of redwood trees, average size and bloom color of various flowers, species profiles of small insects, and models of what the weather might be like in the coming hours based on current readings and historical data.

"Mixture of five kinds of feral grass, low-profile weeds, scattered fallen branches and browned pine needles," Jansee said. "Ideally adapted. Low-water needs; wind resistant. Varied, yet noncompetitive species." After ten meters, Torrance stopped and bent over, rested with her hands on her knees. The air, so rich and moist, felt good but viscous as she inhaled, a little like having a wet cloth over her mouth and nose. She felt claustrophobic for a moment, but her training kicked in, and she stood up and focused on moving forward. This atmosphere was flooding her brain and affecting her vision and other senses.

As they continued toward the residence of one Nicole Tessitore, they weren't sure what they were seeing. The human form in the distance was white — the body, face, hair. Was it a ghost? As children they had heard tales of ghosts, shapes that were thinner than air, but there had never been a single sighting on Kepler-442B. There was conjecture as to why there were no ghosts on the new planet — no wars, not enough dead in the ground, few things to cause the type of trauma that led to "unrest." No one knew why.

Torrance spoke, her voice rang out then flattened against the open space, addressing the ghost woman as if she knew her: "Nix, you promised to finish the final piece in this series by December 2165, and told me to return then, to see if you had changed your mind about leaving Earth. Here I am."

Torrance increased her walking speed, feeling sure of her feet on the ground, her legs finally propelling her with the assured strength she expected from them. "I can't say I understand the significance of them being in a circle."

"Commander, these pieces are all confirmed to be created by the artist Nicole Tessitore, 22nd-century stone sculptor. The pieces to your left are considered highly refined in their technique, number three 'Chances,' number four 'Colossus of Arms,' and number five 'Touched' on your right are considered masterpieces," Fazeef said.

Torrance used her hand for extra shade against the magnified sunlight that reflected off the white stone sculptures and cut through the eye shield like a laser. She continued to walk toward Nix, studied the large stone sculptures that populated the open space as she continued to speak to Nix. "You know I've never had an eye for art, so I'll need to hear from your lips whether your work here is finished or not."

Nix had watched their approach, and petted the stone — one palm flat, fingertips pulling down toward her palm at regular intervals to get a little extra sensation before flattening out and sweeping sideways again — still marveling that it was somehow Italian marble. Then that voice, a rich timbre delivered with the cockiness and command of a military leader, that voice that she hadn't heard in so many years, but with the first notes the decades disappeared. Her hand ceased moving, and her palm forgot the stone and focused on nothing but holding her body upright as she started to collapse slowly from the inside, first the weakness in her legs that rose up through her core and up her shoulders to her neck. *It can't be. Not possible.* Every word from Torrance was an emotional hammer blow to her body. As her neck gave way, she leaned her head against the rock and struggled to hold her body upright with both arms. Still the voice continued, something about 'December 2165.' But Nix was sinking to her knees, the stone scraped her forehead a bit. *Indeed, 'never had an eye for art.'* The last thing she heard was 'your lips,' and it unbalanced her to the point that she fell backward onto the grass, saw the bright blue sky, and lost consciousness.

When Nix awoke, she was surrounded by six haloed faces, tall as trees, looking down at her. Who were they? Young faces. Some of them smiling. Brown people, except the one with delicately curved eyes. The face closest to her, the darkest, with hair cropped and knotted into quarter-inch high nubs on her head, looked familiar. Nix followed the contours of her face — cheekbones formed the widest part, which then narrowed to a round chin that was shadowed by the overly generous pout of lips. When closed, her full lips were as large as most people's open-mouthed smiles. She had puffy lids above almond-shaped eyes and black irises. Her right eyebrow sharply angled down, the left more rounded. *Torr*, Nix thought. The woman stared at Nix without blinking.

"She's conscious," a male voice said. The only male among them. He was kneeling on the grass beside her, holding her hand and passing a looped wand above her arm. As he stared at the device, she noticed his noble profile, a wide flat-bridged nose, a princely mouth — probably inherited from his mother — that dominated the bottom of his face and gave way to the rounded cleft butt of his finely proportioned chin. "Heart rate is 45 BPM, on the low side for an Earthian woman approximately 64 years of age, but she looks very fit, so that could explain it," he said.

Fifty-nine, Nix thought. *Their machines don't know everything.* Nix squinted to extract as many details as she could from the dark woman's face. The perfection of the nose, the center and two nostrils of exactly equal proportions. A round and slightly protruding forehead, her hairline back as far as her temple, looked as regal as the Duchess of

Urbino. Nix stopped. Her heart stopped, her breath. "Torrance?" Nix asked. Her body lightened with the recognition of her face, she was overtaken by ethereal bliss. She was sure the earth had dropped away, that her heart had not resumed beating, that she was…dead, and was in some version of an afterlife seeing Torrance, her long lost love.

Torrance said: "Yes, Nix. Breathe. You're going to be fine." Her voice sank into Nix, weighted her with gravity, and she felt the firm and cool ground materialize beneath her back and shoulders. She blinked her pale blue eyes, only a few shades of blue from being white, and from the collective gasp of the group, she knew that her eyes unsettled them. She scanned the unfamiliar faces around her — a female, maybe twin of the male, her beauty was stunning. Her cheekbones, rounded protrusions right beneath the corners of her eyes, were part of a delicately curved line that ran from her ear to her nostril. Aquiline nose, lush lips of equal size, and her perfectly rounded chin. Was it…Nefertiti? Her eyes wandered to the next, a sharp-faced woman, maybe Indian, with a hawkish nose, blue-green eyes that glowed against the bronzed copper of her face — *Kashmiri* whispered through Nix's mind. And the last had classic East Asian features — milk-white skin, cheekbones high and very wide, an extra curvature to her single eyelids, but unusually luscious lips that were pursed as she studied Nix. Her nose, wide at the bottom, tapered at the bridge to nearly nothing, her eyes were deep chocolate brown. Nix admired the length of her neck and noted a delicate inquisitiveness in the way she moved her head. By this time, the woman was smiling at her, revealing one dimple in the shape of an apostrophe sunk deep into her left cheek, near her jawline.

Nix looked at each face, noted individual details, but still wondered if she knew them. She wanted to look at Torrance again, her eyes were being pulled back to Torrance's face like the moon pulls the tides. She smiled when she saw Torrance's face — the familiar smile of perfect white teeth behind the rich darkness of her lips, her eyes two shades darker still. Just as beautiful as she remembered. Nix wanted to wrap her arms around her.

She had been on her back long enough. She rolled onto her side, pushed herself up, away from the clinging smell of soil and grass that made her think only of her own grave in that moment. She drew in a deep breath, then the ten hands of the visitors reached down and grabbed hold of her shoulders and upper arms and she was effortlessly whisked onto her feet before she could exhale. Once she was stable, the hands uniformly withdrew, like soldiers after folding a flag, and the visitors took two steps back in unison, forming a semi-circle around her. They were nearly the same height and build, all of them, even the one who looked clearly male. They were a sampling of several pre-warming races and very representative of specific classic features from certain geographical regions that had since dissolved.

Torrance stepped sideways so that she stood directly in front of Nix. "Our story was left incomplete. I'm here for a more satisfying ending than we had," Torrance said.

Nix didn't remember her being so eloquent, she had always been more physical than cerebral. But this could be one more thing on a list of many she didn't remember so well anymore. Looking at Torrance's eyes now, how could there be any doubt? Could her youthful appearance be attributed to the difference between her prior sickness and her now vibrant health? Ah, her Torrance. Nix extended her arm, aware and embarrassed of the slight trembling of her hand as she reached forward to touch Torrance's jaw.

Torrance didn't move except to lift her chin a little higher. She could see the fine dust that covered Nix's hand, and as Nix made contact with her face, Torrance could see that her eyes were filled with tears. "I'm here," Torrance said, closing her eyes and bringing her hand up to cover

Nix's hand. Then they hugged for a long time. Torrance could hear the pat-pat of teardrops falling onto the shoulder of her uniform, and she held Nix closer, put her hand on the back of her head and pulled her tight against her body.

Nix looked through her tears at the ship, parked with such precision, that she knew they were here intentionally. She had moved out here to get away, not be on anyone's chosen, or even accidental, path; to be alone with her precious stone, having chosen it over all else, to suffer in her self-constructed open tomb. When Nix finally let go and stepped back, Torrance was smiling at her, her intense eyes locked on Nix.

"Let me introduce my crew," Torrance said.

Nix wiped her eyes and nodded her head and said, "Yes, yes. Who have you brought with you?"

Torrance tilted her head toward the first woman in the semi-circle. "Jansee, ship's engineer. Excellent hands with a laser or anything mechanical. You can thank her for the generously sized rock before you." Jansee produced a curt smile that was enough to show the dimple on her left cheek again. She made brief eye contact with Nix, then bowed her head.

"Gantu, pilot and navigator. And her twin brother Fazeef, scientific payload commander." They made a small bow from the waist in unison. Nix wasn't sure which of them to look at, but she was transfixed for a moment by their sheer beauty, Ramses and Nefertiti incarnate, the colossal gods of the great temple of Ramses II, and carved hieroglyphic panels, standing before her. A logjam of possible poses tumbled through her mind into infinity. Torrance's voice roused her from the engulfing possibilities.

"Derthan. Mission Specialist, in charge of security. Like everyone on the crew, she also has certain scientific mission objectives," Torrance suppressed a smile.

Derthan had an inquisitive face. She smiled at Nix with a bit of mischief.

Security? They're all so young.

"I'm here for everything," Derthan said, a big smile lifted her cheeks up and squeezed her eyes to narrow slits. Torrance turned her head sharply and with one look Derthan dropped her smile. "It's not exactly a vacation," Torrance said in her direction.

"Welcome, all of you," Nix said. "First, thank you for this beautiful piece of stone." She stepped close to it again, her eyes roaming over the surface, then slapped it with her hand and said, "Damn, she's beautiful." She turned to Torrance. "Did you think you could just drop this here and I would leave it unfinished? Hell no, you know me better than that. I mean, god, look at it. Whiter than my thighs." Nix stepped back and gazed at the stone again. "This must mean you're staying for a while, right?"

Torrance smirked and nodded her head affirmatively.

"I'm sure you must've had a long journey," Nix said, putting her arm around Derthan's shoulder, "though *you* look fresh and ready for action." She turned her toward the house.

"739 days," Derthan said. Nix didn't react, she was moving toward the house, toward something that felt more real than the sudden miracles standing before her.

"Yes, but smell this air," Gantu said. "I would travel twice as far to smell air like this."

"It smells green," Jansee said.

"Are you inhaling this air without any conditioning?" Fazeef asked. He was looking out at the tree line. They could all see the image of the trees in one of the six small windows on their retinal screens, images of green on green as deep into the shadows as the integrated camera could go.

"Are you? You were instructed to wait," Torrance said.

"It's too intoxicating. Imagine air... air being intoxicating." Gantu laughed and threw her hands up above her head, her face pointed to the sky.

Torrance wanted to laugh, but she kept it inside. She took a few quick strides forward to catch up with Nix as she continued to direct Derthan toward her home.

"Really, drunk from the air?" Nix asked. "Wait until you try the stuff I've got in the back shed."

"It seems a ridiculous fact — our first hour on this planet and already we are intoxicated by the most basic element," Fazeef said.

"Not only that, but also, tired," Gantu said. "Limbs feel heavy and uncooperative."

"Your readings show normal oxygen saturation levels. Classic acclimation under way," Jansee said. "We've only been out of zero sleep for ten days. Unusual reactions in normal body operating conditions are expected, though this air may put us out of normal operating conditions."

"It's just air. We breathe nearly this same ratio of oxygen to nitrogen at home," Derthan said.

Fazeef ventured, "Maybe it is the Argon in the air here that makes the difference. Yes, it's an inert compound, but metaphysically, consider that you may be breathing the same breath of air that Cleopatra, or Mozart, or Gandhi had breathed."

"I think it's the addition of sunlight, increased gravitational force, and high humidity levels." Jansee said.

"Come on, keep up. We're going to the house," Torrance said. Jansee kept talking behind them, listing symptoms they should be wary of with some of her own thoughts thrown into the mix.

"You all must be hungry," Nix said. "Come inside and I'll make some food." She wanted to sit down at her kitchen table with some food and a drink, to ease all the wonder that had exploded in her yard — giant stone, spaceship, spacewomen. What amazing gifts had come to fill the Colossus' empty arms!

The front door wasn't locked. Nix turned the handle and walked inside. They followed her in and their eyes scanned everything, filled the video feeds with every corner of the room at once. Since there was no one on the ship to monitor incoming data, the vids would go directly into memory for later review. The ceiling was high and pointed with exposed beams every three feet. The dining table was fashioned from a wide redwood slab that still retained the tree's natural wavy edge and bark. Around the table were a motley set of wooden chairs, some simple yet elegant wooden forms, others made of antlers and horns. The wooden chairs looked smooth and blackened as if a thousand hands had touched those places. Deerskin and bearskin rugs hung on the walls, and thick-wooled buffalo skins were draped over a long couch in the adjoining room. Everything was crafted of natural materials with equal amounts of wood and stone, giving the house a rustic, but comfortable feel. Wood was minimally altered to fit a function. Stone, however, was manipulated to masterful purposes — it appeared soft as a chaise longue beside the far wall, flowing and curvaceous as the granite slab of countertop that dipped enough to hold water as a kitchen sink, and light in weight as carved feathers dangling from the antler chandelier. The crew had never associated these applications with stone. The adaptation and elevation of such a basic material was breathtaking to them. They came from a world of metals — steel, aluminum, titanium — refined plastics and advanced glass. Contained spaces and contained air.

"Are we allowed to touch everything?" Torrance asked on behalf of the crew.

"Yes, of course," Nix said. She moved toward the kitchen and started to take out food for dinner, answering their questions while they explored. As she washed some tomatoes in the sink, her mind began to drift. She stopped. *Was it dinnertime?* She had lost track of time, though she didn't really keep track of it on a normal day. As she plucked basil from a small pot on the windowsill, she looked out the west-facing kitchen window, and saw the sun hanging low on the horizon about to disappear into the treetops. Yes, it was dinnertime.

"Is this stone? Is that stone?" they kept asking. "Is *this* stone? Is *this*?" The colors perhaps confused them, there were so many. Nix answered 'yes' each time, and continued to prep and chop until they had touched and inquired about everything in the dining room and kitchen. She carried the plates she had prepared — tomatoes covered in basil leaves, and white disks of cheese she had made herself, then drizzled with black vinegar and olive oil. "Here, start with this," she said, setting down a stack of small plates and a heap of knives and forks.

After some wrangling, she had them all sitting at the table with her. Nix observed them more closely. They had implants under the skin of their forearms, barely raised, but something that they kept touching, pushing at with their fingertips. All but Torrance were very distracted as they sat, not paying any attention to the others. By Nix's standards, they were present but not at all engaged as they looked and pushed at their wrists, or wrote with a fingertip into their palms. Jansee didn't look at anyone; she was scanning the room as if she had single-handedly discovered and was exploring an ancient temple. She touched her temple several times and made comments about the way the local trees had been converted into this dwelling. She spoke at a normal volume as if no one else was present, "...hand-carved, no machine could be so subtle and gentle in respecting the organic shape of the original form." Nix took the first plate off the stack and served herself a portion of the tomatoes, then passed the plate to Gantu who sat to her right. "Take some and pass it," Nix said. Gantu took the dish and passed it to Derthan, who passed it to Fazeef, and so on. None of them had taken any of the food. As the plate arrived to Torrance, she said, "Apologies, Nix, but the crew is still under protocol and not allowed to eat local food for two cycles. But I will try some."

The crew looked distracted, some staring at various points in the room, some with heads tilted down as if reading a book that wasn't there, their teeth chattering as if they were freezing.

"What the hell are they doing?" Nix asked Torrance.

"They are reviewing Lifestream information. It's a networked communications system we are all connected through."

Nix replied, "They seem very unconnected right now, each off in their own world."

"Well, yes. It's like having your phone on all the time — live convos, messages, postings, data inquiries and retrieval, watching real-time vid of what others are seeing. We control and view information inside our eyes through an implanted interface on our retinas. Touch a temple to capture an image, a click of our teeth to pause or review a recording."

"Don't you feel tethered?" Nix stopped eating, though she was so hungry. The food wasn't having the comforting effect she had hoped for. Everywhere she looked she saw some strange behavior. "I mean, do you feel tethered or comforted by the hive-mind?" Nix asked. She focused her attention on Torrance and took another bite.

"We live on a sparsely populated planet, and our connection to others is critical to our survival. Lifestream is part of our society, but each user controls the degree of sharing. It's mostly used for communicating like Earthians use a phone or the Internet. It's also used for location tracking. On an expedition, protocol is to share everything at all times. There is a manual way to temporarily stop the live feed for private moments and actions, but it is temporary and the system will override the disruption within 30 minutes."

Torrance continued her delicate eating, cutting very small portions and placing them into her mouth, chewing the same number of times then swallowing. "We had time to get used to the constant connection during our training for the mission. We were wired into each other for six months prior to leaving. We were still civilians for part of that time, so it made for some embarrassing moments of over-sharing when people forgot that every minute of their lives was being broadcast and recorded. Having four people say simultaneously, 'Ooh, comms out, please!' at the same time taught us to be aware of what the system was doing and how we were going to be 'tethered,' as you call it, to one another. Operating the system is easy, the pupil is used to scroll, a blink is a click. The eye movements for this are obvious, since people tend to only blink on one side, but if info is just flowing and being read, no one would know since both eyes move side to side the same as when you are reading text." Torrance took another bite. "They look strange to you right now?"

"Yes. They are seeing and hearing our conversation through Lifestream instead of just turning and listening to us?"

"It's showing on the screen, but they could be looking at a hundred other things — they could be looking up the black liquid on this plate, or what the white disks are. I know they are cheese, but they have never had this type of food. The system can also display alerts onscreen with their physical statistics. I just got an alert about their blood-sugar levels dropping. They will need to eat soon."

And as if on queue, they each took two packets from their uniforms, poured water from one into the other, mixed them with something that looked like a spork, then began to eat the white paste.

"What are they eating?" Nix asked as politely as she could, but she could feel that her eyebrows and mouth had reflexively puckered at the sight of the paste. "You come here with every conceivable advance and you're eating paste with a spork?" Nix shook her head and laughed.

"This is a highly efficient utensil," Fazeef said. "It's lightweight, practically unbreakable, fits the shape of my mouth and works for a variety of textures. I rather like it."

"But it's a spork," Nix said. Laughing just as long as the first time she had said the word.

"Sorry, I'm not understanding your humor with this object," Fazeef said and held it up to study it seriously for a second.

Nix narrowed her eyes then held up a spoon and fork laid out on each side of her plate. "These two fine instruments produced an offspring called a spork. The thing you have in your hand is a spork."

"Twentieth-century technology?" Fazeef asked.

"Nineteenth-century actually," Jansee said, her eyes tracking from left to right as she read through two paragraphs on the history of the spork.

"Hmmm. It lacks the grace of your two instruments, but is measurably more practical," Fazeef said.

"You must be the art lover in the group," Nix said with sarcasm.

"There is a definite refined beauty to the fork and spoon," Fazeef said.

"Yes, but when you use something every day it's easy to lose your appreciation," Nix replied, looking down at the fork and spoon with new eyes. She tilted the fork, felt the weight of it, held it ready to use, brought the empty fork to her mouth. She looked around the table. The foreigners all sat straight. None rested against the back of their chairs, none leaned on elbows, or even used the arms of the chairs. They waited with sporks poised. Waited for her to start eating before they did. They ate with their sporks, from some kind of soft, silicone-like bowls that flexed slightly in their hands when they picked them up to drink the last of the white liquid.

She asked Torrance, "Why wouldn't they just ask me about the black liquid or the cheese?" Nix said. Her plate was empty, but she eyed the several pieces left on the larger plate.

"It's considered rude to ask such questions. The information is easily accessible, so they should find it themselves, be informed citizens. Ignorance is unacceptable in the new colony," Torrance said. The comment came off as unsympathetic. And the way Torrance delivered it showed a side of her that Nix didn't remember, a harsh authoritarianism that could be easily explained away by the living conditions on a planet Nix knew nothing about.

"Unfortunately ignorance has become more common here," Nix said. "The unpredictability of the weather makes it difficult to ever complete a full school year, even with the elimination of what was once known as 'the summer break.' We live day to day not knowing what the next day or week will bring us. Last year, a stranger came through. Ragged clothes, and dirty in a way that only living outside for weeks at a time can produce. He knocked on the door and Zephyr, ah god, I forgot…" Nix stood suddenly, shaking her head while she took the plates from the table and stacked them carefully on her arm to carry into the kitchen. "Zephyr's out travelling to the exchange to get some supplies. She'll be back in a couple of weeks and I'll introduce her." She dropped the plates a little too heavily into the sink and the clatter of porcelain and silverware made the visitors jump and look toward her — everyone except Torrance, who had already been watching Nix since she'd gotten up.

"Zephyr lives here with you as your only partner?" Torrance asked so cautiously and softly that Nix didn't hear the last few words of the question.

"Yes," Nix replied. She turned on the faucet to rinse the plates. She felt a twist in her stomach. She had been so taken with Torrance's return that she had not once in the course of the day's events thought of her partner of over 30 years.

Torrance walked into the kitchen. She gently took hold of Nix's forearm and pulled it toward her so that Nix would leave the dishwashing and turn to look at her. Nix rinsed her hands quickly, and dried them with a towel as she turned to face Torrance. They stared into each other's eyes for a long moment. Nix bit her bottom lip.

Torrance wasn't sure what that meant, some indicator of desiring a kiss, but not acting on it? She took note to review it later on playback. She said, "Thank you for your hospitality. The food you prepared was delicious, but the crew needs to return to the ship to eat and sleep." She opened her arms and they embraced.

Nix closed her eyes for a second, savoring the pleasure she felt in Torrance's embrace for as long as she could before Torrance released her and pulled away. She erased the emotion from her face before Torrance could see any of it, and replaced it with a cordial smile, "As you can see, it's dark outside, so time for me to get to bed, too. You've got the run of the place. Go have a look around building three." Nix yawned, then pulled her shoulders back and stood at her full height. "In the morning, you can find me working in the metal barn."

"But we…" Derthan started, but was silenced by a subtle wave of Torrance's hand.

"Goodnight," said Fazeef and Gantu in unison, followed a second behind by Jansee, then lastly Derthan in a voice sweeter than the others had ever heard come from her.

Torrance looked from one crewmember to the next. She motioned with her hand again and they all stood silently. She waved for them to follow, and they did, through the cavernous dining room, and out the front door. The sky had faded to a deep absolute black, and they turned toward the sky, looking at the mass of stars and planets above.

Torrance scanned the buildings, some lit with a single mercury light above the main doors, others dark silhouettes. The number three building was easy to spot, marked in white paint with a huge numeral 3. It was also the one farthest from the house. The grass was damp with dew as they crossed the open space in formation, one hand on their weapons, all eyes scanning the perimeter as their flashlights bobbed and cast beams of blue-white light like blind fingers over the land.

Opening the doors of building 3 was a little more challenging than they expected. The doors didn't readily slide open, but didn't appear to have any locking mechanism either. Torrance clenched the flashlight between her bent head and her shoulder to free up her hands. She felt the door handles and a wide plate that had several holes that could be keyholes or just empty holes that had once contained screws. She found a tiny raised knob, which she depressed and then tried to slide the doors again, but they would not move.

Gantu stepped forward, "Let me try," she said. While Torrance shined two lights on the door, the other three crewmembers stood with their backs to them, watching the open space. Gantu wrapped a long, majestic hand around each door handle, depressed the tiny knob with her right thumb and pulled the doors out toward her. As the doors began to swing open, she stepped back, and shone her light beyond the massive doors to the interior. Torrance entered first and found the light switch immediately, though the light only dimly illuminated the deep rectangular building that receded into darkness. Their beams swept the room from side to side, up and down. The room was full of miniature sculptures. They walked down the rows looking at each piece for a few seconds, or longer. Dust particles floated in their beams of light. Within the first few minutes, each of them had stopped, squatted to stare, reached a hand forward to touch a face or hand, or round belly of the tiny humans.

"You know Nix?" Derthan asked Torrance, but loud enough for the others to hear clearly.

"Yes, we have some shared history," Torrance said, bending to look at a clay figure that resembled her.

"Why didn't you disclose that to us prior to the mission?" Derthan pressed.

"No one on the crew asked." Torrance stood up straight and looked Derthan in the eye. "There are some personal matters I need to take care of with Nix. I have approval from mission command for these activities. None of them will affect mission objectives, you have my word on that, but they're something I can't rush, so it's possible that it could affect the length of time we're here," Torrance said.

"Don't be offended if I check in with you on this topic later," Derthan said.

"I won't," Torrance said.

4, THE BASICS

Torrance was awakened by an alarm she had set for ten minutes before sunrise. She would try the method Derthan had suggested to acclimate to this sun-driven planet by setting her circadian system with sunlight. In the faint blue light of her cabin, she struggled to open her eyes for the first nine minutes, then staggered out of bed in her sleeping top and shorts and walked to the window that faced directly east. She stood in front of the blackened glass window, rubbing her eyes as she watched the tiny hot star rising. When she saw the sun had fully crested the horizon, she activated the electrochromic window so that it became clear and allowed the sunlight to come through at full strength to slather her face and closed eyelids. The sun. Behind her closed eyes... tangerine! Glorious, glowing, sweet pure orange. Torrance savored the sensations; the vibrant orange light penetrated her eyes and face, producing a tingle of heat, and she felt herself being fused with the sun itself. The orange became a lemon yellow, followed by further dissolution in the center into irregular green shapes, then white. She opened her eyes and felt a slight vibration through her body, the molten energy of the sun inside her, as if her soul had just been freshly minted. She took a deep breath and raised her arms above her head. This must be what plants felt with the first kiss of sunlight each day. She couldn't feel the heat of it through the glass without reconfiguring the near-infrared frequency settings, so tomorrow she would try this again from outside the ship. "Wake 20 minutes before sunrise," she said. "Noted," replied the ship's computer.

She sat and recorded a vid log of the experience, then reviewed all of the ship's metrics for the past 24 hours, the crew's biometrics, and some of the small vids the crew made on their first night on Earth.

"This is what our planet looks like from here?!" asked Derthan. Her vid zoomed in on a cluster of stars then stayed fixed on the sky. Derthan said nothing more but the vid continued to record for a full ten minutes.

Torrance moved onto the next, this time Jansee's. "I've been sitting on the grass in the open space for over two hours. The barometric pressure has been falling since the sun set. Moisture from the air is settling onto the grass and me." The camera tilted down to her folded legs, her hand wiped at her thigh then turned to show the wetness on the palm of her hand. "All textbook, but fascinating." Torrance laughed a little at this. Seeing the crew so enamored with everything filled her heart with joy. She had chosen them well.

Her empty hands rested on the desk, and she stared out the portside window that curved slightly with the shape of the ship. She had been sitting, fully dressed and ready at her desk for over an hour. Her eyes slowly scanned the trees and hills beyond, absorbing details, colors, and topographical features as if she were studying the landing plan for a new planet. She wondered if she might be lucky enough to see an animal. Beyond the tree line were the softly curved tops of the Sierra Nevada mountains. If she squinted, the thick black line that ran along the ridgeline would sharpen, become prickly with pointed treetops sharp as spears. *Spears?* How did that ancient Earthian weapon even come into her head as a reference? An announcement from the ship's computer, in a disarmingly feminine voice, interrupted her thoughts. "Crew rendezvous at 0800. Ten-minute warning."

"Acknowledged," Torrance said. She forced her eyes away from the distant landscape and went to join the crew in the open space. They were talking among themselves in a circle. She had been watching them via the Lifestream feed as she approached.

"Look at this," Jansee said to the others, pulling a small square container from her pants pocket. She opened the container and produced a flattened, dried daisy. "This is considered an invasive weed, but it's beautiful. So hardy and... look at this shade of yellow. Like the sun itself."

"This is my first treasure," Gantu said. She pulled a broken piece of deer antler, about a finger's length long and white as bone, from the chest pocket of her uniform. "I felt the urge to keep it close to my heart."

"Mine is this beetle," Derthan said, opening her palm to reveal a black-shelled beetle already incased in a cube of Lucite. "This is *Polyphylla decemlineata*, a Ten-lined June Beetle. This is a summer beetle, male. Size range is 22 to 28 millimeters, so he is at the upper limit at 28mm. Thought to be extinct after the warming. A great indicator that things may be getting better here."

They saluted Torrance briefly. To an outsider it would have appeared as a quick casual wave, a flip up of the hand with palm facing the commanding officer.

Torrance stood with her shoulders back, and lifted her chin slightly before she spoke, "Today is the last day for glasses. Tomorrow initial entry protocol will be complete, and we will begin to embrace everything here — the sun, the air, the food. Protocol for the next two weeks requires extra vigilance around biological systems monitoring as we acclimate. The systems will alert on any abnormal readings, but if you see any abnormal behavior, please alert immediately." The crew nodded their understanding. "And no blackouts longer than five minutes for the next two weeks, we need to avoid fatalities at all cost."

Derthan added, "Today we will do a brief exploration of the immediate surrounding area, including the outbuildings, but nothing farther than the tree line. We need to know this area well before we broaden the observation area and begin collecting more samples. Understood?"

The crew nodded.

Torrance smiled and looked from face to face, "Let's get to work then."

Derthan led the way. They walked in close formation to the tree line closest to the ship. The trees were not as tall as they had once been, many of the tops damaged from high winds, and some amount of fire damage at the base marked nearly all of the few remaining older trees. Their eyes were hungry to see this place, their hearts full of excitement to experience the place their ancestors had come from, a rich land that had been paradise for so long, but was now rattled by erratic and uncertain weather patterns as the temperature continued to rise along with the water. They walked as a unit, each set of eyes scanning a different area for maximum coverage, their vids recording a comprehensive vision of the area they covered. They traced the full perimeter around the open grass area and when they arrived back at the ship, they turned their course to the metal barn to find Nix.

They didn't know to knock. The doors were open, so they walked in. The interior of the barn was filled with sunlight that flooded through the open east-facing doors. Their entrance created sharp elongated shadows along the floor, but Nix didn't stop working if she noticed them there. They stood for a few minutes watching her. She was hand-sanding, leaning and bending at strange angles against the piece. She had a wet towel in her left hand that she used to wipe the piece, then sanded for a few seconds before stepping back, looking from several angles and sanding again.

"Ah, yes!" Nix said, standing back and raising her arms above her head.

"Congratulations on finishing the piece," Fazeef said.

"Thank you, sir. This would have been finished yesterday had you not landed in my yard. But, all that aside, it is finished. I'll buff it out tomorrow and then it will be time to start on my next project. But I don't want to get too far ahead of myself. We need to celebrate this, this moment of completion. Let's go for a ride," Nix said. She tossed the wet rag at the small washbasin, and quickly unzipped and shrugged off her work suit.

"A ride of what kind?" Gantu asked, looking around the barn as if there might be something to ride waiting in the shadows.

Nix hung her suit on a nail on the wall beside the workbench. "Well, good question. There are plenty of things to ride around here…"— she looked at Torrance and winked — "but, to be more specific, and I can already tell I'll need to be better at that while you're here, I meant horse riding."

The crew looked at each other. Surprise on Derthan's face, fear on Jansee's, puzzlement on the twins', and a confident smile from Torrance as usual.

"Come on, let's go meet the horses." It was a short walk from the outbuilding to a single-level structure with a slanted metal roof. As soon as they turned the corner and could see the animals, Nix said, "There they are…my beauties."

To see a horse for the first time inspired awe in each of them.

One mare looked up as soon as Nix spoke, as if recognizing her voice, and made a low grumbling noise, four notes that came from low in the mare's chest; the other horses, with various lengths of hay protruding from their muzzles, looked in the direction of the approaching humans and continued to chew, but with ears forward at attention. The group of three mares and a gelding were standing near the feed bins slowly chewing on green hay that was studded with dried purple heads of clover. Every mare was a different color — a black-and-white pinto, black, and blue roan. The gelding was a palomino.

"That one has the pattern of a cow. Is it a cow?" Jansee asked.

"That coloring is called pinto. I can see what you mean about it looking like a cow's coloring. Pintos can be black and white, or brown and white. That mare, the one that looks black underneath but whiter near the surface, she's called blue roan — her pattern is pretty unusual."

"I've only seen vids of these animals," Gantu said. "Their musculature is magnificent; the glassy depth of their eyes makes me think they have feelings." She walked with hand extended toward the enclosure as if mesmerized. "Am I allowed to touch them? Do they bite?" she asked Nix.

"Yes you can touch them, just approach slowly. They need to be able to trust you, so no sudden movements. Go stand next to the fence, then extend your hand and they should come over," Nix said. She headed toward the tack room and came back with a saddle and blanket and placed it over the top rung of the metal gate. She walked back and got another as the crew made their way to the fence and extended their hands.

Nix talked as she carried out the third saddle and blanket, "They're between the ages of three and ten, a mellow bunch. They get along well with each other. We've had some wild horses come near the edges of the property and these guys look out for each other." Then she brought out the fourth saddle, "They're allowed to roam the larger acreage, and I don't see them much during the day, but they always return to be fed and watered every morning and evening."

Nix opened the gate and walked inside. "Please, come in. All of you need to know how to do this. This is our main form of transportation around here."

The visitors followed her inside and stood in a semi-circle around the side of the horse where Nix stood. Nix tossed the blanket and saddle onto the black mare's back. "Blanket first, if it's under the saddle when you put it on, it'll save you a step. Efficiency and confidence are important.

They can sense when you don't know what the hell you're doing, and they'll take advantage of your weaknesses if you let them."

Nix showed them how to tighten the girth strap, and gently kneed the mare's belly and pulled the strap again another few inches before cinching it. Nix grabbed the next saddle and blanket and the visitors followed her like a group of interns, some taking notes by writing into their palms. There weren't any questions, and Nix repeated the process identically each time.

"How can we control such large animals?" Jansee asked.

"Ah, excellent question, which brings us to the next step — bridles." Nix made her way out of the enclosure and went into the tack shed again. She emerged with headgear draped over her left arm. Nix held up one set of headgear and pointed as she spoke. "You'll have reins, the reins are attached to a bit in most cases, which sits in their mouths. Their mouths are generally tender, so using the reins will allow you to communicate with the horse. You won't be fully in control. They aren't machines. It's a relationship." Nix fitted the bit into the gelding's mouth first, then repeated the process with the mares, tossing the long leather reins onto the horses' necks, then looping the reins over the horns of the western saddles.

Jansee looked concerned. She remembered these animals from fairy tales her mothers had read to her, stories of queens and knights carried by these animals. During pre-mission training, she had watched vids of these animals running wild, naked, free of humans, through desert canyons. They would be impossible to control if they didn't want to be controlled. Day two, and she was facing her first dream come true and her first fear.

Nix could see that Jansee was a whiter shade of pale than usual. "You'll be fine, honey. I wouldn't do anything to put any of you in danger."

Jansee forced a smile that only lifted half of her mouth. "I'm ready for the challenge."

"Challenge? Hell, you are going to love this. You're going to wonder how your grandparents could leave behind such a magnificent animal," Nix said, laughing a bit to add levity to the insensitive comment she had just made in front of Torrance. Nix knew exactly the amount of pain and suffering the emigrants had gone through to leave such things behind, and why, all too well. "But since there are six of us, and only four horses, some of us will have to double up."

Torrance said, "Fazeef and Gantu, would you mind riding together? Jansee, you can ride with me this first time, until you get the feel for it. Today we are going to walk the property. I've got work to do, so you need to be able to venture off on your own," Nix said. She quickly finished harnessing the last horse, and helped the riders into the saddles, adjusted the stirrups and asked them to stand up so she could check their clearance from the seat.

The horses were fidgety, reactive, their ears twisting like small satellite dishes, their nostrils flaring, their huffs of breath a language used to offer their commentary. The gelding swung his head over to land gently against Nix's shoulder. He appeared to snuggle against her. As she rechecked all the cinches a second time, he pawed at the ground three times as if counting. "Yes, three horses joining us today," she said to the horse.

The crew looked at each other, confused and unsure whether it was possible for Nix to communicate with these animals or not. But they wanted to believe it.

Nix led the way out of the enclosure, and toward the edge of the woods. She watched the riders carefully, offering advice as they rode along — hold the reins lower, pull back then release to slow them, hold the reins out more to the left or right to steer the horse. The visitors caught on quickly, they were physically adaptable and students of knowledge. It appeared there was nothing they could not do. She pointed out the well behind the horse enclosure, "Pure mountain water that filters through the bedrock beneath and the taste touches the lips with the base, silk smell of calcium. Free samples when we get back," Nix said. They rode past each of the outbuildings, getting a brief description of each. The horses were skittish near the ship, leaning away from it, but sticking to the trail. "There's a creek runs past about quarter mile to the east, but that'll wait until another day." She finally turned and entered the trees. "That smell is balsam, pine needles dried in the sun. I love it. It's like butter and lying on the ground outside on a quiet sunny day alone."

The visitors weren't saying anything. Nix turned to look at them. Their faces were set in concentration, or completely absorbed in looking into the treetops, some of them smiling. Only the horses were relaxed. "Let them pick their way through. Trust them," she said as the horses wound their way through trees, and stepped carefully through the rock-strewn ground. There were no visible markers to them out here, the same type of tree as far as the eye could see, there was no visible trail, and they wondered at how Nix was picking her way through. ":Set Star Location System to local," Derthan said, not ready to put her full trust in Nix or the horses yet.

Nix led them to the second meadow through a distinct double ring of slim, youngish redwood trees, and emerged into a tall grass meadow that was lit brightly compared to the relative darkness inside the trees. The dappling pattern caused by the sunlight on the grassy area stopped Derthan. She pulled back on the reins to stop her horse and stared for a few moments before pointing a small device toward the center of the meadow. Nix didn't know what any of their gadgets did and she didn't care. She wished they would put all those things away and be in the moment. The day was beautiful, and if they were going to measure every step and document every weed, she would rather be working.

"The grass is different here," Jansee said.

"Yes, that's Dallis grass filling the meadow. It can be more beautiful than a woman's hair when it sways in a breeze. And in the shadier areas near the tree-line is rice cut-grass." It looked wider and softer, the upper few inches flopping over.

They stopped and dismounted. Nix tied up the horses. The meadow was still, quiet except for the hissing sound of their pant legs moving through the knee-high grass. There was no destination. Nix set a slow pace, her hands hanging at her sides, her fingertips touching the tops of the grass. The visitors followed silently. Nix felt like she was seeing through their eyes, seeing this place for the first time. She felt the weight of sacredness, the awe this place silently inspired.

As they approached the far edge of the meadow, they passed through another double ring of trees and followed a narrow well-worn trail to a small lake. The water was still, a blue so dark it was nearly black. "If you exit on the southwest side of this lake, there is a small trail that leads back to my house. I've seen mountain lions drink here, and deer markings on the trees," Nix said. She wanted them to know where they were — the beauty and the danger. They didn't appear to be armed, or have any visible weapons. She didn't want to think about it too much. She reminded herself they were only temporary. What a sick thought. Why was that coming into her mind? Because there was a difference between visitors and invaders, and knowing which they were would affect decisions on every level, subconscious and otherwise, wouldn't it? Then all of that patriotic bullshit was flushed from her mind by the true underlying motivation —

she couldn't go through the pain of losing Torrance a second time.

5, STRUCTURE

"**H**ave to repurpose one of these," Nix said as she waved her arm in the direction of the outbuildings. "Tear it down and rebuild a structure around this rock. I've done it before, but with six of us it will go much faster."

Gantu said, "Even if we ignited the ship, we couldn't lower the rock far enough into any of these buildings with the claw. We'd have to drop it through the ceiling."

Torrance started to pace, looking down at her feet. "No," she said, "we can't control the impact if we drop it. Even from 30 feet, the impact would knock all your tools from the tables, and the thrusters would cause some structural damage." She put her hand on her head, cupped the crown of her skull. The gesture, one Nix remembered so clearly, was such a classic Torrance gesture that Nix laughed.

Jansee said, "We don't have to move it or the structure. I can cut the stone from the ship. In half, thirds." She squinted her eyes and moved her head from side to side, tracing the cut marks with her eyes already.

"No, no, no. We aren't cutting this beauty. Back away, point your eyes somewhere else," Nix said. She walked over and stood between Jansee and the stone. "This is a once-in-a-lifetime piece. A gift from the gods." Her laughter burst forth, surprising her as much as the others, but then she let it flow with two smaller bursts. When she'd caught her breath, she repeated, "the gods," and tipped her head toward Gantu and Fazeef. "I mean, shit, look at them. They'd be worthy subjects for this rock, but Egypt beat me too it."

"Is it so obvious that we are descendants of Egypt?" Gantu asked.

"Your particular beauty... Christ, the spitting image of Nefertiti," Nix declared as if it was beyond obvious to anyone with eyes.

"I see," Gantu said. She looked at her retina monitor; small images of her face filled three of the five screens.

"And your brother... Ramses from the Temple of Thebes," Nix added. The screens switched over to images of Fazeef's face as heads turned to see what Nix saw in him.

"Haven't you seen the great monuments?" Nix asked.

"Pictures, yes. But..." Fazeef said, puzzled.

"Well then, don't be so modest. You're endowed with royal genetics," Nix said, as she absorbed the symmetry of his face for the first time. She shook her head after a second, afraid of being pulled any further in by the beauty of it. "Torrance, can you lend me your crew for five days? I know you've just landed, but it will be a great way to get your bodies back in shape for the rest of the mission." Nix slapped her hand flat against the stone. "Once we're done, I can start working on this beast and you'll have the run of the place."

"We'll discuss it tonight and let you know in the morning," Torrance said. She didn't want to force anyone off of mission objectives; working would have to be voluntary. But Nix had a good point, they could use some exercise. The horse riding and the short hike had made them sore, a sign that they were a long way from their standard fitness. If it would help Nix to finish her work sooner, everyone would benefit.

The five crew members arrived in the morning, ready to start. Nix gave them some of her work clothes, but she couldn't get them to part with their boots. The boots were made, no doubt, of something wondrous that functioned in every conceivable environment.

The first hour was a bit maddening; they had to be shown how to do everything. Nix walked from one to the next, adjusting their grip on hammers, crowbars, nail guns. Basic tools. She didn't understand how the new world could function, how space people could function, without such basic tools. But they were incredibly fast learners, and after Nix had showed them how to operate the tools they attacked the old building like hungry locusts and made quick work of stripping the long side boards. The shed had been reduced to a meter-high pile of boards by the middle of the day. Right as the sun reached high noon, the wind announced itself with a violent shaking of the trees. Clouds flowed in and overtook the sun, darkening the sky to near black.

"Take cover!" Nix yelled. "Leave your tools. Double time." The crew filed past Nix as she swayed from side to side in the powerful wind, her feet rooted to the ground, and she shoved each of their shoulders as they passed by her on their way toward the house. Raindrops bombarded the dried ground, bounced ten centimeters off the thirsty earth of the open space, which quickly became a muddy slick covered with matted, limp grass. For a moment, Nix froze as she looked up into the sky and felt the sting of drops pelt her face, gouge at her eyes and lips. It was the kind of torrent that could carve stone if it persisted long enough. She shook her head to clear the water from her eyes, swiped at her eyes with the back of her hand, but she could barely see.

She felt a hand take hold of hers and yank. The rain intensified, she wanted to stay and let it wear her down, to shred her skin and muscle down to bone, down to nothing. The hand pulled her with steady force toward the house. When she squinted in the direction of the hand she could see the silhouette of the human chain the visitors had formed. She took measured steps to keep her footing. The rain continued to rip at her shirt, the impact of it against her skin like children's fingers digging in and temporarily pitting her flesh. The thin tank top did nothing to protect her. At the last agonizing step, just as she reached the house, the rain stopped. She stood in place in the doorframe looking out, her arm outstretched and about to close the door. Not another drop fell. Rays of light pierced the dissipating clouds, illuminating patches of the ground with a glowing golden light. Nix stepped outside, "All clear. Let's get back to work." She turned, left the door open and rubbed her hands over her arms to warm them as she walked back to the building site.

Nix didn't hear any conversation or the closing of the door behind her. She imagined they were stunned by the sudden erratic weather. She felt deficient and slightly guilty in not warning them. She picked up the tools that lay abandoned on the muddy lawn, and dipped them into the three inches of rainwater that filled the bucket they'd been using for nails. The sun had refilled the sky and warmed her skin by the time she had rinsed the last hammer and started removing nails from the first board. The birds chirped raucously, with an intensity usually reserved for recounting the day's events and gossip as they settled into their nests at dusk.

As the crew arrived at the work site, Nix turned to them. "You look surprised. Really? With all your information access and mission prep?" Nix said.

"That is far beyond what we had knowledge of. How long has it been this way?" Fazeef asked.

"Five years at least," Nix said.

"The last mission was seven years ago. There were no reports of such rapid weather events recorded then," Jansee said.

"Everything has accelerated. Mother Nature has lost her patience, and she doesn't hold back anymore, she just lets her moods fly. Frankly, I'm surprised by your surprise," Nix said.

"Thanks, Nix. Surprised by our surprise. Does this mean you've taken us down from the throne you'd put us on?" Gantu asked.

"Hell, this is my everyday world, the norm. I apologize for not warning you sooner. I should have, but the days have just flown by in a blink since you've been here. Look, this just means we'll have to find shelter quickly when it happens next. You're capable of doing that."

"Some warning would be preferable," Derthan said.

"Sorry, sweetie, this is not the kind of thing you can plan for," Nix said.

"We have equipment on the ship, radar that can help with this. I'll make adjustments and set alarms in the Lifestream feed," Fazeef said.

"Dealing with the weather is part of the human experience. You just have to go with it," Nix said.

"And this feeling of my stomach being tensed?" Gantu asked. Her open palm was pressed flat against her stomach, massaging gently up and down.

"It's fear. That's a natural reaction to knowing something is trying to kill you, your warning system. Trust it." Nix handed out the tools. "Let's get back to work while the sky is clear."

The crew silently accepted the tools and completed the teardown by sunset.

Nix was impressed by how much was accomplished in one day, but the ability to destroy was something that every human carried inside from birth. Anyone could do it, even humans born on other planets. The harder part would be constructing a scaffolding that she could trust enough to work on for the next six months, with five inexperienced helpers.

Nix stayed up late drinking tea as she etched an architectural diagram of the structure onto a thin piece of deer hide. Paper was an expensive commodity, possible to make, but she didn't have much use for it anyway.

In her kitchen the next morning, she walked the visitors through the sketched plan, then with a small model she had made from wood splinters. The structure would encircle the rock. Every 15 feet, the planks would ramp upward to the next level. They studied the basic shape, traced it with their fingers and pointed, whispered to each other as Nix spoke. They had no questions or suggestions. They were silent, but nodded a lot as Nix explained her approach and the necessity of the design.

When the crew arrived the next morning, the boards were in several piles that were set on the cardinal direction points. Nix had marked each piece of wood from the torn down building with a letter and a number so that they would know how best to fit the pieces together. "Boards marked with the letter A are the boards for the first level, they are marked sequentially, and they'll form the foundation. I've brought some old fence posts that we'll drive three feet into the ground, then we'll construct the first platform using them as a base." After two hours the posts were set, everyone was sweating and breathing hard. The sky was clear and dominated by the hot sun. They didn't seem to have a slow speed. They went at everything full-bore, then rested and were ready to work again within 30 minutes. Nix was envious of their rapid recovery rate.

Nix brought water from the well, deeply cold, clear and tasting of minerals. She watched them as they drank, inconspicuously tucking small pills into their mouths before raising the cup to their lips, then not putting the cup down until the entire amount was swallowed. Nix wanted to be working more, but her supervision was critical until the first level was complete. She was meticulous about every detail: She demanded a close, but not too tight, fit of each corner piece; the proper number of nails; the addition of reused corner brackets for reinforcement in certain areas. The crew absorbed her instruction with ease and adapted their building skills as they moved forward. After the first level, she expected they would have acquired the necessary skills to finish the rest without any help from her.

The work was hard, and for the first time in months, the sky remained clear for seven days in a row. The visitors worked from sunrise to sunset. She watched them, their muscles becoming more pronounced with each passing day. Their backs never seemed to tire, they handed planks to each other, chucked them from the ground up each ascending level like they were tossing plates. Their physical gifts were far beyond what she had initially imagined. From the outside they looked so human, but they were obviously tuned on every level for optimal performance and adaptability. Each day the women wore less and less clothing, until the final day when they emerged from the ship in uniform shorts and shirts they had modified to resemble Nix's preferred outfit.

The next day, Nix sat for a while and watched them. She sat with her legs crossed as she sketched on a large pad of homemade gray paper with inch-long pieces of charcoal. She started with loose full-body poses, firing them onto the page with such rapidity that the butt of her hand smeared some of the lines. She flipped the page as soon as the sketch was done and started her next one. She didn't look down, her eyes latched onto her subjects while her hand moved on its own, naturally making correct proportions from years of experience. After creating iconic poses of their physical exertion, which thrilled her beyond anything she remembered in recent years, she began to sketch body parts. Fazeef had taken his jacket off and, after the first half hour of work, the musculature of his naked arms, chest and back seemed to have doubled. Nix sketched it and flipped to a new page. Derthan stopped, bent over to roll her shorts up even higher. Her exposed calves, high and as firm as apples, became a three-quarter view sketch from knee to foot. Gantu's flexed biceps and tensed forearms formed an L-shape as she horizontally held boards out in front of her — this sketch crowded the next page. Nix flipped to a new page — the T-shape of Fazeef's shoulders fit nicely within the borders of the page, as his hands held a board aloft. She hadn't had live models in years, and now, she watched them intently — the flexibility of human bodies, the coordination and communication, their teamwork, not much standing still, all motion, all shouts and hand-offs. Nails held in one hand like a bouquet of spiky wild flowers while thundering hammers efficiently pounded another nail into place with only five strokes. Mouths shouted orders she couldn't understand, or lips firmly pressed together in concentration.

After lunch, strong winds came and pushed their clothes tightly against their bodies as they struggled to stand, but this made for new textures — limbs tangled in sheets. Nix started to sketch again. Boards being tossed were caught by the wind, whipped upward as if to take flight in the sky, nearly swept from hands. Fazeef's straight, shoulder-length hair jumped vertically then fell, several times, but he didn't seem to notice. Jansee pushed at the longer pieces of her hair that swirled around her face like wispy reeds. Nix did her best to keep up with the cornucopia of action around her, so much of it that her mind sang with joy. She finally sketched their faces, one per page, large and majestic. Flared nostrils, lips in the shape of an O, eyebrows tilted up from the center like a bridge rising to make way for a passing ship — the moment of fingertips catching hold of a flying board hurtled from below. A bright spot of sunlight on a protruding cheekbone and the rich shadow in the hollow beneath, a herd of sweat beads on a forehead, one a bit larger and poised to drop, which Nix would later transfer into marble retaining the same translucence in stone. Her fingertips felt electric, as if they alone were marking the paper, but the charcoal rasped and hissed with each swift line. Quick short motions, then some longer curved lines up and looping away, like stroking a lover's thigh. Oh, there was a feeling of lightness inside her, warmth in the pit of her stomach, lightning and thunder at once. She could feel it radiating out, a crack in her hardened shell that trumpeted white light — the awakening of her sexuality after a long dormancy.

The next morning, as the sun crested the horizon, as the first light licked the boards at her feet, Nix walked the entire length of the scaffolding, slowly followed the inclining ramp as it rose ever higher toward the top of the stone. She felt the undersides of the joins with her fingers, leaned her weight onto her palms to test the sureness of the railings, bounced on the centers of the longer planks to test their stiffness. The structure was close to perfect. She could find nothing to criticize. Who were these people who so easily acquired knowledge and new skills?

When the visitors came to meet her at the foot of the scaffolding at their usual time, Nix was there waiting. Smiling she announced, "Job well-done. You are officially released from my service and can resume your intended mission."

6, THE VIRTUE OF WORK

Derthan reached above her head to catch the sliding piece of stone in her left hand. She curled her hand into a C-shaped mouth to clamp the marble's thin edge as it separated from the block. Her right hand, palm-up, waited beneath the sliding piece. Gravity pulled the falling piece forward and down, quickly it passed over her palm, until she took hold of the other end.

Nix was one level above on the scaffolding wielding a circular saw with a 20-inch diamond blade. She'd been hacking off large pieces for the better part of two hours, and Derthan assisted with disposal. Derthan's extended arms wavered as she lowered the piece onto the top of her head. She took three steps to the edge of the scaffolding and heaved the stone out and away. The discarded piece entered the ground with a wet thud, the sharp side pierced the earth and left the stone upright at a 45-degree angle. She hadn't realized how heavy the stone was until she was free if it, then her arms and shoulders felt lighter than air, as if they were floating upward for a few magical moments.

As the work continued into the afternoon, Derthan's muscles felt more liquid than solid. The bulky respirator over her mouth and nose seemed to keep the dust out of her lungs, but the clear plastic glasses provided little protection and her eyes felt irritated. She knew better than to rub them. She waited until Nix stopped to drink some water to run a diagnostic on herself. She was concerned that she wasn't adapting as quickly as the rest of the crew. She read the quick burst of scrolling information in real time. There was nothing unusual in her stats. Her stats were comparable to the rest of the crew. Of course they weren't working as hard as she was

– they'd started their mission objectives; scientific pursuits were not nearly so physical as working with Nix.

Nix shouted down at her, "You need a longer break?"

"Sorry, no, I'm fine. I'm ready," Derthan said. She clapped her hands together and smiled up at Nix.

Nix shook her head and turned back to the stone. She started the machine, the screeching sound of steel against stone sung through the air. Dark dust spun from the blade and formed a cloud that began to enclose her. The next cut piece emerged from the cloud and slammed onto the scaffolding near Derthan's feet. The impact was loud and shook the structure. She bent to pick it up. She was unable to get any leverage. She stood and pushed at it with the sole of her boot, but it barely moved. She took a few steps back and thought about how to approach it. Another piece dropped from the dusty haze above and smashed the stone at her feet into pieces.

"What the hell is going on down there?" Nix's voice came thundering from above. The angle grinder whirred to a stop. "You still there, Derthan?"

Derthan watched as Nix's boots, then legs descended the scaffolding. Derthan felt the urge to salute when Nix was finally facing her. "Again, I'm sorry. I wasn't keeping up with your pace."

"Yes, and nearly got yourself killed. I don't think you understand the danger inherent in this process. I can't be responsible for you getting hurt." Nix paced, brushed the small pieces of rock off the side with her boot.

"I'm fit to do this, Nix. I want to do this," Derthan said.

"Then do it. There is no half effort in stone. The unwanted pieces are weighty, not only must you be strong, but agile. You need forethought to move out of the work area if necessary." Nix would not release Derthan from direct eye contact.

"Yes. I'm committed to helping you complete your work."

"If you get injured or die, it's only going to slow things down. And it could be devastating to your mission. You need to be focused."

"I will. I fully understand," Derthan said as she nodded and continued to hold Nix's gaze.

"The 'roughing out' phase won't last forever, but we have a good couple weeks of work left. Are you up for that?"

"Yes, we'll finish this together," Derthan said.

"Alright then. Don't make me come down here again," Nix said as she climbed back to her cutting position on the upper level. She squatted and restarted the saw.

Derthan admired the well-defined muscles in her legs.

Nix was dressed in high-cut jean shorts, a tank top with no bra and leather work boots. She knelt down on one knee on the scaffolding. Her biceps flexed first as she hoisted the saw up, and as she thrust the machine into the face of the stone to cut at an awkward upward angle, she extended her arms, which raised the sizeable horseshoe-shaped muscles of her triceps. Horizontal fingers of muscle spread across her chest as her arms fought against the vibrations of the machine.

"Audio log: She's wiry and lean from years of doing this type of hard labor," Derthan said for her Lifestream. "She fearlessly uses primitive machinery: tractors, chains that can snap, and this archaic saw that looks to have a hundred ways to maim or kill its operator."

Nix called down from the scaffolding, "You'll need to keep your hand close to the bottom of this cut. Yes, there, a little to the left. I can only do this cut from above, and the blade will only be a few millimeters from your fingers in order for it to be effective." Nix revved the saw. "You can trust me."

Derthan kept her flattened hand against the stone close to the separation point. The beastly blade sprayed sparks as it sheared through the stone with ease. With each centimeter the blade descended, she imagined the saw not stopping and cutting her fingers off. Would the crew be able to reattach them before they became infected by the endless bacteria on every surface of this planet? Just then the stone started to slide as Nix pulled the saw dramatically upward. Derthan's reaction was beyond fast, as if she had sensed the stone's movement more than seen it. She caught the painfully thin edge of the stone against the middle joints of her fingers, wedged her fingertips into the separated space between the detached piece and the mother stone. She took hold of the wider horizontal edge further up and gracefully lowered it, keeping the stone close to her body, until she was in a squatting position and the stone rested on her knees. She let it slide down and rest on top of her boots. She took a few deep breaths then pulled the stone back against the tops of her knees. She grasped the bottom edge with both hands and stood up, kept the piece as horizontal as a table pressed into her stomach. At the edge of the scaffolding, she twisted at the waist, used her hips to throw the stone over like a discus. The piece shattered as it impacted the others below. The brutal clacking sound made Derthan flinch and cover her ears. A tiny piece of stone grazed her ear, then popped with a knock against the scaffolding board beneath her. "Hey, can't stone chips be dangerous?" Derthan yelled up at Nix.

Nix switched the saw off, and flipped her respirator up and off her nose and mouth, "Are you kidding me? You fly two years to some place you've never been, may never return home from, and you're worried about a stone chip?"

"Yes. For those reasons. I didn't risk my life to fly here to have some freak accident." She touched her ear, saw a drop of blood on her fingertip.

Nix set the machine down at her feet. "Really, why are you here? You sure as hell didn't come here to learn how to carve a type of stone you likely don't even have on your home planet, and I'm sure my advice wasn't on your list of great discoveries either." Nix took the handkerchief from her back pocket and wiped her face off. The mask kept her lungs safe, but there was plenty of other dust, and the trapped heat made her sweat, leaving vertical streaks of white dried sweat down the sides of her chin and neck. "Let's call it a day. We've been blessed by good weather for this long, let's not push our luck," Nix said.

Derthan was happy to be done. She walked slowly, her muscles already feeling the effects of the short but extreme workload. "Audio log: She wants to know why I would worry over such a small thing as a stone chip. It's the details, right?" She kicked at the grass as she walked, wondered what tiny world she might be affecting with such a thoughtless action. "This world is brutal and beautiful in equal measure. I can't even walk without harming something. What a depressing thought. Every inch is occupied by some life form struggling to live another day, to breathe another breath of this seductive air." She took several deep breaths as she walked, letting the nourishing air cycle through until she felt centered. Once inside her quarters, she collapsed onto the bed. She lay facedown for several minutes. With her left hand close to her face, she wiggled her fingers, watched the movement, mechanical and organic at once, a motion she had done thousands of times in her life, but had never really observed at this level. She turned her hand over, flexed her fingers, felt grateful they were still attached. She thought of everything her hands had done today — an array of subtle and complex motions that had been thoughtless to her, effortless, but had been so hard for robotics engineers to recreate. "Amazing me," she smiled to herself then fell asleep.

Torrance rallied the crew at 1900 hours to meet Nix for dinner in the open space. Derthan managed to wake up and shower in less than 15 minutes. She ran after them across the open space. They saw Nix from a distance, squatting, hunched over a small fire that wafted a long wide flag of blue smoke. She was stirring something. When they were closer, they studied her primitive cooking method — a fire pit, ablaze with orange flames that licked at three pots through a basic grate of iron rods.

"You act like you've never seen fire," Nix said. She watched as they moved to intentionally stand in the smoke, tilted their heads as they sniffed at the air, moved their hands through the smoke as if it was something they could touch.

"We've seen it in the lab and can describe the chemical process," said Fazeef.

But Nix could see from the looks on their faces that the lab experience was nothing compared to this textbook campfire.

Carved stone seats formed a small perimeter around the fire pit. The crew immediately touched the seats with their hands. "Smooth as skin," Torrance said, then when she sat, "slightly indented and surprisingly comfortable. Like it was made for me."

"Mine too," Gantu said.

"Um. Mine too," Jansee said. She laughed a little girl's disbelieving laugh.

"Then you have chosen wisely," Nix said. She laughed to herself, knowing the seats were identical, and lifted the lid off the second pot to stir. She checked to see that everyone was seated. "So the question for the day is, 'Why did you come here?' You can field that collectively or individually."

There was a long silence.

Torrance looked from one face to another, waited to see if anyone would share, but they all seemed transfixed by the fire, staring silently at the flames.

"Fire is so beautiful," Gantu said in a reverential whisper. "You may not know this, Nix, but we don't have fire on our planet due to the need for modulated oxygen levels in our interior living spaces." Then she shook her head, and her eyes regained focus to look at the faces around her, she spoke in her usual measured, perfect diction: "If my mother ever wanted anything, it was to come back to this place. With the stories she told me of her life before leaving — no divorce, genital mutilation, allowed beatings, no public movement without a male escort — I never really understood why she would want to come back." She kicked at something close to her toe, "Until now. Now that I am here, everything that she told me about — the magic of fire, the images seen in clouds, the smell of grass, the twinkling of stars — has become as enchanting to me as they were to her." She looked up at the sky. "Like all of you, I've been in the sky dome and seen clouds, and sniffed vials from the library containing the scent of grass. On some level I felt like the things my mother reminisced about were my own memories from having heard the stories so many times. I've always had an emotional connection to this place. But the reality is a bit overwhelming. The smells are hard to take. The physical sensation of grass on my bare feet, the animals, the texture of foods, the richness of wine."

Derthan reached over and rested her hand on Gantu's shoulder. Gantu continued, "Being here is her dream come true, breathing through my lungs, she lives again." As Gantu said this, a little breeze caused the fire to flare. The crew drew back, turned their shoulders and faces away from the suddenly lively fire. A second gust whipped through and nearly extinguished the flames.

Nix stood up, "Why are you turning away? The wind kicks up, you dig the hole deeper and set the fire lower." Nix stood up and walked to the nearest shed. She returned with a shovel. Nix's physical strength was evident in her digging. She attacked the earth with steady purpose and the smooth regular motions of one of her machines. "You spout facts all day, great to know so much about this place but book facts and stories are only icing — *not* the cake. I wonder if any of you have any common sense." Within minutes, a foot-deep hole with a flat bottom and circular rim was dug. As Nix chucked protesting coals into the new hole with her shovel they sprayed sparky air into the sky. When she was done, she stabbed the shovel into the earth leaving it standing upright. She knelt down, set new logs on end so that they formed a triangle above the coals. With a few directed breaths the coals glowed brightly and the new wood caught aflame. "That is your lesson for today," she said as she stood and snatched the shovel with one hand and walked back to the shed.

When Nix returned they looked up and smiled. She handed each of them a small, handmade wooden spoon — each slightly different in length, width and color. They studied the spoons, smelled them, turned them over in their hands to see the undersides, felt the smooth interior of the cupped end with their thumbs first, then finally put the spoons into their mouths. *Good thing I washed them*, she thought to herself.

"What are you making, Nix? Animal protein, possibly chicken?" Gantu asked, her eyes closed as she attempted to decipher the savory aroma of something that seemed familiar to her. "We have chickens back home. Not sure with their lab grown diets that they will taste like your chickens."

"My chickens will eat anything, best not to think about that too much. This pot is chicken cooked in red wine. The other is vegetable stew from things I foraged. I saw a lot of interesting ingredients when we took the horses out, so I went back to get them. In that respect I'm no better than the chickens, but I'm definitely choosier," Nix said. She filled each bowl with two ladles from the pot filled with simmering chicken, and passed the bowls out in order of rank, starting from the lowest.

Fazeef's brown hand dwarfed the bowl, his fingers extended two inches beyond the lip, like the tines of a wizard's staff grasping a crystal. He held the bowl just under his nose, which had a flat bridge as wide as a woman's finger. His flared nostrils were round as summer peas as he whiffed the curling steam that tumbled up against his closed eyes and forehead. His lips were pursed and still.

Nix said, "Those are your bowls and spoons for the duration of your visit. I made them myself with scraps of exotic wood traded to me. Take good care of them and there's no reason they won't make it all the way back home with you. That also means it's your job to wash them." Nix laughed, and noticed that they had all finished eating. "Time for the second course already?" She filled their bowls again, and watched as pleasure spread over their features with each bite of the complex vegetable stew. They were absorbed in eating when the fire cracked, popped like a gunshot. All of them flinched to some degree. They looked at each other and started to laugh, trying to regain the calm bliss they had before the surprise of the fire. When everyone had eaten their fill, Nix stacked the pans on the grass beside the fire-pit and poked at the flames with an iron rod, sending a waving sheet of sparks ascending into the sky before adding longer pieces of wood to the fire. The fire grew taller, more dramatic. There was silence and awe. All seemed content to recline and stare.

Derthan said, "Our parents spoke of this place, but very little. You put things together over the years. My father was very angry that I was coming. That I might not return after the sacrifices they had made for me. I swore to them I would come back."

"You're a good daughter," Nix said.

"I fell in love 120 cycles before we left. Bad timing some would say. She wasn't angry like my parents, but it was much harder to say goodbye to her. We've spent so little time together, and now such a long separation."

Nix said, "Do you expect she will wait for you until you return?"

"What do you mean by 'wait for me'?" Derthan said.

"Save herself for you, keep her heart and body pure until you return...wait for you. I can't say it any more plainly," Nix said.

Derthan's face was crunched up into a compact mask of confusion. Nix didn't say anything more. No one else talked. The silence stretched as they stared up at the stars. The twinkling stars looked alive, moving, dancing. Though the crew knew it was a trick of the atmosphere, it made it no less special.

Nix was comfortable with the silence. She closed her eyes and felt the night air settling on her face. It was heavy with moisture, still, pressing down on them. So different from earlier in the day when the northeasterly wind had brought a dry warmth that left her thirsty.

Jansee said, "Barometric drop of greater than 15 percent."

"No other alerts. Wind speed has been trending down since sunset," Fazeef added.

"Why couldn't Earthians stop when they were shown so many signs?" Jansee asked.

"Are you ready to get on your ship and take off right now because of the alert you just got? No. You're going to stay here and wait to see what happens. Think about how you are feeling right now, I'd say if you really concentrate you'll notice a feeling of unexplainable hope that things will be OK, that the next reading will be improved, and there won't be another alarm." Nix paused to pour some water from a ceramic jug. "Right? Am I right? *That* is being human. And I don't care if you were born here or not, you have the basics, even if the details are varied. Have you come all this way knowing so little of your ancestors, knowing so little of yourselves?" Nix asked.

"Knowing so little of ourselves? This mission is all we have thought about for years, this is the greatest sacrifice any of us could make for our home planet. We've spent years on education and field training, we've postponed reproduction and left behind mates for this mission," Derthan said.

"Reduce aggression in your tone, Derthan," Torrance growled.

Jansee rapidly followed behind Derthan's response. "The first ships left Earth 35 years ago. We are all 25 to 30 years old, we are all Nautians, no longer attached to a country or region of Earth like our parents were, but still we yearn for our ancestral planet. We speak the languages of Earth but have few social rituals in common. Did you know, when they left, they knew they weren't coming back? They sat on the ship and talked for over three years. They studied humanity from many angles, they had forums every night, listed out the good and bad of our species and changed many things. And when they landed they had architected an entirely new social order."

Gantu drank some water, then looked at the faces of the crew around the fire. "When we were born, no one practiced or spoke of Earth ways except as a former time period, like Victorian or pre-Christian times might be spoken of here — something that once existed but that modern society had moved far beyond."

Fazeef sat with his head lowered. When he spoke, his low voice resonated clearly for all to hear: "We haven't suffered the way the Firsts did. We have nothing to look back at and miss or regret. We've seen pics and vids of this place, but being born there," Fazeef pointed to the sky, then wondered to himself why, "we have known nothing else besides lab-grown food and pressurized interior living beneath organic diode lighting."

"Our food and environment have made us who we are. There is a lack of indulgence, of greed for possessions. Intelligence denotes social status," Gantu said.

"You can see, Nix, that I took the cream of the crop. The sharpest and bravest. This is an all-lesbian crew, except for Fazeef of course. That was a major deciding factor when I chose them," Torrance said.

"In your utopian society, why should that matter or even be any kind of signifier?" Nix asked. "Kinsey proved that sexual preference was a continuum, a scale that most people would fall in the middle of and be considered bisexual." She filled her water glass again, then extended her arm to fill the visitor's glasses.

Jansee said, "We are classified as non-monogamous. On Kepler-442B, monogamy is very rare. Love and sex are known to be separate. Sex can be casual, or for deeper bonding, so having an all-lesbian crew allows for as much bonding as desired. We don't have this expectation of love lasting forever. We stay together as long as it is good, then we tend to find that someone comes into our lives and we move on. There is no mythology of 'the one' in our culture. Life was too harsh at the beginning to foster such expectations. Our paradigm is not 'the one,' but 'the many,' although most of us experience this with one person at a time. They are rare who insist on lifelong monogamy with only one partner."

Gantu added, "How can anyone be hurt or disappointed by love, knowing there are others out there, that there are infinite possibilities for love? I've studied Earth culture for many years, so I know that jealousy and possessiveness are rampant here, though not ubiquitous. Jealousy encroaches on another person's autonomy, and it's looked at as shameful behavior, so nearly nonexistent for us."

Nix was momentarily paralyzed by that last statement. Having a download of an entire alien culture in a nutshell, followed by a philosophical bombshell that left no room for guilt, suspicion, jealousy or destiny. How could that even be possible? How different would her life have been from the beginning with such a radical shift from the fairy tale idea of "the one"? Her mind went through some of her most unpleasant situations — her breakup with Jessica after finding out that she had slept with her best friend… she had wanted to stay with her, but felt such an action meant Jessica wasn't "the one"; the guilt she had felt for years after having slept around in college without thinking how she was hurting each woman; of the fights with her lovers when she stayed out too late with a "friend"; of the many secret affairs, some discovered, others silently cutting up her insides as she led a double life, never letting on because she thought she was with "the one" — all of it would have been so different, but along with the bad came meeting Torrance and feeling that they were made for each other, that the universe had turned to bring them together. Their love was so deep and intense that they both knew that they would never be with another person for the rest of their lives. Did that mean that the foreigners would never have that feeling of destiny of meeting "the one"? The reworked situations were mini atom bombs in her head and produced the sensation of her head lifting off. She shook her head, tried to dislodge the transformed situations she had imagined, knowing that her life would have been so much richer without all that restriction and pain. It was too late to change any of it now. She held up the palm of her hand, wanting them to stop, for there to be silence. And they complied.

Nix lifted the jug slowly, the weight of it reminded her muscles of how hard she'd worked that day. She was comforted by the familiar smell of wet earth the jug emitted. She changed the subject back to something she had a firm understanding of: "I said 'knowing so little of your ancestors,' because I suspect the 'why' and 'from where' are not spoken of on your planet. Like your Earthian ancestors who migrated from one part of the globe to another, perhaps talking about the home and people that were left behind was too painful. But I can tell you why they left. Some were explorers; regardless of the conditions here they felt compelled to go and forge a new future. We've seen this behavior on Earth since people walked on two legs, it's inherent in who we are as a species. There was the simple fact that nothing was predictable anymore; we could have the four seasons in four weeks. Not everyone could handle that and there were suicides — it was just too much for some people to take. For others, including Torrance, the planet had become too toxic."

Nix looked at Torrance, the radiant glow of her skin, her regal cheekbones, the roundness of the bridge of her nose. She had a quick flash of an African Ndebele woman with rings stacked on her stretched neck. Thirty years later, and Torrance looked better than she had when she left. Nix inhaled sharply. She felt exuberant, her own youth rising to the surface in response. She smiled; wanted to keep the joyful feeling of seeing Torrance again to herself for as long as possible. She looked at each of their faces, the way the firelight sometimes distorted or highlighted a feature. They were all so different, beautiful in their own youthful way. Could Torrance have chosen a set of more interestingly featured subjects to bring with her?

Then Nix continued, "New environmental diseases and allergens were afflicting more and more people as the temperature increased. When the fish stocks collapsed, there was a domino effect across the globe, millions of people starved to death. Every nation on Earth poured resources into building space ships, into escaping. So the first ships left in 2130, and over the next ten years dozens and dozens of them left, taking most of the remaining population." Nix turned back to the cooking pots, grabbed handfuls of ash from the far edge of the fire pit and tossed them inside. She swirled her hand around and scraped out the ash, then rinsed the pots with a bit of water from the jug. She tossed the used water with a heaving pitch into the grass and left the pots turned over to drain. Nix turned toward the visitors, stretched her legs out straight in front of her, rested her hands on the tops of her thighs, her shoulders rolled forward. "Some of us stayed. I didn't have the imagination to conceive how I might live as an artist on a distant star. Zephyr was single-minded about staying and trying to fix things. She really started something. Many of the women who've moved to this area over the last 30 years are biologists, zoologists, and botanists. They've kept bee stocks, built bat habitats, raised the most endangered creatures in labs until they could survive again in the wild." Nix let out a heavy sigh, she felt a rush of the old doubt about her decision, but it was gone just as quickly. "So what are your plans?" Nix asked.

"We are here as scientists to collect samples and check on the health of the planet," Jansee said.

"And as adventurers," Fazeef said.

"Casanovas come to conquer another planet. What woman could resist us?" Derthan asked. Laughter spread through the crew.

"Do you like what you've experienced so far?" Nix asked, looking down at her own legs, thin and muscular, but the skin bunched up in an ugly way around her kneecaps. Old-lady knees.

Derthan put her arm over Torrance's shoulder and nuzzled her head against her shoulder. "Yes, very much."

Torrance elbowed Derthan in the ribs, nearly knocking her off her seat. Derthan sprung back to vertical like a weighted target at a county fair, but did not put her arm on Torrance again.

Jansee said, "Though we were trained, and thought of our imaginations as quite extravagant, nothing prepared us for the diversity of life, of textures…even the colors of the sky and sunlight seem endlessly varied."

"You are so right. How arrogant we were," Gantu said. Golden glinting rivers of tears ran silently down each side of her face.

"Come on, honey, no need for tears," Nix said. Seeing Gantu cry made an uncomfortable lump swell in her throat. She had never seen anyone look so thankful and humbled.

"New subject…" Torrance said. "Report your initial ship inspection."

Nix found Torrance's shift of subject jarring. From tears to technical reporting was a long stretch, but the crew pivoted without the slightest hesitation.

Jansee sat up straight, perhaps reading from her screen. "Sector B5 looks pristine, even with the atmospheric entry heat. All windows and ports have minor amounts of micro-meteorite pitting, but nothing outside predicted tolerance. A true genius designed that glass. End report." Jansee winked at Nix.

"Do you have to take credit *every* time you talk about it?" Derthan said, rolling her eyes like a teenager. "The phyto-platinum skin is in very good condition, no remaining evidence of minor nicks or chips from micro asteroids and space detritus. The skin is repairing itself as expected. End report," Derthan said.

"We lost three of the shields on the quad-8 thrusters, but as you know, commander, they're meant to be expendable. I will fabricate new ones in time for our departure. Add reminder: follow-up report when fabrication is complete. End report," Fazeef said.

Nix reached into the flames without any apparent discomfort to add more wood to the fire. She sat back again to listen to them, their perfect English. Who would have predicted that the bastard language that had absorbed so many pieces of German and other early languages, then threw out rules that would have made it easy to learn, would spread on the wings of colonialism and become the international language of commerce, flight and even space. As Nix was contemplating that thought, Jansee cried out, "Can you believe we crossed the flux!"

The crew all came alive with this statement, leaned forward and was suddenly engaged. Derthan said, "I remember fairy tales about it from my youth. A magical place, space thinned almost to nothing, others said it was a nursery for stars, no one really knows, but when the Firsts crossed it, they reported feeling ten years younger, though it wasn't a fountain of youth, since none of them looked any different."

Jansee could barely contain her excitement, "Nix, we actually made a point to come out of zero sleep just to observe this phenomena. And it was so worth it. It's the most spectacular, bizarre place. I was so energized, so awake, like I would never need to sleep again."

Torrance said, "For me, there was a feeling of non-movement, though the ship was moving at the usual speed through that area. I was in a state of confusion. I didn't know how much time had passed. I remember wondering if we had already been to Earth and were returning, if I had already made the trip. I had to keep checking the monitors to confirm our location and route. Thankfully the instruments were not affected."

"I remember looking out the main windows on the bridge, and space was not black, but opaque, deep purple, overlaid with stretched yellow clouds...like vomit, which made me want to vomit," Derthan said.

"Space vomit. Is that from the fairy tale your mother read to you?" Fazeef said. The crew erupted in laughter. He continued, "I stayed in bed, staring out the windows of my chamber, feeling like I was in the gray matter of the universe itself. I had a strange hallucination. I looked down at my legs and I had four, not two. When I reached down with my hands I could feel four legs. I was too disturbed to get up and try to walk, so I stayed still. I listened to Bach and meditated, until I cleared that image from my mind."

"Now *that* sounds like the makings of a fairy tale," Jansee said.

Nix couldn't visualize the place. They had lost her completely. Time for her to go to bed.

7, ALL WORK AND NO PLAY

The next day the crew, except for Torrance, began their planned schedule of collecting samples — plants, water, soil, air. Torrance worked beside Nix, provided tools as Nix asked for them, kept the scaffolding clean of debris. Nix had shifted to a pneumatic angle grinder with a five-inch blade. No longer hacking and slashing large pieces, the stone had a rough shape, though no one but Nix knew what it was or might become. She was cutting in a much smaller capacity, plate-sized pieces that she could send off the platform with a kick, or just ignore. Torrance stood close to her, watched every move Nix made, studied her.

When Nix took a break, Torrance had a cup of water waiting as soon as Nix lifted the mask from her face. Torrance could see that Nix was lost in her thoughts as she continued to stare at the area she had just cut without turning to look at her.

"Here," Torrance said. She held the cup out. Nix clumsily reached for the cup, circled it with her blind fingers and nearly knocked it out of Torrance's hand before finally taking hold of it.

"Thank you," Nix said, without giving Torrance any more of her attention than her reply. Nix stared at the rock with squinted eyes. She held the water without drinking any. After a minute, she turned her head and looked out at the visitors, who were scattered across the open space. She lifted the cup to her lips and drank the water in a series of swallows. They had hardly moved from the places they were in three hours ago when she started working. They appeared to be talking to themselves, and barely moved except to exchange filled containers for empties from their packs. Nix handed the empty tin cup to Torrance and pulled the mask over her face, picked up the saw and started to work.

A week of working closely with Torrance had passed. Nix had cauterized her feelings for Torrance many years ago, and time had completed the deadening of those feelings. She'd been glad when, years later, she realized they were gone. She wanted them to stay gone. These days Torrance was her shadow, there at every break, her face near and smiling whenever Nix looked at her. Her voice was smooth as water, but with none of the nasal timbre and East-Coast accented vowels that Nix remembered. Her intense reaction to Torrance's voice had subsided over the weeks, but it still had some effect on her; it stayed and nested in her chest, coiled warmly around her heart and lungs. Whenever these feelings flared, Nix turned to the rock and sliced faster, pressed the machine into the rock as hard as she dared without damaging either. This was the only way she knew to drown out her feelings, because she couldn't bring herself to tell Torrance to be quiet, to go away, to leave, to let her be.

This morning, Nix was awake before sunrise. She opened her eyes to find the room still dim in the predawn light. Her mind filled with unsolicited thoughts of Torrance. She closed her eyes. A long list of small things Torrance had done over the past week became images, felt like dreams. Why would she remember such mundane daily actions, such small personal interactions, such fresh memories, when she had years of memories to pull from? She was trapped in the state between dreams and wakefulness. Thoughts of the stone came next. Would the dark vein she discovered during yesterday's cutting interfere with the placement of one of the faces? Would she have to change her design? Was she arrogant to not have modeled her concept in clay first?

She pushed the covers off and propped herself up on one elbow. She looked down the length of her naked body. If she was being honest, her physicality was not far from that of the visitors. The difference was 30 years of sunlight and weather on this planet. She had a vision of Torrance's head between her legs, complete with her voluminous afro-styled hair, a hands-length high, the way it used to be when they were a couple. Nix felt a jolt of desire in her abdomen. She reached down and touched herself. Her hand worked thoughtless circles and cross motions. Nix closed her eyes and increased the speed of her movements. She laid her head back on the pillow and opened her legs. Her mind flooded with details of her favorite sex memory of Torrance — in the meadow on a picnic blanket. The grass stood tall all around them, formed a green wall that swayed and rustled in the light breeze. The afternoon sun had been so hot against her exposed breasts and knees and the tops of her feet, as Torrance pleasured her with her mouth. There was no one around for miles. Nix had stared into the blue sky, then down at Torrance, then up at the sky again. She was in the sky and pinned to the Earth at the same time. She loved looking at Torrance, she could fixate on any part of her, trying to preserve her features to later carve in stone. Everything about her was beautiful. In the sun, her skin sparkled with tiny diamonds of sweat.

Post-orgasm, her mind cleared and quieted, she stared at the ceiling, surprised at the power that old memory still held for her. She swung her legs off the edge of the bed and sat up a little too fast. She felt dizzy for a second, but bent forward to pull on her socks. She stood and stumbled as she tried to get her second foot into her underwear. She might as well be drunk. She liked starting the day this way.

Finally fully dressed, Nix stood at the kitchen sink, stared out the window as she ate one of the oatcakes she had made the previous night. As she walked out to the work site, she saw Torrance, the silhouette of her hair and body instantly recognizable in the doorway of the work building. Nix changed her course from the scaffolding and instead walked to the work building. Nix greeted Torrance, tried to keep her smile to a minimum. She certainly didn't want Torrance to know anything about what was going on in her heart and mind. All of those thoughts and feelings would go into her work. She could be very selfish that way.

During the second week of working closely with Torrance, Nix woke each morning as the light seeped around the sides of her bedroom curtains, her heart pounding. She couldn't tell if the compulsion to get up and get going was from the excitement of her new project or to be near Torrance.

They finished the workday without much interaction.

Nix took off her mask and suit, then said, "You're not returning to the ship?"

"No, I thought I'd stay and go to the house with you and prepare food for the returning crew. It's not fair for you to work all day then cook for all of us," Torrance said. "And look at your hands," Torrance said, taking hold of Nix's hands and gently turning them over and back again as she studied at them.

"What about my hands?" Nix said as she looked down at her upturned palms, ignored the deep creases and thick callouses, and studied the shape of Torrance's fingers instead. Torrance's fingers were the same width all the way to the tips. Her fingernails were very rounded in the center, then sloped down on each side. The nails were trimmed short. Nix said, "Your hands are just as beautiful as I remember. Must be easy work flying a ship."

"And your hands are battered from days of cutting. Handling and cutting meat and vegetables will be nearly impossible for you," Torrance said.

"Ah, you remember. But you know this is normal to me. I can still cut vegetables," Nix said.

"After today, I imagine it will be hard for you to even grip the knife," Torrance said.

When they got to the house, Torrance said, "You did a hard day's work, you deserve to take it easy tonight. Go soak your hands in Epsom salts."

Nix got a bowl from the cupboard and filled it with water and a generous helping of salt. She submerged her hands, but kept her eyes on Torrance. She gave Torrance instructions on how to wash the vegetables, and which knife to use. Torrance tolerated it, nodding and smiling. When Torrance finished with the vegetables, she took a wrapped hunk of meat from the refrigerator and cut it into equal pieces.

Nix watched the way she handled the knife with confidence and deft skill. She wished she had a second pair of hands and arms that she could wrap around Torrance. Nix emptied the bowl into the sink and rinsed off her hands. She brushed Torrance's arm as she reached for the hand towel. The feel of her skin made her flinch as if she'd been burned. Her heart thudded, her guts tensed. She stepped away as casually as she could, "Remember, you can't over-season the meat," Nix said. She walked away to shut the feeling down, the towel still clutched in her hand. In the dining room she leaned against the table with both hands. She made a note to herself that from then on she would avoid any physical contact with Torrance.

In the middle of the night, the door to Nix's bedroom opened with its distinct hushed click. She sat up slowly and was unable to see anything in the dark room. When the sheet on the empty side of the bed lifted and a flash of white thigh slid under the sheets, Nix relaxed and lay back down. The warm body settled into the bed beside her. Nix turned toward her, noted the smells of outdoors — fresh air, faint dust, smell of horse sweat — clinging to her hair. She moved closer and pushed her nose to the side of her face, which smelled just washed with the lavender soap from the kitchen. The face beneath her turned and lips feeling so familiar opened and a tongue pushed into Nix's mouth. The kiss was a match on gasoline, a nearly forgotten feeling surged through head and limb. She lifted herself and lay on top of her, still unable to see her face in the dark, but the kisses continued, their lips mashing together harder, as she wrapped her arms around Nix's shoulders, her fingertips running up the back of Nix's neck to comb through the fine ash-colored hair at the base of her neck. She lifted her hips as Nix sunk deeply between her legs and began to press against her; she moaned each time Nix landed. Her fingers traced down from Nix's shoulders along her spine and off near her small ribs. Nix tried to brace herself above so that her chest and upper body were not resting on the woman below her, but the pain of either flattening her palms on the sheets or curling her fists was nearly unbearable. *Is this why they had stopped having sex? No. She could get past the pain, she would never use that as an excuse. Don't think of all the reasons why right now.* Nix's body had plenty of strength to grind out her passion into the body below her. *The body. Just go, just keep following this feeling.* Both of them silent except for exhaled breaths punctuated with moans. *Don't think, just do.* The heat level rose and with it small sweat beads on Nix's shoulders that gathered and slid down her spine, tickled as they ran down the crack of her ass. As Nix held her body up, cool white hands took hold of one hanging breast. She sucked and teased Nix's nipple with her tongue until it gathered into a hardened bud. "Ahhhh..." Nix exhaled to express the feeling that was good beyond words. Her nipple was being lapped and swirled. The sensation traveled like a thread from her nipple to her breastbone, then went up her neck to become a tickle in her jaw. When the sucking stopped, the air felt cool against her wetted skin. The other breast was grabbed and licked horizontally, rubbed over the slicked lips and flattened tongue beneath her, then the tip was playfully nibbled at like fruit dangling from a tree.

Nix's body was hot, her muscles felt loose and flexible. Her pained hands forgotten, she thrust faster, and her lover held on. Nix was driven by a thoughtless determination to climax. She knew she couldn't get off like this, never had, but it felt so reachable that she was determined to try. Then her lover moaned, a higher pitch than usual, a strangled gurgle in her throat as she twisted her hands into the sheets and arched her back. The sound triggered something in Nix's head that felt like an orgasm, but was nothing physical. It had been countless years since Nix had felt such dirty, fucking desire. Her brain was fogged with its aftermath as she rolled off, satisfied with one orgasm between them. She tried to catch her breath.

Nix reached out with a shaking hand to touch the face beside her, to push the matted strands of dark hair back from her moist forehead. A sliver of moonlight had penetrated the room and illuminated the face next to her. Nix noted the deep and perfectly round channel that ran from the bottom of her nose to the top of her upper lip. She imagined carving those lips into clay. She would use the rounded wire tip of the double-end ribbon tool. With a single downward motion, the clay would ripple and gather on the wire, but leave behind the smooth half-pipe shape. Very different from Zephyr's lips.

Nix bent to kiss her, the lips a bit salty after their sweaty effort. The room was so quiet. The sound of their lips parting rasped like a water drop hitting the bottom of a rusted bucket.

"What are you doing here?" Nix asked the intruder in her bed.

"You could have stopped at any time. I wouldn't have been offended," Jansee rested her hand on Nix's shoulder. "But you didn't stop."

"Did you really think I could have mistaken you for Zephyr?" Nix said. She covered her eyes with one hand. It was too late now to see or un-see anything, but the gesture brought comfort.

"I've watched you work, your body is beautiful. And I wanted you. It's that simple," Jansee said.

"Is that how things work in the new utopia — want it and take it?" Nix asked.

"Take it?" Jansee sat up in bed, her white face eerily illuminated in the moonlight, she pushed her stray bangs back from her face and held them in place with her hand. "There was no 'taking' involved. I came here and gave myself to you, and I could feel you above me, driving to be closer. Now, please, relax and let me return the pleasure." She gently moved her fingertips back and forth over Nix's arm.

Nix pushed the covers back and got out of bed. She stood beside the bed shaking her head and looking down at Jansee, her eyes hidden in the shadows beneath her eyebrows. "I don't understand your rules. Motivations, certainly. Though why you would want to have sex with a woman 30 years your senior when you have a whole troop of women your own age is a mystery. Maybe you have mommy issues."

"It's not a matter of choosing over or either. I've had sex with them already, except Fazeef," Jansee said.

"Torrance, too?" Nix was afraid to know, but the words were out.

Jansee hesitated for a second. "Not yet with the commander, but there are no specific mission protocols forbidding sex with the commander. She has chosen to keep herself pure during the mission."

"Do you know why?" Nix asked. She sat down on the bed, a little fascinated, a little sickened, and really confused. The visitors had the same outward appearance as Earthian humans, but at moments like this, when their differing customs and social mores were exposed, they were totally alien to Nix.

"There are many uses for sexual energy. Sometimes it is best to reserve it and channel it to other outlets, which I suspect is what the commander is doing, she wants to 'stay hungry' as this tends to heighten awareness on many levels, especially human interaction. Our intellectuals rarely abstain from sex, since unreleased sexual energy is known to interfere with the flow of analytical thought. But our athletes know the benefits of not indulging in sex before competitive events."

"I'm having a hard time wrapping my head around this. You've had sex with Gantu and Derthan, not Fazeef, and you want to have sex with the commander but haven't had the right opportunity?" Nix asked.

"Yes, and I look forward to meeting your partner when she returns home so we can share some pleasure with her, too," Jansee replied.

"Well, I don't know how that is going to fly," Nix started to laugh, she pushed her hair back and cupped the crown of her head. "Zephyr is so monogamous that she doesn't even like that I have female friends, and she was glad to have never met any of my long string of exes."

"Sounds like a classic description of jealousy to me," Jansee said.

"She's what we call a one-woman-woman," Nix said.

"I'm not familiar with this phrase. Can you say this a different way?" Jansee said. She got out of bed and gathered her uniform from the floor.

Nix said, "It means that she wants only one woman in her life, for the rest of her life. She won't love another woman or have sex with another woman as long as I'm alive."

"What is wrong with her? That sounds dreadful." Jansee reached into her bra to adjust her modest breasts, then stepped into her uniform and pulled it up and over her shoulders.

Nix sat down on the bed and turned toward Jansee and said, "This is a very old romantic idea. I believe, when we were talking by the fire, you called it the paradigm of 'the one.'. Zephyr believes it is destiny that we met, that I'm the only woman for her, that we're meant to be together, and she has sworn to love me, and only me, until I die."

Nix recognized the sweeping upward gesture of Jansee zipping her uniform up to her neck, though it was silent. Jansee shuffled her shoulders, stretched her neck from side to side. "Sounds pathological to me. So limited in possibilities," Jansee said as she walked to Nix's side of the bed. "Thank you for tonight. It was very pleasurable, and I feel we have a great friendship ahead of us. I will remember this night until my ashing."

"Your ashing?" Nix asked.

"When we die we are burned to ash, then mixed with the hydroponic solution that feeds our gardens. It completes the circle," Jansee said.

"That sounded romantic whether you know it or not. And…you will keep this to yourself? I insist it stay between us. And not happen again."

Jansee nodded, and kissed Nix. "I will honor your requests."

"Thank you," Nix said. "I'm going to create your lips in stone. That is how I remember." She reached up and pulled Jansee to her for a long, last kiss.

"Good night, Earth's most talented sculptor," Jansee said as she walked out of the bedroom.

Nix settled back into bed. She stared at the moonlight on the empty rumpled sheets beside her. Her limbs were heavy, and her eyes stayed closed for longer and longer intervals each time she blinked. She would sort it all out in the morning.

During the next week Nix pounded, chiseled, and did her best to work and not be distracted, but she felt Torrance there, both physically from her presence a few feet away, and from the numerous memories that were resurfacing. She planned to exhaust herself, which had worked for the first two weeks, but now it seemed her body was growing stronger, her efforts filled every muscle with blood, she felt a surge of invincibility midway through the day that left her in a vigorous state and wanting sex. Without Zephyr around, she turned to drinking in the early evenings after she had finished working. It helped, and it didn't. The visitors would gather at the fire at the same time each night, and if no fire, they would go directly to the house.

The faces Nix saw around the fire looked that much better after the evening's first drink, and it was harder for her to hold her tongue. She found herself staring, and she knew how they were interpreting it — that she wanted them, which was true on some level. Knowing that they were so fluid and available was a temptation she hadn't expected, and it had a surprising loosening effect on her thoughts. So she drank more, until her brain was fuzzy, neutralized, and her motor functions were a little sloppy. She wasn't sure what they thought of her drinking. They didn't comment and she didn't try to explain. She wanted to keep her hands to herself, on her drinking glass, eat some food, then fall into bed — alone. Her eyes were heavy and she needed an escort back to the house.

Gantu and Fazeef walked her home, one on each side, holding her arms. At the house, they helped her to undress and get beneath the covers.

"Sweetest of dreams," Fazeef said, kissed her forehead and left the room.

Gantu stood above her staring down, but said nothing.

Nix reached up and took hold of her hand. "What are you thinking right now?" Nix asked.

Gantu said, "Is there anything I can do to help you sleep better?"

Nix laughed. "Ah, so polished you are Gantu. There must be a hundred ways to say it, and you choose this way."

"Nix?" Gantu asked, her eyes narrowing.

"Looking at you is enough for me. Your beauty should remain untouched by my hands, so that I may forever long for it, and channel it into my art," Nix said.

"May I kiss you goodnight?" Gantu asked.

"Of course," Nix said. She closed her eyes and waited, but she felt the bed stir next to her. Gantu was naked, had climbed into bed beside her.

"No, you misunderstood. No sex tonight. Just a kiss," Nix said.

"But everything derives from a kiss, let's move forward from there," Gantu said, as she flattened her hand against Nix's sternum and rested it there like the paw of a lioness. "We should have sex, it will be good for you to release some energy. We can all see your unsatisfied physical needs." Gantu moved closer and covered Nix's lips with her own.

The kiss was astonishing. Gantu's lips covered Nix's entire mouth and more. The pillow of soft flesh smothered her mouth and butted up against the bottom of her nostrils, partially blocking them for the few seconds the kiss lasted. Gantu's long spidery fingers moved down Nix's torso, wrapped around her ribs and squeezed, then followed the curve of her waist, then hip, and finally moved between her legs. She ran her hand lightly over the flattened hair until she felt wetness.

Nix felt betrayed by her body's quick response to the kiss. She wanted this woman, who must be a direct descendant of the queens of Egypt, but would rather have had the chance to deny it. Now that was no longer possible. There was an otherworldliness to Gantu, she stood apart — both odd and alluring, like the most exotic flower. Nix wanted to fuck her like a beast from behind until they were sweating and exhausted. But this was not going to happen. She reached down and took hold of Gantu's hand and gently pulled it away. She brought the hand up to her lips and kissed the back of it, then set it on the bed between them. Nix turned to light a candle on her bedside table. In the shadowy light, Gantu's pupils were huge, her head tilted down slightly, she had the look of a panting leopard on the savanna, ready to pounce.

"Gantu, I appreciate your offer, but I can't accept it, or really explain right now why I can't. I'm sorry. You need to go. Now." *God, I need to talk to these women tomorrow and set some rules of how things work here.* "Please get dressed and sleep on the ship tonight."

"I don't understand, but I will wait until you can explain. If I've offended you, or crossed some boundary I wasn't aware of, please forgive me." She got out of bed and stood looking at Nix. Her body was wrapped in smooth curves of muscle, firm, hyper-athletic (as they all were). She was hairless everywhere except the top of her head where a shock of black hair stood straight up from her forehead a few inches, then flowed back in a slim black cascade over her skull and down to her shoulders. She zipped her uniform and ran her fingers through her hair, combing it back three times. "You won't change your mind?"

Nix shook her head. Gantu nodded once and left the room.

As Nix fell asleep that night, her hands twitched. Her right hand curled inward to grip the mallet. The first two fingers and thumb of her left hand closed like a crab's claw on the chisel. Tink, tink, tink. The metallic echoing as regular as seconds passing on a clock. Was that the sound of her hammering or someone else's? No, she was the only creator here. She could feel the solidity of the tools in her hands, the reverberation of each blow rippled through her right arm. She dreamed she was working on the next major area — faces of the visitors emerging. Fazeef, nostrils in a permanent state of flare, his upper lip as curved as a compound bow. He's smiling, biting his bottom lip, the smile pulls his lip into a curved line. Thick eyelashes on the top lid only. His upper lids jut out in a rounded curve and occupy all the space beneath his eyebrows. She mustn't forget the oval cleft in his chin. She had a sudden anxiety — were the visitors meant to be anonymous? Is that why their faces are so pure? Did they know that no one would believe such faces had visited her? Was this their way of obscuring an everlasting record of their visit? The piece would look as if she were praising the pure and lost races of the past. But history would make of it what it would. Masterpiece? Posthumous recognition? She could only control her vision, and the execution of her vision.

8, WINDS OF CHANGE

Nix found herself fighting a daily battle she hadn't anticipated. The beauty of Torrance's face, her restored youth and vitality could be enough, but her smile was like quicksand, and each time Nix saw it she sank in a little deeper. To remedy the feeling that stirred in the pit of her stomach and lit what felt like an always-on fire in her pants, she tried to get ahead of it first thing in the morning, masturbating before she got out of bed.

Nix hadn't gotten a full night's sleep, which showed in her pace. The grinder felt heavier than five pounds when she picked it up to start work, so heavy that she set it back down and tilted it on its side to be sure she hadn't picked up the 12-pound nine-inch grinder by mistake. Model number WS63-125T was correct. Oh, it was going to be a rough day. Her mind was muddled with a hangover from however much booze she had swilled down and that was compounded by lack of sleep. She wasn't sure which was worse, the headache or the sluggishness in her muscles. She flipped the dust mask off, sent it crashing like a giant winged insect swatted to the floor. "Torrance, I need lots of water today. Please fill another cup for me, and when I finish this one I'll take another while you refill this one. I need about ten of these, then I can start working."

Torrance took the empty cup to the edge of the platform where the grubby, ancient-looking plastic water container sat. It held five gallons, usually enough to last Nix for two days. Torrance carried the water container back to where Nix was waiting. She filled the cup and gave it to Nix, then refilled the empty cup. Nix was ahead of her, waiting with the emptied cup held out each time Torrance turned around with a filled cup.

"We have medicine for this," Torrance said. "Would you like some?"

"To cure what? My hangover? My lack of sleep because my bedroom seems to have a revolving door?" As Nix tipped the cup back, the water trailed down the corners of her mouth and spilled onto the front of her work overalls. "Water will do the trick. Water was the first medicine, you know."

"Yes. I know, but we have so much more now," Torrance said.

"Pills to cure everything probably," Nix said. She wiped her mouth with the back of her hand, put her respirator mask on, and got to work.

"Nearly everything," Torrance replied.

Torrance stayed close by, removed pieces of marble as they fell to the scaffolding.

Nix worked without saying anything to Torrance. She had years of practice tamping down her heart with this type of punishing, physically demanding work; she knew this method worked. She fought whole battles in her head while under the mask — wanting to rip it off to stare at Torrance's face, and simultaneously wanting to seal the mask shut over her head, so that she might never have to emerge. Nix felt like she was working in slow motion, everything was more difficult than it should have been. Her work shirt and overalls were dark around the armpits, neck and lower back. She smelled horrible even to herself.

Torrance did everything she could during the day to take care of Nix, kept the water cup full, prepared a lunch of sausage, apples and cheese. Nix ate quickly and with hardly a word spoken between them. She thanked Torrance then went right back to work.

The next time Nix stopped for water she smelled the fire before she could see it. The smoke was nearby. She panicked for a moment. She looked up at the sky, but it was clear in every direction. Torrance was nowhere to be found. She called out to her, but there was no response. Nix made her way around the side of the rock, her heart beating hard, unsure of what she would find. There was a small fire burning in the fire pit in the cleared area. The figure sitting beside it looked like Torrance. A wisp of smoke, opaque as gray wool was being pulled up into the loom of the sky.

Nix tried to calm herself. She took measured breaths until her heart slowed down. There was no way she could work after that. Better to just end the day. She put her tools away and carried her overalls to the wash shed and put them into the wooden hamper. She took a clean pair from the shelf above the hamper and carried them back to the main work building, hung them on their nail. Even from the outbuilding, she could see Torrance still sitting at the fire pit. She walked to the cellar she had built in the base of the hill at the edge of the woods. The door creaked, and she left it open for a little light since there was none inside. Stairs were carved into the earth, and she had fitted them with slabs of slate. The space was small, enough room for two people to stand shoulder to shoulder and turn around. From floor to ceiling, the wooden racks were filled with bottles of wine, some probably turned to vinegar by now, others that she knew to be good enough for anything she would want to barter. She went to the house to get some glasses. She put a fingertip into each, thumb in the last one, then pinched them together to carry.

Nix walked toward the fire, which was now burning above the rim of the pit. Torrance had always been a natural fire-starter. Nix scanned the horizon. There was no wind. Hadn't been any all day. The air felt dry, full of charge and static. Days like this lead to lightning storms, lightning storms to fire, fire to death. Nix looked at the ground around each of the outbuildings, then the house. She had 150 feet of defensible space in every direction. All brush and trees were cleared. Dry creek beds, which could be flooded with water if she had enough warning to activate the pumps, ran along the north and west tree lines. Out here it was just she and an ax. There was only 50 feet of cleared space on the far side of the spaceship. *Hell, if it had made it through the atmosphere, did she really need to ask them if it was fireproof?*

When Nix arrived at the fire pit, she placed the short, cylindrical hand-blown glasses onto each of their stone seats, except for hers and Torrance's. She held a glass out for Torrance to take. Then she sat down on her stone seat, her legs leaned together to hold the bottle between them as she twisted in the corkscrew and pulled the cork free with a shrill pop. Torrance turned to look at her and smiled, then turned back to taste the food in one of the pots. Nix poured herself a glass of wine, swirled it as much as possible in the stunted glass, sniffed at it. The first sip was peppery and silky, not bad for someone who never had taken a single viticulture class. She drank the remaining two ounces without taking a breath. Nix felt drained, a lump of battered flesh. She hoped the wine would transport her to a place of less pain. The wine warmed her insides for a second and made her eyes even heavier. She poured some for Torrance, refilled her own glass, then pushed the cork back into the bottle and set it down. She slid off her stone seat, her body feeling as liquid as the wine. She slipped down the seat until she was horizontal. The stone seat was the only thing preventing her from lying flat, she pushed it over and rolled it away. The thought crossed her mind that this was not proper behavior in front of guests. *Where did that thought even come from? God, it felt good to be flat on the grass-covered earth.* They all knew how hard she'd worked lately, surely they would forgive her for not sitting up for their arrival.

Nix stared vacantly at the sky. It was a little easier to keep her eyes open in this position, which made no sense to her. The only thought in her head was how much she loved this particular type of sky — blue that descended into distinct bands of yellow, orange, pink and purple toward the horizon. The coloration was sometimes seen in the mornings, but mostly before sunset. In all these years, she had never taken the time to find out what conditions caused it, and she considered asking the visitors in their infinite wisdom to explain it to her, but then realized it might take away the magic. She didn't want everything explained. Scientific language was cold and methodical, and did little to express the true nature of things. Right now, all she knew, and wanted to know, was that when she saw this particular type of sky, she was thankful each and every time to be alive to see it again. The beauty of it was simple, a faded color spectrum, but felt deliberate to her on some level. Her eyes went from straight above to the horizon, and back again, tracing the colors as one blended into the next, then became a distinct color before blending into the next color. Simple, yet it made her feel awed, joyous, childlike.

When the visitors arrived, laughing and shoving each other like schoolchildren, she wondered how young they really were. Trained for this mission with books, with pre-recorded vids? How mature where they? What had they experienced socially or sexually? Their bodies were bursting with energy, sexual and otherwise. She pulled herself up to sit on her stone stool. She slumped forward with her elbows resting on her knees, uncorked the wine bottle again and poured a glass for each of them. "I made this last year from the grapes that grow on the side of the hill by the lake we visited on horseback. The soil is very different on that hill."

"Can you taste something as subtle as different soil types in wine?" Jansee asked.

Was she making a reference to the fact that Nix couldn't tell Jansee was in her bed the other night instead of Zephyr? Nix shook her head for a second to rid herself of the thought. "Yes, actually many factors can change the character of the grapes. Soil type, water, sun, when they're picked, how they're prepared."

The visitors moved the glasses under their noses, tasted the wine. Some took another swallow, the rest set their glasses down on the grass at their feet. *Smart of them to wait until after they eat.* They held their bowls out as far as their arms would extend so that Torrance didn't have to reach as far to fill them. As soon as the bowls were filled, and they began to eat, Nix said, "I appreciate your cultural differences. I know everything you do comes from best intentions. But as of this moment, the night visits need to stop." Nix didn't look at anyone directly, but swept slowly around the circle, not giving any face more attention than the rest. "Things work differently here. I thought you guys knew this. Damn, you tell me how much you've studied us, how our paradigm is different from yours, and yet, some of you have chosen to visit my bed in the night."

The visitors were silent, they ate their food and drank their wine hungrily, and otherwise acted as if no one was talking to them, scolding them. Nix continued, "The rules of sex on this planet, in this country, and specifically in my house, and all of the land surrounding my house too, are as follows: I'm with Zephyr. We are a monogamous couple. I know you haven't met her yet, but she does exist, and will be returning home in the coming days, and she will *not* be as understanding or patient as I have been. Actually, there is the possibility that she will throw you off this land if she finds out what you have done or if you violate any of these rules with her. So, the rules: Do not show up uninvited to our bedroom at any time of the day or night. Be sure to double-, no, triple-check if you think that Zephyr or I are giving you signals that we want your intimate company. Ask. Ask very directly. This should help avoid any miscommunications." Nix ate her food in silence. No questions, no comments from the visitors.

Gantu broke the silence: "This might be a planet rich in well-documented history, but it is new to us. Please forgive our social missteps."

Jansee, whose cheeks were flushed, either from her deeds or the wine, continued to drink every time her glass was filled without any hesitation, said, "Yes, if we have offended you, we are deeply regretful. Our mission is important and we hope to continue with our objective to collect samples."

"Of course," Nix said. "I'm not going to get in the way of your mission."

Jansee perhaps a little drunk, continued, "We know a closed system doesn't work. Soil is essential — the bacteria and minerals of soil traveled with our parents, and have contributed to the environment that we survive in. But we need more. We'll take as much as we can." Jansee tilted her head to the side and smiled when she explained something. Nix found the mannerism sweet, some childhood innocence to it, and wondered how the gesture might translate to stone. Would it be interpreted as a question or a statement? Would leaving her lips slightly parted change the perception?

Nix asked for another helping of the stew that Torrance had made with foraged herbs, nettles and honey. She found herself looking at Jansee. Nix liked her eyes, the flat line of the bottom lid, then the upper lid sharply angled up from the inner corner and white at the apex before it dropped down again to the outer corner. She had already imagined how she would shape them in stone with a finger-sized rasp.

"Dr. Jansee, you are sharing classified information," Torrance said.

Nix said, "Don't be such a hard-ass, Torrance. You still don't know when to relax. I can see all of you collecting samples with your tubes and pinchers and swabs. If you weren't, *then* I'd be real nervous."

"Actually, this mission is severely time-boxed since the longer the commander stays here, the more likely she is to die," Derthan said.

"The longer any of us stays the more likely we are to die," Torrance said.

The crew went silent.

The wine was loosening tongues, and Nix wanted it to go on, she lifted the jug and filled the glasses for the third time, and spoke right away to dispel the odd feeling the last statement had produced like a cloud of lethal gas. "So what do you drink back home?" she asked.

"A pure alcohol — clear and flavorless. Nothing like this. This is tart and sweet. It's hard to isolate any specific flavor or smell, so many layers I don't have words for," Gantu said. She studied the liquid through the glass as she held it up to the fire. She brought it back to smell again, then sipped.

Jansee said, "I can taste the earth itself — the dark moistness of dirt, but it isn't unpleasant, it's familiar. And the feeling of this liquid…makes me want to take off my clothes and go run through the woods."

"Let's do it. The moon is full tonight. You won't even need to carry a light," Nix urged them, already bending to loosen the laces of her ankle-high work boots.

"Dance with the devil in the pale moonlight," Torrance said.

"Ah, you still remember that movie?" Nix asked.

"Oh yes, first 'Batman'," Derthan said.

"We've all seen it," Fazeef said.

"We produce very little entertainment, nothing compared to Earth. And even though the Firsts took everything with them, we're about 35 years behind on anything current. Things don't transmit as well as we thought they would," Gantu said. She leaned back, let her head fall back to look up at the sky, the moon having just crested the top of the tree line in a mesmerizing gold color. "Can you imagine if the Firsts had left all that entertainment behind? We have mostly technical-minded people. Artists, musicians, actors weren't so inclined to leave. The old-timers still value art. Sadly we have little new entertainment and even less art."

Fazeef stood for some reason, still holding his wine. He said, "It will be three generations before we are done terra forming. Don't feel sorry for us. We knew nothing else. Returning to Earth wasn't part of the original emigration; they were told it was a one-way ticket to Kepler-442B and they accepted that. On the ship all of the scientists were in serious research and development mode. What else was there for them to do? Once they landed, they stayed in a gathered community, sharing innovations. Some of them had the added hunger of wanting to return to Earth some day, which drove certain individuals to make extraordinary advances. My father, for instance, invented a form of spacecraft propulsion that allowed us to get here in half the time. No ship can carry enough solid fuel for the thrust needed during long trips. His magnetic conducer allows for powerful bursts of thrust that not only propel the ship but also generates electricity as a by-product."

"Your father?" Nix asked.

"He wasn't a father in the traditional sense of donating half of my genetic material, but he did spend a lot of time with me, teaching me, listening to me, giving love and advice. He'd worked like a man obsessed most of his life, had never had children of his own, but since the day he'd heard about a young boy in the nursery making complex arrangements with blocks, he had taken an interest in me. He allowed me to be an observer in his lab from the time I was 5.

I became his assistant by age 7, and led my own experiments by age 9."

"Fazeef, that is fascinating. You were a bit of a boy wonder." Nix smiled brightly at him. He gave a smile and nodded, then looked down at his wine glass.

The wine had caught up with Nix, and she was getting sleepy. She stood, her legs unsteady for a second. "Torrance, thank you for such a delicious meal, and all your help today. I really appreciate everything you do. I'll be back to myself tomorrow. Sleep well everyone..." then she started slowly walking toward the house, "...and in your own beds!" She held up her right hand and wagged her finger, but didn't turn around. She could hear them giggling. Sweet laughter of young women who are at once innocent and rebellious.

Nix focused on the soft glow of light in the house windows. She made her way toward it like a battered moth to a dim, distant moon, her feet practiced and sure. Inside she dropped her clothes outside the bathroom and closed the door. She leaned forward on the sink, letting her weight rest on the palms of her hands. Her naked body in the mirror — mostly firm, but sagging in her once firm breasts, and stomach, the skin of her face also submitting to gravity on both sides of her chin. Yes, she had gotten too much sun on her fair skin over the years, it wasn't that she didn't know the damage it would cause, it was just that she didn't care. You're born into skin on this Earth, it's meant to be used, not saved up and babied. Still, seeing it now, she considered that her philosophy was flawed. She reached up to touch the side of her neck — it felt soft even though the look of it was parched and deeply creased. What did she know of soft skin? Her fingers touched stone all day, her fingertips were hardened and a bit numb most of the time. She was old. The mirror spoke truths that were irrefutable; she was on the down slope to death. Oh, she knew better than to look at herself when she was this tired. Something about exhaustion took away any kindness she would otherwise allow herself. She wasn't 40 anymore; hell, even 50 was long gone in the rear-view mirror. The sun had left its mark on her now browned face and neck and hands.

She turned the shower on and immediately stepped under the water. The chilled water sprayed against her face and chest, an unpleasant sensation that overrode every thought of being old and dying. A cold shower could make anyone feel 20 again. There would be no more looking in the mirror. She needed to focus every ounce of energy she had left on washing herself and getting to bed. The water warmed, but was running more slowly than usual from the solar-heated tank on the roof. She tilted her face up. She had to move her head three times to wet all of her hair, but the warmth and feeling of the silken water rinsing the stone dust away was pure pleasure, a reward she deserved at the end of her work day. Her hands could barely hold the bar of soap, the muscles of her palm and the base of her thumb on her right hand were deeply bruised. She dropped the soap several times, but forced her right hand to close around it and resume soaping. She dropped the soap again. The new bar of soap hit the slate tiles of the bathroom floor with a loud thud. She had soap everywhere it needed to be, she wasn't going to bend over to pick up the soap again, it was too much. When she tried to flatten her right hand to scrub her body, the pain was too intense. She washed herself with her left hand, but it was challenging in terms of mechanical coordination. She sat on the slate floor for a minute, let the water rinse the soap off. She shaved her legs with her left hand, taking twice as long as usual. She rubbed between her toes, behind and inside her ears where the marble dust liked to hide, then tilted her face up again and closed her eyes. The pleasure of a thousand warm fingertips touching her face, enveloping it, running into her ears and blocking all sound.

She heard a knock on the door.

"Nix?" The voice sounded familiar, but the water could be distorting it. Then she heard it again, "Nix?"

She was sure it was Zephyr knocking and calling to her. Her first reaction was to be angry with her for disturbing the primal ecstasy she was experiencing, but she heard herself replying, "Yes, come in."

"I'm just hanging a clean towel for you. The bed is turned down too. Whenever you're ready," Zephyr said.

"Thank you. I'll be right out," Nix said. She closed her eyes and tilted her head back one last time to enjoy the sensation of the water on her skin. She wondered if she started breathing, if she would drown. Instead her hand came up and wiped the excess water from her nose and forehead, cleared a space to breathe. She turned the water off and stood up. She should be excited. But she was anxious. She toweled dry, and wrapped the towel around her torso as she walked to the bedroom where Zephyr was unpacking some clothes from her saddlebag and tossing them into the hamper. Nix walked closer and turned Zephyr's body toward her so that she could kiss her.

"Welcome home," Nix said and kissed her again on the side of her neck. Ah, her hair smelled of the road — fresh air, dust, and horse sweat. Nix opened her eyes to vanquish the memory of Jansee's recent night visit.

"Oh, look at you," Zephyr said. She put a hand on each side of Nix's face. "Trying to work yourself to death again? Look at your eyes, such dark circles." She bent forward and kissed the area just beneath each of Nix's eyes. "Did you sleep at all while I was gone?"

Nix was silent. She didn't want to talk, she just wanted to go to bed. She pulled herself away as casually as she could and made her way to the other side of the bed.

"I noticed some people sitting around a fire out in the open space. Do we have travelers passing through?" Zephyr asked.

"Yes. A band of five from very far away. I don't know how long they'll stay, but they're self-sufficient, and...interesting. They've been great company while you were gone. I'll introduce you in the morning," Nix said. She got into bed and pulled the blanket close under her chin. Her eyes were barely open.

"Did you leave me any hot water?" Zephyr asked.

"Sorry, I was extra dirty today," Nix said.

"Right. You didn't know when I was going to be home," Zephyr said. She hung the empty saddlebag onto a hook on the wall, then crossed the room to Nix's side of the bed. She stood above her for a few moments, just staring, she pursed her lips, then bent to kiss Nix. "I'll be quick."

When Zephyr returned, Nix was sleeping on her back. Her snoring was impossible to fall asleep next to. Zephyr got into bed and pushed at Nix's shoulder. "Honey, you're snoring, roll over." And Nix did. The snoring stopped and Zephyr turned her back to Nix and was asleep before she realized it.

In the night, Nix woke and reached for Zephyr, slid her hand between her legs. Zephyr moaned a little, turned toward Nix and kissed her. Lips she knew from years of kissing mashed against hers. Some spark caught between them. Half asleep, their bodies touched under the covers. Nix's fingers slid into her. Zephyr moaned in a way Nix hadn't heard in so long. Nix put her leg over Zephyr's, and she welcomed her by opening her legs so that Nix fit squarely between them. Blind passion in the dark. Nix began to thrust, possessed by a lust whose origins she didn't want to think about. *Thinking is the lust-killer, just feel and move.* Nix gulped breaths between thrusts. She wanted to remain in this half-conscious state, her body running on instinct and the accumulated knowledge of years of sex. She knew how to make a woman come. Zephyr clutched her shoulder blades, nails pressed into the skin as she pulled Nix closer. Nix kept pushing, a steady rolling rhythm, toward a finish that she needed more than she needed air, sleep or food, until she felt Zephyr tense then relax away from her. She slowed to a stop within a beat. Nix rolled off of her and onto her back, breathing hard.

Zephyr nuzzled Nix's shoulder, kissed and rubbed her cheek against her. "That's quite a welcome home," she said.

Nix was silent for a long moment, her breath fast and heavy in the dark. "I love you," she said. The words faded into the darkness and, within a minute, Nix was snoring again.

9, MUSE

In the morning, Nix felt rejuvenated. Her muscles should have been sore but weren't. Her mind was sharp and clear. She slipped out of bed, snatched her clothes from the floor and left Zephyr to sleep. She dressed in the kitchen, pulling on her socks while chewing a strip of dried venison that worked her jaws to near cramping. She stared at the strip of dried meat dangling from her mouth like a cigarette and wondered why it was so tough. At any rate, it was the last of the batch, and she'd need to get a deer soon. She stuffed two apples into her shorts' pocket, carried two raw eggs in her hand. When she opened the front door, the deep blue night air already had the distinct smell that foretold of a hot day about to arrive. She walked slowly toward the scaffolding, trying to be as objective as possible about the large stone in front of her. It was still lacking details, but some rough shapes were emerging. In the near dark, it looked dynamic, a round shape that exploded but was frozen before any of the pieces separated from the whole. Explosion. Separated. Launching. Expanding. She sat on the edge of the scaffolding, cracked the eggs and held them above her mouth to catch the falling white and yolk. The apples, from the wild trees on the east side of the property, were tart and a perfect finish to her breakfast. She ate the apple cores too, tossed away only the stick-like stems. She put the eggshells under a heavy piece of discarded marble.

She had had a proper breakfast today. She needed to take better care of herself. Zephyr was back, the balance would be restored, she would find her center, and her life would resume to something she thought of as normal — work, lunch, work, bed, a trip into town once a month, three days of stone work then one day of clay sculpting. Repeat. Clay was like hand yoga: Using very small, precise, and subtle movements, it provided a balance to the heavy cutting and pounding with the pneumatic tools and mallet. Nix had hundreds of clay sculptures — sometimes they were nothing more than doodles, sometimes extreme new forms and shapes or the germination of an idea that would become a grand sculpture. She had been hesitant to work with clay since the visitors arrived. For one, the sculptures were so intimate. They were her thoughts, good and bad, the contents of her head for anyone to see like pages in a journal. Of course, she didn't expect that the visitors would have the visual language to understand in any real sense what was going on in her head just by looking at these small clay creations, but…oh, *if they did* she would be so exposed. Now that she was rested and had a clear head, she also realized that she had been avoiding working in clay because it would leave her so much more accessible to Torrance. She wouldn't be able to hide behind the noise and the dust, behind the mask, and pure exhaustion of stone work. Any of them would be able to talk to her, ask her questions, stand, sit, be close to her for hours and hours. Touch her even.

The sun was coming up. Orange light quickly diluted the dark blue of the twilight sky. The air temperature was rising with it. Amazing what that fireball did on a daily basis. Nix looked at the tops of the trees, the ridgelines of the hills behind her, everything tinged in coppery orange. She needed the light to start working. She had about 15 minutes until it crested the horizon and blasted everything with daylight. She looked directly at it, her feet swinging beneath her. When had she changed from wanting to sleep as late as possible to getting up before the sun to wait for it, to wring every moment of workable daylight out of each day? She had been such a night owl the first part of her life. Now she rose before the sun, prepared everything in advance of the light-giving rays, ready to begin as soon as she could see, utilizing every minute available. For the work she did, this was the most sustainable way. To generate enough power to light her work area on the large sculptures would take more resources than it was worth. The solar panels that covered the roofs of every building could only do so much, and she needed that power for the power tools. Whatever was left was for things around the house — warm water, reading light, playing music — things that sometimes had to be sacrificed in the name of art. The clay sculptures she sometimes made an exception for. She primarily worked in the daylight on those too, but if she needed to work in the pre-dawn hours, past sunset, or on a particularly rainy day, she preferred to use candlelight. Those sculptures were more about feeling than seeing most of the time anyway.

The sun came quickly, vanquishing the navy blue in a blast of whites and oranges. Nix stood and began her daily review of the piece. She leisurely walked around the scaffolding three times, bottom to top, back down again, and repeated. She inspected with her eyes, felt with her hands, squatted, stood on her tiptoes, stuck her fingers into cuts and chops. The sun warmed her legs. If she stood still for a moment she could feel it on her back through her thin T-shirt. She walked to the bottom of the scaffolding, stepped into her suit and zipped in. She walked toward the house, turned and walked around the whole piece from a distance. Not a cloud in the sky, but she felt suspicious. The weather had been clear too long.

She started work slowly, but within an hour she was back to the exhausting pace she had been keeping. This time for different reasons — there was a lot to be done and she was falling into the grip of her vision. Once under the spell of her creation there was no room to think or feel anything else. Even the tiny, unpredictable chips that flew back from the angle grinder and smacked her face shield barely roused a reaction.

When Nix finally stopped for some food, she saw Torrance standing on the platform beside her. Torrance's mask and suit were covered with a fair amount of dust, so she must have been standing there for some time. Nix pushed her mask up and smiled at Torrance. She kept it as cordial as possible. She felt like she was being watched from the house, suddenly aware of every word and gesture she shared with Torrance. Irrational paranoia, but since Zephyr had come home last night, she felt tense, on alert. Some freedom felt gone, though she knew nothing had been taken away. It was as if she saw her actions from the outside, objectively, and she knew that the smiles she had given Torrance, the way she had looked into her eyes when they talked, the way she looked at her when they were not talking — all of it was suspect behavior that would raise uncomfortable questions from Zephyr.

"Lunchtime already? Great, let's eat," Nix said, wanting to deflect any and all conversation.

Torrance nodded without replying. Nix remembered well Torrance's ability to know when to leave her alone and not probe. Nix pulled at the neck of her jumpsuit, damp with the day's third round of sweat, trying to get some airflow to her skin.

"I prepared some rabbit and carrots for you," Torrance said, pointing to two identically made plates set on the stone seats. "Lots of water too," she said, her eyes wandering over the white salt rings on Nix's suit.

Nix removed her mask and carried it under her arm down the scaffolding.

She put her mask beside her seat, unzipped her suit and peeled it off. She laid the suit flat on the grass so that it could dry in the sun. Torrance had already filled the water glasses. Nix poured a small amount of water into her hand, washed her face and the back of her neck, then a little more water for both hands. Torrance refilled the water glass, and Nix drank like a desert wanderer. As Torrance refilled her glass again, Nix looked toward the plates. A nicely charred piece of meat and sliced carrots sprinkled with some green herb on the other half of the plate. "Food looks delicious. You must have built a good cooking fire to get that char," Nix said.

"Come on, Nix, give me some credit," Torrance said, lifting Nix's plate from the seat so she could sit down.

"It's not that, I just...you know I've been in the stone all morning," Nix said.

"More like a vortex," Torrance said.

"I didn't even notice you were making lunch. And how long were you standing next to me?" Nix asked.

"Few hours. I thought we had a set schedule, so I showed up as usual, but you were already working, the back of your suit was soaked along your shoulders and spine. I didn't want to touch you and have you jerk the saw, so I waited until you took a break, but you didn't. You always work like this?"

"No, just since you've been here. I thought I was too old for this pace, but it turns out I just needed a little inspiration." Nix picked up the rabbit leg with her fingers and bit into it. Clear juice ran down her chin as she bit down a second time to shear the meat from the bone. She wiped at her chin with the back of her hand, looked at Torrance as she chewed, glanced toward the house, and back to Torrance. She couldn't stop looking at Torrance's face, but still felt she was being watched.

"The stone, of course. I'm so grateful that you love it," Torrance said. "Required some challenging maneuvers for the ship to get it here, but it was imperative. As critical as the mission itself."

"No, not the stone, though I have to say it is one hell of piece." Nix looked over her shoulder toward the house once more, then looked Torrance in the eye. "My muse has returned," Nix said and pushed the last of the meat into her mouth with her fingers. She smiled as she chewed, but stomped her foot on the ground to admonish herself for letting that slip out. She needed to keep her mouth shut — she picked up a few carrot pieces and stuffed them into her already full mouth; one fell back down onto her plate.

"Your muse?" Torrance said, pursing her lips, her eyes looking skyward and to the right for a second and back at Nix.

Nix pointed at her mouth and shrugged. She picked up her water glass and held it out for a refill. She swallowed some water, and stood up. She grabbed her mask, and swooped quickly to grab her suit and started walking back toward the scaffolding. Nix called out, "Thanks for lunch. Come join me when you're finished. No rush. I've still got a few more hours left in these arms." At the base of the scaffolding she stepped into her suit and pulled it up over her shoulders. She turned around quickly and smiled back at Torrance as she zipped up, and made her way up the scaffolding.

Torrance watched her go. She gathered the plates, then sat down on the grass. "Retrieve: Muse," Torrance said.

"Definition: In ancient Greece, daughters of Zeus and Mnemosyne, nine sister goddesses who…" Torrance watched the images of toga-clad women scroll over her retina.

"Stop:" The screen froze on her command. "Provide alternate definition:"

"Alternate definition: Muse, a person, usually a woman, who inspires an artist to create."

Torrance watched as Nix picked up the tool and started cutting. The shrill sound of saw slicing rock kept Torrance from further research. She knew firsthand how heavy the tool was, and yet Nix sometimes held it with one hand, making sweeping cuts from above, under, side-to-side with what looked like the ease of trimming vegetation. What she didn't know was that as Nix twisted and turned in odd positions, sustained those positions a second longer than truly needed to complete the cut, she was doing it just to prove to herself she still could. Cut pieces fell onto the scaffolding, against Nix's knees, the tops of her boots. She didn't seem to notice.

Torrance observed her for some time, she sipped at her water, one leg crossed over the other, her elbow resting on top of one thigh. The sun was declining in the sky. Nix was operating on the shadowed side. Torrance knew she would be moving in a moment to maximize the remaining light. When Nix moved, Torrance got up and found another vantage point on the western side of the stone. She repeatedly touched her left temple to capture images and some vids of Nix in action.

The crew arrived as the sun dipped down to the horizon. They set their packs down and each bent to kiss Torrance's cheek before they sat on the grass beside her. Within moments of watching, they were as transfixed by Nix as Torrance was.

"Can you believe this tempo? She's been working like this for over four weeks," Torrance said.

Fazeef said, "Well beyond expectations for a woman of her age. But that pace is necessary if someone is to be such a prolific artist, is it not?"

"Are we disturbing her by being here?" Gantu asked Torrance.

At this question, which Nix could not have heard, she stopped and flipped her mask up, looked their way, but made no acknowledgement of their presence. The light was going and she needed to stop. She glanced toward the house. The lights were on in a few windows. She had told Zephyr that she would introduce her to the visitors and she hadn't, now the day had passed. Nix had eaten dinner with them every night since they had landed. Why should that be any different tonight? It wouldn't unless she lied to them. She would go get Zephyr and bring her out here to meet them, then they could all eat together.

Nix turned off the saw and set it on the scaffolding between her feet. She fought with her stiff index finger and thumb to clasp the zipper, once she had hold of it she struggled to pull the zipper down from her collar to the bottom of the work suit, but she managed. The next step was to shrug the suit off of her shoulders, something that should have been easy. "Torrance, I'm done for the day. Can you come up here and help me with something?" Oh, she felt humiliated to have to ask. She had overworked her arms, and this was the price for that foolishness — she should have known better.

Torrance smiled and climbed up the outside of the scaffolding instead of taking the longer way up the circular ramp. She folded her body and slipped between the outer railings to arrive beside Nix. She brushed gray dust from the shoulders of her suit, which she had been wearing all day. Torrance stood behind Nix and gently unpeeled the suit from one shoulder, then the other, as if any indelicate move might hurt her. Torrance stood face-to-face with Nix to push the suit down over her body to her feet. She paused for a moment on her haunches and looked up at Nix. Their eyes met. Torrance licked her bottom lip, then stood and removed her own suit with her eyes still locked on Nix. Nix watched her without moving.

"Can't step out either?" Torrance asked as she bent to pull her boots free of the suit.

"No," Nix said flatly, embarrassed by the vulnerable position she was in. Now Torrance would have to touch Nix's skin repeatedly. Torrance took hold of the back of

Nix's left thigh and pulled the leg up until the loose-fitting pant leg dropped away from her boot, then repeated with Nix's right leg.

Nix looked over Torrance's shoulder at the visitors, and saw that there was one more person among them, someone standing. It was Zephyr. *Oh god, how long had she been standing there?* Nix replayed the past five minutes in her mind. Was Zephyr standing there when Nix called Torrance to help her? All of this would look bad from down there, undressing so close to each other. "Zephyr!" Nix called out. She waved her arm just once. "I'll be right down to introduce you to everyone." She could see Zephyr was standing back, slightly apart from the others, her arms crossed over her chest. Some of the visitors turned to look at her.

Jansee whispered, "Inquiry: all information on long-term partner of Nicole Tessitore." Her screen flashed more youthful images of the woman standing behind her. In one picture Zephyr stood with her hand raised, her mouth twisted as she shouted during a protest, streams of smoke billowing behind her, tanks off to one side. Private audio told Jansee, "Zephyr Zahradnik, born 2100. Twenty-second century biologist and gene hacker, best known for her radical plant experiments. Recluse since 2133. No known images available beyond 2132. End record." Jansee turned and looked up at Zephyr, though she was now 65 years old, it was unmistakably her, wide-set eyes with strong brows, a heart-shaped face with a round chin. She looked fragile and vulnerable standing here. Her hair was longer and all gray now, pulled back from her face and left in a long, low ponytail that made Jansee think of their planet's brave founder, Thomas R.

Torrance picked up the suits and hung them over the railing, spread them open and slapped at them with her hand to knock the dust free. She gathered the mallets and chisels into the wooden carpenter's box and carried it in one hand, the angle grinder in the other. At the bottom of the scaffolding, she put the tools into the waterproof crate they had made so that they wouldn't have to move the tools back and forth from the work barn to the stone each morning and evening.

Nix followed behind her as quickly as she could force her body to move. The muscles of her legs ached, her knees refused to bend, so she walked stiff-legged like a bear. As soon as she stepped off the scaffolding she said, "Everyone, this is Zephyr. I was planning to introduce you at the house, but, here she is. Zephyr and I will make dinner in the house tonight. If anyone needs to wash up, please go now. I have to shower too, so the timing should work out." Nix secured the lid of the tool crate with a twig through the latch.

Zephyr smiled and raised her hand up to her shoulder. "Hello. I'm looking forward to getting to know each of you over dinner. See you inside soon." She came close and hugged Nix, kissed her cheek, whispered, "They're so young."

Nix smiled and left one arm around Zephyr's shoulder. They turned and started walking to the house together. Nix did her best not to show her pain outwardly. But the way she was walking was ridiculous. She riveted the smile to her face and forced her legs to continue on Zephyr's pace, but they felt as clunky and uncooperative.

The colors of the sunset were reaching their most saturated — orange and pink clouds smeared erratically as if by an impatient two-year-old across the darkening sky. Nix turned back to see Torrance. Her silhouette — high forehead topped with knobby, tufted hair, slim neck — against the last light was like an ancient cameo.

"Nix you're pulling on my neck," Zephyr said.

"Sorry. I may have overdone it today," Nix said. She pried her eyes from Torrance and faced the house. She took her arm from Zephyr's shoulder and instead rested her hand on the curve of her waist.

"That was a lame introduction. You didn't even tell me their names. They're odd-looking enough that I certainly won't forget their faces, but still, when they're in the house, you owe me a proper introduction."

Nix nodded. Each step that matched Zephyr's pace was a major accomplishment of will, she refused to wince. Once inside, Nix went directly to the bathroom to shower. The first challenge was getting undressed — she twisted at odd angles to escape her clothes, even used her teeth to pull the fabric of her shirt down from her elbow. The next challenge was turning the shower handles to start the water. The pain in her hands made it difficult to close her grip enough to get any leverage, but wasn't that why Zephyr had forged the X-shaped handles? She grabbed the old ax handle she kept in the far corner near the toilet and used it to lever the knobs. When she stepped under the water of the shower she started to call out "Torr... ." She wanted Torrance to help her. *Wash me, rinse me, rub my shoulders, dry me, swaddle me in a towel.* In the few minutes she had alone, she tried to clear her head. *What was I thinking looking back at Torrance? I blew the intro, it was too casual. Not sure if Zephyr recognized Torrance or not, but once she hears her name, she certainly will.* The water drops, blissful little indentations on her cheeks, eyelids, forehead, a steady beat of hot water. Her mind drifted to a clear white space of no thought. She leaned against the wall, her forehead holding her weight, her arms hanging useless at her sides. The water came down like rain from the wide showerhead — a luxury she had never given up from before the warming. Her left hand was slightly more useable, since it held the barrel-shaped body of the saw and not the narrow handle. She managed to grab the soap and wash the dust from the finer crevices of her body. When she was done, she dried herself with her left hand, then headed directly to the bedroom where she faced the challenge of putting clothes on.

It took a while, but she got dressed and was sitting at the table a moment before the visitors arrived. There was faint music playing in the kitchen. Nix exhaled and closed her eyes. Zephyr came to the table and kissed Nix's cheek. She set down a short, thin-walled glass and poured Nix three fingers of whiskey — whiskey she made and whiskey only she was allowed to pour. *She knows how bad I'm hurting or she's looking for a fast way to loosen my tongue. Either way it's trouble.*

As Zephyr prepared plates for everyone in the kitchen, the visitors talked excitedly with one another about their day's findings. Nix could do little more than listen as she stared at her deeply tanned arms that rested like lead on the table. She contemplated whether she would be able to lift them to eat or if she would have to lean forward and lick up her food like a dog. She laughed a little to herself at this thought. She remembered nights when she could only use her face during sex because her arms were so exhausted and beaten down, like they were tonight. Women seemed to love her in this state; she didn't know if it was the vulnerability they saw or maybe just bad timing on her part — whatever it was she had had a lot of sex in this condition. Nix heard things like "mixed evergreen forest," "ancillary food source," "attenuated nitrogen levels." She knew what all of it meant, she just didn't want to think that hard right now. She tuned out their conversation and stared at the deep amber whiskey that waited to touch her lips, if only she could pick it up and hold it with any confidence. She waited as Zephyr served their guests first.

Zephyr set the last plate in front of Nix, then took her seat at the opposite end of the table. Nix stood and said, "Everyone, everyone, please. You remember Zephyr." The visitors quieted and promptly stood at attention. Nix said,

"Please sit down, no need for such formality here. Please introduce yourselves in turn." Nix sat.

"Commander Torrance Whitney." She smiled first at Zephyr, nodded her head, and looked at Jansee.

"Jansee." She bowed her head more deeply, as was her custom.

"Gantu." She extended her long thin arm and hand for Zephyr to take, and wrapped her other hand over Zephyr's. "Thank you for allowing us into your home and for preparing such beautiful food for us."

"Fazeef. I've read some of your biological theories, and I'm particularly fond of Nix's art. I feel honored to be in the presence of such beings." He smiled as he bowed first toward Zephyr, then toward Nix.

Nix recalled the stern faces of his ancestors carved into the temple of Thebes, and realized what a revelation Fazeef's smile was — something humans hadn't seen in thousands of years.

"Derthan. My interests are various, and I, um, am mostly fascinated by the air." Her eyes were a mesmerizing yellow-green in the light of 20 candles that burned down the length of the table. She smiled broadly, showing a beautiful set of especially white teeth.

They held up their water glasses and smiled first toward Zephyr, then toward Nix, then drank.

Nix said, "Thank you all. Now, let's enjoy this wonderful meal."

Small sweet tomatoes, creamy avocados, and flaky smoked salmon on their plates — such simple things, but so excellent and pure in taste. Eaten together, they became something greater than the sum of the parts.

The table was covered in small bowls and plates — olives, raisins that were plump as a half-deflated grape with a short shriveled stem on top, almonds, lemons cut into wedges and drizzled with honey, dates filled with white cheese, apples cut in half and sprinkled with cinnamon. The visitors ignored all of the silverware on the sides of their plates, except when taking a portion from the common dishes. Anything on their plates they ate with their fingers. Nix felt responsible for this, but only for a second until she realized she would like to be eating with her fingers too, as she had been for weeks now, but felt stilted knowing that Zephyr would judge her.

Each table setting had two sets of clear glasses. One filled with water, the other with wine. Bottles of both were on the table. The visitors were drinking slowly, but steadily, equal proportions of water and wine.

"This wine tastes different from the other you served before. More earth, but also more silk and fruit," Gantu said.

"Very well-described," Nix said.

"I love when you talk so sensuously," Jansee said, turned Gantu's face with her hands and kissed her on the mouth. Gantu took it one step further and pushed her tongue into Jansee's mouth. Nix looked away and cleared her throat. *What the hell was going on with them?* She stared at her plate, then smiled at Zephyr and shrugged her shoulders. Nix held her glass up as if toasting toward Zephyr, but didn't wait for anyone else, or say anything, and took a swallow of wine. *Is having them in the house with Zephyr a bad idea?* Everything they did made Nix so self-conscious, like she was responsible for them. But that wasn't true.

When she looked at Zephyr a second time, Zephyr was staring at Torrance. Oh, she must have recognized her. There was no doubt. They hadn't talked about Torrance in over a decade, but that didn't make the wound any less fresh; it was just ignored, not healed. Nix had carefully watched Zephyr's face when Torrance introduced herself, but she didn't notice anything unusual. Now, Zephyr's head was turned to the left, her eyes squinted, her bottom lip was sucked in and undulated against her upper teeth. Nix knew what she was thinking — *it's Torrance, but it can't be Torrance.*

"The wine is good. I can feel it already," Derthan said. A drunken half-smile on her face, she turned her attention to her left side and started to tap her forearm, pushed at it as if she were typing. When Derthan looked up, Nix was staring at her. "My defenses are compromised. I had to set an extra layer of alarms for us and the transport." She winked at Nix and shaped her hands into pistols and made shooting sounds with her mouth.

Nix shook her head. She couldn't help it. They probably had enough munitions to blow up half the state.

"Thank you, Zephyr, for providing such delicious food for us tonight. Am I correct that nothing is cooked?" Gantu asked.

"Yes. All raw, all local. In the old days we said 'seasonal' too, but now the growing patterns are not reliable. You saw the greenhouse on the back lot?" she asked.

Nix interrupted, "Not yet. I was waiting for your return." Her rationale was that the greenhouse was one of their key food sources, and she didn't know if she could trust the visitors. They outnumbered her. Now those thoughts seemed ludicrous.

"I'd be happy to show it to you in the morning," Zephyr said. "Do you know much about gardening?"

Gantu lifted her large hand to delicately stroke the top of her ear. "We are taught from a young age about plants. We've heard that Earth children are more inclined to animal pets, but we are given plants. Oh, I've loved many plants." She tilted her head up and to the right. "Basic, hardy plants to start, then we are granted more exotic species with very specific soil, light, and water requirements as we prove our skills at sustaining them."

"Plants do have a beautiful silence and stillness that animals do not," Zephyr said. She looked at Nix and smiled.

Nix saw Zephyr's face change, turn suddenly pale, as something crossed her mind, "Did you say 'Earth children?' "

"I did," Gantu said. "As we are not."

"Zephyr," Nix said as she stood, her aching limbs forgotten as her heart filled with panic at her oversight. "They arrived by ship, the large silver bullet at the far end of the open space. I thought you'd seen it since you always return from that direction." Nix rushed to Zephyr's side faster than she thought her legs could carry her. She put one hand on her back between her shoulders. "Look at them, they are us, they're not little green men with slanted black eyes and no noses. They're human. They've just been away for a while and now they've returned."

"Then this..." Zephyr stood up, pushed the chair so violently with her legs that it fell over with a loud crash. She pointed her finger at Torrance. "*This* Torrance... is somehow *your* Torrance." Nix moved quickly to straighten the chair and get it behind her before her legs gave out. Nix pushed the chair slightly forward just as Zephyr sat down heavily. She continued to stare at Torrance, her eyebrows expressing her confusion.

Nix put one hand over Zephyr's, wrapped her fingers around and squeezed.

"Zephyr, we come in peace," Torrance said. The crew laughed, Nix laughed, but Zephyr did not.

Nix said, "Come on, honey, that was funny."

Zephyr stood and stared at the faces at her table, in her house. She had made food for them. How could Nix have left out such important facts? She felt shaken. She was an adult woman with years of social skills from things as vicious as the art world of the pre-warming, who had adapted her instincts and skills into things that made her a very successful barterer in the region. But this was too much for her. "Good night," Zephyr said to no one in particular as she walked toward the bedroom. She heard the clink of glasses, and some laughter in the seconds following the brief silence.

10, GRINDING IT OUT

Sometime in the night, Nix got into bed. In her half-conscious state, she saw that Zephyr was turned away from her. She lay down and closed her eyes.

Zephyr's voice like a shadow, "Torrance…" but that was the only word. Hearing it was enough. A few thoughts of Torrance and Nix's body responded, and she felt no guilt. No words needed to be said, after so many years, some understood signal was given and their naked bodies met under the sheets and Zephyr opened her legs. It was practiced and predictable, one of the three positions they had in their repertoire.

This brief, intense sexual release turned into an every night event. Nix tried to get off, ramming and rubbing her body against Zephyr. It didn't matter the position, she pushed her body, her hands, her fingers, her tongue — to satisfy the desire that was the master of her mind. In the dark of the night, the sex felt anonymous in the best possible way, heated and self-gratifying. Losing herself in the purely physical, the pain of her hands dissolved in the heated pleasure of her body, which emanated the intensity of an angle grinder with a friction that threatened to wear down the organic shells of their bodies. The forgotten pain of her tortured hands and Zephyr's receptive silence made for a powerful and addictive mixture. But satisfaction was elusive; even after an orgasm, the watchful beast of lust stared out through her eyes, wanting still more. Only after a second orgasm did her mind relent, and her body, too sensitive to be touched again for several hours, would settle into post-orgasmic sleep. The sleep she got between midnight and dawn was deep and dreamless. Nix made it through the next two weeks without any dreams of Torrance, without any daytime stirrings of desire.

But two weeks was as long as it lasted. For the past two mornings after Zephyr had gotten up to start her day, Nix had smoothed her hand over the sheet beside her, wondering what it would be like to have Torrance there. She remembered a dream of Torrance from the previous night — she had been tricked somehow, suddenly both of them were naked in each other's arms. She remembered thinking in the dream *I'm here now, I might as well keep going — just live with what you are* — her subconscious trying to tell her of the inevitable slide to do what her body insisted must be done. All the old energy was still there between them, magnetic and forceful. Nix started to panic. *How will I resist, is there any way to resist, what if I can't resist?*

She had hoped with each new relationship that it would be different, that it would last, that her curiosity would settle and she would find a way to still desire a woman beyond knowing her, in spite of knowing her. Her longest stretch had been with Torrance, she had never gotten enough of her, but after eight years, Torrance's request to be part of the colonization was approved. She'd had three months to prepare for her departure. It may as well have been death that separated them — same outcome of complete and utter separation with no chance of return, and it felt as horrible. She had begged Nix to go with her, but she couldn't leave. At the time she didn't know if it was fear, or her love of stone. How could she give up her love for something as esoteric as art? But since Torrance's departure, she had thought on it long and hard, and could acknowledge now that she loved the Earth at its deepest level — the stone — and she would not be separated from it at any cost. She had to admit that she loved it more than any woman. Instead Nix had focused on her own grand gesture — that she loved Torrance enough to let her leave, to go to a place where she could live.

After Torrance had left, Nix was alone for a time, never staying with anyone beyond a week or two. If she started to feel any kind of affection or attachment, she left. At the last gallery showing of her work, she met Zephyr, who was running the gallery to make a living, and at night working to master gardening at one of the most challenging times in human history. Nix was amazed by the journals she kept, full of precise measurements, breeding logs, and details of radical experiments, as she attempted to adapt plant species before they died off. Nix told her that this show would be her last, that she had recently purchased 20 acres in Northern California, a place were she would have space to work on her next set of pieces, which would be too large for any work space in the city. She had already ordered the massive stones, and they would be delivered before she arrived. Zephyr loved the idea of the extra large sculptures, and asked if she could visit to see the progress of the pieces. They got close slowly, so slowly that Nix didn't notice, and so didn't push her away. Zephyr was her only visitor for the first year and never stayed longer than to see the pieces and have lunch. When Zephyr finally stated her wish to set up a full lab and greenhouse on Nix's land, it took another year before she untangled herself from all her obligations and moved in with Nix.

In the self-sufficient isolation they created, Nix was finally monogamous (though it took moving to the middle of nowhere and only going into town once a month). She smiled to herself. She *had* found a way. Then she considered that the other night while making love to Zephyr she could only think of Torrance beneath her, imagined Torrance's nipple in her mouth, closed her eyes and let her mind have what it wanted. What happened in her mind was hers, every long marriage required some fantasizing to get through the lean times, which for Nix tended to accelerate around year seven and went off the cliff shortly after. She sat up in bed suddenly. She needed to get to work. Too much thinking so early could ruin her whole day.

Nix got to the worksite and put her work coveralls on and was quickly reminded of how bruised the front of her pelvic bone was. She reached down and delicately touched the bruised area, tested the tolerance. Torrance arrived as the sun rose, and Nix did her best to hide her discomfort, but all it took was a turn to the left or right, enough to pull the material across her crotch and the coveralls reminded her of the recent night's desires. She turned to reach for a chisel and for a split second her flesh was bound, pinched. She dropped the chisel, grimaced and reached down to pull the suit down and away.

Torrance asked, "What's wrong? Ants in your pants?" They both laughed. Nix bent to pick up the chisel.

"Sun's up. Time to get to work," Nix replied.

As each day passed, Nix continued to circle the rock with the pneumatic saw in hand, but made fewer and fewer cuts. She checked, double-checked, examined the stone from every angle. Then one gloomy morning, the sky blocked out by dark gray clouds and ready to burst with rain, Nix set the grinder down at her feet. "We did it, Torrance. Ha ha!" She put her arms up in a V, smiled, closed her eyes.

Nix walked over and hugged Torrance. Plumes of white dust rose from Nix's shoulders, Torrance coughed instead of hugging her. Nix stepped back, kept hold of the round perfection of Torrance's shoulders, "We've completed the first phase. This is huge. We are going to celebrate. Fuck. I would have never guessed we'd get this far in four months."

"You know the process so well now that you have recognizable phases?" Torrance asked. She unplugged the grinder from the extension cord, was startled by the raw spark of blue electricity that jumped between the steel-tipped end of the plug and the cord's socket. She wrapped the cord around her elbow and upturned palm, then set the bundled cord on the ground beside the tool crate.

"Yes, I do. That is one of the benefits of living so long — knowledge that is enlightening to the individual, but completely useless to other humans, accumulates in the mind. That's 'wisdom.' But in all seriousness, I can predict that with a stone of this size, this upcoming phase, which is always the longest phase of any project — pure chisel and mallet — will last 12 to 18 months."

"But that calculation is based on you working alone, right?" Torrance asked.

"Of course, but there is really nothing that untrained labor can do in the next phase. I appreciate all you and your crew did during the first phase — the scaffolding, the initial roughing out, all the clean up. All of those things did cut time off of the project as a whole. But..."

"But what?" Torrance asked as she picked up the grinder.

"But, even if I have all of you help me, we won't be able to accelerate this phase in the same way. When we get past this phase and move to polishing, then you'll be able to assist me again," Nix said. "Like I said, we need to celebrate the end of the first phase." *Because who knows if you'll be around for the final celebration.*

"Do you have a certain ritual?" Torrance said.

"You know me too well, my girl." *Why did she say that?* She chose to move past it without showing her surprise or explaining to Torrance. "Phase one is celebrated with a bonfire under the full moon. I'll invite some people who live within a day's ride, and they'll come here and eat and drink with us."

"And when they see the ship?" Torrance asked.

"Can't you make it invisible or something?" Nix laughed to herself.

"Yes, by activating the infrared molecules in the phyto-platinum skin. Birds will be able to see the ship, so they won't fly into it. But humans won't see it at all."

"There you go." Nix put the grinder into the crate. She closed the lid and sat on it facing Torrance. "Let me ask you this: Are you going to wait here for a year or more until this is finished? If not, then it really doesn't matter if anyone sees the ship, and if you are, then it matters even less."

Torrance turned her whole body away from Nix. The thought of staying here for another year made her feel sick to her stomach. She turned back to Nix, "Do you think we are prepared to protect this ship that long from whatever hostiles are here?"

"God, don't let Derthan's fear infect you. No one cares that you're here. No one is going to rush the ship to get off this planet. Everyone who wanted to leave has left." Nix hung her head down, looked at her hands resting on the crate. "But I guess that answers my question. You're not staying, so what is the rush on getting this piece done?"

Torrance stood back and crossed her arms across her chest, "Have you thought about anyone but yourself here? Have you forgotten why I had to leave? Do you know how many pills I have to take every day to live in this air?"

Nix stood and put her hand on her forehead. "I thought...I mean, look at you, you still look 30 years old, and more beautiful than the day you left...no, I didn't think you would come back here and still be sick...make yourself sick to be here with me." She could feel a throbbing under her brows. She closed her eyes and squatted down onto her haunches, sat on the grass, and finally gave in and lay down on the grass. She was so physically exhausted from the last phase of the project and wasn't expecting to have this conversation so soon. Or was it late? It felt soon. Oh, she didn't know what the visitors wanted, beyond their tidy explanations of checking on the planet's health and collecting samples. Inside she was still suspicious of it all — the "gift" they had brought for her, their looks, their landing here of all places. And Torrance who looked too young and healthy now saying that she was slowly being poisoned by the air. Thump, inhale, thump, thump, exhale — she could hear her heart beat in her ears. A raging headache was almost upon her, smothering her slowly like a coiling python. "Torrance, will you get me some water?" Prone and flat she stared up at the sky, which looked like a crumpled dirty blanket. Wispy fingers of fog blew over the treetops. She focused on breathing the cool, brined air in through her nose and out through her mouth.

Torrance returned with water and sat on the ground beside Nix's head, "Here," she said. She picked up her head and held the water cup to her lips.

"Oh, darling, I've overdone it. Older but not always wiser." She said, and sipped more water. She didn't look at Torrance, she kept her eyes closed. The feel of Torrance's hand cupping the back of her head provided a level of comfort that Nix savored even through the pain.

Torrance said, "Yes, look at you. Splayed in the grass. Down like a dog that's run too far. Swear to me that you'll take it easy the next week, then we'll talk about this celebration more."

"I promise, I will," Nix said. She could hear Torrance breathing. She could feel the pulse of Torrance's heartbeat in the palm that supported her head.

"Water is the first medicine. Have some more, then I'll walk you back to the house so you can rest," Torrance said.

" 'Water is the first medicine.' You talk like an old woman sometimes," Nix said. "I'm ready to go in now."

"I'm only quoting you," Torrance said.

"I'm ready to go in now," Nix replied.

Torrance helped her up, and walked with Nix's arm over her shoulder. Zephyr was not in the house when they entered. Nix called out to her, but no answer. "I'll sit on the couch for a while," Nix said.

Torrance walked her over, but let her sit on her own. "I'll get more water." She walked to the kitchen and filled a ceramic pitcher, set it on the table next to Nix. "Drink it all. Sleep if you can." Torrance leaned forward and kissed Nix's forehead, then pressed her hand flat against Nix's breastbone and held it there for a few seconds. "I have things to do on the ship. I'll see you for dinner tonight."

11, *LIKE* US, BUT *NOT* US

Nix rested for several days, sleeping well past sunrise. She was never seen without a cup of water in her hand, a ceramic jug in the other. During the day she walked around the stone, she spent hours looking at it — at times just standing without moving, her eyes shaded against the sun. She moved her head from side to side, looked for things only she could see, or squatted very close to the rock face and rubbed her hand over the stone; occasionally she would wet her hand and rub it over the surface. She spent one entire day sitting on the grass staring at it, moving as the sun moved until she had made a complete circle. None of the crew understood the reason for this. She could be seen mumbling to herself. No one knew what the stone was saying to her, whatever she was hearing or seeing, and she didn't mention any of it to the crew during their shared dinnertime. Instead Nix quoted from the many books she was reading simultaneously, and ideas that came from deep in her mind. At times she brought art books to the dinner table, held them up, and lectured — completely ignoring the food. She didn't seem to notice the way she monopolized the conversation to explain a technique. After dinner she sat on the couch and read until she fell asleep.

On Torrance's orders, the crew stayed clear of Nix and Zephyr aside from dinnertime. Their fieldwork was taking them farther out from the open space. At sunrise they set out in separate directions or sometimes in pairs. Torrance spent most of her day on the ship, processing logs and samples, reviewing ship stats and the crew's vids.

But after a week of reading and lying around, Nix was ready to engage in some physical activity again. She was craving movement, sweat, thoughtlessness.

When the visitors came by for dinner that night, they settled into their chairs quickly. They were remarkably punctual, and Nix admired that. She had also noticed that they sat in the same chairs that they had from their very first visit to the house. It must be based on rank.

"I'd like to see some variation in the seating arrangements. Is that possible Torrance?" Nix asked.

"We sit according to rank and security," Torrance replied.

"I'd like for everyone to get a chance to talk to Zephyr, since she hasn't had as much time to talk with the crew as I have," Nix said.

"That's a reasonable request," Torrance said. "We'll start with a new arrangement now." The crew stood and shuffled to the seat on their right side. Once seated, they adjusted plates and silverware. Everything impressively coordinated with minimal disruption. Nix had imagined something more extreme than one seat to the right, but it would do for now. She enjoyed seeing how they reacted to things. And this was a clear sign of serious hierarchy, but she didn't know if it was cultural or mission-based. She wondered if Torrance was messing with her. But now that the visitors were in the 'saying yes' mood, Nix asked for more.

"I'm looking for a couple of volunteers who would like to work with the animals this week. Duties could include, but not limited to — paddock maintenance, feeding, washing. Ah, also some horse riding. I know it sounds grand, so don't all volunteer at once." None of them were looking at her, they were looking at Torrance. There were no hands raised. There was no outward sign of communication.

"Gantu and Fazeef have volunteered," Torrance said.

Nix nodded in acknowledgement, but didn't understand how they had communicated that or if Torrance had just ordered them to do it. She looked at Zephyr, who rolled her eyes. The trick here was to realize the visitors were *like* them, but *not* them. The surface was comforting, but very little about them was similar to an Earth-raised human. How could something so fascinating deserve an eye roll from Zephyr?

They finished dinner in silence. Gantu was sitting beside Nix since they shuffled seats. Nix reached over and stroked her arm and smiled. "Don't stay up too late tonight. I've got a full day of activities planned for you two."

Gantu turned as slowly as a preying mantis to look at her, a smile curling only the corners of her wide mouth. "We will be fully prepared."

"You feel some unexplainable connection to the horses, don't you?"

"It is a difficult feeling to explain. I've seen pictures and vids of these animals, but being near them, I feel an urge to touch their noses and stroke their necks. And the feeling of sitting atop one… I feel connected to the earth, but so high, powerful. How can such a thing feel so natural to me? So familiar?"

No one answered. Nix stood up and walked around the table gathering plates onto a stack on her left arm. Most of the visitors were staring blankly ahead. "Let's explore it further tomorrow," Nix said.

In the morning, Gantu and Fazeef met Nix at the horse paddock dressed in their pristine white uniforms and issued boots. Nix laughed when she looked at them. "I have extra boots and coveralls inside. I'd suggest changing. This is dirty work, and smelly. I don't know what kind of detergent you brought with you, but horseshit is one of the toughest staining agents on the planet," Nix said.

They took Nix's advice and changed. Nix handed them pitchforks, and gave a demonstration of how to hold it, the best way to get leverage it, how to scoop and pitch without hurting their backs. As they started to pitch, Nix was again awed with their physical strength and endurance. They moved so smoothly, pitch after pitch executed just as she had shown them. They kept a quick and steady pace. The horses stood in the adjacent paddock and watched them work. After 20 minutes, they were sweating, and Nix was too. She had kept her own pace, feeling no pressure to keep up with them. She was happy just to have some help and get this done after neglecting it for too long. Then something spooked the horses, one of them reared, at the same time the other violently kicked the fence. Gantu turned to see what was happening, her pitchfork went through Fazeef's calf. Nix saw it happen. Fazeef barely winced, but bit his lip and looked down at his leg. Gantu quickly pulled the pitchfork out, and thrust it into the manure pile beside her. She took a few steps closer to her brother and looked into his eyes.

"I'm fine. I'm fine," Fazeef said.

Nix bent down, took hold of Fazeef's leg. It felt warm, muscular, pliable. She squeezed the tissue, but he didn't react. There was no blood. "What do you mean you're fine? You could get sepsis from this. I need to find some antibiotics for you. Come on, I have some in the shed." Nix stood squarely, offered her shoulder for him to lean on, but he didn't show a single sign of pain on his face. She started to question what she'd seen.

"He's fine. No need for any medication," Gantu said.

"Yes, I'm immune," Fazeef said. He gently put his hand on Nix's shoulder. "Trust me, Nix. I'm good to keep working. If only she'll be less skittish." He leaned his head toward his sister. "Gantu, really, why such a reaction?"

What the hell? Nix was very confused. So confused that she couldn't even formulate another question.

Gantu tilted her head all the way to the left and frowned. "I'm not fully adapted to them yet." She grabbed her pitchfork and started to pitch as if nothing had happened. Fazeef reached down and brushed the side of the coverall where there was a puncture hole from the tine. "Sorry to have damaged your suit," he said.

They resumed their pace and pitched manure with the same enthusiasm that they had shown when tearing down the old shed and constructing the scaffolding. Nix worked beside them for another hour until the paddock was cleaned down to the dirt floor.

Fazeef showed no sign of discomfort the rest of the afternoon. Nix didn't dwell on it, but once in a while she watched him walk. He remained unaffected.

They spent the next several mornings feeding and grooming the animals. Nix taught them using as many scientific words as possible, realizing how much slang and local dialect — words not likely to be deciphered through Lifestream — had crept into her vocabulary over the years. By the end of the week, Nix could see a noticeable difference in their interactions. They were at ease, the animals trusted them. Gantu brushed the horse's manes down in long strokes, smiled as she talked to Nix. She was attentive but assertive; a good mix when dealing with horses.

One morning they prepared for a long horseback ride. They saddled the horses, and packed the saddlebags with water and food. They rode in the open space first, walked the horses in simple patterns. Nix watched them execute different signals to the horses to see if they were comfortable with one another.

When Nix was satisfied, she waved for them to follow her into the forest. There was no trail. They walked silently across the spongy forest floor, stepped over fallen trees, picked their way through the trees until they arrived at the lake. The water was calm, a deep green color. They walked along the edge of the water until the horses were in the water up to their stomachs. Nix turned in her saddle, watched them. They sat majestically straight, but not stiff, their bodies swayed forward and back with the horses' gate. Nix led them over a small feeder stream and back into the woods.

Gantu's horse stumbled, its front leg collapsing, the body rolling to the right. Gantu leaped off to the left, rolled on her side. The horse scrambled to catch its balance, dashed straight ahead and to the left, slowed and came to a stop, looked back at them, tossed its head up and down, snorted. Nix dismounted immediately. "Are you alright?" she asked Gantu. The horse trotted by Nix. Nix said 'whoa' in her deepest voice and the horse slowed and stopped. Nix took hold of the horse's reins, stroked the long part of the mare's face, then neck. Nix reached down and slid her hand down the horse's front leg, picked it up and looked at the bottom of the hoof. She led the horse in a small circle, watched her walk. Everything appeared to be normal.

Gantu pushed herself up and sat with her arms on her knees for a second. She smiled up at Nix with her hands upturned. Gantu froze for a second, stared straight ahead as she reviewed the diagnostic information scrolling over her retinal screen. "No broken bones, some deep tissue bruising near my left hip. Fingernail on right hand is producing a small amount of blood beneath the nail. Three times normal adrenaline levels. Otherwise good." She stood up and looked at her fingernail, then brushed the pine needles and dust from her uniform.

"Get back on," Nix said.

"Of course, that is the ancient adage. I'm happy to have a chance to understand it finally," Gantu replied. She put her foot into the stirrup, grabbed the saddle horn and the rear of the saddle, bounced once and threw her leg over. It was a graceful, powerful movement. She landed in the saddle with such confidence. Nix handed her the reins. The rest of the ride was uneventful.

When they returned, they stopped at the barn to unsaddle the horses. The day had gone so well, that they were ready for the next level — bareback riding. The crew stripped everything from the horses except their bridles. They had no problem grabbing a handful of the mane and swinging a leg over. They rocked forward and back to get a feel for how to sit, how their legs could hang or squeeze the horse.

"Feels right, doesn't it?" Nix asked. She circled around them on her horse. "Everything works the same — the way you sit and move with the horse, the signals you send through your legs and the reins. You're much closer to them now, but there is no saddle horn to hold onto."

"There is so much heat coming from them," Fazeef said.

"They've had a bit more of a workout than they're used to. It's hard for us to ride all of them as much as they need," Nix said.

"I could ride for days," Fazeef said. "The feeling is very enjoyable."

"Let's take them for a little run to the woods," Nix said. "Keep both hands in the middle of the neck, loose, floaty, don't lean on her neck. Hold on with your legs, rock with the motion of the gallop."

Gantu jabbed her heels into her horse's ribs, and instinctively leaned forward as the horse sprang into a full gallop. Fazeef was only a split second behind her. Nix gave full rein to her horse to catch up, and rode beside Gantu at breakneck speed across the open space, her horse so close that Gantu could hear the snorting breaths, feel the heat of its body on her leg. Gantu laughed out loud. She looked over at her brother beside her to the left, then at Nix on her right. The feeling of the muscular mass thundering beneath her caused a surge of emotions — joy, freedom, pride in being able to ride this animal on Earth like so many of her ancestors had.

"Dinner tastes very good tonight, thank you for taking the time to cook for us, Zephyr," Gantu said, looking at Zephyr and bowing her head.

"You are welcome. I saw you riding today. I think you have some natural abilities. You too, Fazeef."

"I wouldn't go that far. But we are nearly identical genetically," Fazeef said.

Near the end of the meal, Nix said, "One more thing. I'd like the rest of you to start doing various things around the property — to give Zephyr a break and also to get more of a feel for life here, the simple rewards of work, the cycle of life, and so forth." Nix took a long swallow of wine and sat back to hear their responses.

"Agreed. We'll start as soon as you are ready to teach us," Torrance said.

Nix took another swallow of wine. "And one other thing, I'm going to throw a party to celebrate progress on the sculpture. The invitations will have to be delivered by hand, there's no postal service out here. I'd like Gantu and Derthan to ride with me. Fazeef will continue to care for the animals. He'll teach Jansee what he knows while we're gone. When we return from the ride, I'll be doing some work in my studio — the small building with no windows on the far edge of the property. I have a few ideas to work out, so it's time to get back into the clay. I'm looking for a couple of volunteers to help harvest the clay from a place near the lake. It's dirty, difficult work. Whoever is inclined to help will get to learn the basics of clay sculpting when I start."

"And how is that benefiting *me*?" Zephyr asked.

12, THE LONG RIDE

Nix saddled her horse, made a quick second pass to test the tightness of the billet strap, bent to check the clearance of the rear cinch, then watched Gantu and Derthan saddle their horses. She wanted to take some credit for teaching them, but they learned so quickly and easily that she could only justify a modest smile.

The plan was to ride together to deliver invitations to women who lived in the area. She couldn't take Fazeef; a man on the trail would raise questions that Nix didn't want to answer. She'd have to answer them eventually when the guests arrived. She couldn't just ask him to hide out on the ship for two days until everyone left. Or could she? She would have plenty of time to figure that out during the ride.

Nix strapped on her saddlebags. She lifted the flaps and checked the contents once more.

"We brought food for the expedition. We don't want to impose on your resources any more than necessary," Gantu said.

Derthan held up green and red foil pouches she was about to shove into her saddlebag. "Some of the tastiest food in the universe," Derthan said. She raised her eyebrows as she made an exaggerated smirk and licked her lips. "I can bring enough for you too, Nix. Greens are plant-based, reds are lab-grown protein."

Nix shook her head. "That puts a whole new perspective on 'local.' You got enough water? I told you three days' worth, but you look light." She expected the ride to be one day out, eat and drink at the farthest house, then one day back, but she had to plan for contingencies. The woods had been clear of hostiles for years, but it was prudent to be on guard.

"We have water purifiers, so if there is water along the way, we would prefer to refill," Derthan said. "It means less weight. Maybe it doesn't matter so much with these animals, but we have resource conservation pounded into our heads from birth. We have an extra filter. It even desalinates."

"Bring the extra, but I won't use it. There'll be water, questionable for drinking. But if your filter is as described, there'll be plenty."

"The filters are proven technology, they eliminate all contaminants and enhance the flavor to something we are accustomed to," Derthan said.

"Killing germs I understand, but don't you think changing the taste defeats the purpose of exploration?" Nix asked.

"It's water. Our bodies need it, best to have it be palatable," Gantu said.

The sun was beginning to lighten the sky. Blue-black was streaked with deep red gashes. Nix watched the clouds to see if they would thicken or evaporate. Packing finished on schedule. The rest of the crew and Zephyr had gathered in the open space beside the horse paddock. They talked among themselves until the women mounted their horses and rode out to say goodbye. Gantu bent from her saddle to kiss Jansee. Torrance patted Derthan's leg. "Protect them," she said in a voice only Derthan could hear.

Nix lead the way toward a point in the forest only she saw, though she was sure that one of the other two would be able to lead on the way back, if they wanted.

Gantu felt a pulling emotion in her chest, a physical pain of separation from the crew. She hadn't ever felt such a sentimental moment. Even when she had left Kepler-442B, her guardians smiling and waving, there had been no tears, no fear of never seeing them again. This was a short, low-risk trip. There was no reason to feel this way. Then the saddle reminded Gantu of the previous day's ride, an inventory of painful places she hadn't even realized were damaged on her rear and inner thighs. She sat up straight and held her head with her chin extended, her arms relaxed, the reins in her upturned right hand that rested on the saddle horn. "Audio log: Day 148. Seasons are irrelevant as a marker of time passing here. It feels as if time passes more quickly on this planet, even when the weather is challenging or threatening, our days are so full, and our nights just as fulfilling, that days are over in a flash. I could stay here forever, I think. Today we are leaving on a two-day trip to deliver party invitations by horseback. It sounds so primitive, but I'm thrilled to have a chance to do it. What wonders lay beyond Nix's land? I am fully open to see whatever is presented. End log:"

Nix heard Gantu talking and turned around in her saddle, grabbed the back with one hand as she twisted her upper body around to look behind her. She had given them a couple of beat-up straw hats she had in the barn. The hat suited Derthan, who wore it tipped down to keep the sun out of her eyes. She rode with her shoulders rolled forward, slightly hunched over like an old farmhand. On Gantu the hat couldn't have looked more ill-placed, a thing that belonged to someone else that she had been forced to wear out of necessity. She had regal riding posture, more expected of someone riding in a carriage, but she smiled at Nix and leaned forward to stroke her horse's neck.

The sky was filled with high clouds, the slight northwesterly breeze was as cool as water against exposed skin. Good riding weather, but it couldn't be trusted to hold for the entire trip. They walked into the second forest, slightly higher as the hills rose up out of Nix's valley. The temperature was much cooler out of the sun. Pastel green moss hung loosely from branches. Beneath the horses' hooves fallen branches crunched and cracked, muffled by a cinnamon blanket of pine needles. The horses seemed to know where they were going and required no effort to guide. The three rode in silence. Derthan scanned, her ears and eyes carefully processing every noise, movement, or shift of shadow. She was in hostile territory, just because the woods were quiet and empty it meant nothing. Anything could happen at any time.

Gantu was also very alert, but for different reasons. She felt no signs of danger and trusted her intuition. Instead of worrying about threats, she was listening to the aggressive chirp of the large blue jay that hopped from tree to tree until they were out of his territory. That bird should be neutralized, it could be giving away their position. But she would leave such things to Derthan. Once clear of the screeching jay, she preferred to observe the way the sunlight fell onto the forest floor, and savored the delicious smell of fallen pine needles warmed in the sun. She watched for plants and animals. When they passed from the woods to a clearing, a large predatory bird flew overhead. The bird glided on fully extended wings, its red tail feathers tilting to make small adjustments. She stopped her horse so she could watch with her full attention. She touched the side of her temple. "Identify:" she said as the picture was captured.

":Red-tailed hawk, male. Weight range is 690 to 1300 grams. Height range is 45 to 60 centimeters. Wingspan ranges from 105 to 141 centimeters. Sexual dimorphism favors females with a 25 percent larger body than males. Adapted to all biomes in North America. Trained for falconry…"

"Stop:" Gantu said. Her eyes were pulled like magnets to watch the bird circle above. In the moment the bird was directly over her, something that felt like a memory — an image of a man's body with a hawk's head — was quickly displaced when the hawk banked and left her staring directly into the sun. She looked away quickly, seeing great red-orange spots everywhere she looked.

"Come on, you have to keep pace," Nix said, completely dislodging the memory from Gantu's grasp.

"Yes, pic it and keep moving. This isn't a nature ride," Derthan said. Tension was evident in her tone.

Gantu made a clicking sound with her mouth and squeezed her horse with her legs as she lifted the reins higher up onto the horse's mane. She bounced with the canter until she neared the rear of Nix's horse. Derthan's horse cantered to close the distance. Gantu looked back and said, "I don't know how you enjoy anything."

Derthan smirked, but said nothing.

"No fighting," Nix said. "Christ. Should I have picked two others? Really, was I just too dense to see that you two would be a major pain in the ass on this trip?"

"We're fine," Derthan said. "Ms. Spock doesn't know how to handle her overflowing emotions."

Gantu squeezed her horse again, urging it forward so that she could ride beside Nix. When they reached the far side of the meadow they entered forest again, but this time there was a very distinct, narrow, single trail in the forest floor. It was too worn and obvious to be a game trail. "Nix, is this for horse or human use?"

"Both," Nix said flatly.

They had been riding for almost two hours. Derthan felt like they were in the middle of nowhere. She turned in her saddle to check the trail behind her, rode for a long while turned around, then touched her forearm.

"Why are you setting a perimeter alarm?" Gantu asked as she saw it flash in the corner of her retina screen.

"Have you noticed the trail we're on? It's heavily trafficked. Sign of possible predators or hostiles," Derthan said.

"I can assure you, there are no hostiles in this area," Nix said.

"How can you be so sure?" Derthan asked.

"We've eliminated them," Nix said.

"You've what?" Derthan said.

"No more talking. Please. Try to enjoy the ride," Nix said.

They delivered the invitations to six houses in total. Six houses that looked more like shacks — slanted and leaning, gaps in the outer boards that must let in the wind and rain, doors ill-fitted to frames. Gantu and Derthan didn't actually go inside these places, so they chose to believe that looks were deceiving. For all they knew these facades were meant to dissuade entry, they could be filled with high-tech labs or equipment. Nix always went to the door alone, embraced a woman, talked for a few moments, handed off the invitation, embraced again, then returned to mount her horse and ride off.

As soon as they were out of earshot of the third house, Gantu asked, "Do they live so poorly compared to you?"

"They live as they choose," Nix said. "Not everyone desires such things as you see at my house."

"You do have many beautiful things. I think you live a rich life," Gantu said. She sat tall in her saddle, her hat cast a dark band over her eyes and nose.

As the day went on, they saw that the houses were quite varied — built high into trees, into the base of a hill, inside a natural cave. They each had some piece of cleared land, covered with a mixed-species grass like Nix had in her open space, and a water source nearby. Horses, and lots of dogs. Some houses had scrap metal and junk piled to one side of the house, others had yards filled with countless pots of various plants. Three greenhouses. Water catchment and reserve tanks. Solar panels that looked ancient to Gantu and Derthan. Nix made the visitors wait far enough away from the houses that they could see that the people answering the doors were women, but not close enough to see details of their faces or clothes.

Derthan scanned the houses and got readings indicating that two to four women were inside each house. She messaged Gantu's screen, ":Do you think it odd that we wait so far back from the house?"

Gantu made tiny, imperceptible movements with her eye to type her reply, ":Yes. Implies some fear, security concern," Gantu replied. But they said nothing to Nix.

At the final house, which looked abandoned, Nix instructed them to wait at the farthest edge of the property, to unsaddle the horses and make a fire. Nix tied up her horse and walked to the house. A woman with matted-looking hair and ragged work clothes that were too big for her, could be seen as a murky shadow on the other side of the screen door. A gun barrel protruded slowly through the ripped screen door.

"What did you come for?" they heard the woman ask. Derthan and Gantu stared, wondered how Nix could stand and talk to the woman as if there were no gun pointed at her belly. They couldn't hear anything else they discussed. Nix turned and pointed toward them. They smiled, but didn't wave. Derthan felt the urge to mount her horse and charge into the woods. Gantu made very slow motions, stooped to add wood to the fire, then took hold of Derthan's hand and pulled her down close to the fire. Gantu looked from the corners of her eyes without turning her head in the direction of the house. The sky was darkening. Soon the light of the fire would expose them more than hide them.

Nix returned, smiling and nodding her head. "You comfortable sleeping here?"

"You're asking us?" Derthan said, her voice pitched up at the end so it sounded like a teenage whine of disbelief. "How should we know if it is safe to sleep here?" She jammed a stick into the fire and caused a spurt of sparks to rise.

"You're not listening to what I asked," Nix said, trying to be patient with Derthan's paranoia.

"Then try again in simple English that I can understand," Derthan said.

"It's safe to sleep here. We're going to sleep here," Nix said slowly, patronizing in her simple delivery.

"Sleep on the grass?" Derthan said.

"Why is it any different from sleeping on my grass?" Nix asked.

"I don't know, why is it?" Derthan said. She looked around, scanning everything with quick turns of her head.

"What the hell is wrong with you? I'm not talking some secret code. I asked you a simple question," Nix reached over and put her palm on Derthan's forehead. "You feel warm. What are your gadgets telling you?"

Derthan was still for a moment as her bio results posted to her screen. "Elevated by point six degrees Celsius, which is essentially a non-indicator," Derthan said.

"Then get your food out and let's eat. It's almost dark, we need to sleep and ride out before the sun rises."

"Why?" Gantu asked, already laying down her reflective sleeping pouch that absorbed every nearby color and became close to invisible.

"Just do as I say," Nix said. There was an odd silence after she said this. The women lay down, not bothering to eat. Nix ate some of her dried fruit and nuts, washed it down with some water. She wondered if they were silently communicating over their comms systems, or even communicating with the crewmembers on the ship. Damn, she didn't care. She lay down and pulled the blanket up to her neck, looked up — the cold, black void of the sky, the pinpricks of light, the sparkling orbs, the snowy field of the Milky Way. She knew little about it, had never had the urge to go up or even look through a telescope. Would that change?

In the predawn darkness, as the first bird began to sing, they woke and ate in silence. Nix didn't speak, but made gestures with her hands for them to break camp. Derthan pressed her boot sole into the smoldering coals, extinguished most, then smothered the rest with damp earth. They saddled the horses and were riding through the woods before Nix could see well. She trusted her horse to see better than she could in the dark.

They rode through the day without stopping; they ate and drank while in the saddle, an urge in all of them to get back to more familiar surroundings. When they reached the lake, Nix abruptly stopped her horse. She raised her hand to her mouth to signal for silence. A deep snuffle, pause, more snuffling, wet sounds of open-mouthed chewing. The crew could not identify the animal purely from the sounds. Nix dismounted and tied her horse to the nearest tree. She unsheathed her rifle and motioned for the women to stay on their horses. She pointed two fingers toward her eyes, then out toward the lake. Nix motioned again for them to stay. They would be much safer on the horses if the boar went wild and charged. She walked with her gun pointed in front of her, sighting down the barrel, slightly crouched and rolling her footsteps from heel to toe until she saw the animal's rounded black back shivering with the effort of its thick neck and powerful snout as it tossed up great handfuls of clay from the bank of the lake. Why hadn't she thought to harness such an animal for her own clay harvesting? She was lucky to be down wind during her approach. He would be hard to pull out of the thick mud, but if he started to run, she might miss the shot. She kneeled onto on one knee and took the shot.

Gantu covered her ears a second too late. The shot was unexpectedly loud considering how far away Nix was.

The pig squealed and began to jump back out of the clay as if stung by a mighty bee. His shoulder was bloodied and his front leg was no longer functioning. He wrenched with his back legs to pull his body away from the lake. Nix considered a second shot, not wanting to damage the meat, but knowing the tenacity of feral pigs, she stood, walked toward it, and fired again.

The second shot was more unexpected than the first. The sound of the pig's cries, shrill and terror-filled, entered Gantu's ears and travelled down into her heart. She dismounted and ran to where Nix was standing. Nix turned, alarmed by the sound of Gantu's approach, she swung the gun and aimed it at her. Nix wanted to yell at her, to remind her that she was instructed to wait on her horse, but Gantu's face was twisted, her mouth open, brows slanted down, her right hand extended toward the pig, but it was too late, the kill was done.

Nix lowered the gun and laid it on the ground. She paced in a circle with her hands on her hips, took a deep breath, and sighed. "Christ, don't ever run up on me like that. I damn near could have shot you." She looked up at the sky and took another breath. She paced in wider and wider circles until her breathing and heart rate returned to normal. She took hold of Gantu's hand and walked toward the pig — still on all fours in the clay, its head forward as if drinking from the lake. "Damn, this is a fine gift. Enough to feed everyone at the party."

Gantu lifted Nix's hand and kissed the back of it as she stared at the animal. "For days."

13, BACCHANALIA

The day of the party arrived. Preparations had been finished in the days prior, because Nix didn't want anyone working on the day of the party. Firewood was stacked next to several fire pits dispersed across the open space. Nix had picked locations so that the fires would accentuate her sculptures, and also to keep people from creating their own fires. The open space and immediate perimeter of trees had been cleared and cleaned up for guests to sleep overnight. She knew these parties lasted through the night, at least until the sun came up, sometimes into the next day. They had built some temporary structures — four poles with a flat corrugated metal roof and three sides covered with tautly drawn canvas, the fourth wall draped with loose canvas — in case of bad weather, and because there was only enough room for four people to stay in the house. The guests would come well-prepared; they were all living in the same world, they knew what to expect — unpredictable weather, predators (man and animal) — they knew how to take care of themselves. Those that didn't had perished already.

"The guests will arrive relatively on time. I know them all well enough to know who will be here when," Nix told the crew as she lit the tinder under the waist-high pyramid of logs in the largest pit in the middle of the open space. The hardwood would create a substantial base of coals that Nix would continue to build into a roaring fire over 15 feet tall once the sun went down. She sat beside the fire pit to tend the fire, in between she sketched with a thin piece of charcoal on sheets of homemade paper. The crew joined her, sat on what they had come to think of as *their* stone stumps.

They talked quietly with one another, or stared at the fire, or into space.

On the far side of the open space was an old oil barrel cut in half lengthwise and hinged at the back. Zephyr had constructed it with a blowtorch and an arc welder. The roasting barrel sat about four feet above the ground on legs made of rusting, heavy-gauge steel pipe. Inside the smoking barrel was one of the largest pigs that Nix had ever killed on the far side of the lake. Its hollowed-out gut had been stuffed with whole apples and onions before being sewn shut.

"I thought Zephyr was making dinner for us tonight," Jansee said.

"Well, it's still daylight, dinner at the house will be within the hour. This pig will take another four hours to cook. You'll be ready for it by then." Nix looked over at Jansee. Her intelligent and gentle eyes had a mesmerizing shape that she quickly rendered onto the sketchpad, over and over, just the right eye, no pupil. She picked a feature from each of the visitors in turn and sketched it — Fazeef's nose, Gantu's hand, Derthan's chin, Torrance's...what part of Torrance to choose? She was frozen for a moment as whole images of Torrance's naked body flashed and paused for a moment in her mind like slides on a carousel. *Pick something. Pick anything. Unstick your gaze.*

Nix heard a murmur from the visitors and turned to see what was going on. The first guest entered the open space on foot just as the sun was descending toward the top of the trees. Nix stood and raised her hand high above her head, spread her fingers wide, in greeting. But before the first guest reached them, another guest made a strange call like the ancient cowboys and galloped into the open space on a thick-legged auburn horse, whose mane flowed down in kinked waves to the middle of its muscled shoulder. The horse braced its back legs and came to an abrupt stop a few feet from their fire, then snorted. The rider was slight, pixie-sized compared with her horse; she dismounted easily, but stood for a moment shaking her legs and stretching.

"Welcome, Serentia. Been a while since you've ridden this far?" Nix hugged her and the woman kissed Nix's cheek.

Gantu greeted the rider with a nod, not recognizing her from any of the houses they had delivered to, then let Derthan take the horse's reins.

"Thanks, dear. Let me keep those saddlebags with me," Serentia said. With fast fingers, she untied thin leather straps and the bags slid off of the horse. She heaved them onto her right shoulder, then turned back to Nix. "Yes, the longest trip I've had in a year." She hugged Nix again, slapped Nix's back several times. "Damn good to see you, old neighbor. Congratulations on your latest work. I'm excited to help you celebrate." She was the same height as Nix, had the same lean build and once fair skin that had seen too much sun over the years. Her fiery red hair matched her horse, and her eyes were green as grass. Her upper body was encased in a form-fitted green leather vest that covered her shoulders, then scooped low at the neck and pushed her breasts up so that they rose above the top seam and jiggled ever so slightly when she laughed or moved. "Brought some newly made mugs with me." She patted a saddlebag, "Mostly ceramic, some wood, some horn. They'll fit your hand like they were made for you." She winked at Nix then laughed. "Zephyr will be joining us tonight, or is she travelling?"

"She's in the house, fixing the last bit of food. She should be out soon."

"Ah, alright then, I'll go in and see if I can help with anything." Serentia adjusted the saddlebags higher onto her shoulder, then started toward the house. "Save me the place closest to the fire. Christ, I see you're prepared to burn a week's worth of wood in a night. Such decadence, I love it."

The guest who had entered the open space on foot was nearing the fire. She was laden with a backpack made of hides topped by a bedroll. "Nicole... Nicole," she called and waved both arms above her head like she was drowning. Nix started to walk toward her, then ran. Seeing Nix move so fast surprised Torrance. She knew she had strength and endurance, but not that kind of speed in her old body. The force of their embrace nearly knocked them over, they appeared to be dancing as their feet shuffled to keep them upright. They laughed and twirled in a circle, still hugging.

As other guests arrived, Derthan walked their horses to the paddock. She was responsible for prepping them for their overnight stay. She noticed that every guest had brought soft skins filled with liquid. She had seen skin bags strung together on a single piece of rope, hung from belts, backpacks, over saddle horns, or on each side of the back of the saddle like saddlebags. She was concerned that what was inside could be incendiary. After unsaddling and brushing the latest horse, giving it hay and water, she left the barn to find Nix, then discreetly asked her what was in the bags. Nix said aloud, "Wine."

"Looks like enough for all of us to bathe in," Derthan said.

"That's the point," Nix said. She took Derthan's hands and started to waltz with her, and sing, "In the pale moon light." Derthan moved stiffly. Nix shoved and pulled at her arms to get through the basic steps, humming, "La da dee, la dee dum." Derthan had watched vids of this ancient form of dancing. She tried, but couldn't concentrate on the steps because she was uneasy about what was to come with so much drinking among so many strangers. She looked toward the ship.

"Don't worry. It's going to be the most fun you've ever had. Come on, let's have dinner. Zephyr made something special for us tonight," Nix said. She looked at the open space and saw that a couple more guests had arrived. They didn't need anyone to introduce them, they were already talking with the visitors. Nix waved her open-palmed greeting to them, then started to gather everyone to walk to the house. They held hands or had their arms around waists. They talked easily and joked with each other. The crew wondered at this closeness of women who didn't see each other often. Gantu thought they might all be old lovers. There was some intimacy, a deep bond between them, but she didn't know yet what it was.

Inside, the table was set, covered with silver candelabras, black slate plates with their names written in white chalk. The guests, interspersed with the crew, took their seats. Crystal wine glasses with thin stems, and substantial silverware — four forks, two knives, two spoons per plate — everything looked so antique, like in the old vids the crew had seen. Nix walked around the table with a wine bottle that was twice the size of a normal bottle. Her thumb was inserted into the deeply indented bottom, her fingers spread wide on the underside to hold it as she gently tilted the bottle over each glass. She returned the bottle to the hutch behind her — a massive antique wood cabinet with smaller side cabinets and shelves that held various types of glasses and some mismatched cups and saucers made of white and blue patterned china behind clear glass-leaded doors. Each lower cabinet door was adorned with leaf and acorn patterns along the edges. On the hutch sat several extra large bottles like the one Nix had poured from, some clear, others made of deep green or brown glass, their tops sealed with wax. The bottles were marked with letters and numbers, which meant nothing to anyone but Nix and Zephyr.

The sunset painted the upper walls of the dining room with the last rays of hot orange and searing red. The level of conversation grew heated and loud. Every tongue felt the effects of the wine. Zephyr brought bowl after bowl and plate after plate of food — raw and cooked vegetables, cheese, olives, shelled almonds roasted with herbs, apples, walnuts smothered in honey. Then venison steaks and smoked whole ducks. Dishes were passed from person to person. Nix watched the visitors as much as was polite. She watched Torrance take second and third helpings of tomatoes and cheese, not touching the venison or duck. Each new dish was a surprise in presentation — adorned with coin-sized edible flowers or dusted with cylindrical clover petals, or wispy green scallion blades. Then came a single biscuit, lumpy and substantial, cracked open and overflowing with wild berries and topped with honeycombs that dripped golden dew.

It was a beautiful feast, and the crew was high with the pure tastes of Earth-grown food — the taste of soil in the skin of apples, the essence of sheep in the cubes of salty cheese, scent of meadow flowers in the honey, wood smoke in the duck meat. Each taste so different from the next. The crew touched their temples to take pics as dishes passed into their hands. They savored each bite slowly. Jansee excitedly pointed across the table for more of the things she liked, Gantu pressed her hands together then pointed them toward the dishes she wanted more of then nodded in gratitude to the person who handed it to her. While they ate, their eyes feasted on the faces around the table. They ignored the silverware and used their fingers to eat, tore things into bite-size pieces and pushed them into their mouths, chewing and smiling at the same time, making eye contact and laughing at the appropriate time when jokes were told. Nix was impressed with their integration. They were perfectly social in this moment. No one would believe they were off-landers if she told them.

":Old lovers?" flashed across all of their retina screens. Heads slowly turned toward Gantu. A sly smile spread her lips thinner. Jansee nodded. Derthan nodded. Torrance cleared her throat. They shouldn't be communicating like this in such mixed company. She made a gesture with her hand — a closed fist that she quickly tilted back up.

The gesture must have caught Nix's eye; she turned toward Torrance.

Torrance started to say, "We were wondering..." Derthan started to laugh, then Jansee. Nix assumed they were well on their way to being drunk.

"What is the question?" Nix said.

Gantu, wine-loosened, said, "What intimacy bonds you together with the women at this table?"

All of the conversations around the table ceased. The crew looked at the guests, trying to understand the situation. The guests smiled and sat back in their chairs, looked at Nix.

Nix cleared her throat, looked down at her plate, then back at Gantu, "We've done many things together, there isn't just one thing."

"Hunting," Serentia said.

"Killing," said another.

"And close quarter...interactions," said Zephyr.

"Of a sexual nature?" Gantu probed.

"Yes," many replied and nodded at once.

"Then Nix's house rules do not apply to these women?" Jansee asked.

"That is a true statement," Nix said.

Jansee turned to the woman next to her and kissed her. Gantu did the same thing, and so did Derthan. The situation looked so choreographed that Nix laughed out loud. "Starting the night off right, I'm happy to see you're getting into the spirit of the evening."

The crew stopped and smiled to each other, stood suddenly, picked up their wine glasses. The other guests stood a little more slowly, but also held their glasses aloft as Torrance said, "Zephyr, thank you for the sublime meal. We will be forever grateful." She bowed and turned to Nix, "We are ready for the festivities to begin." They all clinked their glasses together and drank.

When they emerged from the house, the crew was shocked to see that the open space fire pits were all lit with blazing fires surrounded by people. There was music being played and dancing. The moon was golden on the horizon.

Nix put her hand on Torrance's shoulder and said, "I'm glad you're ready. The party has started without us. Go enjoy yourself." Torrance led the crew toward the less populated edge of the open space. Nix walked into the fray with her guests. Nix had her rituals, first she would walk from fire pit to fire pit carrying a long, thin pike against her shoulder like a rifle. She would use it to move logs into better burning positions. The jostling of the logs sent rippling sheets of sparks skyward where they dissolved into the midnight blue sky. She talked to guests as she tended each fire, pointed out the high poles that were draped with venison sausages and whole smoked salmon, told them when the pig would be ready, and let them know where the shelters were located, then moved on to the next fire. Once she had made her rounds, she would leave the pike beside the front door of her house and carry bottles of wine from pit to pit.

Torrance huddled the crew around her, they put their arms over each other's shoulders and formed a tight circle. "Have a good time tonight. Do as you wish, alert if you need anything. I'll be around, observing, ready to assist if needed. We are too intimidating as a group, so let's break apart and do whatever brings you the most pleasure. No more than 30 minutes max on blackouts please. That should be enough time for any acts you wish to keep private." Torrance broke the huddle and walked away from them, smiling, into the crowd. Every retina screen displayed four live video streams of different slices of the party — people eating, dancing, sweating, pouring the contents of skin bags into each other's mouths. Wine overflowed and spilled like blood down chins and throats. Shirts came off.

At the southern end of the open space, Nix had hung a simple swing made from two pieces of rope and a board from a massive live oak. The trunk was thick and bulging with two burls. The tree's powerful horizontal branches were perfect for hanging a swing. Torrance sat on the swing and watched the guests. She looked toward the ship once, wondering what Fazeef was doing during the "watch duty" she had assigned him until the open space was clear of all guests. She didn't want to think why she had been forced into such a request by Nix. She didn't understand the rules here and had decided it was best to listen to Nix's advice. As she contemplated this, someone gently pushed her forward — hands briefly against her back — and the swing started to move. She smiled and held the ropes tightly. At intervals she glided forward, then back, slowly gaining altitude with each push. The feeling of flying above the Earth, simple and free. She put her feet out straight in front of her as she went up, then tucked them beneath her as she went back. She didn't want to turn around to see who was there. She didn't care. She just wanted to enjoy this feeling that felt so natural to her, like a memory. Eventually, the pushing from the unknown hands ended, and she slowed down, eventually stopped. Her feet came to rest flat on the ground beneath the swing, she sat staring up at the moon, or out into the open space for over an hour. That was as long as she would allow herself to relax.

Torrance requested information about the ship, some reports on the total number of humans in the area. She noticed her retina screen only had three feeds. She didn't remember hearing a blackout notification from anyone. She had told the crew before they split off "blackouts no longer than 30 minutes."

"Log recall: time of blackout of any crewmember in last three hours."

":Jansee's Lifestream went offline 29 minutes, 35 seconds ago."

"Last known location:" Torrance said.

":27.4 meters from the ship."

Torrance stood and began to walk, her mind filling with possibilities forced her to jog, then run toward the ship. There was no one else on the outskirts of the party. Fire pits and shelters were kept out of this area. She stopped as she got closer. Was she making a mistake charging over here? The crewmember could have lost track of time with wine and women everywhere. She could be interrupting a sexual encounter. She paced in a small circle.

She heard footsteps behind her and turned to see Nix.

"What are you doing here?" Torrance asked.

"I saw someone approaching the ship, so I came to check it out," Nix said.

Torrance put her hand on Nix's shoulder and whispered in her ear, "One of the crew is on blackout, last location was near here. I'm making sure everything is in order."

"Really, you're playing commander tonight? You should relax and enjoy the party like everyone else," Nix said. In the moonlight Nix looked rugged and chiseled, her cheeks hollow, her lips pushed out as if expecting a kiss. "She's not here."

"I know that," Torrance said. She could inquire further, scan for heartbeats or heat signatures, but she took Nix's advice and decided not to pursue it any further. Tonight was special. The crew could take care of themselves among the natives.

Nix took Torrance's hand and led her back toward the swing. "You should have some food. And less wine," Nix said. She walked ahead of Torrance, the distance of their extended arms. When they got to the darkest point of the open space, Torrance stopped and when Nix's arm pulled sharply she turned to see why. Torrance pulled Nix's hand propelling her body back toward her, she wrapped her arms around Nix and kissed her.

Nix was shocked, tried to push her away. But Torrance held on.

Nix tried to duck out of her arms. She slid down toward the ground, but Torrance sank with her. Torrance exhaled a wine-laced laugh as she landed on the ground beside Nix. Torrance pushed herself up and kissed Nix's neck, nipped a little too hard. Nix pushed her shoulder hard and Torrance fell backward and flat onto her back. She laughed again. Torrance came up one more time, pulled the neck of Nix's shirt down, kissed her collarbones. "Stop. You've had too much to drink. This is not the time," Nix said in a weak voice.

Torrance listened. She pushed herself up and kneeled beside Nix.

Nix lay still for a few minutes. The solid earth against her back, the sky above. Everything in its rightful place. She took deep breaths, tried to calm her heart. The moon behind Torrance hid the details of her face, but lined her head and shoulders with a silver luminosity. Tears overflowed down the sides of Nix's face.

Torrance leaned forward and tenderly pushed the tears away. She lifted her hand to her mouth and tasted the tears. "You want me, don't you?"

"It's so much more complicated than that," Nix said.

"Tonight is not a night for tears," Torrance said. "Come on, let's go to the swing and I'll push you this time."

Nix rolled onto her side, feeling the effects of the night's wine. She moved slowly to her hands and knees, then stood up. She laughed a little as she dusted off her shirt and pants. "How did you know that was me?"

"The feel of your hands," Torrance said. Torrance took hold of Nix's hand and they walked together. The sounds of the party were close by, the volume of laughter and talking was now at the raucous level it had been before the kiss. The moon was slowly becoming more reddish as it settled toward the horizon.

When they arrived at the swing, Jansee was sitting on it, both hands holding the ropes, shoulders slumped, limp head fallen forward. Torrance stood in front of her and gently lifted her head. "Are you OK?"

"Commander. Yes. Better now," Jansee said. Her eyes blinked slowly.

"Do you realize you have been on blacked-out comms for over 60 minutes?" Torrance's voice shook with authority.

"I apologize. I was so sick. I didn't want the crew to see me vomiting. I tried to make it back to the ship, but didn't."

"You should have alerted," Torrance said.

"Have you had any water since?" Nix asked.

"No," Jansee said.

Torrance ordered, "Re-engage your comms system," Jansee complied, and Torrance watched her vitals roll over her retina screen. "You're dehydrated. Slight arrhythmia. Blood pressure is elevated."

"I started toward the house, but I ended up here. So I sat down to rest," Jansee said to no one in particular.

Nix gently stroked the side of Jansee's face. "You're with us now. We'll take care of you."

"I'll go get some water and aspirin," Nix said. She looked at Torrance, and bit her bottom lip, hesitated for a moment as she fought the urge to kiss her goodbye.

"I've comm'd the crew to bring water and medicine for her, Nix. Go enjoy the remainder of the party. We'll take care of her," Torrance said. She smiled, her eyes somehow bright in the darkness.

Nix shrugged and walked toward the party.

Torrance helped Jansee from the swing and they sat on the grass together. Jansee lay down, put her head in Torrance's lap. Torrance stroked her hair and said, "Sleep if you can. I'll watch over you." She looked down at Jansee, wondered if the rest of the crew was overindulging in the same or worse ways. Were they howling at the moon? Running naked through the woods? This place was affecting them much more deeply than anyone had predicted. It wasn't just the air, the food, the alcohol. It was everything down to the blades of grass.

Torrance felt Jansee twitch, then become still. She leaned back on her hands to look up at the sky that was darkening as the moon neared the horizon. If she sat here long enough the sky would turn black and she could see the Milky Way. *To come all this way...*

Derthan and Gantu emerged from the night, giggling, clothed, intact. They set a container of water onto the grass within reach of Jansee, then dropped a tiny pouch of pills. "As requested, Commander," Derthan said. She saluted, holding the pose until Torrance acknowledged her. "Five hours until sunrise, Commander. I thought she would last longer," Derthan said.

"How long has she been sleeping?" Gantu asked.

"Not long," Torrance said. She shook Jansee's shoulder. "Wake up. Jansee. Come on. Time to take some medicine."

Jansee opened her eyes, pushed herself up with her arms until she was sitting upright. She looked at the faces around her.

"Here, take these. Three of them," Torrance said, holding out the green and black pills. Jansee bent her head down to Torrance's palm and closed her mouth over them. She grabbed for the water at the same time. She drank enough water to swallow the pills. "Swallowing water is unpleasant," Jansee said.

"You'll feel better soon. Lie down and look at the sky with us," Gantu said.

They sat down beside Torrance and looked up at the sky. They were silent. All lost in their own thoughts.

Torrance said, "You still have time left, you should go enjoy the party. You may never have another party like this in your lifetime. I'll sit with her until she's recovered, then I'll comm you." And so they left.

After sleeping for two hours, Jansee sat up and looked around. She was alert, recovered. Torrance comm'd the crew that she had recovered. Gantu and Derthan returned, slightly drunker than earlier. Gantu's lips were red, her cheeks flushed. Torrance didn't ask what conspired during the three 15-minute comms blackouts she had had since last being together. She smelled of sex and wine.

None of them were used to being up so late into the night. They had adapted to the Earth's light patterns. As they sat together on the grass, they sighed and looked at Jansee. Past the edges of the open space were the silhouettes of several old wooden buildings they hadn't been inside. Jansee stood up, "Let's do some exploring tonight. I want to see what's in some of these buildings."

"You're still drunk. We haven't asked permission from Nix," Gantu said.

Derthan said, "I think we should return to the ship tonight. I highly advise against sleeping out here with so many strangers." She shot a look toward Gantu to see if she had her support. She felt exposed in the large open space.

"Are they strangers? We've talked and drank with them, and some of you have shared your bodies with them," Torrance said.

"Scan confirms there are no apex predators in the vicinity. Or human males," Gantu said.

"Might explain why Fazeef was asked to stay in the ship tonight," Jansee said.

Derthan added, "Also confirming 32 additional warm bodies in the 500-meter radius." She let her body fall back onto the grass.

"Jansee, give me your hand," Torrance said.

Jansee gladly gave it, but scanned the commander's face, wondering why she would suddenly choose to ask for a third mate's hand. "Certainly, Commander." She looked up at the sky as she waited for Torrance to take her offered hand. The sky was open to them here, to look at or ignore as they chose, there were no walls, everything was wide open allowing for an overwhelming number of choices and possibilities. Nothing during her training prepared her for the freedom that had engulfed her mind, or the feeling in her chest — of enlargement, opening, rising without any way to compress, deflate, or descend. She felt like she was lifting off the ground. Torrance grabbed her hand then, and started to pull herself up.

"Jansee, are you feeling this too? A little drunk, I know, but everything above my waist feels light as a feather. The rest of me, so firmly on the ground," Torrance said.

"Yes, Commander. I imagine this is what plants must feel every day, rooted yet stretching upward toward the sky. That we grow, and plants grow, and humans have no thoughts or recognition of this growing as it is happening. Just an upward stretch toward the sun. The basic destiny of Earthians. But for me, this is the first time in my life to have such a feeling of openness, of…expansion. It's like I've dreamed this feeling, this place, but now that it's happening, it's so much better than any dream." Jansee squeezed the Commander's hand firmly. "Perhaps a silver-blue would help restore balance to your mind, Commander." Jansee offered two pills with her left hand, silver capsules with a blue band around the center.

"Silver blues are for disorientation and anxiety. I have neither. It's more as you described, the sky open and pulling us up as far as we dare to reach." Torrance leaned and kissed Jansee's cheek. "Anyone who chooses can sleep out here with the natives. I want to return to the ship."

Jansee walked beside the Commander, all the while sneaking looks skyward to admire the splayed universe above them. She didn't have time to spot their home, but she wanted to, just a small glance to know it was still there and waiting for them. She felt aware of the night in a way she never had on her home planet, here it wasn't perpetual, but a pause between light-filled days.

On the ship, Torrance said, "We need a bit of home tonight." She stood still for a second. "Set: breathable atmosphere to 20 percent oxygen. Humidity to 50 percent, temperature to 22.2 Celsius." A female voice replied, ":Ship's atmospheric level set. Confirmed."

"Good night, Jansee," Torrance said. She hugged her and kissed her forehead, then made her way up the narrow aluminum stairs to her room.

In the morning the open space was covered with sleeping women. Against orders, Fazeef walked silently among them, noting their strange clothes, mussed hair, their faces expressionless in deep sleep. He bent to touch one of the deflated skin bags. The fire pits smoldered, the humid morning air had flattened the thin trails of smoke into horizontal gray lines. He had watched them most of the night from the windows of the ship. He didn't understand, every body he scanned was female. A mass of Earth women...

14, RECOVERY IN CLAY

In Nix's working studio were two rows of very long tables that receded into the darkness. The tables were covered with clay models of various sizes from ten centimeters to half a meter high. One wall displayed clay and plaster faces, two walls were stacked with shelves filled with more figures of humans and animals, and even a few machines.

Nix was going through the steps of her artistic process backward. She normally started with clay then moved to stone, but this time she had seen the whole thing in her head so clearly. She was concerned that if she didn't make the requisite clay sculptures, there might be some question of the sculpture's authenticity, or worse yet, if anything happened to her, there would be no blueprint for another artist to finish the piece.

Jansee had volunteered. She was genuinely interested to learn about sculpting and seemed keen to harvest clay. She would start working on a figure of Jansee first. After their brief sexual encounter, Nix knew the shapes of her body. And now as she sat waiting for Jansee to arrive, she marveled at how there had never been any awkwardness between them. She wondered how Torrance had made the transition from the rules of Earth to the rules of Kepler-442B. Torrance had wanted marriage and vows and all the things that Nix wanted to give her, but never did. How had she fared on the new outpost with their lack of tradition and commitment?

Jansee said, "Sorry I'm 32 seconds late. I was nearly defeated by the door. I thought I'd covered all of them in my ancient locking mechanisms class." She pointed with one hand over her shoulder toward the door behind her. Nix laughed with her.

"Have a look around, then come get settled by me and we'll start," Nix said.

Jansee smiled, was already looking around with wide eyes. She was filled with such childlike joy that she started to walk on the tips of her toes. When a particular sculpture caught her eye, she would bend to inspect the miniature humans. Their rendering so lifelike, every muscle realized, the surface so soft-looking that it fooled the brain into thinking that if touched they would be warm. They were perfectly accepted by the mind as human despite their diminutive size. Jansee sometimes extended her hand to one because she expected them to reach out to her, then she would pull back in the second before her hand touched the clay. She smiled and bowed in front of one that had demanded a more formal greeting. Then to Nix without taking her eyes from the sculpture before her, "They look alive. Their skin... You are everything they said you would be," Jansee said.

Nix wondered if Jansee would notice that the figure she had started to carve was of her. Nix wasn't going to mention it. At the moment it was unrecognizable, the head and shoulders were square, the rest nothing more than a square brick. Nix worked quickly, sliced off excess to make the smooth curve of legs, a small bump for an ass, and the indentations of her waist.

Jansee continued to make her way around each table, sometimes shining a light (Nix wasn't sure where the light was coming from) onto a piece and squatting to really inspect it. Time was not something that Jansee was concerned with on a daily basis. She looked back toward Nix occasionally, then when she was ready, she took the seat that Nix had arranged directly across from her. Between them was a knee-high table with a rotating tabletop. The area where Nix was working was lit from above and from the sides by canned lights mounted on the ceiling and on opposing walls. The figure on the tabletop cast no shadows, it was lit well from top to bottom.

"I noticed you spent a lot of time with Gantu during the party," Nix said.

"We had the most amazing sex in the woods right after dinner. Her body is breathtaking. And she is so flexible. The smell of pine everywhere, and her above me, holding my knee as she slid her sex over mine."

Nix cleared her throat. Jansee understood this signal and curbed further sexual description. "You should have seen the orange light from the bonfire shimmer against her face and upper body. I can still see it in my mind." Jansee let out a heavy sigh.

"You don't want to be with Gantu all the time?" Nix asked. As she pressed a new bit of clay onto the thumb-sized thigh she was sculpting.

"You mean have sex with her all the time? You've seen her, who wouldn't? But I'm happy with the time we have together. I don't need more than that," Jansee said.

"No, I mean live your life with her," Nix said.

"Every minute of the day and night? No! Why would I want to do that to her? Holding on to something so tightly is selfish, and sure to smother the freedom that is granted to us from birth."

"I see it as wanting to devote your life to a person and build all your memories with them," Nix said.

"Are you listening to yourself? That sounds ridiculous. We don't build a life with any single person, but with all of those we choose to connect with. Next you'll be saying 'only have sex with one person for your whole life.' Am I right?" Jansee laughed a bit, then grew serious, she bit her lower lip and stared hard at Nix as she waited to hear Nix's answer.

"You've done your homework. That's for sure," Nix said.

"Believe it or not, we also have homework on our planet," Jansee smiled. "You know, Gantu told me that you kicked her out of your bed before anything even started."

Nix rolled her eyes, but quickly checked herself. "Yes. I did. It's certainly not because I don't find her attractive, but it's not appropriate for you guys to just jump into my bed at night. As I said..."

"Yes, you lectured us about this already. But the rules seemed different at the party. I had sex with two other women besides Gantu that night, and neither of them protested in such as manner as you had. They showed me techniques I had not experienced before."

"You slept with two at once, or separately?" Nix asked.

"That hardly seems worth answering, but yes, both at once," Jansee said.

"Move your chair to this side, I want you to get your hands on this," Nix said.

Jansee moved her chair so that it bumped against Nix's chair. She leaned forward, rested her elbows on her thighs. Nix put a wooden tool into Jansee's hand, then pulled her hand down so that the stick left an indentation in the outside of the sculpture's thigh. The head was a round shape, no facial details or hair yet. Nix continued to guide Jansee's hand over the thigh, pressed the clay down at key points on the sides and at the top of the knee so that the muscles were pronounced. She helped her to shape the calves as she remembered them, slightly elongated and not so spherical. "Now we're going to do the feet. Take your boot off."

Jansee did as instructed. She was surprised, pleasantly. A sly smile, devilish curiosity about whether this would become her next sexual encounter with Nix.

Nix shook her head. *She can easily sleep with two women, but is surprised that her foot is worthy of sculpting.* "Use this tool now. I want you to use your own foot as the model. Really look at your toes. Are they square or round? Are the nails wide or small? Are any of your toes longer? Look closely and do your best to reproduce it." Nix sat back. She looked at Jansee's very white foot perched on the sculpting table, the toes rounded and clinging to the edge, the joints two shades whiter than her skin; her nails slightly more narrow near the tops.

"Ah, good start. Yes, they are slightly square," Nix said.

Jansee used the wire end of the tool to make a line on the surface between each toe. "The toes are so small. Should I go all the way through the clay? What level of detail are you expecting?" Jansee asked.

Nix tilted her head and looked at Jansee's clay foot. She took the spoon-like tool and rounded the fronts of the toes. "Just like you have it. Adding space between them wouldn't help any, it would only make them smaller. This section is good. Let's move up now that the base is set." Nix quickly finished the other foot.

As Jansee put her boot back on, she watched Nix start to shape the breasts. Nix didn't offer any explanation or instruction as she scooped under each orb to form perfect half-circles, then pressed at the breastbone with the side of her thumb. She added a pebble of clay to each breast and used a thinner, pointed tool, to shape the additions into nipples.

Jansee squinted her eyes and pursed her lips, moved her face closer to her likeness. The feet and the breasts looked like hers, exactly what she saw in the mirror every day, or when she looked down at herself. She smiled and laughed a little, put her hands on her breasts. "How'd you do that? It was dark in the room that night."

"Not everything is seen with the eyes," Nix said.

This woman was brilliant. Jansee felt the urge to kiss her. Their faces were very close. She resisted the impulse to take Nix's face and turn it toward her so that she could kiss her lips. Instead, she kissed Nix's cheek.

Nix sighed. "What's that for?" She looked at Jansee's face, really looked, noting her long cheeks, black bangs that hung across her forehead, her caterpillar-width eyebrows.

"Expressing my feeling of admiration. Little overwhelmed right now." Jansee rubbed her hand on Nix's thigh.

"At least you're honest," Nix said.

"We're taught to be completely honest about what we want. Life is short and too hard for it to be otherwise," Jansee said.

"Hand off my inner thigh please, it's distracting," Nix said. She kept working, leaned forward a little and tilted her head to get a better view of the clay ribs. "Are you like this with everyone?"

Jansee moved her hand off Nix's thigh. "Not everyone, but on this mission, I've been especially lucky with attraction. Based on my level of attraction to you, I would expect our genetics are highly compatible."

Nix nudged the point of her wooden tool into the belly of the figure to make a belly button.

"I don't have one of those. They're not required for gestation outside the womb. See," Jansee said as she lifted her shirt to show Nix her flat stomach that was devoid of a belly button.

Nix wanted to stare, but instead returned to the sculpture and with one upsweep of the tool the belly button was gone. "OK. Anything else I might have missed in the dark?" Nix asked.

"Let me show you," Jansee bent to take her boots off, then stood up and started to undress. She pulled her shirt up and off and Nix felt some erotic charge when she saw Jansee's collarbones. She dropped her pants before Nix could protest. Nix studied her, scanned her skin from head to toe for any distinguishing marks (small moles here and there), looked at the skin of her elbows and knees (taut), her ribs (barely visible), breasts (as sculpted). Jansee pushed off her sheer underwear that hid nothing, but no doubt were regulation issue. She stood with her arms straight up above her head, underwear dangling from her left hand. She smiled at Nix, no shyness at all, just pure sexual display, then looked up at the ceiling and twirled slowly on the balls of her feet like a ballerina.

"You're beautiful. No doubt," Nix said as she picked up another tool, and turned the table to the right until the miniature figure's back was facing her. "I'll do the backside while you're here. Would you mind turning around?"

Jansee turned. She was silent as her eyes wandered over the rows of figures in the room. Her heart thudded in her chest at the thought of her figure being here among the others. "Tell me what you're feeling while you look at me," Jansee said.

"It's hard to say. It's more thinking than feeling. I'm looking at you, and your image is passing through me. My hand is working without me thinking about it, no feeling there. The feeling comes when I look from you to the sculpture and see that they are the same. That is one of the best feelings there is for me. But that feeling is not for you, or your body, but the transference of your image into something that has come from my hands."

"So you are looking at me now, but not feeling any sexual arousal? I don't understand how that is possible," Jansee said.

"You're young. Everything is sexual to you now," Nix said.

Jansee replied, "Everything is sexual to everyone. This is the basis of all human interaction. Upon meeting anyone you evaluate whether he or she is a potential sexual partner or not. Example, a heterosexual man walks into a room of other heterosexual men, he says 'Ah, a room full of men.' And by this he means there are no sexual partners for him in this room. He has made a sexual judgment and moves forward from there."

"I see," Nix said. Human sexuality was not something she wanted to discuss at this moment. "Please turn to your right, lower your arms."

Jansee lowered her arms.

Nix cleared her throat when she saw the perfect slope of Jansee's breast again. Some memory from their night together made Nix feel pressure on her tongue, then her mouth began watering. She reached for the water jug and took a swallow to displace the sensation.

Jansee smiled to herself, she knew what throat-clearing meant in a situation like this. She closed her eyes to try to feel Nix's gaze moving over her. She imagined it would produce the feeling of heat on her skin. She felt no such thing, but her maroon-colored nipples had hardened, and she could feel a swelling between her legs.

"Can you squat, then put your right knee onto the floor for a minute, arms horizontal and out, hold that position for a minute, then switch to your left knee?" Nix said.

"May I ask what purpose this will serve if you are sculpting a standing figure?" Jansee said.

"After you hold each pose I'll ask you to stand and your muscles will be more defined from the strain. This will help me see the shape of your legs and arms better."

Jansee obediently followed Nix's requests. She couldn't remember anyone ever having looked at her this long, with such concentration, with such thwarted desire.

15, IN THE TALL GRASS

Tall grass formed a wall around where Torrance and Derthan sat in the meadow. A breeze made the grass sway toward the east, and a soft 'shush' was the only sound, then birdsongs at intervals. Derthan imagined that the birds were here solely for the same reason that she and Torrance were, to enjoy the beauty, and that their songs were to express their appreciation, not merely an instinctual action to announce territory or call a mate. The landscape beyond the tops of the grass was treetops on three sides, and rounded, golden mountains on the fourth side.

Derthan tore off a stalk of the reedy grass. She bent the stalk over and over, watching the chlorophyll pool at the wounded spot like green blood. She stripped layers of dermis from the grass. Then she lay back onto the grass, felt it crumple beneath her uniform, some rough pieces resisted and poked her. She thought to stand and crush them, but instead rolled from side to side, using her back to soften her newly created bed.

Torrance followed and lay down beside her. She closed her eyes, and was hypnotized by the brilliant red she saw, her blood illuminated with the fire of the sun, her head full of nothing but the intense color. Then the most comforting feeling swept over her.

Derthan said nothing, her head supported by her folded arms, her unfocused eyes stared blankly into the pale green grass, until a buzzing bee caught her attention. The bee hovered near a tear-shaped purple flower. "Retrieve:" she said, rolling onto her stomach to get a better view.

":Common name Clover. Genus Trifolium, Fabaceae family." Derthan smiled and pushed herself up onto her hands and knees. She touched her temple to capture an image from the bee's perspective. ":Africanized honey bee, Apis mellifera scutellata." Derthan watched as the pollen clung to the bee's legs as it stood on one stamen long enough to take a drink of the nectar, then flew off to the next one. She mimicked its movements by moving her fingers in the same probing-then-retracting motion.

With each passing second, Torrance relaxed into the earth. It was softening — or was it her imagination?

"Are you feeling this?" Derthan said. She was standing now, her eyes closed, her hands raised above her head, as she took one deep breath after another.

Torrance sat up and looked at Derthan. "Feeling what?" Torrance asked. She stretched her arms out in front of her, flexed her fingers and watched the movement of her bones beneath her skin. The sun reflected off of her skin as a silver disk beside her thumb. "We both have extremely high levels of vitamin D, but I don't see anything else. Nothing unusual from the feeds."

"Exactly," Derthan said. "It's bliss, and that doesn't register on the monitors."

Torrance lay back down again and closed her eyes. There was a long silence.

Derthan said, "Why shouldn't we just stay?"

To Torrance's ears, it sounded like Derthan was talking to herself, so she didn't answer. When Torrance felt that the sun had suddenly become dark she opened her eyes; Derthan was looking down at her.

She sat up. "We have no reason to stay here. The mission was to come, get the samples and go back. The samples are valuable to our people's survival," Torrance said.

"They don't care about us. When we left we were heroes because they knew we might never return. Don't you remember the way people looked at us when we were walking out to the ship? Like we were already dead," Derthan said.

"How can you be in such a paradise and say such ugly things?" Torrance asked.

"That is precisely why. Everything is clear here. I can think, I can see, and I can't understand why the founders ever left this place — so that we could live indoors with filters and no sunlight for generations?"

"My genes can't survive on this planet," Torrance said.

"What do you mean? You were modified like the rest of us, your genes were cleaned and repaired prior to regeneration," Derthan said. But inside she was alarmed, her stomach knotted.

"Come and lie down with me. Put your head on my lap."

Derthan obeyed, lay on her side, curled into a ball. Torrance stroked her head. "That's what they told me, but if they changed me, then my chemical signature should have been different, and I wouldn't be falling in love with Nix. I've been taking dopamine suppressants, but even with those, my feelings for her are interfering with my ability to think clearly."

Derthan turned so that her head was in Torrance's lap and looked up at her. "In love? You want to fuck her is all, that's all that adrenaline rush means. That's not love. And with the dopamine suppressants how would you even know what you're feeling? You know how crabby those things make people. Oh, but it explains a lot about your reactions since we arrived. You're not getting much pleasure out of anything, are you?" Derthan turned back onto her side, and said, "I could argue that you're letting your feelings for her jeopardize our mission. Do you realize we've been here for seven months already? At this rate, we will be here longer than a year...and whatever it is that is hindering you from completing your personal mission, could you resolve it? By all calculations, a year was more than we would ever need for this mission. And do I have to remind you that if they don't get some ping from us by the 18th month, they will deploy retrieval ships to extract us and the samples."

Torrance said, "No, you don't have to remind me. You don't think it weighs on my mind every day? But this is not about me stalling, or whether I want to fuck Nix, it's about love, a very important love that I swore I would..." But she stopped there for a moment. "I could die for this. I'm in love with her, so I likely will. That's what you should really think about. And to answer your next two questions — I can live for 20 years on this planet. And there is no cure." She moved Derthan's head from her lap and stood up. She brushed the grass from her uniform, then stalked off into the field of grass.

Torrance didn't know where she was going. She walked with no intentional direction, but kept her eyes on the sun. As the yellow light began to fade, dissolving into layers of orange and purple toward the horizon, she stopped and rested with her back against a tree. She stared at the sunset, and its beauty filled her with peace. She wanted to remember the feeling. She touched her temple to record the image. ":Comms off." When she took her next breath she coughed, one cough became three, followed by a set of five. Her eyes filled with tears, which overflowed and ran down her face. She was having difficulty breathing. She coughed again to clear whatever was inside her lungs. The coughs made her throat raw, and left her gasping in short, quick breaths. She bent forward to catch her breath, focused on taking longer breaths, each one slightly longer. When she could breathe again, she wiped the tears from her face and leaned against the tree. The sun had set. The air was starting to cool. She knew somehow that the cold air could bring back her cough. She took the long way back to the ship.

No one saw Torrance for an hour. Derthan returned to the ship alone after having fallen asleep in the tall grass and waking up as the air began to cool. This was the longest blackout any of the crew had used since their arrival, and the feeling of being disconnected, especially from the commander, left them all feeling anxious, unsure. Jansee spotted Torrance with an infrared camera at the edge of the woods and notified the rest of the crew that she was approaching. Torrance walked in her loping gait toward the main house, not toward the ship. "She'll come back when she's ready," Derthan said.

Some time later, Torrance returned to the ship and went straight to her chamber. The crew had the ship announce that they were leaving for dinner. Torrance's voice came over the ship's comm, "Go ahead without me. I have logs to review, and vids to watch. I'm behind and need to use this evening to catch up."

The crew left without her.

16, LOOSENING UP

Nix cried into her tea. Outside the sun was rising, a slow assault of wide orange slashes penetrating the tree line. She could feel the light, the sting of the sun's energy on her left cheek, and welcomed it after the past five days of heavy rain and wind.

The weather had served as a clear distinction between phase one and phase two of her project. The wind and rain had cleared the air and washed the ground, soaked the earth until it squished underfoot and earthworms beached themselves on anything to keep from drowning. Nix felt like she was drowning. She had dreamed about Torrance last night again. Since the party, each night in dreams — the two of them young and tangled together in every sexual position, or with hands threaded together as they walked and talked, or love passing through their eyes as they sat at the kitchen table drinking tea, which they had never done in this house. She could tell she was losing the battle to subdue her feelings. Feelings were nature, and nature will only be denied for so long.

She wiped her eyes and made her way outside. She walked around the scaffolding. Changes were required to the structure to give her the kind of access she would need for the next phase of work. There would be no need for heavy saws in this phase, it would all be done with smaller pneumatic tools and chisels and mallets. She would work on a two-meter-by-two-meter piece of the surface at a time. The structure they had built to give her 360-degree access around the rock was no longer needed. *Fuck it. The whole thing needed to come down.* She would construct a rolling painter's scaffolding, then she could sit in one place for hours, with some kind of roof over her head, and she could adjust the space between herself and the rock to allow small chips to fall to the ground below.

She was contemplative, her mind replaying the dreams that took her to places with Torrance that she had refused to go to during her waking hours. All this thinking slowed her down. She was having a hard time focusing on work. She lightly slapped her own cheek, took some paper and a pencil from her pocket and made some notes. The day had barely started and she was already thinking about the evening. Tonight she wanted to be outside. The weather appeared to be holding, and she expected a warm, clear night. They should be outside, even if it would be a bit soggy in the open space. She would cook venison — cubed and skewered and seasoned with salt and pepper — over the fire. She would bring two jugs of wine from the root cellar. She wanted to feel the warm oblivion of meat and alcohol. With wine in hand, she went and sat in her working studio. She opened one of the bottles and stared at the finished sculptures of Jansee. They preserved the fine details and forms she would reference for the remaining stonework. She started a new block of clay for Gantu and spent the rest of the day sipping wine and finishing two different poses of her.

When she was finished, she went to the house to prepare dinner. As she rinsed the meat under the faucet, then chopped vegetables, she started thinking about how she would ask the visitors to help her with preparations for the next phase.

The crew returned from their day in the field to wash up and debrief in the ship as usual. The sun was setting, the sky changed from blue to shades of red and purple as the crew set off across the open space toward the small fire they saw burning in the usual spot, with the figure of Nix once again hunched forward as she cooked something that caused the flames to jump erratically and flick at her hands like orange reptile tongues. A soft breeze blowing from the northeast carried the luscious smells of roasting meat and wood smoke toward them.

Everyone settled onto their seats, pulled them closer to the fire. A few of the crew lifted their boots for inspection, noted the water's depth marked halfway up the thick soles, then commented about the excessive water in the open space.

Nix was happy to see them, she turned and smiled, noticed that they each held their wooden bowls and spoons. "Ready to eat I see." Everyone nodded. She used a wide-tined fork to push the meat from the skewers into their bowls. The visitors ate with their fingers, which was now their standard for everything but liquids. "It's hot," Nix warned. They popped the cubes of meat into their mouths and blew out tiny puffs of steam before chewing a couple times, then puffed more steam. They laughed and hurriedly drank water to stop the burning. "Hot, yes, but too good to wait," Derthan said.

"I've got more. Eat your fill," Nix said. But tonight was the last of the venison and she would need to hunt in the morning.

"After that rain, you should have enough water for months in the tanks," Fazeef said. He thought about little else besides the party since it happened. He had made vids of his experience and had lingering questions, but would wait until the right moment to ask Nix for answers. He wanted things to return to the way they were before the party.

"Yes, definitely. I filled every tank and container I had," Nix said. She laid fresh skewers onto the metal rack over the fire. "There's wine too, help yourselves." She handed the jug to Gantu who then kneeled before each of the crew and poured wine into the small glasses that Nix had placed beside their stone seats. Nix watched them between turning the meat or as she drank her wine. The wine was spreading its warmth through her limbs, she wanted to close her eyes and sleep so she could dream. She had the urge to chug the tart red liquid, to lift the jug to her lips and drink it like water; but she sipped and looked, let her eyes drink instead. *God, what do they think of me? Some perverse old woman with weathered skin staring at them with wine-glazed eyes.* They sat differently than they did in the house, was it all of the manual labor they had done, had such efforts of the body contributed to their relaxed postures? Were they finally here, in the moment, ignoring all the rules? She was puzzled. Oh, whatever it was, there was no denying that they were slouching and reclining while eating, and Nix liked it. Their uniforms were unzipped to below their breasts, their collars folded down. They had become more sensual, trusting their senses and relying less on their instruments for analysis; yes, she was sure of it.

"Thank you for this meal, Nix. The taste of deer meat is something I like very much. I could eat this every day if I lived here," Fazeef said. That was what Nix wanted to hear. A simple compliment, thankfulness.

"You are welcome, Fazeef. I still owe you for complying with my wishes during the party."

"Oh, I've been meaning to ask about this..." he said, but Derthan, without any notice that he had not finished, charged in with her own thoughts, "I thought, when we left home, or maybe all of us did, that I might never return." She talked around a hunk of venison as she chewed. "I'm the only one that has someone waiting at home, and she knows there is a 43.6 percent chance that I may not return," Derthan said.

Gantu finished chewing before she added, "No, that was never part of my thoughts. With all of our resources and training, I have only envisioned this mission as a success ending in our eminent return home." She held out her bowl for Nix to refill.

Torrance said, "You never stopped to think there is a very real chance that we could be trapped here! This is the dilemma that comes with the desire for exploration — seeking new places means you may have to sacrifice everything, never return, or never see home in the same way again. These are the risks explorers accept. Was this not part of your training?"

"Yes, Commander, it was. But I have chosen to apply creative visualization to the entire mission from takeoff to my return home. I have seen these things happen successfully in my mind. And so they shall be," Gantu replied.

" 'And so they shall be.' This is the kind of thinking that makes reality," Nix said as she leaned forward to fill glasses with more wine, then turned the remaining skewers over the fire. "And speaking of making ideas into reality, let's talk about phase two, shall we? The current structure isn't suitable for phase two work."

"You have plans for what needs to be built?" Fazeef asked. He extended his bowl to Nix.

"Still in my head," Nix said as she pushed another skewer of meat into his bowl. "I'll get them out tonight."

"We start tomorrow?" Torrance asked.

"If you can," Nix said.

"I'll do the teardown with Gantu and Jansee," Torrance said. "Fazeef and Derthan can review the construction plan and prepare things for the build. Fazeef, I'd like you to lead the build effort."

Nix sighed, and held up her glass toward Fazeef. "I'll teach them how to weld, too. I've got the parts lying around — pipes, planks, casters. Shouldn't take more than a day."

"Yes, we're in," Torrance said, and the crew nodded with her.

The teardown started the next morning at daybreak. Nix took Fazeef and Derthan to the work shed to gather the tools. She plucked tools from drawers, off the walls, and handed them back to waiting hands. Once gathered, she instructed them on what each would be used for. They knew how to weld before the sun set.

The teardown needed one more day. Fazeef and Derthan assembled the rolling scaffolding — a sturdy three-story, square, metal skeleton.

By day three everything was in place for phase two to begin.

17, ARTEMIS UNLEASHED

Nix rose before the sun was up. She dressed in the living room, having laid out her hunting clothes and supplies the night before, everything readied to make the process quiet and easy in the dark. She didn't want to wake Zephyr. Every time they had a few moments alone, they argued about the amount of food the visitors consumed, about the lack of privacy, about the length of their stay. Zephyr complained that she couldn't look in any direction without seeing one of them, and she was very unhappy about the amount of time Nix spent with them, leaving nearly no time for her. Seeing Zephyr's jealousy tore at Nix's heart. She had tried to reassure her that the visitors' stay was temporary, though in all honesty she didn't know how long that meant. The mood between them had become so strained that Zephyr spent every waking hour in the greenhouse, and no longer ate dinner with Nix and the visitors.

Nix shook her head to clear it. She couldn't be in this mindset and have a good hunt. She shouldered her rifle and shoved the two leather pouches stuffed with dried fruit and nuts into her coat pockets and silently left the house.

She saddled the palomino and harnessed a second horse to follow behind. She was armed with a handgun holstered to her thigh, a knife strapped to her calf under her pants, a bowie knife on her belt. She always hunted alone. She didn't want to talk, she needed to keep her energy inside and concentrate on the environment around her.

Nix nudged her horse to trot across the open space. She wanted to be far into the woods before there was more light. As she rode past the first elevated hunting stand, one of 50 she had scattered over the surrounding lands, she looked up at it, ensuring it was unoccupied, but didn't stop. She had a feeling about the lake, so she would go there first. With the new scaffolding and the stone waiting for her she felt tense, like she had deserted her post. She was hyper-aware of time passing. She wanted to get the hunt over as quickly as possible. Every minute she spent hunting meant a delay on starting phase two.

The lake was flat and as smooth as black glass. Nix tied up the horses and walked 100 feet to a slight ridge with a stand of youngish pine trees. From here she would be able to see the horses and most of the surrounding area. She climbed a tree, sat on the first limb large enough to support her. She was ten feet above the forest floor, a good vantage point for seeing and shooting. She laid the rifle across her lap and listened to the song of an early bird. She loaded a shell into the chamber of the gun, then picked at the bark of the tree for a moment, until she realized how loud this was, so instead plucked an infant branch with miniature flat needles from the trunk and held it in her hand, stroked it with her thumb.

She wasn't used to being still for so long; this was the most challenging aspect of hunting for her, not the waiting, not being in one place, but the lack of motion. She would rather be tracking, in pursuit. She closed her eyes and took a deep breath, imagined herself to be invisible.

The sun was coming, the sky above was a deep purple, and more birds were starting to sing. There was so much happening — changing light, rising temperature, birds announcing every subtle change in their own language, alerting all creatures to rise and live. She scanned the area without moving her head. Nothing. She lowered her head slowly, stared at the engraving on the metal plates above the trigger. When her head was down, her ears were more alert. She sorted through the forest sounds of rustling leaves, branches snapping, the occasional thud of her horse's front hoof on the forest floor.

Her eyes felt heavy. She leaned back, found the trunk strangely comfortable. A falling pinecone startled her right as she was drifting off. To stay awake, she took out a small cloth, and barely moving it back and forth polished the metal parts of the gun near her hand. The volume of the forest was changing, hard to explain with no humans or machines for miles, but the activity of creatures produced its own hum, the great machine of life ignited for another day on the planet.

Her horse made rumbling sounds. Nix looked behind her and saw some motion. She steadied her back against the trunk of the tree, and slowly turned with the rifle pointed toward the small group of deer headed toward her. She waited. The gun was getting heavy. She realized she was holding her breath. She exhaled and closed her eyes for a second, took a deep inhale. When she opened her eyes, a buck and three does were grazing 50 feet away.

Nix shot and the stag leaped in an attempt to scatter with the others as the shot rang out through the forest. The stag stumbled, his front legs crumpling unable to hold any weight, but he tossed his head up and back, perhaps struggling for breath, then collapsed. Nix descended from the tree as quickly as she could with her stiffened, cold legs, glancing toward the stag every few seconds. She readied the rifle for a second shot as she walked to where he lay. The tips of his antlers penetrated the earth and his head twisted skyward, glazed eyes reflecting the blue sky above. On a cold morning, she would have seen his breath and known if he was still alive. She stopped a few feet away and stared, watched for any movement of the chest or hide, but there was none. Nix waved her hand in the air and stomped the ground, sure to rouse a reflexive reaction, but nothing. She shouldered her rifle and stepped close to grab the antlers near the base, and pulled his head forward to free the antler tines from the dirt. She unsheathed her knife with her free hand and slit his throat, allowing the blood to drain until the heavy flow became a trickle. Within moments she had the head wrapped in rope. She dragged the deer far from the water and several feet into the forest. She threw the rope over the nearest horizontal branch and brought the horse over to hoist the carcass up.

She eased the knife under the skin at the bottom of the chest. With the knife edge turned toward her, she sliced all the way down, careful not to puncture any organs, then delicately circled the anus. The guts spilled like a great vat of hot stew onto the forest floor. She would leave them for animals to eat. Her fingers blindly felt inside the cavity for anything that was still attached, assuring it was hollow and clean. Nix tied the rear legs together and lowered the hanging deer onto the canvas-covered back of the packhorse. The impressive antlers dangled like a chandelier of dark icicles. She roped the antlers to the deer's front legs to keep the head from swinging, since there was some danger that the horse could be injured if the head were to catch on a tree or something inflexible. She would leave the woods carefully and take the long way home, which was more open.

Derthan was alerted of the shot by an alarm in her chamber. She stumbled out of bed and manipulated the exterior cameras in the direction of the shot. She was able to locate the exact coordinates of origin, but it was well beyond the camera's reach. She started to panic. "Display level one security protocol:" *I should have memorized this manual.* She set alarms in concentric rings around the ship. She drummed her fingers on her desk. *What would be the purpose of a single shot 31 minutes after sunrise?* Protocol for a far-off, single shot was not in the manual. She tried to get a reading on the type of weapon, but there was no match in the system. She would have to wait for more information, like a second shot or a perimeter violation alarm. Derthan played the recording of the shot and listened to it over and over. She thought she recognized the sound. She had only ever heard one combustion weapon in her life, two shots that Nix had fired at the wild boar. She adjusted the levels, and listened again. She requested the Lifestream logs from the day that Nix shot the pig by the lake. She searched through the logs until she found the hunt and kill. As she compared the two shots, she heard the same almost imperceptible pre-sound before the bang. Not only were the sound profiles of this morning's shot and the pig kill approximately the same, but so were the location coordinates. She felt better; it was most certainly Nix, but in case she was wrong, she set alerts on any motion or infrared signature bigger than a bird that entered the camera's range.

The motion-activated alarm sounded 90 minutes after the weapon discharge alarm had sounded. Derthan dashed to the monitor and saw a figure emerge from the tree line on horseback. She zoomed and saw that it was Nix, holding reins in her bloody right hand, a sheathed rifle slanted downward on the left side of her saddle. There was a riderless horse trailing Nix's horse; slung over its back was an animal form whose gut area was gashed and bloody even from a distance. Red stains ran down the rear leg of the horse to the hoof.

Nix walked the horses to the wooden shed and tied them up. She brought a bucket of water for each horse, looked over the packhorse to make sure she hadn't been injured by the antlers. Next she carried wood into the shed and made a fire in the cast-iron stove in the corner. The butchering work would be wet, and she wanted warmth in the room.

She rinsed the blood off her hands and went out for the deer. She untied the ropes, and as she made her way around to the other side of the horse, she noticed the visitors running across the open space toward her. She wasn't feeling like human company right now, she was still too far inside herself. She went about her business, pulled the deer's head toward her with both hands. As the body began to slide down, she got her shoulder under it, then she backed up allowing the hindquarters to drape down the front of her body. She adjusted the carcass on her shoulder. The head snapped back and an antler gouged her calf. God, it hurt. She didn't think it pierced her jeans or the skin, but it would leave a deep bruise. Their combined bodies were wider than the door would allow; she struggled to find the right angle to get through. She exhaled and tried to make herself as thin as possible, scraped the back of her hand on the wooden door frame as she turned and finally pulled her prize through. She let the head sink down toward the floor behind her and heaved the deer's bound back legs upward so that she could loop them over a thick metal hook attached to a strong crossbeam. For butchering purposes it didn't matter if the legs were apart or not, the hook usually left some clearance from the floor so that a deer's head didn't drag on the dirt floor. This deer was larger than the others. She retied the spread legs to a thin metal rod with a loop welded in the center and rehung the deer. When the visitors gathered at the shed door, the deer's legs were apart, the raw red gash of its empty interior facing them. They turned away, shielded their eyes as if blinded by a noon sun. Nix wasn't sure if they were more bothered by the wood smoke released as she stoked the fire or the sight of the slaughtered animal. She had shut off all feelings of sympathy before she left that morning, and she hadn't come to a place yet where she was ready to allow herself to feel such feelings — they needed to remain off until she was done with the butchering.

With the deer prepped, it could hang while she took care of the horses. The visitors followed her like puppies, taking notes or chattering to themselves. She led the horses to the barn and removed their tack. She pumped water into a bucket, then used the tin cup she usually drank from to scoop water and pour it over the packhorse's haunches. Blood reddened the water as Nix rubbed the horse's stained hide with her hand. The ground quickly absorbed the shimmering red lines. None of them had ever seen so much blood running. When the packhorse was clean and dried, Nix brushed her out and released her into the paddock with the palomino. She dumped half a bale of hay into the feeder and headed back to the shed to finish the deer.

Nix used a small D-shaped knife to skin the animal. How different this was from working in marble. This was utter ease, the softness of the flesh, the knife an extension of her index finger like an ancient claw, reaching out a few inches to easily separate the hide from the deep purplish-red muscle meat beneath. She was always amazed that simply peeling back a thin layer of skin could reveal a masterpiece of sculpted muscle and the brilliantly engineered bands of grayish sinew that raced to their connecting points. Never in stone had she been so lucky to peel back so little and reveal so much, but maybe this stone would be the one. She took her time. This was a subtle art that required great delicacy. The blade was razor-sharp, and she knew the power of it, so she made each slice in a slow, dream-like motion. Some of the cuts were like long strokes of a painter's brush, sweeping continuously downward; Nix bent at her waist, stretched her arm until the blade completed the work at the crook of the deer's leg. Her hands were red from fingertips to wrists, and her forearms streaked with blood. The apron she was wearing was splattered, and she had wiped her hands on it so many times that it resembled the stripes of the old American flag. Nix was too engrossed to notice whether the visitors had stayed to watch or left.

After the skinning was complete, she tacked the skin to the far wall, flesh side out. She would scrape any reaming meat and fat off later. She cleaned her hands in a bucket of water, rinsed the skinning knife and sharpened it on a whetstone before setting it on the table. Now that the meat was exposed, she would carve off steaks for her guests, though looking at the once-crowded doorframe it seemed only half the visitors were still here to receive such a bounty.

She cut the steaks with a filet knife. The table behind her was covered with grape leaves. She placed a steak onto each leaf. When she was done with five steaks, Nix wrapped them in the grape leaves and handed one to each of the visitors as if she were handing them the most precious jewels, even bowing to Jansee as she handed over hers. Seven steaks made little difference to the mass of the stag.

"Fazeef, will you hold the two for me and Zephyr, and the extras?" Nix asked, knowing with his large hands he could carry twice as much as anyone else, but that he would have to use both hands and hold the meat against his body to carry it all.

Fazeef nodded and extended his arms. Nix stacked the leaf-covered steaks onto the ones he was already holding. "You know, we have no firearms, or wild animals," he said.

"Yes, I figured," Nix said. She hoped that her feelings might emerge soon so that this experience might be a little more pleasant for her guests.

"What is this place?" Derthan asked.

"A butchering shed, smokehouse. Usually filled with venison, sometimes fish, or boar," Nix said. "Can you grab more wood and add it to the stove?" Nix went back to cutting.

Derthan returned with an armful of wood. Nix didn't see her, but heard the latch to the stove open, the thud and hiss of wood being dropped in.

Nix said, "Take the iron rod and poke the bright orange coals on the bottom, stir them a little to allow some oxygen to get in there."

Derthan did as instructed.

A sooty cloud filled the room, and Nix knew that Derthan had done it right. She also heard the new logs catch fire, a few crackles that became a dull roar. "OK, you can close the door now. Good job," Nix said.

Nix was cutting faster now; as large blocks and strips of meat fell into her left hand, she turned and slapped each piece onto the table.

"Anyone interested in the antlers?" Nix asked. Fazeef and Derthan both raised their hands. "Any ideas what they could be used for?"

"Weapons," Fazeef said.

Nix turned to look at him and the blade nicked her finger. She held the half detached steak in her left hand, wiped at her cheek with the back of her right hand, leaving a broad red mark from nose to ear.

18, SHARP EDGES

Nix started with a heavy-gauge carbide-tipped chisel, and an iron hammer that she thought of as Thor's hammer — able to hit anything as hard as she liked and it would not fail. With the rock's shape roughed out, she would crack and chip off saucer-sized pieces, which would take several weeks, then she would move to using narrower chisels to nick off smaller pieces, smaller and smaller until it was time for sanding. It was a simple plan. She could only approximate how long it would take to get through this phase. She wasn't in a hurry. The duration of the visitors' stay was unknown. She preferred to operate without thinking about time, but everything about the visitors brought time to mind — their youth, their daily activities, their very presence.

With everything prepped and ready for Nix to simply step up and get to it, the work started well. Separated by layers of protection, their faces masked, their hands gloved, and still Nix could feel Torrance's presence, closer than ever with the pneumatic tools out of the way, as if they were naked and alone in a silent room. What else could Nix do to stop thinking about this woman? Work harder, pound harder, cut faster.

At the end of the first day, as the sun began to set behind layers of gold-tipped purple clouds, Nix was completely exhausted, her body, weighted by the oppressive hands of gravity, insisted that she find a place to sleep and soon. Finally her mind was at ease. She looked at Torrance and felt nothing. She took off her gloves and slapped them against the top of her thigh. Dust puffed and dissolved. She couldn't say *Hallelujah, it worked!* — but she wanted to. She shucked off her work suit. She sat down on the wooden planks of the scaffolding. "Would you mind cleaning up?" Nix asked Torrance without turning around, then she leaped off the scaffolding to the ground below. She landed heavily and started toward the house without looking back, for fear she might lose her resolve. She heard Torrance cough a couple times, but no more than that. She kept walking.

Morning came abruptly to Nix, who had slept hard with no dreams. She looked over at Zephyr's tranquil face, she was sleeping so peacefully. Nix thought about reaching over to touch her, but slipped out of bed slowly, taking extra care to not wake her. She dressed in the kitchen, ate breakfast without delay and was out the door before the sun was up. Across the open space the ship looked dark and silent, a shadow that extended up instead of lying on the ground. For all she knew, every light was on inside and they had partied through the night.

She arrived at the scaffolding, climbed to the first level of boards, slipped her suit on. The sky was beginning to lighten. She sat facing the sun, her legs dangling over the edge. She sipped some water and waited for the light to overtake the horizon and warm her face. She closed her eyes and imagined the work she would do today, thought about the hammer strikes, the wonderful steadiness of her pounding. Oh, pounding. A flash of a woman beneath her, her head back, lips open. *Damn it. It was going so well for a few minutes.* The sun's rays struck her face then temporarily blinded her unprotected eyes. Two hands came around from behind and covered her eyes before she could do it herself. She was so startled she couldn't move. Her breath stopped.

Nix reached up and took hold of the hands. She pulled one down to her mouth and kissed the palm. "Torrance, you scared the hell out of me. Why would you do that to an old lady so early in the morning?"

Torrance waited for Nix to release her hand, then she sat down next to her. "I often sit in the ship and wait for this same moment, for the sun to rise and flash against my face, to see the glowing tangerine against my closed eyelids. But enough of poetry." She stood. "Let's get to work."

Day after day the carving continued. Rough shapes were starting to appear — elongated ovals and blocks that might become faces or fists or feet. Nix moved the scaffolding slowly. If she made what she considered good progress, she would move the scaffolding a meter every day.

The weather raised some hell at the end of the third week. The winds knocked over the scaffolding. Nix left it lying in the muddy yard until the rain stopped on the third day. In the brief respite between torrential downpours, she widened the base by adding four retractable legs that doubled the circumference of the base and would prevent the scaffolding from falling again. On the fourth day, she watched helplessly from the window as the wind's invisible hands pushed the scaffolding like a Trojan horse, its slowness belying its forward speed, until it collided with the rock. It did not fall over. But she cursed the next day when she saw the impact cracks that went several inches deep. The damage was something she could work around. She considered whether she should make the scaffolding collapsible or build a permanent structure around the rock. She had never been at the whim of the elements like this, but then, she had never had a piece of rock this size. She looked over at the ship. How the hell did that thing remain stable in the last round of winds? Rain started to fall again, large drops pelted her head and shoulders, the most pregnant raindrops she had ever felt. She pushed the scaffolding across the open space, her feet lost traction, she fell to her knees several times. Her boots and pants caked with mud up to her knees. She pushed the moveable structure until it was hugging the side of her working studio, the least likely part of the yard to get strong crosswinds. She stuffed old two-by-fours under each wheel assuring it would not move. She called off all work until the weather cleared.

Nix felt trapped in the house after a day of reading; she was tired of it. She considered going to the greenhouse to visit Zephyr, but now that Zephyr was working on a new set of experiments, she knew she would be interrupting her work. Not respecting her work in the same way that Nix demanded her own work to be respected would not help their already strained relationship. The second day she went to the clay studio. She evaluated the Jansee figures, and decided they were done. Then she prepared two wire frames that would become dynamic poses of Gantu and Fazeef. She hadn't seen either of them naked, but she had a good sense of their proportions from watching them during the demolition of the old shed and construction of the wrap-around scaffolding. She was interested in their complete likeness expressed in both female and male form. Sculpting them together, side by side, would give her a chance to explore the absoluteness of their similarities and differences. She got as far as she could that day, leaving the rest until she could get them to model for her.

At the start of the following week, the weather cleared and Nix went back to work. The open space was a slop of mud; the grass was waterlogged. At the tool chest, she shoved chisels and hammers into her leather tool belt, called out the type and size of each, not giving Torrance much time to absorb it all. She was short on patience to teach today, she wanted to work, to be deep into the physicality of it. Strange, because during the rainy days, she had imagined explaining to Torrance the use for each tool, having her hold them and say the type and size back to her. When her belt was loaded, she nodded to Torrance and walked past her, careful not to make contact with her skin.

Torrance worked beside her every day. She watched Nix work, made vids and pics of her process, but never let documentation get in the way of handing over chisels, clean rags, wet rags, or drinking water when Nix requested.

Music played from a dented silver box covered in scratched-up solar panels during specific daylight hours. Once the sun declined to a certain angle, the music would stop until the next morning when the sun made another pass. The tink of single chisel blows or the rhythmic piston clack-clacking of the pneumatic chisel were the primary sounds throughout the day and the only sounds on the extreme ends of the day.

There was a constant haze of dust around Nix, chips of stone rained from her hands at rhythmic intervals. Through her dust-covered face shield, she kept catching the ghostly profile of Torrance in her peripheral vision. She heard her laughter over the noise of the machine. And noticed that Torrance smiled pleasantly if Nix turned toward her or said her name.

Whenever Torrance walked on the scaffolding, her weight bowed the planks. Nix was very sensitive to such fluctuations and would hold the pneumatic chisel, the heated machine, like an impatient child in her arms, until the platform was still again.

Torrance took hold of Nix's bicep and tugged gently. Nix turned the chisel off and lifted her hood. Her face was studded with diamond-like beads of sweat. She wanted to take a deep breath, but dust was still suspended in the air around her. She opened her eyes wide to look at Torrance's bare brown arms and face against the white stone backdrop. The dust gave Torrance's image a glittering, mirage-like quality, made her appear vaporous and unreal. Then Nix felt a surge of emotion, the adrenaline rush of a crush. It shouldn't have taken her by surprise, but it did. She looked away, hoping to hide the softened look in her eyes from Torrance.

Torrance said, "Come on. Climb down with me and get some fresh air. How do you do this every day?" She tugged on Nix's arm again to shake her from her trance.

Nix nodded, set the tool down. Torrance climbed over and down the outside of the scaffolding; Nix nearly matched her speed. At the bottom, Nix dusted herself off, and followed Torrance to their usual sitting area. "My father was a daredevil, unafraid or inconsiderate of physical pain. And my mother — an uncrowned beauty queen who would have greatly benefitted from the discipline and confidence of a college education — was more interested in enjoying her youth than sacrificing such gifts to motherhood. This magical combination can be used to explain a lot of things about me — my stubbornness, self-sufficiency, but *not* why I'm an artist." She stopped to unzip her suit and started to shrug it off her shoulders, "Why I feel compelled to live in the middle of nowhere might be another interesting question you should want an answer to."

Torrance tilted her head, bit her bottom lip as she contemplated Nix. "I know when to back off. I get it. I'll give you some space. Doesn't look like you need me, or anyone, during this phase, so it could be a long, lonely, two years for you." Torrance turned and walked toward the ship.

Nix sat on the grass staring at her white-dusted boots, wondered what the hell just happened. She ate both lunches that Torrance had set out for them, then returned to work.

Torrance returned to the ship. She could still feel the adrenaline that had surged inside her when Nix had lifted her mask a few hours ago and their eyes had met. *How many times had she looked at Nix's eyes since they had landed? Why was this time any different?* She had gone from knowing that Nix had light-colored eyes, to really looking at them, to finding the washed-out blue beautiful beyond any she had ever seen. She worked late into the evening reviewing the crew's vid streams and research logs from the past week.

They were making great progress; if they left now they would have enough to make the mission worthwhile.

It wasn't surprising to her that she was feeling like she was falling in love. But she was angry that she had fallen when it was so preventable. She had been so careful. Had she forgotten to take the medication this week? She thought back, and no one thing seemed to have triggered it. Once she had completed all of the official mission work, she stayed up to review her own Lifestream logs. The feelings had started some weeks back, but they were dismissible, easily suppressed by the medication. The feeling today, so amplified, had come out of nowhere, suddenly flooding her mind with a mixture of excitement, then panic at the strength of it, enough to make her question her mental stability.

"Condensed log chart by day for Commander Whitney:" Torrance requested. She reviewed the accumulated data of her vital stats, looked for some correlation of elevated heart rate, adrenaline levels, pupil dilation that might have occurred during a particular interaction with Nix. She was surprised to find a pattern — upon seeing Nix each morning, there were elevated adrenaline and dopamine readings, heart rate. She hadn't noticed it while it was happening, but the sensors had logged it. A noticeable spike earlier in the day — when she had climbed onto the scaffolding and Nix had raised her mask to look at her. The look had triggered a multitude of physical reactions inside her, a swelling wave of emotions that pressed to get out, that off-balanced her body and caused her mind to go blank for a second in the undertow. *Had Nix felt something similar?* It felt like they had had a fight, but maybe she had misunderstood the underlying causes, their sudden collision and withdrawal. Now, with the benefit of a many hours since the occurrence, it seemed very likely that Nix's expository "personality" speech was her way of covering her own surging feelings. Some distance between them would be a good thing. Torrance would show Nix that she could throw herself into her work just as deeply as Nix could.

19, VISIBLE CRACKS

Torrance had been sitting at her desk since the previous evening. She had assessed and reassessed the charts of her biological reactions, tried to sort them out and the night had passed into morning. And the morning into the early evening. In her unusual state, the sunset seemed magnificent beyond words. She stared at the orange fireball as it set down in a controlled impact onto the horizon.

Derthan had returned to the ship first after completing her daily duties. She hadn't seen Torrance all day, and felt compelled to check on her. But aside from the brief greeting when Derthan had entered her chamber, Torrance said nothing, just stared blankly forward. Her hand in her pocket absently fondled a metal container that rattled with something inside. Derthan walked closer, watched her. The moment Torrance took her hand out of her pocket, Derthan thrust her hand into the pocket and pulled out a tiny aluminum box. Derthan took a few steps back and opened the box before Torrance could turn in her chair and try to take it back. "I can't believe you're still taking dopamine blockers." She closed the lid and slammed the case onto the tabletop. "So you won't fall in love during the mission, right?"

Torrance was slightly relieved to have her secret finally shared. She looked at Derthan and nodded her head.

Derthan kneeled between Torrance's legs and looked up into her eyes. "Why are you doing this?"

"I've been taking them the whole time, but recently they haven't been working. Logs confirm I'm falling in love with Nix," Torrance said.

"I thought the point of being here was *to be here*, do as the natives do — no chemical manipulation — just pure emotion."

Torrance didn't want to listen. What did Derthan know of this feeling that had the power to make the strong weak and the sighted blind? Nothing. "Easy words to fall from your mouth. You haven't felt emotion like this. You don't know the addictive joy that I crave more than anything else, and I can only get it from being near her. My nonexistent resistance makes me feel as weak as a baby. The way I feel scares me to death. This is the most powerful happiness I've ever felt. I'm afraid of losing it. Of losing her, of losing myself."

A pleasant sounding bell chimed, and the female voice of the ship said, "Gantu and Fazeef have entered the ship, main entrance."

"Announce: Gantu and Fazeef to report to Commander's chamber," Torrance said, and as Torrance spoke the words they were instantly announced through the ship's voice over the comms system.

Their approaching footsteps sounded like one set to Torrance. They greeted Torrance and Derthan with their customary greeting, smiled and bowed slightly. "What is the conversation today?" Fazeef asked.

"Love," Torrance said.

"Sex," Derthan blurted.

"Such corruptive forces," Fazeef said as he set his bag full of specimen tubes onto the floor. A jingle of glass. His hand opened like a lotus flower blooming in fast-motion to reveal triangular, striped pills. "Look, I have yellow-blacks right here. Take as many as you like, I brought enough for years."

"You don't have to be a slave to biology," Gantu added.

He said, "At this point, I'm down to one per week, and not a single sexual thought enters my mind, and if it does, no physical correlation. One can be incredibly productive once one directs that powerful energy into other endeavors." He tilted his head toward the bag on the floor.

"Yes Fazeef, but your choice to be celibate was well-established on Kepler-442B before we even left. We respect it, but I don't want it for myself or Torrance," Derthan said.

He urged Torrance again, "Take some, two a day to start, absolute galvanization of your mind and body." He pursed his lips and tilted his head up.

Torrance reached out to the open hand that looked so much like a sunflower with ripe seeds ready to pick.

"Don't, Torrance," Derthan said. She gently pushed Fazeef's hand away. "We're here to feel. To feel everything, the good and the bad."

"I don't think you understand how terrifying this feeling is, how vulnerable it makes me feel. I did not sign up for this shit, Derthan," Torrance said, but she also didn't take any pills from Fazeef's open hand.

"All is clear in the yellow-black," Fazeef said, a pleasant smile stretched his broad lips thin, his eyes half closed. He pinched a pill between his finger and thumb and tossed it into his mouth.

"Clear and boring. A half-life," Derthan said. "Show me one couple that is happier without sex than with it. Have you even tried it? Your perfect body with so many possibilities, and you choose denial for yourself instead. We are physical creatures. Imagining is only half of it." Derthan had gone too far, she knew even as the sentences escaped through her lips. She was already forming her apology.

"I do not like your tone," Gantu said.

"I'm sorry. Too far. I know. I know," Derthan said. "But we're not taking any yellow-blacks. Torrance and I are going to do this clean, as planned, no matter how difficult it gets."

"Understood," said Gantu and Fazeef in tandem.

"What will you do when it hurts too much?" Gantu asked. "Will you stop talking to her? Do you have the strength to initiate the takeoff sequence and end the mission without her?"

Torrance thought for a moment, "There's never been a pain too intense for me to endure if I wanted something badly enough. I will finish this mission with or without her." She put her hand on the back of her head and shook her head back and forth slowly.

"You're saying you won't jeopardize the mission, but you're shaking your head. Which is it?" Gantu asked.

Torrance straightened herself, set her hands on her hips and put her shoulders back. "I will see this mission through successfully. You have my word that my feelings will not interfere with mission objectives. Now please, all of you, leave my chamber. I need to get some sleep before dinner."

They each nodded and bowed, leaving the chamber in an orderly line.

"Close door: Dim lights: Set alarm for 60 minutes:"

":Yes, Commander. Preferences set." The voice confirmed.

Torrance removed her boots and sat on the bed. She unzipped her uniform and collapsed onto the bed, sprawled her limbs in the cardinal directions.

":Commander, time to wake," the soft voice of the ship said. This was repeated every 15 seconds in the same inflection, but louder volume, until Torrance replied for it to stop. She felt dazed. Had she already slept for one Earth hour? She sat up. She was naked, but didn't remember taking her uniform off. She lifted her right arm and whiffed at her armpit. She would need to clean up before going to dinner.

"Lights 40 percent brighter:" She said as she walked toward the room that contained heated water, mirrors, cleaners for her hair and skin that didn't require water but were much more pleasant in combination with it.

The mirror told the story in exactly the same way she perceived it — her eyes had dark circles beneath from a night of not sleeping, her cheeks a bit hollow from a day of not eating. She looked depleted. She ran water into her cupped hands and splashed her face over and again, massaged the skin with her fingertips to rub out the sleep lines. The next time she saw herself there was some improvement, and that would be as good as it would get without food and more sleep. She dressed quickly in a black uniform, leaving the white one to be laundered in the ultraviolet chamber.

"Announce: crew ready and rendezvous in five minutes at ship's entrance:"

The bell sounded and the announcement was made. Torrance checked her hair one last time before she left her chamber. She knew exactly why she had checked it and her first reaction was to be upset with herself, but she got past it. *Let it flow*, she thought and made her way to the entrance of the ship.

The crew was assembled as ordered. They were talking and laughing. Torrance was the last to arrive. She liked seeing them like this — happy and enjoying each other's company, beaming with the day's accomplishments. "Did you have a productive day? Anything you'd like to share on the way over?" Torrance asked. She started walking toward the house before anyone answered.

They followed closely behind her in a loose formation. Jansee said, "Today, I heard a wonderful bird song. I analyzed a clip and learned that it was a *Melospiza melodia*, a song sparrow. Which seems a very fitting name. The song clip is logged. Human language doesn't have words to explain these sounds. If anyone would like to hear it from the source, I will gladly take you."

Gantu said, "I've logged and stored living fern samples from three different species — five-finger, western sword, and giant chain. The leaves look similar from a distance, but the intricacies of the leaves are so varied. They are all high oxygen-production species. Also of note, the sky looks clear for the evening meteor shower. Anyone interested in staying up with me to watch it?" She tilted her face upward, the skin stretched even tighter over her prominent cheekbones, making her face as sharp as a poised arrow.

20, TRUTH BEYOND WORDS

In bed beside Zephyr, Nix lay awake, sleep elusive, with her mind in a downward spiral of dark thoughts. She could only think of the distance between them, which had existed for some time, but was so much more evident in the spotlight of her feelings for Torrance. Then the anchor of her body rapidly pulled her into the abyss of sleep.

She woke groggy. Dressed in a half-awake state. Zephyr was sitting at the dining table drinking coffee and making notes. Nix ate silently, not wanting to stir any conversation. As Nix opened the front door, Zephyr reached over and took hold of her arm. Nix turned and gave her an obligatory kiss, a small reassurance of her primary place in Nix's heart, then she smiled, gently pulled away.

Nix couldn't be in the house a moment longer than necessary with Zephyr there. Zephyr would want to talk, to ask about the progress of the work, about Torrance. There was nothing between her and Torrance, there wasn't going to be anything, so there was no point discussing it. Nix was either in the house or working on the stone, and in both places a woman wanted something from her. They wanted too much. They wanted every waking minute. She didn't want to talk to either of them. She wanted to be alone, to have the stone as her lover.

"You're just going to walk out and not say goodbye?" Zephyr said. She took hold of Nix's hand, so that she would stop and turn around. "I'm packed. I leave this morning on my annual trading trip to the coast."

"Oh, that's today?" Nix said. She'd lost track of time completely lately.

"Yes. And can you believe it's been a year since the space women landed? Or at least that's my estimate since I was at the coast when they arrived. Hard to believe." Zephyr shook her head, then squeezed Nix's hand tighter. "Oh, and I forgot to tell you, I'm extending my trip, I'll be gone twice as long as usual. I'm going farther north, I hear there are some communities that have recently opened to trade."

"I see," Nix pulled her hand free, bent to hug Zephyr. "I love you. Have safe travels."

Zephyr tried to kiss her, but Nix turned her head, so that Zephyr's lips could only land on her cheek. "Oh, you won't even kiss me?"

"I was hugging you. Why are you being so sensitive?" Nix stepped back and looked at her.

"Being around her is changing you. I want them gone when I return. Promise me."

"I don't have any control over their departure schedule," Nix said.

"I want you back, our lives back," Zephyr said.

"I don't want to fight. Take care of business and we'll discuss it when you return." Nix looked out the kitchen window, the sun was coming over the horizon.

"Tell them to move on or I may not be coming back."

Nix sighed heavily and clenched her teeth together. "Let's discuss it when you get back."

"You are fucking impossible sometimes. Do you want to save this relationship or not?"

"I want to finish the stone. That is all I'm thinking about right now. I'm sorry if you think that's selfish, but this isn't the first big piece you've been around for," Nix said.

"Oh, yes, simple Nicole, just wants to work. Slave to her art. Beyond her control. All else be damned. Hurts to hear the truth, doesn't it? Well, contemplate it while I'm gone. Take your head out of that fucking rock and think about your feelings for me. We'll discuss *that* when I return."

Nix nodded, and silently turned and went out the door.

That afternoon, Nix set-up high-lumen lights to cover a five-foot by five-foot area from three angles — above (hanging from a pole extended out from the top level of the scaffolding), direct (beside her, and a burning hazard), and below (anchored to the ground with a giant wooden spike). She repurposed two sheets of solar panels, did a little geometry to decide where they should be placed and hoped they would be enough to power all three lights for three to four hours after sunset.

By the time she was done, the sky had turned deep purple. She turned the lights on and started working. The air felt dry. In the far distance, she saw a white pulse of lightning inside a tall fluffy cloud. She waited, but there was no thunder. A shrill call from the house reminded her it was time to go inside and eat.

It was past midnight when she sat down for the first time since dinner. With trembling hands she drank a ladle of water. Her fingers were scuffed and bleeding in a few places. She turned off the lights, and walked to the workshop. She washed her hands, then wrapped them in strips of ointment-soaked cloth. She would start wearing gloves tomorrow.

For days she worked morning until late at night, alone. Torrance kept her distance. Since their intense interaction on the scaffolding, Nix had a tremendous amount of energy and chose to put all of it into her work. She refused to let her mind dwell on any thoughts of Torrance, but she could not stop images that briefly flashed in her mind — her lips pressing against Torrance's neck, Torrance turning to look at her and smile, looking down to see the tip of Torrance's tongue sliding into the top of her underwear. Some of these were actual memories, some masturbation fantasies, but most were new — made up by the power of her mind. She found switching from carnal images of Torrance then back to the cold stone as exhausting as the work itself.

Each night, the crew greeted her when she came into the house for dinner. They looked at her and smiled, tried to make eye contact. She was too far into her head, distracted, anti-social, an island of one. She smiled and nodded and took her seat at the head of the table.

Gantu brought a plate of food and set it in front of Nix. She smiled and bowed her head.

"Thank you," Nix said. Her hunger threatened to override her manners. She felt herself hunching over and shoveling the food into her mouth like an animal. She forced herself to slow and chew, then to wait before taking another bite. She stared blankly forward, took smaller bites of food, noted the taste, her mind emptied except as a receiver for the feeling of her body — a great hunk of bruised pulsating meat. "You've learned well over these months. Your food is delicious and my body is singing with pleasure," Nix said to all of them. She finished her plate before everyone else. If she sat for too long she would start to settle. She stood up. "If you'll excuse me, I'm going back to work. You can't imagine how much is left to do."

Torrance looked at her and nodded silently. There was no voice of reason in the house with Zephyr gone. Nix could work herself to the bone and the visitors would just nod. They would let her do whatever she thought best.

At the end of a week, Nix threw an old tarp over the music machine, starving it of life-giving sun. Every song had reminded her of Torrance. She squeezed the chisel, focused on its solidity, the inflexibility that forced the soft parts of her hand to make room around it. She placed the chisel onto the stone with her left hand and struck it with the hammer in her right. She tilted the chisel and struck again. Her eyes gauged her next move, her hands executed, working as a single entity.

She stopped for a drink of water, drank so thirstily that water ran down both sides of her mouth, her chin, her throat. She wiped the sweat from her face and turned back to the stone. She resumed her rhythm, forgot to put her mask down, made minor adjustments with the chisel and continued to strike it hard. A small chip hit her lip with a scissoring pain. She wasn't sure what had happened. She instinctually spit first, in case it was an insect. She continued to work as her tongue inspected her lip. No swelling, diagonal indentation. Taste of blood. Clink, clink, clink. Not enough to stop her hands from their important work. She flipped her mask down and kept working. Chips fell onto her thighs and boots, some as delicate as a fish scale, some as large as a baseball. She focused on her work, chiseled twice as fast and hard, felt the aching reverberation in the bones of her hands and forearms. She was so successful at times that when the visitors came by to watch her she didn't even notice them standing nearby and talking about her. They were in awe of the magnificent artist at the height of her talent, pouring herself into her work with a devotion they could only hope to attain at some point in their lives.

She worked until it was too dark to see. The chisel felt less effective so she stopped. It would be difficult to explain if she had to put it into words, but there was a subtle change in results. Nix knew this feeling well. She hadn't changed, the chisel had. She rubbed her thumb over the carbide tip, confirming her suspicion that the tip was beginning to round. She'd caught it before it had gone to the more damaging "mushrooming" condition. She walked to the machine shop. The air in the building was dank, pungent with oil and steel, the smell of blood and guts of machines that she loved. She could fix anything in this quiet place, one of her sanctuaries where time ceased. She turned on the industrial bell-shaped lights that hung from the ceiling, then flipped the chrome switch to start the green sanding-wheel. Nix held the chisel firmly with both hands as she pressed it against the spinning wheel. Beneath the machine, a spray of orange sparks shot out like accelerated falling stars that bounced and died against the blackened cement floor. Nix flipped the chisel over, worked both sides several times to ensure the tip was beveled evenly and as sharp as it had been before her hammering marathon. When she was happy with the renewed tip, she turned off the machine, then the lights, and closed the door behind her — all while keeping her eyes and one thumb on the tip of the chisel.

When Nix finally looked up, Torrance, a dark silhouette in the twilight, was standing in front of her. She felt a smile overtake her mouth. Her heart was betraying her and charging full-gallop across the field into battle. She found it difficult to speak. She swallowed for the third time, licked her lips. "Hello." The word sounded gruff and miserly to her ears. She looked for something else for her eyes to focus on — the different insignia on Torrance's uniform, the crescent moon rising just above her shoulder — anything to give her some room to breathe and get her head right. *How does this happen? I fall in love too easily. God, I'm old now, old enough to know better, old enough to recognize the pattern. But helpless to stop it.*

Voices came from across the lawn as the crew dashed like a herd of young deer toward the house for dinner. "Torrance, Nix, come on," Derthan shouted first. "Time to eat," Fazeef said. "We worked all day too. Don't make us wait," Gantu said.

Torrance and Nix turned toward them. Nix felt suddenly sad, then giddy, then like she might cry, all in a matter of seconds. She ran her fingers through her hair, which was gritty with powdered stone. She started walking toward the house, relieved to have an excuse to turn away from Torrance. She wouldn't look over at her, didn't wanting to feel the magnetic pull of Torrance's eyes again. *Cursed love. Only a fool would give her heart twice to the same woman, knowing the outcome would be the same.*

In the house, the temperature felt overly warm, smothering. Nix's cheeks felt ablaze. She gripped the high back of the chair, stared at the table laid with bowls and spoons.

"Sit down, Nix. Everything is ready. I made venison stew," Torrance said, smiling. She moved casually around the table as if she were in her own home. Nix sat, and though she was curious to see the smiling faces of the visitors, she wouldn't look up because she knew her eyes would go directly to Torrance. And once they were there, she wouldn't just look at her, she would *look* at her as if under a spell — study the contours of her eyelids, the way her cheeks plumped when she laughed, admire her chalk-white smile.

Nix drank her entire glass of water without stopping. "Nice table you've set." She made a point to look anywhere but at Torrance. Her hands were grubby. "And look at me, I didn't even have a chance to take a shower yet. I'm a little embarrassed."

"Don't be. It was supposed to be a surprise," Torrance said, refilling Nix's water glass. "Besides, the failure is mine. I couldn't think of a tactful way to ask you to take a shower." She winked, and set her hand on top of Nix's for a second before turning back toward the kitchen.

The heat in Nix's body went up a notch. She reached up and touched her right ear; it was hot. "Keep the stew on for five more minutes," she said, "it won't take me longer than that." She stood abruptly, not waiting for permission, and walked toward the bathroom.

"No, come on Nix, stay," Derthan said.

"Nix, come back," Torrance said.

She ignored their jeers and pleadings. "Have some wine, I just need five minutes." Nix turned the corner into the hallway.

Torrance said, "Fine as summer wine." A cork popped.

Nix froze in mid-step, one hand gripped the nearest doorframe to keep her steady. That old phrase from their summer weekends at the beach. Tears welled into her eyes, stinging. She knew better than to rub them. She stumbled into the bathroom and turned on the shower, dropped her clothes in four fast movements. The water sluiced over her face and drowned out all sound. She rinsed her shoulder-length hair, pulled and combed the cleaning paste vigorously through. She washed the front of her body, not lingering a second longer than was necessary, but she was surprised by the level of her arousal as she rinsed. She rubbed the bar of homemade soap between her cheeks, rinsed and re-lathered, finished with armpits, feet. Then splashed a few handfuls onto her face. Her face. *Her* face.

Nix rejoined the laughing crew at the table. They had waited to eat, but they had started drinking. Torrance served everyone, and refilled glasses before sitting at the far end of the table (Zephyr's usual seat). Nix ate, smiled politely, and drank more wine than she should have. What else was there to do? Now that she was showered, she would not be returning to the stone tonight. They had tricked her with food, and the only way she could tolerate being trapped inside with Torrance was to drink. She thought of Zephyr, a sobering thought. Wondered how her trip was progressing, how far away she might be after two weeks of travel. She had taken two additional horses, so she would be many, many miles away. When Nix could no longer keep her eyes open, she excused herself and walked into the bedroom, within seconds she had her clothes off, and collapsed face-first onto the bed.

21, DON'T SAY YOU LOVE ME

Nix was conscious, awake only on the lowest level. She didn't know who she was, where she was, or which woman she was sharing her life with. *Is this what they mean by "sleeping like the dead"?* Her eyes remained closed and her sluggish flesh insisted she fall asleep. She resisted. *Why do I have to fight my own body?* Her heavy limbs wanted to remain prone, sprawled as they were across the bed. *The entire lovely bed.* Her mind was a resident only, not yet fully integrated into the control seat. She took a deep breath, opened her eyes. She recognized the ceiling immediately. She was Nix, this was her house in the wilderness of Northern California, Zephyr was her partner. She reached over, but the bed beside her was empty.

After a few more minutes, her eyes remained open without a constant struggle between blinks. She pushed the covers off her body, lifted herself onto her right elbow. She looked down at the sculpture her body had become as of late — the scalloped sides of her flat stomach, especially the definition of her external obliques that formed inverted L-shaped indentations on her lower stomach, so prevalent on Greek male sculptures. She turned onto her side, propped herself up with her left leg. The quad muscle hung heavily, pulled by gravity toward the bed. Her right hand was puffy, still curled as if holding an invisible mallet. She lay back down and tried to open her right hand, but it was locked. She took a deep breath, grabbed her right hand with her left. The two grappled like ancient wrestlers until the left hand won the battle and the right opened, showing its palm in surrender.

She sat up and absently rubbed the back of her neck with her right hand, her fingers loosened with every motion against the warm skin. She sat on the edge of the bed and stared at her feet. They weren't complaining, which was surprising. She wiggled her toes and mumbled "thank you" to show her gratitude. She put on the clothes that were in a pile on the floor. All she remembered from last night was Torrance saying that old expression, then she had showered, had dinner with them, drank too much wine.

She ate venison jerky leaning against the kitchen sink. No sign of anyone inside or out. The visitors were probably still tucked-in inside their tin can. She cracked two eggs into a glass, added a shake of salt, a grind of pepper, and swallowed it down. She drank two cups of coffee and was ready to work.

The morning air was soupy; heavy white fog shrouded all of the buildings. She had entered an opaque dream world and could only see a few feet in front of her. Her breath was visible as she exhaled. She had a sudden chill that shook her shoulders and traveled down her ribs. She should have brought another layer of clothes, but she was anxious to get to work. No birds sang, there was light enough to see that everything had vanished into a gray-white void. Nix headed to the workshop first, hoping the fog would lift in an hour. It was early enough that she would have the place to herself, but the door was ajar, so she knew Torrance or someone from the crew was already inside. She turned on her heel and headed in the direction of the woods, suddenly wanting to go for a long walk instead. She looked over her shoulder as she made her escape.

Torrance walked out of the workshop, squinted a bit against the diffused light. She shielded her eyes in Nix's direction, "Nix, wait." Torrance broke into a loping run.

Nix waited, watching and comparing the ease of her run to the lightness of a deer running through a field. When

Torrance caught up, Nix tried not to look into her eyes, she knew that the small action would cause a little rush of desire, and she didn't want it, she liked the coolness of her heart, her hands would stay at her sides, they were for work only. Another side of her was surveying hungrily, ready to touch, to feel some union of skin. *How can I stay monogamous with Torrance here?* Being this close to her was painful. Pre-tears clawed across the surface of her eyes, etched like acid. She looked skyward, her old habit to allay tears. She took a few steps back, then turned and started walking into the trees. She held her hands out, let them graze tree trunks as she weaved in and out. *Can I be as strong as these rooted trees in the ground?* She had to admit that her mind was infected, obsessed, no matter how hard she chiseled. The only relief seemed to come when she was sleeping or when she injured herself. Her dreams were filled with water — flooded roads, the house filling with water, diving into a deep lake.

Nix emerged from the trees into the tall grass of the meadow. Her fingertips brushed the grass, a sensation delicate as feathers after the rough bark of the trees. Torrance had stayed close behind her, silent until they came to the old fence built from field rock and mud, which had been standing for hundreds of years. The fog lifted as swiftly as a sheet pulled from a bed, leaving higher clouds like horsetails, ripples of ghost waves, trumpets stretched long with curved, cupped ends against the blue sky. Nix looked up, enchanted by the white wisps of clouds that were as fine as pencil lines.

Torrance stood beside her, looked back across the wide meadow they had crossed, the enclosure of trees. "I recognize this place."

"You should, this is your third time here," Nix said flatly.

"You just won't give me a break, will you?" Torrance said.

"Sorry, but the brightest pupils deserve the most scrutiny."

The tall yellow-green grass waved in the wind. They leaned their forearms on the top of the rough wall and looked out at the changing scene — the grass and trees tinged with golden morning light. The morning sun painted warmth over their stretched backs and the backs of their legs. Their shoulders relaxed in the joy that standing next to each other brought, and the hardness of the wall melted away, transforming into the most comfortable place to be in this moment of togetherness and privacy.

Torrance wished they could stand there all day. "There is no wild grass on our planet. This place is like a dream — it starts with the smell of the air, the blue of the sky, then the sunlight and infinite colors of everything around, every inch covered with magnificent species. I feel like I'm living in a painting."

"Tell me more about your new home," Nix said.

Torrance said, "The promise of off-world was equality. And they've delivered for the most part. Our culture is free of the racial and gender inequalities that still plague Earth in the remote regions. But what we encountered instead was a lack of health equity. The first generation of off-worlders were scrubbed clean to prepare for the long flight, and vaccinated with antibiotics and antimicrobials to bolster the immune system, but within a generation we found our numbers diminishing, even with all the advances we'd made with gene manipulation and cloning. Yes, we knew a closed system doesn't work, that soil with all of its bacteria and minerals was essential if we were to create an environment that could sustain us, and when the ships left Earth we thought we were taking enough, but somehow we underestimated the complexity and importance of our own microbiome. We've cultured what good bacteria we could, but the varieties are few and in the confined atmosphere of the new colony, it has proved more than challenging to proliferate. Our best chance of survival meant that we needed to return to Earth for more and varied samples. So the decision was made to send us here."

"Are you expected to bring back biome samples from humans?" Nix pushed her hand back through her silvery hair.

"Not *from* humans. *As* humans. This mission is important on many levels. To survive we need to return to Kepler-442B with biome specimens. We'll use our own bodies to transport the biomes as a safeguard against losing the specimens. This is the reason for the genetic diversity of the crew, in case you hadn't noticed — we cover a sample set of genes. We are not only useful as carriers, but we will also log our individual reactions to the current atmosphere here."

"That's a huge responsibility on you and the crew. You all look so young." Nix was floored by the importance of their mission, the willing sacrifice of their bodies.

"Who better than the young to want to fight for life? They have their whole lives ahead of them, and will do anything, endure anything to preserve it," Torrance said.

"Tune to five:" Jansee said through the comms system. She had been watching Torrance's monitor for the past hour, and she saw some change in Nix's face that made her anticipate what she suspected — that something was about to happen between the two of them. Torrance heard "Tune to five:" over her internal speaker and knew she had missed something in Nix's reaction. She replayed the last minute in fast motion on her retina screen. *The subtle smile? The way Nix rubbed her lip absently with her index finger while I was talking?*

"Earth to Torrance," Nix said, waving her hand in front of Torrance's vacant Lifestream stare.

Torrance turned away and said in a lower volume, "Blackout: max temporal limit." Her screens went dark.

Something important was about to happen, and she hoped 15 minutes would be long enough for her to have it to herself. "Sorry Nix, something important. But I'm here now."

Torrance put her hand over Nix's and stepped forward to close the gap between them.

Nix thought of her sculpture "Touched," the embodiment of her first, long ago kiss with Torrance. When she looked at that piece, she could still remember how all the world fell away when their lips touched. They became the only two beings in the universe, time ceased. Her body had fallen away and her entire being inhabited her lips. For years she wondered how they had only known each other from days and weeks of talking and then had had a kiss like that. Could it be that way again?

Torrance leaned in to her. There was some matter of mechanics. As Torrance tilted her head, Nix closed her eyes and felt Torrance's lips land on hers. Nix heard the hush of a breeze over the grass. Felt the sunlight on the side of her face. Mouths wet with wanting, sliding. The ease of it was ancient, implanted inside them and emerging to reform their connection.

This kiss, somehow the same as the first, was more perfect. Torrance's lips — nirvana-esque, a plush familiarity — put Nix into a kind of ecstasy she thought was no longer possible to feel. Then Torrance delivered a crushingly passionate kiss, her hands cupping the sides of Nix's head and pulling her closer like she needed her life-giving breath. They breathed through their noses, long inhales, short bursts of exhalation. The spark was delicious, one of the best feelings of being alive, this shared sensation multiplied by another. Body heat increased, hands clutched, grabbed, and greedily pulled their bodies together like atoms wanting to collide. Nix's legs became liquid, unsteady. She needed to get low, to lie down, to have the solidity of the earth beneath her.

Had Torrance become untethered? Gravity disappeared. Was she floating up or down? She didn't know anymore. Then she felt Nix disengaging, untangling her hands and arms from her and stepping back.

Nix's chest rose and fell as she tried to catch her breath. She could feel the animal inside her, her eyes wide and unblinking with the enlarged pupils of a hungry tiger. She leaned forward with her hands on her knees and looked at the ground, shook her head to extinguish the fire inside. "Let's head back," Nix said.

"Let's stay," Torrance looked at Nix, hesitantly touched her hand.

"I can't stay here alone with you. We should go. I could barely stop," Nix said. She turned and started across the meadow.

Torrance picked up her pace to catch up with her. She walked silently beside her, no touching. "I love you," Torrance said.

Nix kept walking. No reaction visible on the outside. *Where was that coming from? That was such a serious thing for anyone to say.* She wouldn't say it back, but suspected that deep inside she felt the same.

When they reached the edge of the forest and were about to enter the open space, Nix stopped and turned, meeting Torrance's gaze, "You said you *love me*. You love me? How can you say such a thing? You know I'm not single. I'm with Zephyr."

Torrance made some erratic gestures, pushed the keyboard in her forearm, looked back at Nix, "My comms will re-activate in 19 seconds."

"Just turn it off again." Nix said.

"I can't. I'd have to override the system, which would look even more suspicious than the last blackout," Torrance said.

Nix wanted to care, but she didn't. The past 15 minutes were enough for her. She kept walking, turned her head enough to see Torrance walking in her peripheral vision. She was relieved to have this come, and pass, and know that she had the discipline to hold back. To not indulge. Nothing more than a kiss. She had a choice this time. *It's controllable, I'm not an animal compelled to follow my instinct.* She jumped up and grabbed some leaves from a branch.

To Torrance it looked like an expression of pure joy.

22, HANDS ON ME

Toward the end of the week, well after dinnertime, Torrance noticed the lights were still on in the clay studio and went in to see if Nix was still working. The room was dimly lit, except for a spotlight over a single posed clay figure on the rotating table. Nix sat mostly in shadow, only the tip of her nose and her hands illuminated as she worked.

"Hello?" Torrance said.

"What brings you out so late?" Nix asked.

"The moon looked interesting on the monitors." *I couldn't sleep, I was thinking about so many things.* She sat on a stool next to Nix, so close that their legs touched.

Nix nodded her head, then turned the table half a turn, tilted her head to the side, paused for a second, then turned it back and continued to work.

"The moon is setting now, a beautiful red. You should see it," Torrance said, leaning her knee into Nix's.

Nix looked at her, smiled as best as she could through her resentment at being interrupted. "I'm a little busy right now."

Torrance stood, walked slowly around the shop until her eyes adjusted to the relative darkness away from the sculpture's light. "I noticed the lights are on in the house too. I wasn't sure if you'd be in here," Torrance said.

Nix continued to work for a minute before answering, "Zephyr's back. She got home last night."

"Oh," Torrance said. "Why didn't you mention it today at the work site?"

Nix didn't answer, and Torrance's attention shifted to a sturdy granite slab fitted into one corner. It looked like a tabletop, polished glass-smooth, the edges ground into rounded lips. Torrance imagined this was used as a multipurpose table for eating, drawing, writing. But something more interesting also came to mind. With her arm outstretched in front of her, she pushed the contents of the table gently to the side, then wiped the thin layer of dust from the table with a cloth she found on the nearby bench.

"Nix, come sit over here. Please," Torrance said from the dark corner.

Nix didn't move immediately, she looked in Torrance's direction, eyes squinted and full of questions.

"Just for a little while," Torrance said.

Nix stood and walked over. If she didn't do it, she would never get back to sculpting tonight. She looked at Torrance disapprovingly and sat on the slab, her hands flat next to her thighs, her legs open.

"Move back a little. Make room for me too," Torrance said.

Nix glanced over the familiar beauty of her face, but something seemed different. She ventured, "I guess my memory is a little off, because I swear you look shorter."

"The crew is all the same relative height and build, though we are varied in ethnicity and gender. The mission required that we undergo some basic genetic changes through a gene standardization process to reduce variances in our uniforms, quarters, caloric intake," Torrance stepped forward to the edge of the slab, turned her back to Nix, placed her palms on either side of Nix's thighs and easily pulled herself up.

Torrance covered Nix's right hand with her own, but the hand felt rigid, frozen. "Don't be afraid," Torrance whispered. She eased her fingertips under Nix's palm.

Nix forced the pleasure of the tender action to the back of her mind. Torrance's hand was supple. She had the hands of a young woman. It made no sense.

"Put your arms around me," Torrance said.

Nix encircled her in her arms, felt her trembling.

"Tonight I want to be the clay," Torrance said.

"Torrance. Let me up. I need to get back to work." She tried to push her forward, but she couldn't move her.

Torrance pressed back against Nix, assuring her that she wasn't going anywhere until she decided to let her. "Slide your hand inside my uniform, touch my skin."

Nix heard the sound of Torrance opening the front of her uniform. Nix reached with her right hand and slid her fingertips between the layers of fabric, the fine knit caught on the tiny nicks and abrasions on her fingers, and she touched the bare skin beneath. Her fingers were as stiff as chisels; she couldn't bend them. The moist soft skin of Torrance's belly made Nix even more aware of her rough hands and she was ashamed. She tried to withdraw her hand, but Torrance's hand staid hers. "What's going on here, Torrance?" Nix asked.

Torrance leaned her head back and rested it on Nix's shoulder. "I'm seducing you."

Torrance reached down and unfastened her uniform down to mid-thigh. Torrance took hold of Nix's hand and moved it down, left it resting on the waistband of her undergarment. Nix moved her fingers over the delicate skin of Torrance's stomach, whispered, "Softer than silk."

Nix pressed her nose to the side of Torrance's head, her hair smelled clean, botanical. "It's been a long time, but I never forgot the way you smell."

"You talk too much," Torrance said. She put her hand over Nix's and pushed it down inside her underwear. Nix hesitated, and Torrance turned and kissed her cheek. "You know what to do. Don't be shy. I can feel your heart beating against by back."

Nix's blunt fingers parted the trimmed hair and made contact with the skin beneath. Torrance sighed and the weight of her body slouched against Nix. Nix touched everything, her fingers pressed, her whole hand stretched over her, felt her wetness briefly, spread it with her fingertips, moved out and up, then back to touch the inner folds again.

Torrance writhed against her, impatient. She put her hand over Nix's and moved it in a masturbatory motion. "Please," she said. "Faster. We can do it again later."

Nix reached and slid her index and middle fingers down until they touched wetness.

Torrance whispered to Nix, "Use two fingers."

Nix did as Torrance insisted, pushed inside up to her knuckles. With her inserted hand she pulled Torrance's body back toward her until there wasn't a sliver of air between their bodies.

"Uh," Torrance moaned. She grabbed Nix's thighs with both hands to brace herself. Her breathing was changing. Nix moved her hand up and out, then slowly slid it down and in again, hesitating at the top. Her fingers straddled each side of the opening, massaged the tender flesh, moved side to side before entering again. Torrance made a deep short growl in her throat. Nix wrapped her left arm around Torrance, pinning her shoulders against her, continued the back and up motion. Torrance undulated her hips, rode Nix's hand. They found a rhythm. The smell of sex filled the space around them.

Torrance reached up and pulled Nix to her for a kiss. She slid forward, pushed herself down onto Nix's hand, rocked her hips up and down to double the pleasure as they ground against each other. "You're so good," Torrance breathed heavily into Nix's ear, the volume increasing as her breath became faster and faster, until she felt the ignition of an orgasm. She arched her back away from Nix, moaned through clenched teeth. Her orgasm trembled the flesh of her thighs and ass, reverberated into Nix's lower body.

She leaned back against Nix. Her breathing returned to normal. She pulled Nix down for another kiss, bit her lip, then rubbed her head against Nix's shoulder, her eyes closed, a big smile on her face.

"Your turn," Torrance said, easing both hands into the space behind her, she followed the convergence of Nix's thighs, then curled her fingers and rubbed her knuckles over the heated seam of Nix's work pants.

"I'd prefer to be somewhere more comfortable," Nix said.

"Then let's go to the ship," Torrance said and retracted her hands.

"Later. Just close your eyes and enjoy the moment." Nix put her arms around her.

They sat in silence, the air motionless around them. Soon Nix could feel the small twitches of Torrance's body as she fell asleep.

Nix closed her eyes, not tired, but to better see the images in her mind, the memories that flashed and faded at lightning speed. Memories triggered by the smell of fresh sweat on Torrance's skin, the taste of her lips, even the sounds she'd made.

When Torrance woke up, she seemed disoriented. Her head darted from side to side as she turned toward the walls and ceiling to get some idea of where she was.

"Torrance. You're here with me," Nix whispered, and Torrance relaxed, but only for a second before sitting upright, breaking free of the loose embrace, and vaulting from the slab to standing. She turned and looked at Nix. She fastened her uniform from thigh to collar. "I don't know if my comms was on or off." She paced in a tight circle. "I need to get back to the ship."

"You can't sleep here anyway," Nix said. "Go, go back to the ship." Nix stood and kissed her cheek, then followed her to the door.

"It's just sex. Don't read more into it than that," Torrance said, she put her hand on Nix's cheek and stared into her eyes for a long moment, then turned and made her way to the ship.

Nix leaned in the doorframe for a while, watched Torrance's form until she disappeared into the darkness.

The air was moist and damp on Torrance's bare skin, clinging in an unpleasant way. She walked until she was out of Nix's sight, then she started running full speed toward the ship. Had the whole crew watched it, heard it? Were they watching it over and over in the vid logs? She slowed to a walk as she neared the ship. With every footstep a new question entered her mind, but her mind felt so relaxed, feeble even, that it refused to answer any of them or even remember the previous one once a new one arrived.

Nix sat in the workshop for hours afterward. She started working on a new clay figure of Torrance, but she couldn't hold any kind of focus. She kept drifting, staring at things around her — the finished and unfinished pieces, the long table of tools, the wood beams of the ceiling. *How did I let Torrance leave the first time, even encouraged her, ultimately pushed her away? God, it was so many years ago, I've forgotten the most painful details or pounded them out of my body with years of chiseling until there was nothing left but dust. This time it could be different.* Her eyes were getting heavy. And she couldn't sleep in the clay studio tonight either. She roused herself and headed for the house.

She stopped outside the kitchen window and tore off some strands of lavender from the bush. She crushed the stalks and pill-shaped purple flowers in her hands first, then rubbed them against her cheeks and chin, her neck. Rubbed until there was nothing left but shreds of fiber. The pungent earthy spice made her nose twitch. She discarded the remnants on the ground and slid her hands through her hair, pushed her hair down flat against her scalp and held the crown of her skull with both hands. She wished she could push herself down, grind herself in, disappear into the earth. She squeezed her skull, took a deep breath, and walked toward the house.

She got as far as taking off her clothes, showering and walking into the bedroom before she realized Zephyr was sitting on their bed. "You must think I'm blind, which is insulting enough. I've seen the clay models in the studio. Tell me that you at least feel a little guilt for spending so much time with her."

"Am I not supposed to look at her?" Nix said. She pushed her hair back from her face and kept going over the top of her skull until her hand rested on the back of her neck.

"You've done more than look. You don't think I can still smell her on you?"

"Yes, I had sex with her." Nix slammed her open palm against the doorframe beside her. She moved into the room toward her dresser to get a pair of shorts and a shirt. "Maybe it's been too long since we've discussed such things. Did I ever swear to not have sex with another woman for the rest of my life?"

"I thought you'd fucked enough!" Zephyr said. She crossed her arms over her chest.

"Is that even possible?" Nix turned her back to Zephyr; she didn't want to see the ugliness that was oozing from her eyes, the noxious jealousy that twisted her mouth. "I've never asked or accused you of *anything* during your travels. Are you going to tell me that you've been as celibate as a nun?"

"This is our home. We were living here in peace, happiness. And now she's here, they're here. And they're ruining everything — investigating, analyzing, notating, eating dinner in our house every night. I can't take it anymore. I don't want them here. Tell them to leave tonight," Zephyr said.

Nix pulled a T-shirt over her head, sat on the bed. There needed to be more discussion, but she wasn't sure if she had the energy left to talk anymore. "They're staying as long as they need to. I won't tell them to leave. And you should think about what I said. I've got another 40 years of life left in me. You knew what I was like when you met me."

"Yes, when I met you, but you've changed. You've been happy here."

"My self-imposed exile; removed from any chance of ever meeting anyone I find remotely attractive. You're right, there is no one out here. No need to worry about my eyes wandering. But I'm not made of stone."

"Nix, that isn't fair. You've been around many women since we've moved here."

"I moved here to get away from the world, to forget who I was. This is not news to you. You know how broken I was when we met."

"Yes, broken. And I was here for you. I helped make you strong again. *She* wasn't here for you when your hands were so bruised at the end of the day that you could barely undress yourself or hold a glass of water. Do you think she cares that the only way you could make love then was with your mouth, because you worked until your hands were useless?"

"Zephyr, I'm exhausted. All the things you think are in my past — my aching hands, the pure exhaustion, the obsession — is all happening right now. It's been happening for months, and you're just now noticing?" Nix curled her hands in her lap. *Why did pleasure always come at such a cost?* She had done her best to keep it inside, to bear the burden herself, knowing it was temporary. The visitors would leave at some point and that would be the end, and she wouldn't mention Torrance ever again.

Zephyr said, "You want to sleep, to rest, to act like nothing happened. You want the stability of our relationship so you can continue the work, but the passion and sex from someone else to fuel your inspiration."

Nix couldn't argue. Zephyr's assessment was correct. She said nothing, and lay down on the bed hoping to disarm some of the rising tension.

Zephyr stood up, started to undress. "So, you'll start sanding soon?"

Nix kept her eyes closed, spoke in a soft voice. "Still a bit of refining to do first, but yes, soon. The sanding machines are prepped. I've taught most of the visitors how to use them, so they'll help with the upcoming phase. I mapped everything out, what they can and cannot sand," Nix said. "They've been doing maintenance on my chisels, too."

"Your own private army. Impressive," Zephyr said. She slipped into bed, turned off the light, turned on her side and said nothing more.

In the morning, the guilt and anger had faded and Nix woke feeling good. She hadn't felt this way in a long time. An unexplainable lightness and sense of how good things were going to be. *How could I have ignored my own physical needs for so long?*

As Nix and Zephyr ate breakfast, Nix noticed that Zephyr was wearing several silver necklaces, she was showered and dressed in riding clothes. She bent forward in her chair to strap her favorite blade to the outside of her calf.

"All that for around here today?" Nix asked.

"I need to go into town for some supplies," Zephyr said. She hadn't made eye contact with Nix since she'd entered the room.

"But you just got back," Nix said.

"Maybe I've been gone too long, already," Zephyr said under her breath as she stood and tugged her pant leg down over the top of her boot. She looked down to make sure the knife was indistinguishable beneath.

"Are you going to ask me if I need anything?" Nix said.

But Zephyr didn't ask if she needed anything, just stepped close and kissed Nix on the cheek and went out the door.

"When will you be back?" Nix called after her.

"When I get back."

Nix closed the door behind her, didn't bother to go back inside.

The air outside smelled of the sea. The blue sky was hazy, the ocean air had managed to hold a tremendous amount of moisture this far inland. Birds sang, the grass looked greener. She put on her suit and mask and got to work. She noticed even the slight hiss of the chisel on the rock. She was moving more freely, turning her shoulders and twisting at the waist as she sledged rhythmically. She felt so much more aware of every sensation, awake. *Amazing how a little sex changes your perspective.*

Everything she saw during the day became sexual. The curved end of the mallet made her think of a breast, a point in the stone looked like a nipple, the smooth lip of the drinking cup made her think of lips. She laughed to herself. She had long ago laid out the scene on the other side of the sculpture, so the timing was perfect. She could put her flowing desire into carving sexual desire.

Images of the previous night with Torrance pushed their way to the front of her thoughts. The memories were flash points that would cause her body to be filled with a sensation like the third wave of a fading orgasm. When this happened, she would hold the chisel still and close her eyes for a second to enjoy the sweet and sharp sensation that was like placing a piece of dark chocolate onto her tongue.

23, SHAPING

Each day, Nix spent a couple of hours with Jansee in the clay studio, furthering her student's sculpting skills. Since Nix had slaughtered the deer, Jansee had developed a small obsession with deer. She would often spend whole days watching their behavior, returning with tales of close encounters — coming upon a sleeping fawn in the tall grass, arriving at a ridge and startling a herd grazing a few meters away, watching from a tree perch at the lake when they approached to drink — sharing the details at the dinner table. Her other interest was clouds, she would lay in the open space for the better part of the day just staring up at the sky. And though Nix had plenty of ideas about how to sculpt clouds, she wanted Jansee to continue to master more anatomical and solid forms first. She had already completed several sculptures of fawns, some with does, others nestled in grass or springing into the air. She was currently struggling on the much more complex form of a leaping stag.

They had developed a comfortable friendship. Jansee respected Nix's boundaries, for the most part, but she still flirted and touched Nix more than any friend she had ever had. Nix was accustomed to it now, had relaxed about every touch having to mean something. And for all the subjects they discussed, it seemed at some point every conversation ended up being about sex. Tonight's conversation could be classified as "ruminations on the power of a kiss."

Nix had been skirting the subject, very abstract, referring to famous sculptures of kisses, and movie kisses, and kisses in literature before finally stating her personal experience. "For me, the physical is the connection. A simple kiss is usually the first point of connection." Thinking of it, just mentioning it, sent memories of the kiss with Torrance zinging through her body, a lightning bolt to her second chakra. She started to imagine more, but she stopped and came back to her conversation with Jansee, not wanting to be rude. "Those kisses used to feel so harmless to me. I'd wonder why everyone made such a big deal out of something that felt so small. I guess I thought of it as small compared to what I *wanted* to do, hell, even congratulated myself for keeping it under control. But maybe I should have been thinking of it compared to zero. I'll tell you this — every one of those amazing first kisses, that didn't go any further than kissing when they happened, turned into great relationships, eventually."

Nix handed Jansee a different tool, then moved her hand in a sweeping gesture to demonstrate how to use it to form the texture of the deer's fine hide and splayed tail.

"I've hidden things, like the kiss, through omission from my lovers," Nix said. "I've told half-truths because I desired to keep something to, and for, myself. They're *my* memories. Moments that pass and didn't need to be discussed, because there is no discussion about desire without jealousy. And if you want to feel it, no words can dissuade you." Nix stopped talking, ran her hand through her hair, which bristled softly and stuck up from between her fingers like gray feathers. "I've come to that place in my life, where words from my elders are starting to make sense. Late, for sure. But one particular piece of advice — to wait, to not sleep with someone right away, get to know them first. Looking back, it would have kept me from having sex with at least a few women. And saved me a lot of drama. Women take sex so personally here. Most of them can't see the difference between sex and love, and bad sex is no excuse for not loving them."

"So you have regrets about some of your sexual encounters?" Jansee asked. She leaned forward, her face inches from the deer sculpture as she worked on the details of the hide.

"I wouldn't say 'regret.' But I have *not once* held back when the feeling was reciprocated. *Not once*. And it's made for some painful exits, what we call 'breaking hearts,' " Nix said as she shook her head, then looked up toward the ceiling as if she were remembering something. She stood up and stretched her arms above her head.

"Ah. We have this same phrase, but it is only used when someone you love dies, not because you've ended or started a new relationship," Jansee said.

Nix liked to see the focus Jansee had, much like her own in the early days of learning, putting every effort into making sure it was the best she could make it.

"Would you say you fall in love easily?" Jansee asked.

"I'd say most people do. We all want to feel love, to know that someone thinks we are special. Our species is so full of hope."

"Indeed, that is true. But this specialness you speak of brings pain and denial of other encounters in your life," Jansee said. "In my opinion, there is plenty of love in the world, and the more people you have feelings for, the more blessed you are — these connections are more precious than gold. They are not something to push away because you already have love."

Jansee stopped for a moment, set her tool down and sat back. She sat for a while with her fingers intertwined, her hands folded flat over her lower stomach, letting her sculpture wait as she contemplated everything Nix had said. Jansee had had more lovers than she could count, not remembering the faces or names of most of them. But the complications that Nix spoke of had not presented themselves to her. Feelings yes, love sometimes, but never jealousy or pain.

Nix made note of her body language. *Does the position of her hands signify holding something sexual inside or some more general feeling?* She had never seen this gesture before, and found it endearing that she would forever associate it with Jansee. Nix said, "Sex and love...they can be so hard to tell apart at the beginning, those overwhelming feelings of connectedness, the drive to be together. Yet we never know why sometimes out of this grows a deep caring, a desire to stay together, and at other times to be done with the person after a few couplings." As she explained it, Nix felt like a hypocrite. *God, I know these things as facts but I still struggle and act the fool!*

Jansee yawned. And this was always Nix's signal to end the lessons and send her back to the ship.

Nix would keep working until she fell asleep with a tool still in her hand. There was no point in stopping early. Having free time only left her to wonder when Zephyr would return home or when Torrance would leave.

For the next several weeks, the carving continued. With Nix's blazing pace, her tools needed constant maintenance, no carbide tip lasted more than half a day under her usage. She was glad she had assigned this work to the visitors. When she came outside to work in the morning, her sharpened tools were already stuffed into her leather belt; she simply removed the tarp that covered it and put the belt on over her work suit. Her body also needed daily maintenance. For the first time in her life, an orgasm in the morning felt necessary to get through the days she spent with Torrance at her side. But it felt like a temporary fix, and some days she had to return to the house during lunch to have another to quiet her rising desire.

Nix changed her tool set to diamond-pointed grinders of various, diminutive shapes. Her tool belt was stuffed with every length and texture of file, and diamond rasps, which she kept bundled by coarseness/fineness in leather straps. She used the rasps to level uneven high and low spots left from the earlier phases of chiseling and grinding. Her left hand constantly rubbed and felt the surface until she was satisfied. The dust was less, but the strain on her forearm and eyes was greater. At this level of detail she couldn't be switching over to her left hand. *Why didn't I teach myself to be ambidextrous over the years?* Her right arm could only do so much, and she hoped it would last through the end of this project. She would be forced to rest at some point. She iced it at night, slathered it with ground arnica paste before bed, whatever it took to keep going.

Recognizable shapes had emerged — cheekbones, the tips of noses, the details of hands, various shapes of eyes. She was more than satisfied with her progress. Any stranger could walk around this sculpture and tell what it was, maybe even feel some impact from it. *God, and for the first time I can see the end. Yes, there's a lot of work left to get there, but it's visible.*

But it wasn't done. It would not stand as a masterpiece in this condition, so the filing began. And for weeks on end refinement, refinement, refinement. Her face always close to the rock, her eyes focused directly in front of her. Her neck and various other parts of her body ached from the odd positions she got into, and her failure to notice how long she had held the positions. She settled into a routine, absorbed in her work, everything else faded away. She had three meals a day only because she had to fuel her body. She thought of herself as a machine, not a thinking, feeling woman. She was chained to this stone, this art that she had birthed, and must now raise to a level of genius. Every little detail — the width of eyelids, diameter of nostrils, fingernails, hairlines — all must be as perfect as she could make them.

In places she had gone deep, 24 inches into the stone to form reaching hands, raised arms, thighs that one could entirely wrap a hand around. All of the visitor's beautiful bodies, a Gordian knot made of young, prime flesh, entwined together, threaded in each other's arms with Fazeef's noble face looking away, his arms crossed over his bare chest. On the other side of the rock, the theme was very different — the crew dynamically bursting out, charging forward, springing from the ground toward the sky, not a single foot bound by gravity to the ground. Her masterwork of flesh and intellect, earth and sky, was ready and waiting to enter the final stage — sanding.

24, SMOOTHING

For days, Nix had circled the rock, stopped, moved a few inches, touched it, shined a light into each crevice, moved on. She hadn't found anything that needed changing in the past 24 hours, but she would continue to circumnavigate the stone until she was satisfied.

She stepped outside and the sweet morning air made her smile. She stepped out prepared for her daily battle with herself — how to be around Torrance without physically touching her, to work without thinking of her. But when she saw Torrance standing in her crisp white uniform in front of the machine shop with her eyes closed, enjoying the morning sun on her face, Nix felt nothing, no stirrings of desire. It was gone.

Nix walked past her, pleasantly said, "Good morning." As she put her work coat on, she could see Torrance's shadow on the floor beside her. "You ready to get started?" Nix paid careful attention when she turned and looked Torrance in the eye, but again, no reaction. The feeling of elation was gone, a cooled memory. Finally the day had come. Nix's heart had cooled and she didn't need Torrance or Zephyr. It was like the relief she felt when diving into lake water on a hot day — her hands registered the violent impact of entering, maybe she felt a knock on the top of your head, but her face felt it most — the enveloping chill, a quick clap against both cheeks — then the coolness would ripple over the rest of her body like a close-fitting sheath being pulled over her from head to foot. Nix was now chilled against the fear of where her relationship with Torrance was going, against the guilt of enjoying Torrance's company and every word. She felt free of the responsibility for the inevitable crushing future pain their relationship would produce for at least one party.

Nix fitted a cone/bullet attachment to the small angle grinder first. She stood for a moment, torqueing the attachment to test the fitting, her eyes unfocused, as she inventoried her mind — she was alone in her head again, no lingering thoughts and bubbling memories, no deep waters of contemplation, just a clear running stream of the present moment. She didn't know what had changed inside her. *Hormones? Wasn't that what everything came down to?* Whatever it was, best to finish Torrance's training as soon as possible.

Nix handed the grinder to Torrance. She led her over to a set of four stone pillars along the wall. "These are marble, and as you likely know from your Lifestream, it's a form of crystalline limestone." Two were pure white and two were jet black. "You can see that I've carved the top half of each pillar in a consistent finish — rough to fine. The bottoms are completely raw, they're shaped and that's all. Come up and touch them."

Torrance inspected the pillars. The first was rough, gouged deeply, the rows of indentations were deep and jagged, but square as if the pillar were a bone gnawed by a giant's square teeth. The next was less rough, much shallower indentations than the previous pillar, consistently and uniformly pitted. The third was smooth, but the finish was matte. The last pillar was smooth as the skin inside the mouth, and glossy as a wetted lip. When Torrance realized how she was delicately stroking the last pillar, she stopped herself. Nix didn't seem to notice and continued the lesson, "You'll master different attachments with the smaller machine on each pillar, then move on to other attachments on larger machines. This is the opposite of how I work, but this is the best approach when learning." Nix stood behind Torrance, took hold of her arms, made sure she was the proper distance from the stone. "Drop your right elbow lower and keep it close to your side. You'll have more control if your arms stay bent instead of extended. And two more things: We wet-sand, so use your hand to dip some water and apply to the surface before you start…and always make sure you are masked. If you thought there was dust before…" Nix laughed, handed Torrance a full-face respirator mask with two large circular disks on each side. "This is rated at P3, it will keep your nose and lungs clean."

"Thanks. Have you always worn a mask?" Torrance said.

"And by 'always' do you mean since I've been working in stone?" Nix said. She laughed, but the laugh turned into a cough. She covered her mouth and coughed a couple more times before she was done. She looked at Torrance and half-smiled as she raised her eyebrows.

"I see," Torrance said. She put the mask on, adjusted the filter straps. Once it was tight, she nudged it into a good fit with the back of her hand.

"Something has to kill you. At least I picked my own poison," Nix said. She stepped away to turn on the massive fans that were mounted on each end of the building.

Torrance adapted the improved position Nix had shown her and guided the grinder over the pillar in front of her. It produced an immense amount of dust. Nix returned with a plastic tub filled with a few inches of water and set it between Torrance's feet and the pillar. She reached into the tub, then bathed the rock with the water that clung to her hand. She shouted through her mask, "Remember to do this often, keeps the dust down."

Torrance developed a rhythm, a steady side-to-side motion. When white dust spun off the machine in furious, roiling clouds, she would reach down and wet the stone. After what felt like many minutes of grinding, the polished surface was only the size of a coin. The feeling under her fingertips was exquisitely smooth. "How will I know when it's done?" Torrance asked, her fingertip continued to rub the spot. She couldn't stop touching it.

"That spot is finished. Expand out from there, keep the same pressure and motions," Nix said.

Torrance started again. Nix watched, "Hold the grinder as you would a gun handle, not a hammer. This will prevent unnecessary strain in your wrist."

Torrance tried, then shrugged, not fully understanding, so Nix moved behind her again, reached around and put her hands over Torrance's hands, molded her hands into place, then let go; she didn't linger. "OK, keep going." Nix continued to observe her. "Yes, now you have it. Vary your movements to include some up and down, too. It's tedious, but you can see the results are worth the effort."

Torrance smiled. She reached down to wet the stone again.

Nix left Torrance to practice by herself the rest of the day. She would need at least a week of practice before Nix would let her, or any of them near the stone.

Nix started sanding on the sculpture that day. She leaned with her body, was very conscious of every movement and pose so that she could prolong working. Her increased work output had ramped up her hunger, which twisted her gut like a waking dragon. She hadn't realized how hungry she was after having skipped lunch. She took her mask off and rinsed her face with fresh water, then dusted out her hair. She waved her hand in front of her face to disperse the dust. She coughed. Damn, she had never gotten used to the mask, and usually took it off when she most needed it, and lately the cough had returned.

Torrance brought her lunch, bent close enough for Nix to smell the scent of her hair, even through the marble dust. Still Nix's heart was cool. She hoped it would last at least through the day.

Sanding — lots and lots of sanding. The visitors came in shifts during the day, doing no more than two hours of work. Nix did a quick debriefing when the new person arrived, went over the 'sanding map' first, then walked over to the rock and discussed exactly what needed to be done, and the level of polish she wanted. Nix supervised, not only to save her own arms for the critical parts that needed more subtle sanding, but also because this was a skill, something they would have for the rest of their lives and she wanted them to be damn good at it when they left. Sanding could only happen during the day, and Nix cut it down to days with a certain amount of light, no rain. Wind was OK, even preferred, but still there were only so many hours in the day, so they did as much as they could. She made sheets and sheets of sandpaper every evening.

With all of them working, the final phase was tremendously accelerated. Nix began to step in more and more, the finishing touches would all be done with her own hands.

As Torrance approached one late afternoon to check on Nix, she found her sitting on the ground, knees bent, covered in white dust. From a distance, she looked still, turned to stone. Torrance stopped walking and just stared. But Nix must have heard her because she looked up and smiled in her direction.

"Come and sit with me, feel the sun on your skin." Nix said. She patted the ground beside her and small cloud of white dust rose up from her arm and from the grass.

No sign of Zephyr. Nix wondered if she would ever return.

25, SHIP TOUR

When Nix entered the workshop, Torrance was listening to music that came from a device the size of a fingertip, but filled the room with voluminous, layered sounds. The song sounded like English, last century, full of synths and drum machine beats. Torrance moved her body from side to side, not really dancing, as she sang to herself. Nix watched her move while she put her work coat on, but before she had her arm through the second sleeve, Torrance said, "Can we get out of here? It reeks of industry."

"OK," Nix said, noting a shift in Torrance's behavior, a playfulness she had rarely seen since Torrance's arrival.

"You won't mind starting work a bit later?" Torrance's voice was lilting, playful. She looked at Nix, tilted her head to one side, curled the front of her tongue up and pressed it against her upper teeth, which threw sparks of lust into the pit of Nix's stomach like a chisel's tip against a grinding wheel.

Nix gave in first and looked away. "What's the rest of the crew doing today?" she asked, having to raise her voice to be heard over the new song.

"They can resume mission directives, or whatever they want, but I've ordered them not to return to base or to comm me before sunset."

"Sounds like you've got serious plans," Nix said, as she hung her work coat back on its nail.

Torrance laid two fingers flat against her left temple. "Going dark for remaining daylight hours:" She kept her eyes closed for a long moment. "Sorry, give me a few seconds. Sometimes the sudden darkness behind my closed eyes…" She shook her head and took a deep breath. "I'm ready now."

Nix smiled, let the elation of the moment fill her — a pure ignition point of life in all her cells that electrified her. Such a dangerous feeling… crowding out caution, guilt, and logic. How long had it been since she'd felt excitement like this? Everything be damned, she was going out onto the ice. "I'm all yours. Let's go."

Torrance led the way to the ship. Nix followed a few steps behind and admired the physicality of Torrance's backside. Her calves and hamstrings were well-muscled and strained against the efficient tailoring of her uniform. Higher up, two round symmetrical cheeks, no wider on the top or bottom, contracted and hollowed on the sides as she walked. Her narrow waist angled up into strong shoulders. The uniform was tailored so precisely that it didn't take much to imagine what Torrance would look like without it. The wide-cut neckline allowed Nix to study the sinuous muscles that flared on each side of her neck, and finally she noted the roundness of the back of her head beneath the pyramidal nubs her hair had been twisted into.

At the ship, a panel opened as they approached and Torrance's voice resumed its normal matter-of-fact tone. "The ship's skin is a combination of organic and non-organic materials called phyto-platinum. The microorganisms that live inside the metal are capable of rebuilding the metal if it's damaged, and they also generate energy, much more when we're near a star, but enough to keep the ship moving even when we're in the darkest depths of space. The collected energy from the skin is converted to electricity. The energy is stored in a collection of batteries that run in a spiral configuration along the core of the ship, distributing the weight throughout, and allowing for multiple access points to the energy from anywhere on the ship."

Nix followed Torrance inside. The door slid shut behind them, enclosed them in a scarlet-lit room. Another door opened and they walked into a second entry chamber lit by pale blue light, where Nix's utter lack of eye color made her appear to be completely blind. Torrance reached for Nix's hands to shake the thought from her mind. "Almost through. One more second." The door opened into a large circular chamber. Torrance walked out first and spread her arms wide, "Welcome to the Azalea."

Immediately Nix noticed that every wall was covered in electronics — switches, cables, tiny monitors, blinking lights — like the innards of a pinball machine but on a larger scale. The ceiling was low, silver hoses and black pipes snaked over one another. Aluminum ladders ran diagonally and vertically on the walls, making everything accessible. She turned in a circle on her heels, felt the urge to touch things, but kept her hands at her sides. It was the most inorganic thing she had ever seen. "It feels good in here." It was the only nice thing Nix could say.

"We retain a constant temperature of 22..." she corrected herself, "72 degrees inside." With restrained enthusiasm Torrance said, "Let me show you the other levels."

They climbed ladders, passed through several floors that looked the same as the first floor. On the bridge, tall tables with no chairs, the walls covered in screens that wrapped with the curved shape of the ship, more switches in between, not an inch of unused space. Torrance watched Nix, and narrated, "We cruised over the Earth at 28,000 kilometers, sorry, 17,400 *miles* per hour at 100 miles above the Earth. Hard to believe a non-metric system still exists here. The windows are made of...I'll call it 'bulletproof' glass to retain a reference point for you, it's incredibly strong and able to resist impacts from micro-meteorites." Nix looked puzzled. "You thought the windows were display monitors because they're dark and opaque?"

Nix nodded, walked to a window and touched it.

"With a switch we control how dark or light the windows are. We also use them as display monitors," Torrance said. She waved her hand over one of the tables and made hand gestures in the air. "Since we are in the Northern Hemisphere, this seems appropriate." An image appeared on the screen closest to Nix. "This is barely visible to the naked eye, but I'm sure you've seen the constellation Hercules, so imagine his body, and this particular cluster would be found in his armpit."

"Funny how we anthropomorphize everything, even the stars," Nix said.

"This globular cluster was first discovered by Edmond Halley in 1714, but cataloged and named by Messier. This is M13." Torrance stood behind Nix and gently wrapped her arms around her waist. "Zoom and center:" She said quietly, and the screen filled with thousands of gem-colored stars — whites, blues, yellows, reds.

Nix was awed to silence. So many luminous stars, some marked with a cross-hairs effect from the angle of the lens. Some that looked like candle flames, others blue as a natural gas flame. "Imagine the minerals and textures of rock in those far away places…"

"It could be possible for you to discover exactly what those minerals and textures are. Does it make you want to come to our world?" Torrance asked.

Nix stared at the screen for several minutes. The pure blackness was captivating, the stars even more. Her mind stretched to imagine how alike or different those materials might be from all the rocks she'd seen and held on Earth. *But leave here, leave the rock that flows in my veins? Could my rock be replaced by another? That's what Torrance is asking, isn't it?* Nix said, "There's more you wanted to show me?"

"Yes, so much more." Torrance took her hand and led her back to the ladder and they climbed down two levels, stepped off into a circular hall of metal doors. "Behind these doors are the crew's private quarters. I'm sure they would be happy to show you, if you're interested enough to ask." Torrance said, laying her palm on one door. "This one is mine, same size, only the contents vary."

Nix had to lift her feet and bend her head to step through the door. She wondered if everything would be diminutive inside.

Torrance's room contained a desk with a surface covered in tiny winking lights, a star map embedded within. When Nix came in for a closer look, the map expanded up and to the sides, surrounded her head with a galaxy of stars. When she looked down, the stars receded far into the desk with a plunging 3-D effect that made her feel vertigo for a moment. She stepped backward and the map shrank back into the desktop.

On the opposite side of the room was Torrance's bed, barely wide enough for two people to lie side by side and with metal doors for storage beneath. At eye-level, large square windows — one to look out while seated at the desk, and one near the head of the bed. Nix imagined Torrance lying in bed, watching the stars through this window as she cruised through space.

"Has it been difficult to adjust to such confined spaces?" Nix asked. She made her third trip around the room, touched and held things, stopped to look at anything unfamiliar, which was everything.

"The interior of this ship looks very much like the cities we live in — filled with technology. Nearly everything serves two or more purposes. We pride ourselves on efficiency of design. Children play in hallways between labs when they're not in school. If they're lucky, they get to play in the greenhouses. They think it's normal that there are no animals. It's amazing how they adapt to anything. I believe, because we are the only animal species there, we need to be more connected to each other. The policy is for children to be comm'd at birth. It can feel like hive-mind sometimes, but without it, we feel lost; reminded, in the silence, of our utter aloneness." She exhaled and put her hand on the back of her head. "There is no rain, grass, or outdoor life. Here, everything is calling to you, connecting with you — the animals and insects, leaves on trees, the sky, the wind. The crew wants more and more to be alone in nature, to connect with it in a private, singular way without comms."

"That explains a lot," Nix said. "You have nothing more than the essentials."

"There is water on our planet in liquid form half the year. The other half we melt snow and ice inside our black container environments. So plenty of water, enough to create hydroelectric power, and we found several types of bacteria on the planet that generate cold light, so no need to use any power supply for lighting. But heated water, more than a cup or pot, is a true luxury. And everything gets cycled through the greenhouses. In 50 years, we may start producing small mammals and fish from genetic material we took with us."

"Sounds like hell or prison. Except for the children and greenhouses." Nix put her hand on Torrance's desk, traced a constellation pattern over the surface, and it rose and hovered in front of her eyes, but her fingers started to curl in toward her palm. Her hand tightened into a fist and locked up. She pried her fingers out one at a time, pressed them against the table to slowly force them open, the white-on-white of her fingers and knuckle skin made her hand look more like stone than flesh; stone that could crack at any moment as it flexed beyond its tolerance.

"Let me help," Torrance said, as she took Nix's hand in both of hers and gently opened Nix's hand while looking at her.

Nix said, "How can there be so much love in your eyes when you look at me? It makes me uncomfortable."

"Uncomfortable how? You've seen it before. It should feel familiar." She moved her thumbs slowly back and forth, soothing Nix's palm.

"Looking into your eyes gives me the same feeling as looking at deep sapphire blue ocean water. It's gorgeous and beckoning, but also terrifying with its promise to consume anything that enters."

Torrance exhaled, shook her head. "Is that what you think? That my love will consume you?"

Nix didn't reply. She looked down at her hand, craving more of Torrance's touch.

"Then look at my body for a while instead." Torrance slipped her arms out of her uniform, naked beneath, and let it hang from her waist.

Nix stopped breathing. She was freezing in place. Surely the myth of Medusa was about seeing beauty, not ugliness.

Torrance closed the distance between them. She took Nix's hands and pressed them against her breasts. Nix's palms were dry; rough calloused at the base of each finger scuffed Torrance's tender nipple skin, but she held the hands in place as she stared into Nix's eyes. "We'll go slowly this time, like I promised." Torrance lifted Nix's hand to her mouth and closed her lips over her index finger. She sucked on it gently, tickled the imperceptible fingerprint with her tongue.

Nix closed her eyes, her left hand closed over Torrance's right breast. Her lips parted, created a dark opening from which a soft moan escaped like a halted breath. "Torrance...we shouldn't do this again."

"Why not? You want me, I can feel it whenever I'm around you." Torrance began to run her fingers through Nix's hair. "I'm in love with you."

Adrenaline sparked Nix's heart, she opened her eyes. Torrance's face was inches away, her eyes closed, her lips pursed as if she were about to kiss her.

"Say you love me," Torrance said, needing to know that what she felt was real, the connection they had was mutual.

"Why would you want this to happen again? Why did you come back?" Nix asked. Torrance's brown eyes bored into her, searched for some confirmation of how Nix felt, but neither eyes nor lips gave any sign.

"Does it matter at this point? This is our reality," Torrance said.

"We should stay friends for the duration of your mission," Nix said. *And somehow endure the most exquisite wanting I've ever felt.*

"Stay friends for the duration of my mission?" Torrance stepped back and pulled her top up and over her shoulders, but left it unfastened. "Do you realize that when I leave, you will *never* see me again?" Torrance asked.

"I've always done everything I've wanted, followed my heart or my cunt, and to hell with the casualties. This time I'm going to do the right thing. Zephyr is a good woman. She adores me, she has never hurt me, and it would break her if I left." *That is real love.*

"I'm being punished because you've never made yourself wait?" Torrance turned away, disturbed by the energy that bounced through her like a reflected laser, multiplying until she felt she would burst. Nix was making no sense.

"Because it's the right thing to do." *But the cunning desires of my body don't care about the consequences.*

Torrance stood near her again, the skin of her exposed breasts and stomach only a hands-length away from Nix's face, her voice soft and calm. "Did you hear me? I said I love you." She stroked Nix's hair from her temple down to the base of her neck, then started at her temple again.

If Nix thought about this old habit of Torrance's too much, she would cry. She could feel this delicate care, this intimate comfort all day every day and never tire of it. "Yes, I did, Torrance." *Your voice went right through me.* She stilled Torrance's hand, then kissed her palm. "I'm not single. I've been with Zephyr for over 30 years." She looked Torrance in the eye until Torrance broke their gaze.

Torrance looked at the floor for a moment, inhaled deeply and looked at Nix again. "But you love me, Nix. I can feel it. Tell me," Torrance said.

"I have feelings for you, yes," Nix said. "Strong feelings, but I can't call it love."

"Then what would you call it?" Torrance demanded, her voice deeper and shaking.

"It's lust, desire, needs of the body," Nix said. She turned her head, unable to look at Torrance as she tried to explain away the feelings surging inside her.

"Really? You are calling this, this energy that I can feel like a magnet between our souls 'lust'?" She pressed her hand against Nix's chest. "Tell me you don't feel it here."

"Had you returned sooner! For five years I held out hope, even while I was falling in love with Zephyr, I thought of *you* every day. Then I had to start untangling myself from you, from the memories, the wanting, the loss. Now I don't have the right to tell you that I love you anymore. I'm committed to my relationship. And until you came, I thought I was pretty damn content to live the rest of my life here with Zephyr."

"You think if you don't say it that it won't be true, that it won't exist?" Torrance asked.

"Torrance, we've been through this, both of us. You know how it works. This feeling, this elation, it doesn't last."

Though it seems a miracle that I would feel it twice with the same woman.

"No, I haven't been through this as many times as you have. I've never felt this way with anyone. Fuck. I've had to medicate myself since the first night I saw you to suppress this feeling and function as the commander of this mission." Torrance took Nix's face in her hands and stared into her eyes. "Nix, tell me. I don't think you realize how far I've traveled to be here with you." She cleared her throat, "Yes. I made a commitment to this mission; but you are the real treasure."

Nix dropped any emotion from her face and didn't move. Inside she prepared to get her back against the nearest wall and draw her knife. Her gut was telling her that Torrance was about to make a hostile move toward her. She hadn't suspected they would try to take her. "And if I choose not to go with you? Is your mission a failure?" She reached down slowly and touched the knife on her calf. "What is waiting for you when you get home, Torrance? I would say nothing is waiting; without art, there is no life."

Torrance's arms darted forward like cobras, took hold of Nix's face, and she kissed her. Nix's hand was equally fast to draw her knife, but she re-sheathed it as the kiss went on. Torrance kissed her for the length of several breaths. When she stopped they both gasped, inhaling like they had just surfaced from great depths of water.

Nix grabbed Torrance's shoulders and kissed her with a force that pushed Torrance back. With equal force Torrance leaned into Nix, and they fell back onto the bed. Torrance straddled her, her hands on each side of Nix's head. Nix took hold of Torrance's thighs and pulled her body forward, then pushed it back, created heat where they touched. Lips reddened by speed and passion, their mouths became increasingly dry. Nix struggled to stop, but pleasure had flooded her brain and senses. Her heart was beating rapidly.

She wanted this. Torrance was right: When she left, Nix would never see her again. It would be painful. She should be making new memories to hold onto, she should have her as much as possible, she should be fucking her every day.

Torrance slid down between Nix's legs and yanked her jeans open with one rough tug. She pulled her pants down to her knees, pushed them down to her ankles, not hesitating for a moment to ask permission. Her mouth tasted the salt of Nix's flesh and didn't stop until Nix climaxed.

Afterward, they lay together in silence on the small bed that demanded they be wrapped in each other's arms. Nix fell asleep. When she woke up, Torrance was sleeping on her side. Nix rolled off the bed, tried not to wake her. As she buttoned her pants, she looked at Torrance's sleeping face. She was beautiful in every light, every situation she had seen her in. She wondered if she would be able to leave the ship without Torrance's assistance. Then Torrance slowly opened her eyes. She patted the bed beside her. "You can sleep here."

Nix bent over and kissed her. "Your bed isn't big enough for both of us."

Torrance laughed, sat up, moved her hand over her head, yawned. She stood up, fastened her uniform. She was all smiles again. She put an arm over Nix's shoulders, and led her to the exit.

At the door, Torrance kissed Nix. "Promise you'll return soon. There is one more thing we need to discuss."

"I will," Nix said. "There are things I need to say too."

26, MECHANICAL STRANDING

"The major transducer on the ship is broken. Actually completely melted on one side," Jansee revealed to Nix after trying four different fixes and failing each time. She set the melted form of the transducer on the table in front of Nix, then spun away to land roughly, though precisely, in a sitting position on one of the seats. "Usually we would print a replacement, but the last one was printed en route and it didn't need to do much while we were cruising. It's mainly used to regulate immense energy surges during takeoff, keeps them from damaging any of the main systems. Likely we fried it when we lifted the stone, but it must have been damaged before that. This time, I'd prefer to find a conductive stone and have you fabricate the part. That will assure that we make it home." She flashed a pixie smile for the moment that she looked at Nix.

As the thought of being stranded entered her mind, Jansee squinted her eyes and ended her hopeful smile by biting her lip. She sat with her legs shoulder-length apart, bent forward, planted her elbows on top of her knees and rested her head in her hands. She massaged her scalp with her fingers, causing long tendrils of black hair to spill forward and stripe her hands. "Nix, I can't tell you how important this part is, and we need to have it fixed as soon as possible. Our mission is not sanctioned to last more than 18 months. Not departing and notifying base by that time could have serious repercussions. I haven't calculated lately, but I know we're getting close to the cut-off," Jansee said.

Nix examined the part. It was lighter than it looked. The melted mess made it challenging to imagine what it might have looked like.

After a minute, Jansee sat up. "OK, I'm done whining. I have calipers for measuring, but no stone-specific tools. The size and shape of it will be hard to fabricate with the imprecise tools of Earth."

"Imprecise? You start that way and expect me to be successful? Come on, let's go see what I've got." Nix left the building not bothering to notice if Jansee was following or not.

In a poorly constructed room off of the main outbuilding, Nix stored a variety of stone samples she had collected over the years. Everything in the room was covered with white marble dust that entered easily through the gaps in the wallboards. The rocks varied in size from a cherry to a car tire. Nix knew there were many pieces containing silver, gold and copper, but she wasn't going to make it so easy for Jansee.

Jansee held a glowing square instrument with flexible probes. She went from stone to stone pressing the spring-loaded needles against each sample. She stood longer in front of the hematite (green stone containing copper), then for a while in front of the turquoise (blue stone containing copper). *Clever girl. She's on the right path.*

Jansee's expression flattened. She blinked several times in a row and sighed heavily. Frustrated. "None of these are conductive enough. Overall metal content needs to be higher."

"Wait here," Nix said.

When Nix returned, she held a piece of quartz, bigger than a loaf of bread, with an impressive gold vein running through it. "My great, great grandfather left this to me. Never had any use for it. It's been sitting in the safe for decades."

Jansee's eyes brightened and widened. A sly smile pushed her cheeks up, her deep dimples on full display. "Superb specimen ..." She touched the stone with her machine, it made a clicking sound like a Geiger counter.

"Can you carve this to these specifications?" Jansee projected a schematic into the air between them. "There is a .01 percent tolerance allowed on any of the exterior edges. The interior can be less precise."

Nix felt ill, like her stomach had dropped to her knees. She leaned against the wall beside her. She couldn't take her eyes off the schematic — it was ghostly and transparent but also sharp and clear. *Can I possibly carve a piece of stone that will fix a broken space ship?* "Everything I've ever made was for art, aesthetics, not precision. And without this? I mean, what if I just can't do it?" She tensed in anticipation of the answer.

"We can't leave," Jansee said. "No pressure, eh?" She sighed deeply. Feeling the gravity of the situation in her bones, she slid off the stone seat to squat on her haunches.

Nix cradled the stone in her arms like a baby. "Come on, let's get started." She carried the stone to the workshop where she instructed Jansee to drape the vice with a scrap piece of soft leather. "We will focus on success, nothing else," Nix said.

Jansee slowly turned the vice lever while Nix kept one hand beneath the stone.

"OK, that's good. Stop." Nix tested the fit. It didn't slip at all. She knew that the gold vein made the quartz very unstable, just one badly placed hammer stroke could ruin the entire piece, and melting it down wouldn't produce enough mass for the schematic dimensions. "I'll have to work slowly," Nix said. She bent forward and eyed the stone from several angles.

Jansee rubbed her hand over the five by six by ten inch piece of quartz shot through with lustrous gold veins — their only way home. She wondered if Nix would choose Torrance over this piece of gold, or if she might end up with neither. "We're in no hurry. Even though staying longer could make things worse for the commander."

"What?" Nix sensed that something important had been said, but she continued to bob her head, looking at the stone from different angles to see how the part would best present itself from the stone.

Jansee changed the subject. "Nix, I'm 31. I've trained my whole life, all of my teens and 20s, for this mission. Everything in my life leading up to this point has felt like destiny. I left my partner behind with full confidence that I would return home. I didn't say goodbye too seriously. I knew I would see her again. Now I'm not as sure, and I regret my rushed goodbye to her."

"I'll do my best to make sure you all get home," Nix said. She stepped away from the stone and began to search through deep wooden drawers for what she needed, creating a raucous clanging of metal tools. Nix nodded her head and said, "yes," to show Jansee that she was listening as she continued to gather what she needed.

"Since I've been here, I've become more and more confused about everything," Jansee said. "So many times over the past months I've wondered if I would choose to stay here, if perhaps my subconscious mind had already decided. The ship could return without me. By design it only needs one crew member to fly home; a precaution in case of 'eventualities.' 'Eventualities' being various things including fatalities. But now, I might not have that choice. I may be stuck here."

Nix wanted to keep plucking tools from the drawers, but she couldn't hold one more in either hand, and this subject matter was too serious. She turned, set the tools on the table beside the vice and gave her full attention to Jansee.

Jansee continued, "I don't even know what I'm feeling — a crisis of conscious, existential crisis, midlife crisis. I'm questioning everything — I'm sure this wasn't one of the 'eventualities' the designing engineers had considered. But they should have."

Yes. They should have. "Come sit by me, Jansee," Nix said. She took Jansee by the arm and led her to the elegant stone seats, identical to the ones they used in the open space. When they were seated facing each other, Nix said, "Ah, stay or go. Decisions don't get any harder than that."

Jansee spoke softly. "I can't decide on anything. How could they send us here and not think we would want to stay? This place is so beautiful, more than any vid could ever convey. Every day there is something new, miraculous, fascinating. It makes me want to be immortal. How can one lifetime be enough?" Jansee twisted her hands together in her lap. "My feelings are complicating everything, clouding my rational mind."

"We aren't made to be completely rational," Nix said. She put her hand onto Jansee's shoulder and rubbed, and she visibly relaxed. "Don't disregard your heart too quickly, it's the only thing that can lead you to happiness."

Jansee sighed, and the tension melted from her shoulders. She wanted to fall into Nix's arms and cry, but she didn't want Nix to see her weakness.

Nix moved her seat closer, wrapped her arms around Jansee and hugged her close. "The answers will come. Don't be so hard on yourself." She leaned forward and kissed her cheek. "It will take me a while to finish the part. That should give you enough time to decide."

Jansee arrived at the ship as it was getting dark, giving her just enough time to wash up before dinner.

"Where've you been all day? We ran the maintenance test suite on the ship and the major transducer is missing. And you haven't responded to my calls in hours!" Torrance said. She was a master of hiding her emotions, all cloaked under layers of professional protocol, but unmistakable traces of anger sharpened her delivery.

"In the shop working on a fix for the transducer with Nix all day. Where'd you think?" Jansee said.

"Out with the deer again for all we knew," Derthan said.

"Wasn't anyone watching my stream?" Jansee asked, wondering why anyone would question her if they had bothered to watch any of it.

"A stone with highly conductive metal saturation?" Gantu asked.

"Yes, it's actually native, though mined out 50 years ago. There's a limited quantity, unfortunately. Just enough to make the part once," Jansee said. "You realize if she fails, we're stuck here until we find the next solution?"

Torrance smiled, which seemed like an odd response to several of the crewmembers who noticed. "Yes. It's ironic that everything is in her hands now," Torrance said.

"Literally in her hands," Derthan said. She took her handmade knife from its sheath and began to clean her fingernails.

"I want a Plan B and C," Torrance said.

"The part has to be fabricated somehow, which is why the solution is stone," Jansee said. "We'd have to venture out from here to see what other solutions we could find."

"No! Wait. I won't authorize that," Derthan said, emotion warped her voice to a higher pitch than normal. She inhaled sharply and continued, "I'm not comfortable with that. We don't know who or what is out there. We could come back and the ship could be damaged or dismantled, we could run into hostiles."

"Easy, Derthan. Yes, those are all possibilities, but we need to get home. Risks must be taken." Torrance was back to her steady, sober tone.

Gantu tried to further diffuse the tension. "Please, Derthan, from what we've seen on our previous travels with

Nix, there are only women for miles around. And none of them hostile. Let's see whether Nix can do it. I'd rather spend my time collecting more data than constructing a plan that may not even be needed."

Fazeef stepped closer to his sister. "I agree. Let's give her some time. I have confidence in her. Look at those pieces out there — massive and without a single flaw."

"We've all seen what she can do with her hands," Torrance said, shooting a quick look to Jansee, who smiled.

"Yes. She's our best hope," Jansee said.

27, COLOSSUS OF ARMS

After working on prototypes in the clay studio for a couple days, and not letting her mind wander to a single thought beyond how she was going to accomplish the replacement part for the ship, Nix was ready to revisit Torrance and finish her conversation.

Torrance met Nix at the entrance door and they climbed in silence to the living quarters. Once Nix and Torrance were comfortably seated in her chamber, Nix started. "I'm going to be very frank. It's important for you to know what happened after you left Earth, how I felt, since I never wrote." She straightened her posture and looked at Torrance, took hold of her hand. "I was miserable, and I wanted to die. I left the city a few weeks after your ship was confirmed to be outside our atmosphere. I only stayed long enough to pack my tools and clothes and pull my money out of the bank. I had no intention of ever coming back. I came to Weaverville sight unseen based solely on the name and the elevation on the map. In those first years, I worked in granite. It was like a self-imposed hard labor camp. That stone is extremely hard and yields very little even to carbide-tipped chisels. I used iron mallets. The reverb was torturous to my hands, but it took the pain from my mind. It was hell from the early roughing out stages to the bitter end, but once those pieces were polished to a gleaming gloss — I was ready to start on the next one. My hands were so bruised at the end of the day that I could barely undress myself and had to use both hands to hold a glass of water. And forget about masturbating." She laughed, but saw a slight lift of Torrance's eyebrows. "Am I making you uncomfortable?"

"No. Please go on. I should hear it all," Torrance said. She moved her desk chair closer to Nix.

"I just wanted to be alone with the stone. I couldn't bear to have another person ask me about you. I didn't care if I ever heard another human voice at that point. And for at least a year, I didn't. Amazing what you can shut out if you try — the whole world if you want to bad enough. There were years after you left, that I dreamed about you night after night. Always the same thing — we had been separated but we were together again because you were my true love, then I'd wake up and I'd be in my bed alone, or with whatever woman I was with, and even later with Zephyr. And every time it happened, I'd be so confused for a second when I woke up, thinking there must be some mistake, that you should be in the bed beside me, but you weren't."

"For the first four weeks I sat among monoliths, raw stone that I'd ordered from Italy months before you left. I stared at them with no thought of what they might become. I'd spent the better part of my savings on those precious stones. I didn't panic at my lack of vision. The plan was to be here for a while."

"Nothing between you and your art," Torrance said. "Isn't that what you always wanted?"

"No, I wanted you, a whole lifetime with you. What woman in her right mind would choose the cold, hardened earth over her lover?" Nix spoke in a low, measured voice, shook her head back and forth. "Nothing between me and my art. God knows I'd thought it enough times, so... there it was — exactly what I'd asked for. Morning after morning I did nothing but stare at them. I didn't know what to do with the stones, they felt funereal. My muse was gone, all my passion gone with her. I moved them around the yard with a tractor, formed a geometrically accurate replica of Stonehenge as a satire. Materials were hard to come by then, with most of the trees having died out, so I could only have a structure around one stone at a time. It forced me to focus."

"But there are many, many trees here. Where did they come from?" Torrance asked.

"About a year after Zephyr and I finally settled here, this group of women came by. I thought they were travelers, but over the years I realized they were our far-scattered neighbors. They had a vast seed bank, and they also had a lot of saplings. They gave us so many trees, a couple hundred; we just had to promise we would plant them and care for them. Zephyr modified them in her lab, made them more wind-resistant, able to survive with less water by adding some evergreen traits, that's why their leaves look so strange, some hybrid between deciduous and evergreen. She even tried to make some of them fire-resistant but it caused a mutation in their ability to absorb sunlight, so they grew less than an inch a year. The others grew fast, and after 20 years, even with the violent weather and unpredictable rain, this area has become a forest of trees."

Nix put her hand on the back of her neck, pulled her head forward. "I've never felt anything like the love I felt for you." Tears fell from her eyes onto her pant legs. "Do you remember, how crazy in love we were?" Nix lifted her head and smiled a bit remembering the happier times. Torrance looked down instead of to the side, where she should have been looking if she were searching her memory. Nix said, "I see; maybe not. It was a long time ago. I'm sure you've loved many others since those days. I wanted you to, I expected you to. But I never, *never*, expected you to be here again." She stood, afraid of an uncontrollable outpouring of tears, she walked to the door, took hold of the handle, then changed her mind, got her emotions under control, and walked back to Torrance. "I was haunted for years with the thought that it would have been better if you had stayed here and died with me, then I would have had some closure. God, it's selfish, I know." Nix kneeled in front of Torrance. "And now, I'm in this improbable situation. The gods must be laughing at me. This is not something that has been written about. I have no reference — ancient or modern." Nix put her hand over her mouth, kept her eyes locked on Torrance. She pulled herself up, then sat heavily onto the corner of Torrance's bed. "Fucked up is what this is."

"I've never felt like this in my life," Torrance said. She put her hand on Nix's thigh.

"Wait. Why would you say you've never felt this way before?" Nix said. She placed her hand over Torrance's and squeezed it tightly.

"I...feel like we're meeting for the first time again," Torrance said.

"Again, or for the first time?" Nix squeezed a little harder.

Torrance winced. "Nix, you're hurting me." Her eyebrows knitted together, her eyes clouded with anger.

Nix released her grip. "Tell me, Torrance, that you've loved me before."

There was a long silence.

"My *mother* always said that without the world being so fucked up, the human race would have no challenges to rise to." Torrance coughed, a deep cough that rattled her chest. "I'm a lot like her. The longer I stay here, the sicker I'll get." She stood up and put some distance between herself and Nix. "The other clones weren't enough like *your* Torrance; physically yes, but their souls were very different. They're still up there." She said, tilting her head and raising her eyebrows toward the ceiling. Torrance's bay brown eyes filled with sympathy as she saw a storm of emotions race over Nix's face and eyes. She bent and kissed Nix's cheek. "I need to show you something. And remember, I'm showing you this out of love. Real love, *my* own love for you, not my *mother's*." Torrance touched the screen beside the bed and a vid started to play. "I watched these vids on the way here. She made most of them on her journey to Kepler-442B, some right after arrival, and the last one right before our ship left for Earth. They were hard for me to watch, so I don't know how they will affect you, but she wanted you to see them. There are hours and hours of vids, so tell me when you'd like a break."

Nix nodded. The screen filled with Torrance's face, a plain white background behind her, a soft light on her face so that every detail was well defined. "Hello, Nix. How are you, my love?" Her hand reached up and touched the screen, reaching out to Nix. "There are so many things that I'm experiencing, and I wish you could be here with me, but that ship has sailed, as they say. I've never been afraid during this journey; I know that I'm going to be alive in a whole new way, that I am choosing to live, even though my heart is telling me otherwise. I'll try to start at the beginning."

"I cried during the violent shaking of launch, tears whipped horizontally across my face. My body was strapped to my seat with a six-point harness. I screamed as I was being physically ripped away from Earth; from you, Nix." She bit her lip and looked down for a moment. "I watched Earth grow smaller, the light faded and faded, and darkness filled the periphery of my vision. The only light was from the gauges and monitors." Her eyes looked to the side, then back to the camera. "The great enveloping womb of space, quiet beyond understanding, is never warm or comforting. It is a black, horizonless ocean filled with invisible waves." She touched her hair, twisted down a tuft near her temple, but it sprang back up as soon as she let it go. The screen went dark.

A few seconds passed, and Torrance reappeared on the monitor. She was no longer wearing a space suit, but a bulky sweater. "The initial flight was nothing but endless violent shaking as we pulled away from Earth. I thought for sure the ship would come apart. Loud popping, cracking of metal as the ship went from extreme heat to extreme cold. Then once we were beyond the reaches of Earth's atmosphere and gravitational pull, we were all so relieved, you could hear cheers coming from every direction as the commander made the announcement. It was only the first of many milestones, but it felt good to have success on the first day. But with that milestone, I also realized that none of us could go back. There was no going back. I've heard other passengers wonder the same thing — will we make it to our destination? It's terrifying. I think about it every minute of every day. But there is so much work to do, so many things we all have to maintain and prepare. The constant monitoring of systems and cargo. I'm so tired sometimes. Hell, look at me, my eyes have circles under circles. You'd think I was up all night having sex." She laughed as she closed her eyes and rubbed them with her fingers. "We work in 12-hour shifts. I manage to lose myself in work most of the time." Torrance paused for a moment and smiled. She lifted a container to her lips and drank. "God, I miss you. Every day, every minute, every second."

Though the things Torrance was saying were difficult to listen to, were dredging up old memories by the bucketful, and left Nix feeling helpless, to see Torrance smile soothed Nix's heart in a way she hadn't thought possible from something as simple as a vid.

"But I'm trying hard, baby, I'm doing my best to live like you wanted me to. I know you're thinking of me right now, I can feel it. I know you're hurting, and it's so hard for me to be here, knowing I can't do anything for you, that I'm moving in the opposite direction, putting distance between us." She rubbed her eyes again, and tears spilled down her face. "I can't imagine what you're doing to get through this. Knowing you, you're working yourself to death...crashing the ship of your body against the not-so-proverbial rocks. Damn, that was grim." Torrance laughed, and tossed her head to the side. "In space you get sick of every song. Thousands of songs were loaded into the ship from every era, every country and you'd be surprised how many your mind can store, recognize on the first few notes, and *hate*. You know I've loved music since I was a baby girl. So, I'm learning the music of Earth, even without knowing the language of the lyrics, I can still love a song. Music connects the people on the ship. We sing when we pass each other in the halls, and after meals, and when we drink together. I can sing in 15 different languages. I don't know what I'm saying, but I can sing along."

"My health improved during the flight. By the time we arrived on the new planet, I had so much more energy. My physical body felt *incredibly* good. It's strange, but feeling good distracted me every moment until I grew used to it. I kept wondering if it would suddenly vanish and I would go back to my old self. I'd walk a little and think, 'Wow, this is effortless.' Then I'd run through the halls for an hour and still be thinking, 'This is effortless.' I was so happy that I didn't wheeze at all after running. Eventually it became the norm." She smiled and the screen went dark.

Nix looked at Torrance. "Is there more?"

"Yes. It should start momentarily. I've queued them to play in the order my mother dictated. They are not sequential."

The screen became white again, but no Torrance. Nix stared at the room, noted the metal walls, the back of a chair. Torrance entered the room and sat down immediately. The Torrance on the vid screen looked straight out at Nix, she said, "*This* Torrance is smart. I've educated her on all the things you love, and my hope is that when she meets you, and spends time with you, she will fall in love with you, as I did. She will finish what I started. And if that never happens, if love is some magical thing and not purely chemical, then at least she will deliver these vids to you."

Nix sat for hours watching the videos. The Torrance on the screen continued to talk, always looking straight out at Nix. In a confessional tone, she said, "It felt like the pain would never end. When we entered the third quarter of the trip, I confined myself to my quarters and slept half of each day, cried the other half. I ate little food and lost most of the fat on my body. The withdrawal, the internalization, the crying. It concerned the others. Crying was a waste of water, they told me. I needed to be more disciplined and stop. I started training with short, intense workouts, twice a cycle, every cycle. That cleared my mind of any thought, gave me some peace and took you out of my dreams. My body was finally something enviable. And with the great change of my body, the taming of my mind, I finally let go. I'm sorry, baby. I had to let you go." She started to cry, she closed her eyes and her lip quivered. Tears flowed down her face for a moment, then she inhaled a short, sharp breath. She wiped the tears from her face with the back of her hand. "Hardest thing I ever had to do. I hope you'll forgive me." She stared out at Nix for half a minute in silence, her eyes looking for the forgiveness she sought, then the screen went dark.

Torrance sat beside Nix through all of the vids, sometimes holding her hand, sometimes kissing her cheek. Nix struggled with the extreme emotions of watching the vids while at the same time being able to turn and see Torrance in the flesh. She could touch her, kiss her lips, like she used to. A beautiful and torturous gift. In some ways like heaven. But then like a living ghost, the body near, but the soul long gone.

Had this Torrance really fallen in love with her? She certainly acted as if she had. "You've delivered the stone and the vids, why would you want to stay? Yes, the physical beauty of Earth is alluring. I get that. But you'll die if you stay here."

"Nix, at first it was strange to know so much about someone, and yet not know them at all, just facts and stories, nothing shared through actual memory or physical bodies. I didn't want to love you. I came here to fulfill my mother's last wish. I never expected to love you, but I do, and I have never felt anything like it."

Nix's head started to spin like a rocket gone haywire, skittering over the ground. She lay back onto the bed, because it felt like she had just jumped off the moon and was plummeting toward Earth, about to lose consciousness.

Torrance straddled Nix's hips and looked at Nix with searing eyes, "My heart is for you, my blood is for you. I will stay here with you until I die, if that is your wish."

Nix squirmed beneath her, instinctually tried to buck her off. "I need air, *my* air. Please take me out of here. Now!" Did she want to cry, laugh, cough, scream? Yes, all at once.

Torrance led the way out in silence, then walked with Nix into the open space, sure that she shouldn't leave her alone.

"This is how I chose to show my love," Nix said while gesturing to the sculptures around her, tears making her voice waver. "At times Zephyr has been a little starved for it, and I regret that, but I was never able to fully let go of my love for you. But I don't know who you are. You look like her, you smell like her, your eyes are her eyes, and it feels like you love me, but I don't trust it. God, the way you are looking at me right now — she looked at me just like *that*."

"Nix, I *am* her. Touch me." Torrance grabbed Nix's hand and put it to her cheek, pulled it down over the softness of her neck.

"I loved more than her physical body." She grabbed Torrance's wrist. "Come with me!"

Torrance stumbled as Nix led her across the open space to the Colossus of Arms — a perfect replica of her own smooth arms from 20 years ago; round shoulders capped curvy biceps that sloped down to elbows that sunk two feet deep into the earth, then her especially ropey forearms and vein-addled hands rose again at a 45-degree angle toward the sky. The hands — palms facing each other, but tilted slightly out, scuffs and nicks in the skin — captured in the moment after something had been torn from them.

"Do you see that?" Nix pointed with her free hand at the Colossus.

And Torrance realized that those arms belonged to Nix. Why hadn't she noticed sooner?

"Can you feel that emotion? That is more than a longing for the physical. That is a longing that my human-sized arms could not express. I put *everything* into it, four years of work — all of my love, longing, sorrow, tears. Through tears, then anger, then depression, I hammered. I punished my body with long hours, beat everything out of myself and into the stone. I worked through my loss of you, chipped away at it, cut the bonds between us with each swing of the mallet." She slapped her palm against Torrance's stomach. "A sickening feeling of separation, like starvation eating my gut, but it ate my heart instead."

Torrance turned her torso to free herself of Nix's insinuating touch. She couldn't bear it a second longer. She pulled her hand from Nix's grip too, and started to walk toward the woods. "I didn't come for this!" she screamed loudly enough for Nix to hear her without having to turn around. "Comms off."

"No? No? Then why the fuck did you come here? You think you can just drop into my life, make me fall in love with you, then walk away? You could have said 'no' to her, you could have declined the mission. This was *your* choice Torrance, you came here, now come back here and deal with it, feel it, all of it."

Torrance walked until she couldn't hear Nix's yelling anymore. She was compelled to escape a pain she didn't even know she could feel. The sun was beginning to set, casting deep orange light onto the tree trunks, but Torrance's vision had narrowed to see only what was immediately in her path. She took a deep breath when she stepped inside the darkness of the tree line, but she didn't slow her pace. Branches scratched her face and the backs of her hands. The air inside the woods was damp, saturated with newly made oxygen, the scent of moldering pine needles. The sky was darkening. Torrance walked until she couldn't see more than a foot in front of her. She stood still, bent over, and rested her hands on her knees. She was completely out of breath, wheezing as she inhaled. It was happening much more frequently in the last few months, the environment was no longer her friend. She wanted to keep walking to see where she would end up, but decided that with no water or supplies, she should sit down, be still and become part of the forest. She knew the consequences if the air chilled her, but she didn't care. Perhaps she had not suffered enough in her life. She didn't know what Nix meant by starving, or having such colossal longing, or the feeling of her heart being eaten. She sat for a long time and heard nothing. The wind was still. No creatures stirred. How long had she been sitting when she heard some twigs break, and a low snuffling? Long enough for her senses to adjust to the darkness. Something heavy walked on the forest floor toward her. She turned slowly and saw a black horse stomp the forest floor with one hoof and huffle, huffle. She crouched to make herself ready to leap to the side or dash behind a tree. The horse came toward her and drummed its hoof on the ground three times, then exhaled white jets of breath through flared nostrils. Maybe it didn't like the smell of her. She didn't know all of the abilities that this specific beast possessed, but she recognized the threat in its actions. She stood and slowly stepped backward. It reared. A majestic and frightening black mass that blotted out the shadowy shapes behind it. The horse let out a surprisingly shrill sound for such a large creature. When it landed on the ground it turned and ran hard away from her. She closed her eyes and listened to the receding thunder of its hooves. She fell to her knees and cried.

Nix stumbled across the open space. When she arrived at her latest work, she began walking in circles around it. When the sun had been gone for some time, and the blood-red moon was barely visible between the clouds on the horizon, she saw bursts of heat lightning, far off. She counted the time from the lightning to the thunder. More than five minutes. Quick flash of a thick red root at the base of a cloud, and veins, just as red, that branched and fanned up and out into thinner veins. Nix was dazed. She had never seen red lightning in her life. She started to walk quickly toward the house for fear that death itself was stalking her. She went into the house and straight to her bedroom. She undressed and lay down. There would be no eating, no reading after such an encounter as she had had with Torrance. The lightning came more often, white now; through the window she saw it drop from the confines of the clouds, stretching skeletal fingers to touch far off hillsides. The thunder got closer and louder, then seemed to lessen and quiet down. She was relieved that it was moving away. Then there was a bright flash of white lightning that lit the entire inside of the house. The thunder was immediate. A mighty boom that shook the house and made her heart jump into a galloping rhythm.

The storm lasted most of the night. Thunder rumbled the house, the sound impact threatened to collapse the walls. Lightning, with the brightness of midday sun, banished the darkness every few minutes and made it impossible for her to sleep. She was alone in the tumble and blaze of her thoughts, a castaway tossed by rough seas. Her eyes would grow heavy, she would almost find peace, then a blinding flash of lightning, followed by thunder that pummeled the house and the very Earth. Mother Nature would not be outdone by the priceless gifts from the stars.

To Nix, it was too close to call.

28, TREE CLIMB

Nix had been working since before sunup. She hadn't gotten much sleep due to the flash and bang of the previous night's storm, and in her current state, she didn't trust herself to work on the replacement part. She could, however, work on her own piece. During her lifetime she had worked on her art in every state of body and every emotion of her mind. She didn't allow herself the luxury of only working in her best states. All the remaining sanding would be done with her own hands. And so she sanded. The repeated strokes fatigued the muscles in her forearms and fingers. Her index finger had locked up twice — a straightened, open position that she was unable to bend when she flexed the others.

It was midday when she stopped for some water. She surveyed the open space, and noticed Torrance emerging from the ship.

When the sun reached midday, Torrance left the ship and strode purposefully across the open space. The storm hadn't kept her up, but the situation with Nix had. She looked at the Colossus with its arms thrust in a great "V" toward heaven. The sculpture dominated the open space, not only in size, but presence. It was impossible to ignore such pleading, such longing that had been made so real to her through the stories of her mother and Nix. Her head turned sharply to her right as she walked in a swift march. She kept her eyes locked on the Colossus — open mouthed, in something between a howl and slack-jawed disbelief, the pupil-less eyes a wide expanse of sadness and loss that could cry no more tears.

Torrance could make no sense of the feeling that was driving her, which felt like anger, revenge, something aggressive that needed physical satisfaction. Her destination was the curtain of trees that fronted the forest. She pulled her gaze away from the Colossus with some effort and studied the trees ahead. The tops of the trees swayed in a breeze not felt at ground level. She assessed how high the lowest branches were from the ground, how far apart the ascending branches were as they rose up the trunks. She would take the tree left of center, which was one of the tallest and appeared to have the most consistent branches. She started to jog. With a good enough jump, she could reach the lowest branch; then the next two or three, estimated by her Lifestream to have one and a half meters of spacing between them, would be easy. There were branches farther up that were more than two meters apart, but she would worry about those when she got there.

The first branch appeared to move up and away as she got closer. She took a couple of deep breaths then started to sprint. When she neared the base of the tree, she directed her energy from one foot to the other in a few well-placed leaps, then sprung upward and grabbed for the branch. Her left hand caught hold of it, but barely, the weight of her body hung on her wrist, the bark scraped the tender skin, but she didn't let go. She reached with her right hand, fought for a good grip. She flexed her shoulders toward her spine and pulled herself up and over the branch.

She stood on top of the first branch to catch her breath, then turned and reached for the next, and the next. Easy now that she was up. She disappeared into the vertical heights.

As soon as Fazeef saw what Torrance was doing on his Lifestream, he left his fieldwork and made his way to the tree. He climbed with a strength that awed Nix, who had initially stopped all work to watch Torrance from her perch on the scaffolding. His ascent was rapid. His body stretched

— left, right, left, right — proficient as a spider, no motion wasted.

Torrance saw the difficult branches above. Lifestream warned her that she had passed the height from which a fall would be survivable. She stopped for a moment, then leaped for the branch above and grappled with it, her feet striving for some traction against the trunk. The skin of her wrists not covered by her uniform sleeves was slashed by the rough bark again, plentiful shallow cuts, but she didn't register the pain. She climbed without fear, up and up.

Eventually, the branches became too small and thin to support her weight. So she straddled a branch and swayed with the treetop in the breeze. Her retina screen showed her heartbeat as 175 BPM. VO_2 max reached four minutes ago, currently two minutes into recovery. Beyond trying to catch her breath, she felt the solidity of the branch supporting her, and was profoundly grateful to the tree. Climbing the tree had felt like the most natural thing to do. These feelings of joy and familiarity confused her. She had never done such a thing on Kepler-442B. The smell of the pine tree itself — the amber sap, the countless needles, the dusty bark — permeated the air around her. She enjoyed feeling like a fly compared to this giant. She rubbed one hand against the trunk. She wouldn't have been surprised to feel a heartbeat. But the trunk and branch beneath her were still, no pulse or vibration or any sign that it was alive.

Her limbs were tired. She knew it would take some effort to get down, but that was far from her mind. The whole valley was laid out before her — mountains to the east and north, the ocean to the west, the small lake beyond the meadow to the southwest. She closed her eyes and inhaled. Her mind was clear. The air was nourishing.

"Torrance," Fazeef called out even before he could see her, not wanting to startle her in this precarious environment.

"Fazeef! Come to escape with me? You've put yourself in danger now, too. I felt like I was climbing into the sky, an unexplainable joy, invincible. A freedom I've never felt from any other physical activity." Torrance looked down, trying to locate him based on his initial call to her. His head and hands were indistinguishable against the tree, but she caught glimpses of his white uniform as he continued to climb.

When he was on the branch beneath her, she did not make eye contact with him, but instead stared out or up as if seeing the landscape and the sky for the first time. "Commander, I've come of my own will, purely for the experience. I accept the risk."

Torrance said, "Like with any climb, we are only halfway there. There is still the way down."

"I have enough for the way back," Fazeef said. "The sky looks bluer up here."

"I expected to feel anxious up here, but I feel safe, like I'm part of this organism. Nothing can touch us up here," Torrance said.

"Lightning could," Fazeef said. "We shouldn't stay long, an unexpected storm could mean death."

Torrance continued to stare out. "Not a cloud in the sky as far as I can see."

"You know a clear sky is no prediction of permanence here. Rain, wind — either could exponentially increase the risk of this endeavor."

"Beauty of this magnitude is something worth dying for," Torrance said.

"Let's not die for it today," Fazeef replied.

"I need to stay a little longer. You don't know what I've been feeling lately. Tangled, complex emotions that make death look attractive."

"Then let's stay for as long as you need." Fazeef moved down one branch to give her more space, and as he settled in and looked out, he was soon just as hypnotized by the surrounding landscape and blue sky that enveloped them.

"Fazeef, have you ever thought about reincarnation? Wondered why some things seem familiar to us — the love of flowers, an affinity toward a trade, or love of a certain kind of music, or art. Is it something magical to do with our souls? Or simply passed down through our genes?"

"Of course I have thought about this. There are many things that are unexplainable in our lives. We try to find meaning and patterns, it's part of what makes us human. But that is not why you climbed an 80-meter tree with no safety equipment. What is on your mind?"

"I can't live without her," Torrance said.

"You're in love with her?" Fazeef said.

"I haven't ever felt anything like this. But all projected outcomes are negative."

"Have you had sex with her?" he asked, already knowing the answer.

"Of course. How long did you think I would wait?" Torrance said.

"I didn't expect you to wait. It's only that it intensifies the connection."

"My rational mind can't overcome these feelings and has failed to adapt to them. I feel trapped by them."

"Commander, the heart is the strongest part of the body. Don't resist it."

"Fazeef, it's infinitely more complicated than following my heart."

"I'm not so versed in love, but I know you will find the most fitting resolution."

They sat in silence. The tree swayed. Dappled patterns of sunlight danced over their uniforms.

Torrance closed her eyes and listened to the very specific sound of wind blowing through pine needles. She wanted to remember this sound forever. She touched her temple and recorded it.

The tree continued to be moved by the invisible wind. Fazeef touched his temple to capture the landscape below. He rubbed the back of his head against the tree trunk, which caught his hair and caused tiny pinpricks of pain. He put his hand on the back of his head to provide some cushion. He checked on Torrance. He expected they would be here for a while.

Torrance dropped a piece of bark onto Fazeef's head. He looked up at her and smiled. "Are you ready to climb down?"

Ten meters from the ground, Fazeef lost his footing and did not catch the branch with his hands either. He plunged swiftly. His body rebounded helplessly against the next three branches. He heard a wet snapping sound as his ribs broke on the second impact. His arms spun like windmills trying to catch hold of something, but this only left his hands and wrists vulnerable to being smashed against the third branch. He was able to catch himself by hooking his forearm over the next branch. His right arm from shoulder to wrist was torn and bloody — a thousand shallow scrapes filled with reddish specs of bark. He swung his leg up onto the branch, his stomach flat against it. He clung as if his life depended on it, so thankful to have stopped, relieved and surprised to be alive, then he realized that there was no farther to fall, that he was on the branch closest to the ground. Damn, for several moments he had thought he was going to die. The free fall seemed impossible to stop and his only thought was a hope that he would still be alive when he hit the ground, and they would be able to fix him. He laughed to himself. It was difficult to breathe around the stabbing pain in his left lung. *Stupid and careless to miss that step.* He would review the vids later to see what had gone wrong.

He didn't need to look at himself to know how battered he was. His legs pulsed with pain from hips to ankles. He held on with both hands, let his weight, feet-first, slide off the branch in a very controlled motion. The downward momentum caused his body to swing back and forth until he was hanging still, then he dropped gracefully to the ground. He straightened to his full height, unzipped his uniform and cautiously peeled off what was left of his sleeve over his wounded arm. He winced as he bent forward to push the uniform farther down past his knees, then pulled his feet free of it. With his uniform off, it was plain to see that the color of his legs didn't match the darker chestnut brown of the rest of his body. A lighter shade of brown flesh, which conducted feeling through advanced synthetic skin, hung in thick shreds, peeled down from his right hip to knee, exposing a metal skeleton. His upper body was a wonderful display of majestic pectorals that swelled outward creating a deep shadow beneath that capped eight distinct abdominal muscles separated by an inch-deep valley.

Nix had been waiting at the bottom of the tree with the others. She made an inventory of his musculature, said each muscle name in her mind as her eyes moved from one to the next. She had seen less than a handful of men in her lifetime with such a god-like physique. Masculine in every way. Not sexually exciting to her, but artistically attractive.

Fazeef surveyed his body, made note of the damage, touched each wound, then looked up into the tree at Torrance, who was sitting on the branch he had miscalculated and fallen from. "You coming down or do I have to come back up there?" he said, laughed a bit, but winced and grabbed his side.

"I think I got all that on cam," Torrance said. She slapped the tree trunk beside her. "I thought you were dead for sure."

"Part of me is, I fear." Fazeef reached down between his legs where his uniform pant leg had been ripped away during the fall and examined his injured penis, which hung to one side, semi-hard and bloody. He pushed it up with his hand, held it for a second. He let it drop and looked at Gantu, who made an exaggerated frown. The veins in his neck and on one side of his forehead bulged as he clenched his teeth and tried to contain his erupting anger. With a bit of a growl he said, "UH! Do you know how difficult it will be to fix this thing?"

"We aren't exactly a breeding pair," Gantu said to Nix. She crossed her arms over her chest. "My eggs were harvested early, then I chose endometrial ablution — no bleeding ever after."

"Sterile?" Nix asked.

"Most definitely." Gantu nodded her head four times as she watched Fazeef continue with his personal inspection.

Gantu continued to stare at her brother, not noticing the way that Nix studied her. "Not many of us carry children anymore. It all happens outside our bodies. Raising children is the responsibility of the entire community, though children tend to bond to an adult who spends more time with them, and they refer to those special adults as their parents. But the children live in their own quarters, separate from the adults. They learn to rely on each other. They have a great amount of freedom to explore and be independent, producing a strong culture of risk-taking and innovation. As demonstrated here." She pointed at the tree. "But sometimes, as evidenced by Fazeef's metallic..." She rolled her hand in his direction without specifying anything else, "You can also see ours is a culture of consequences."

Fazeef chimed in, "Loading dock accident as a child, trapped between a steel pallet and a concrete wall while playing alien-fighter with friends." He winked when he said this, but there was no delight behind the gesture. After a few moments he added, "I'm not a machine. I'm fully human, just mechanically enhanced."

The entire crew waited at the base of the tree for Torrance to finish her descent. Jansee looked concerned, Derthan worried, and Nix smiled up at Torrance.

Torrance was crouched on the lowest branch, and leapt to the ground with the grace of a panther. There was a thud of her weight and a rustling of her uniform as she landed on her feet. Her flattened palms touched the ground briefly as the shock was fully absorbed by her legs, then she stood and straightened her uniform. She looked at her bloodied wrists and sighed.

29, THE FIX

Before the sun rose, Nix was at work in the clay studio. She bent and turned her arms like a ballerina, like loops of smoke, coiling around the quartz, nicking off pieces until she had the rough shape.

She went outside to get some fresh air, stretched as she walked to the house to make herself tea. Within the hour, she was refocused and refining the part with a variety of rasps, measuring with Jansee's calipers after every pass. Then she sanded vigorously, leveling rough spots. She tested with her fingertips, and also with the calipers, arriving at the specified exterior dimensions by noon.

She enjoyed a solitary lunch sitting in the open space. She looked for the visitors, but they were seldom seen from dawn until dinnertime. Since the final phase of sanding had begun on her sculpture, the visitors had removed every obstacle from her daily life — prep, cooking, cleaning, hunting, tending the garden, caring for the animals, even laundry — so that she could focus on her art, and now their replacement part.

She kept her eyes on her sculpture — luminous, white, the new dominance in the open space. *God, it's beautiful.* She flexed her toes while she chewed cold, leftover rabbit, then pushed a few grapes into her mouth. *I wish my Torrance could have been here to see this.* She remembered Torrance's face on the vids, and her mind started spinning daydreams. She lay back on the grass, let her eyes unfocus and fill with the blue of the sky, the earth beneath her back a singular, reassuring comfort.

After lunch, Nix began the tedious task of removing sand-grain sized pieces of quartz from the center of the part with dental instruments — pencil-thin tools with tips as fine as needles. This meticulous work was necessary to prevent cracks from forming and compromising the outer shell. She thought through every move she made. This was not her normal way of working, nothing was free and flowing, it was contemplated, validated, then executed. This was not art, it was craft at its highest level, and it was difficult, uninteresting, and required a level of concentration that zapped her strength so that she arrived at dinner grumpy and uncommunicative. But once she ate the tasty food that the visitors had become so good at preparing, she felt re-energized and returned to the clay studio for a couple more hours of work.

*   *   *

Fazeef waited until the ship was quiet, until the rest of the crew was sleeping. He had been up late fixing himself. He had brought tools and materials to repair any damages he might sustain during the expedition, but every time he touched his shredded skin or looked at it, dark memories, which he had thought were long forgotten, stirred. He could walk and run, his penis still functioned, but every hour that he was not fixed meant he had to deal with the loose skin's abnormal bulges in his uniform; he felt more like a monster than a man, at odds with every living thing around him, aware that if he was truly from this planet he wouldn't have survived his childhood accident, or the tree fall. He changed his washing routine to protect the delicate, exposed circuits near his hip and knee, but ultimately his skin was cosmetic, so it would be the last thing he repaired. He had completed the last of the major fixes to the large pistons and joints, and was near optimal operating efficiency; now it was a matter of minor tweaks before superheating his skin and sealing in his metal bones.

He went for a walk in the open space to test the changes he had made, and to see the night sky. If he was having difficulty of any kind, the sky soothed him. At home, he would walk down the long glass hallways, glancing up at the stars until he found a quiet place to sit on the floor and look skyward — the immensity of the black sky and shimmering stars reminded him of his smallness, of the insignificance of his problems, but also his limitless potential; one person could change their people, a planet, a universe.

He looked up, saw a spattering of white and blue stars, smiled to himself. He tried a slow jog, but his ankle only flexed half as far as it should. He stopped and bent forward, inserted a slender hex tool into the skin of his ankle joint and turned it a half turn. He tried to jog again. His foot flexed farther up, but needed another half-turn. He walked over the damp grass, watched the action of his foot as he made deliberate steps of different kinds — toes first, heel then roll forward, jogging in place — as he tried to find the exact location of the catch. His walking brought him close to the clay studio, its windows illuminated by yellow light, and he felt compelled to visit. He stood at the door, lifted his foot and pointed his toes down, noted stickiness in the plantar flexion of his ankle. He raised his toes up again, wondered if he should disturb Nix or turn around and head back to the ship to get the tool he needed. Two of the three times that he flexed his ankle it did not stick, he took this as a sign and knocked on the door.

A shout of "It's open!" came from inside. He walked in and tried not to think about the act of walking. He sat down on a stool just outside the circle of light that Nix was working in. He didn't want to disturb her, he wanted to watch the master work.

Nix didn't acknowledge him, she squinted at the piece of stone that she had fabricated into the replacement part — a hollow cylinder with flared ends that narrowed in the middle like an hourglass. She was using sandpaper so fine that it required several passes over the part to produce any visible dust.

On the table beside her were no less than 20 clay models of the part. All virtually the same dimensions. Fazeef could see no difference between them, no flaws or the slightest size variance, even when scanned by his Lifestream. "Twenty seems excessive," he said, picking one up to examine it.

"Oh, it does? What data are you basing 'excessive' on?" she asked.

"Ha ha. You become more like us as time goes by. You're right. I have no basis for such a statement," he said. "I apologize."

"No need to apologize. None of you know much about my process. There is more to it than walking up to a stone and *freeing* the thing inside." She rolled her eyes and waved her hands in the air as she said this last bit.

"Well, freeing something from the stone sounds romantic. Mystical, really. Oh, this was said by Michelangelo," Fazeef said, his eyes stared straight ahead as he read from his retina screen.

"Artists have been haunted by that saying since it passed his lips," Nix said.

"If you don't free things from the stone, how do you approach it?" Fazeef asked.

"Everything starts with clay. Sketches sometimes, but always miniatures before a single hammer blow," Nix said.

"*These* are not miniatures. Are they a form of pre-work? Prototypes? Why have you started over so many times? I didn't see so many copies of other pieces when we visited the other building — I only saw one of each thing," Fazeef said.

"This is a special project, my usual process won't get it done. But tell me about you. We've had few opportunities to talk since you've been here. I'll keep working if you don't mind," Nix said.

"I'll start with the accident. It happened when I was 13. Everything profoundly shifted. I didn't want it to define my hopes and dreams, but I experimented on myself a lot. I wanted to have my legs back so badly. I studied robotics all the way through to my post-doctorate. Please, no jokes about Dr. Roboto."

Nix allowed a small chuckle, but contained the rest so that her torso didn't make any movements that could travel through her arms and hands into the tools.

He flexed his foot, "There are a lot of industrial accidents on the new planet. We rely on machines for almost everything, and with a culture that was bred for pushing limits, many people have benefited from my research."

"Your walk looks very natural. I wasn't aware of your circumstances until the tree accident. Have you recovered your normal state since the fall?" She had noticed a slight limp when he walked in. "Tell me how they work."

He pulled his leg up and rested it on top of his other thigh. "Yes, the movements are fluid. For everyday activities, like walking and sitting, you'd never know that my legs are robotic." He held onto his shin with both hands. "My muscles and tendons have been replaced by springs and compressors. Near my trunk, those substitutes are hardwired directly to my nerves. Hips, knees, and ankles are controlled by microprocessors that communicate with each other to coordinate balance, speed, and movement. There are micro-gyroscopes on every joint. A tri-axis accelerometer tracks speed and vibration. Motion is converted into an electrical signal that is fed into the microprocessors, which then fire motors of various sizes, and…I walk, run, even climb."

"And sex?" Nix asked.

"I'm hydraulically performant, but nonreproductive." He looked down at the bulge in his lap.

He's a eunuch. Who on the crew knows this?

He asked, "Why can't we only experience love in our minds, through our eyes? That is enough for me — the hope, the elation that love generates."

"The high of just looking at someone?" Nix asked, knowing the feeling so well over the course of her life.

"Yes, exactly. This type of love is no different than physically expressed love."

"Are there others on your planet who share this philosophy?" Nix asked.

"Dismally few, I'm afraid." He absently shook his foot back and forth.

"Fazeef, touching, and I don't mean sex per se, any touching — a caress of the face, a kiss, someone's skin pressing against yours — makes it different, takes it to another level that the mind is rarely satisfied with."

"That other people are rarely satisfied with." He adjusted his skin where it had clumped at the bend of his knee. "I saw how the commander changed when you started sleeping together, something resolved. Then while we were sitting in the tree, she talked of an unbearable pain from being in love with you. Sex complicates things. I know Zephyr left and stayed away for many weeks, we assume because of Torrance, but none of us knows for sure. Why can't it work for you to love both of them?"

"Zephyr and I are not of your planet. We can't love two people at the same time. *But I do.* Some people from every generation continue to try, but I've never heard of it working. Our culture, from the time we are very young, pressures us to find and pair with 'the one.' We move through various levels of serious relationships, trying to find this person. Then people stay together when they no longer bring each other happiness because they believe that there is no other 'one' out there, and if there is, they are admitting that they chose wrong in the first place. It leaves hurt feelings all the way around," Nix said.

"Hmm. I see. A primitive archetypal belief, enforced by societal norms, with failure to comply resulting in pain. Very powerful."

Nix sighed. "It fails far more often than it works." She moved her head so that the full power of the overhead lamps brightened the piece.

He stood up. "After the celebration of phase one, I woke before dawn and watched from a darkened window in the ship. I scanned the area until I was sure everyone was asleep, then I walked through the open space. Why is it that I did not see one man among the guests?"

Nix kept sanding. "Alright, it's getting late. I need to focus on this part, so you should head back to the ship and take care of that foot."

"Nix…" He wanted to push, but knew he would have time to bring it up again before they left. "You're right. I'll see you tomorrow at dinner." He quietly closed the door on his way out.

*   *   *

Jansee continued to come to the clay studio every day and work on her clay pieces. Though she hoped for more instruction from Nix, with the fabrication under way she knew it was unlikely. And Nix was way beyond the point of needing anything from her, since she had already answered all questions about the schematic and handed over her calipers.

The crew paid careful attention to Nix's progress through Jansee's feed. They could see that Nix was nearing the final stage. She was "licking" the fabricated part with the finest sandpaper she could make. This was the only one of her works that would return to their planet. They knew people would ask about how it was made, and by whom. They needed to be able to answer those questions, so they gathered in the clay studio, and respectfully sat or stood in silence at the boundary of her work area.

Torrance was the last to arrive at the studio. The tree climb had been cathartic on many levels — she felt purified from the physical effort, grounded by her communion with the tree, alive in a way she hadn't been before — and she had her feelings for Nix under control. But when she saw Nix her heart stopped, then rebounded with a punching thump against her breastbone. A feeling of happiness flooded into every limb, and tugged the corners of her mouth up and out, exposing her teeth. She tried to extinguish it, though she didn't know why. Everyone knew what was going on between them.

One stroke of the sandpaper, and Nix measured. Two swipes, then she measured again. She didn't notice the coming and going of the visitors, her focus was as sharp as chipped glass. At this scale she could see nearly the entirety of the part at all times. She loomed over the comparatively tiny piece of stone like an immense god over a pebble-sized planet whose creation, she alone, was responsible for.

The crew talked softly among themselves.

"She's doing it."

"One slip and it could all be for nothing."

"She's going to come through for us."

"As I predicted."

They made vids of Nix, each of them posing close to her for future proof that they would share with their progeny. But Nix didn't give them a second of her time, and after a few hours everyone went to the house to prepare dinner, leaving Torrance and Nix alone.

Torrance sat on the bench nearest to Nix, watched her work, watched the movement of her hands, her eyes, watched her breathe. Sometimes she typed on the keyboard in her forearm, or leaned forward to watch Nix with passionate interest, touching her temple to make a vid when the light was good.

It was the end of a long week of picking and sanding, and Nix's arm was about finished. She turned to Torrance. "What the hell are you smiling about? This is a serious situation."

Torrance shook her head, and when she stopped her face was expressionless. She sniffed one quick breath and sat straighter, as if readying for inspection. "Is that better?"

Nix looked into Torrance's eyes, wrapped sandpaper around her four fingers and inserted them into the concave center of the piece, applied even pressure as she traced the curves of the interior surface. Torrance smiled again, a dirty smirk that told Nix everything she needed to know. She placed the part onto a small piece of deer hide, and folded the edges over it. She set the sandpaper, light as a feather, on top. She turned and put her dusty hands on both sides of Torrance's face and kissed her. A slow, deep kiss.

Torrance melted. *Is this my kiss goodbye?*

"There's more," Nix said, as if reading Torrance's mind. She went to the sink and washed her hands, then locked the studio door and turned out the lights. Nix took Torrance's hand and led her through the darkness to the marble slab fitted into the corner, lifted her and set her on the cool, slick surface. "Remember this corner?" Nix said in a voice lowered by days of fine dust.

"How could I forget?" Torrance wrapped her legs around Nix and pulled her close.

*   *   *

Near sunset, as the crew was wrapping up dinner preparation, Torrance called an emergency meeting in the woods behind the ship. "Comms off for max temporal limit."

The crew did as ordered.

All of them, except Torrance, closed their eyes for a few seconds to adjust to the sudden disconnect from Lifestream.

Derthan was the first to open her eyes. She scanned the woods around them, feeling frighteningly diminished without her Lifestream-enhanced vision and data access. There was no movement in any direction. She twirled a knife, which she had fashioned out of deer antler and a repurposed digging probe, in her hand, always catching the handle. When the others opened their eyes, Derthan stabbed the knife into the tree stump that the crew had circled around.

Torrance said, "I'm fully confident that Nix is about to deliver the replacement part to spec. The reason I've called this meeting is to ask one question. Would you choose to stay on Earth if you could?"

Gantu had folded herself into a cross-legged position on the forest floor. Her eyes were still closed. She inhaled very deeply, then exhaled, three times in a row. When she opened her eyes, the sun's rays lined her upper and lower lids in glowing orange. "I'm sure all of you have thought about it. But if we stay here, then I will be the last of my kind, extinct after only one generation." She swept her elegant hand across her body to include herself, Fazeef, and Torrance. "Earth doesn't have the technology to propagate any of us, and even if we could let go of that, what contributions could we make to this place and these people?"

Jansee said, "We belong here. Our bodies, our genes, are built for this planet. Think about something as simple as breathing, the varieties of moisture and temperature of the air. You don't think about it, you just breathe. We've adapted. Think about the hours we've all spent outside — in the sun, under the stars, in the rain. You know the feelings — relaxed and pleasurable like nothing you've ever felt before — to the point that you could just melt, letting the animals and bugs and elements take you back into the earth. Is there anyone who doesn't acknowledge that?"

Derthan moved closer to her knife. "Beautiful scenery is only beautiful if you have food and fuel," she said. "Any thoughts you've had about staying here have all been predicated on the fact that you *could* leave. We don't know if that part will even work. It could overheat, it could short-out the entire ship and we'll all be stuck here. The question should be who is willing to do whatever it takes to get home."

Torrance said, "All of you are ordered to think about whether you would choose to stay. You have tonight to make your decision. We'll meet back here tomorrow night after Nix has announced that the piece is finished. And you'll each announce your decision. OK, comms back on."

As soon as they were back online, a message scrolled on their Lifestream screens, a woman's voice, not the ship's voice, more passionate, said into their ears, "Azalea 549, the time limit of 18 months sanctioned for your mission is about to expire. You have 168 hours to reach an off-planet transmission point and notify us of your return or status. If no transmission is received, dispatch of a retrieval ship will commence." The message was clear and concise, but something no one expected.

Torrance turned her back to everyone. She curled her hand into a fist and rested it against her pursed lips. *My time with Nix is up.*

Derthan pulled on Torrance's shoulder to turn her around to face the group.

Torrance turned after some resistance, then covered Derthan's knife with her hand to keep it out of play.

The message faded, but after a few seconds of silence, repeated. This time, the voice was accompanied by flashing red text. "Azalea 549, the time limit of 18 months sanctioned for your mission is about to expire. You have 168 hours to

288 | MADELEINE LYCKA

reach an off-planet transmission point and notify us of your return or status. If no transmission is received, dispatch of a retrieval ship will commence."

Torrance silently gave the hand signal for "Comms off."

Everyone complied.

Torrance said, "Did any of you know we were so close to the cut-off?"

Derthan shrugged, the others shook their heads to indicate no.

Torrance coiled her arm back, wanting to hit something. She forced herself to stand down. But with the action of resisting her urge, she had used up all of her control, and as she spoke, rage turned her words into shouts. "How did I not get this piece of information sooner? No one thought to tell me?" But she was angriest at herself. She should have been on top of it, she should have been the one to notice.

Derthan said, "Commander, we thought you knew. You ordered us to run the maintenance test suite last week. We assumed that was done in preparation for departure."

Torrance pulled Derthan's knife from the stump and threw it at a far off tree, embedding the blade an inch deep into the bark, then she started to pace.

"Torrance. Please calm yourself," Gantu said, which elicited a snap of Torrance's head in her direction, the bridge of her nose wrinkled like a snarling lion.

"Do you realize the gravity of this situation?" Torrance shouted to no one in particular.

Jansee calmly said, "If the part is ready, we'll have no problem making the deadline."

"I love your optimism," Torrance said. "But the consequences if it doesn't…" Torrance put her hands on her hips and stood very still. She looked from face to face, "I was going to ask each of you to tell me now, to decide now if you're going stay on Earth, but we'll delay that decision until we hear from Nix, and have tested the part. OK, comms on."

Torrance looked up toward the sky. She took a deep breath and pulled her shoulders back. "Gantu, I want a full inventory of all specimens. Is there anything we haven't collected, are the specimens are still viable, the quantities ample? Jansee, the sculptures — scan all of them immediately, and prepare to run full analysis on the part once it's complete. Fazeef, you're responsible for evaluating the scans and deciding whether they're satisfactory for any future printing, reproduction, and archiving. When you're done with that, assist Gantu. Derthan, set up perimeter scans with alerts to run every hour over a 50 kilometer radius, I don't want anyone or anything surprising us." Torrance turned and started to jog toward the house. When she saw the movement of the crew on her retina screen, she ran faster, and they sprinted through the woods like a pack of wolves. There was suddenly so much to do and so little time, but first they needed to have dinner.

30, IGNITION POINT

Over dinner, when the crew expected the big announcement that the part was finally done, their glasses full of golden wine, ready to toast, Nix said, "Creating the part for your ship has been draining…I can't tell you how hard…how with every touch of a tool, with every swipe of the sandpaper…as I try to achieve your insane hair-width specifications…the implications of failure…and I know how important this is to you guys, but…" She sat back from the table, leaving her plate half full. She pushed her hand through her hair and sighed. "I'll be working on my sculpture for the next few days. I'm taking a break, effective immediately."

Gasps, head-shaking, eye-rolling from the crew. Torrance lifted her glass to her lips, closed her eyes as she drank slowly, hoped that no one would mention the seven-day countdown that had started an hour ago.

Derthan stood up, pushed her chair back, extended her arms and hands toward Nix. "Nix, you're so close to finishing. It can't be more than a few more hours of work. Push yourself a little for our sake."

Torrance gave Derthan a warning look, subtle, but noted. Derthan sat down, bit the inside of her cheek.

Torrance sent a message to the crew's retina screens, "Pushing Nix and having her make a mistake isn't worth it."

Fazeef said, "No, let it rest. Come back to it when you're ready." His chest swelled as he inhaled, inflating his smile. He pushed his chair back so that he had space to cross his legs, then sat back like he had all the time in the world.

Jansee said, "If you want to work on your own piece, of course we understand. We'll wait."

Gantu looked at Nix and nodded.

"Thank you for understanding," Nix said, she felt her shoulders lighten, the burden lifted temporarily. "Having you here has been one of the best times of my life. Everything you've done for me, all the respect and kindness..." Nix sniffled, tears were close, she was teetering on the edge of a deeply sad canyon, so she inhaled and stood up from the table, giving herself a moment to recover. "I'm going to bed. I wish things were different, and I could invite all of you to join me, but..." And she laughed at having even said it, "I need some actual sleep tonight." Nix winked at Torrance, then turned and left the table.

The crew left the house after they'd cleaned up, leaving Nix to rest. They had spent a good part of the day gathering firewood from around the open space, and preparing the main pit for a celebratory fire. Torrance stopped at the pit, studied the wooden pyramid, bluish-silver in the moonlight with velvety black interior shadows. "Let's light it anyway," she said. The others nodded, and Torrance leaned forward and ignited the base of the kindling, which rapidly swelled with bright yellow-orange flames, illuminating the inside.

"Did you put accelerant on it?" Fazeef asked.

"No. Nothing in there besides what we gathered," Torrance said.

"It's very dry," Jansee said.

"Beyond," Derthan said.

They watched the flames grow and rise, entwine the wood like ravenous orange-blue snakes.

"Something really shifted this evening," Jansee said. "Time is flying past at a maddening rate."

Derthan said, "More like time has started to drag unbearably." She threw a stone into the fire. "Tonight's dinner took forever, and I don't know what Nix was trying to explain to us. How can one type of carving be draining and another not be?"

"You've obviously learned nothing here," Gantu said. She held her hands out to warm them on the fire.

"Regardless, I'm hoping we'll be on our way home very soon," Derthan said, chucking a second stone into the fire.

"When Nix finishes the part, I'll need three hours to test it," Jansee said. She sat down on the coarse grass, put her arms out straight behind her to lean on.

Gantu sat beside her, rested her head on Jansee's shoulder. Jansee reached up and stroked Gantu's hair, which had not been cut in since their arrival and was so long that it coiled on the ground behind her and brushed Jansee's other hand.

Torrance squinted and stepped closer to the fire until the heat became uncomfortable against her face. The pyramid's thicker, outer logs were burning at full force. The heat was stealing her breath away. She coughed. *If I stay here I'll die. I will never see my mother again.* Her mouth was dry, tasted of ash. She stared down at the ground, the earth below her a place that felt like home, but wasn't. The intense heat of the fire cupped the top of her head, forced her to step back. "I'll see you all back at the ship." She started walking toward the house. She was going to sleep in Nix's bed tonight, and every night, and to hell with the consequences.

For the next several days, Nix worked on her sculpture (and each night Torrance slept with her). In some ways, she kept working because she wanted to prolong the visitor's stay as much as possible. But she also needed to find herself in her own work before she could complete the part. Finishing the part would seal their fate — return Torrance to her home, and leave Nix with a second, hopefully smaller, hole in her heart.

Nightly dinners were awkward, the entire crew had a nervous energy, or else they would be non-responsive, lost in their thoughts, not sure what to say to one another or Nix; the conversation sputtered. Nix attributed their behavior to realizing that after nearly a year and a half of being around her every day, they would at some point have to say goodbye, and for all their technological advances, their human hearts were just as primitive as hers.

Toward the end of the week, late one afternoon, the sky piled high with pewter clouds, Torrance came across the open space as usual to deliver Nix's lunch. She saw Nix sitting still on the ground as an exhausted cowboy, knees bent as she stared at the ground between her feet. Her hair, face, shoulders, and hands dusted in white. It felt like a memory, but she wasn't sure if it was hers or her mother's. She stopped and stared, touched her temple to activate vid mode, remembering the day they landed, the ghost woman they had seen walking across the open space to the stone, the way she'd touched the stone with her hands, oblivious to the ship a hundred meters away, had made them wonder if she was blind.

Nix absently pushed her hand through her hair, unleashed an ashen trail of dust that settled down her back. She lifted the cup beside her, took a sip, then splashed the water directly into her face. She cleared the water off, from forehead to chin, with one hand, spit to the side, and stared blankly out across the open space, not smiling.

Torrance approached slowly, still in vid mode, and sat down next to her, put her arm over her shoulder, and kissed her cheek. The chalky residue tasted alkaline, mineral, induced memories of the night on the marble slab in the corner of the clay studio. She smiled. "How's it coming?"

"The last little bit can be the hardest. I'm struggling to be patient and not push too hard, and also not to give up too quickly and call it 'done' until it is." She rubbed both eyes with one hand, then pushed her hair back. "Rain is coming. Seeing the piece wet is the last test. The water will tell me how it might age, where I've left a vulnerable low spot where a torrent of water can wear it down slowly over time, smooth it, erode it, eventually break it." Nix turned and looked into Torrance's eyes, raised her eyebrows. "A clever sculptor takes the flow of water into account, especially with faces, because eventually, with air pollution and time, those water pathways become dark lines. And, as you've seen with your own eyes, no one on *this* sculpture is crying. The only lines I'll allow are mud on the boots, or to deepen the cleavage." Nix smiled and kissed Torrance. An easy kiss, without a single thought about who might be watching.

*   *   *

After a day of rain had come and gone, Nix returned to the clay studio and unwrapped the deerskin to examine the fabricated part. She ran her hands over every surface, then a second time with her eyes closed, which confirmed that there were no more changes to be made. With a damp cloth she carefully cleaned the fine layer of dust from the deerskin and the part. She rummaged through the tool drawers until she found her leather tools, then punched holes into each corner of the deerskin, and tooled a filigree design onto each corner. From the far wall she retrieved the hawk feather that she had found the previous year while delivering the party invitations to her neighbors. The feather was extra long, half striped in black. She stroked it, and the separated segments instantly resealed. "Ready to fly," she said to the feather. She set the part onto the deerskin, creased each fold before gathering the corners, and gently threaded the quill of the hawk feather through the holes.

Nix sat down on one of the stone stools and stared at the part, admired the teardrop-shaped shadows between the folds of the buckskin-colored leather, the rich auburn-brown of the hawk's feather. It was a beautiful gift. She rested her elbows on the tops of her thighs, hung her head down. She wanted to be happy, proud, but tears fell. She said out loud, so that her voice might offer some comfort as the voice of a friend might, "Hard part is over, just hand it to her." She struggled to breathe through her dripping nose, "You're an old fool. Don't do it." Then Nix heard the clack of the door latch and sat up. She wiped the wetness from her eyes and nose with her sleeve.

Torrance looked for Nix at the sculpture first, then found her in the clay studio. She sat on a stone stool next to Nix, and put a large plate piled with a variety of one-bite items — cherry tomatoes, olives, cheese, venison salami, smoked fish — onto the table between them. Torrance held out a slice of apple for Nix, who took it delicately with her mouth. Nix chewed while she reached down for a cube of goat cheese without taking her eyes from Torrance's. She held the soft square in front of Torrance's lips, but her bite was hard and fast, a little reckless, she nipped the end of Nix's finger.

Nix pulled her hand back to see if she had drawn blood. She laughed. "Easy tiger."

"Tigers are best kept in bed," Torrance said. "You have time?"

"Not right now." She leaned to kiss Torrance's cheek. "Finish lunch with me, then I need you to call the crew to come meet us here." Her eyes flashed for a moment toward the deerskin.

Torrance noticed, but didn't look in that direction until Nix looked down at the plate for her next bite.

"I'll make it up to you tonight," Nix said. She held a red grape in front of Torrance's lips.

Torrance leaned forward slowly, closed her substantial lips over the grape and the finger and thumb that held it, bathed them in warm wet tongue.

The concentrated, suggestive sensation made Nix want to pull away, it was too much, too intense, too good.

Instead she closed her eyes, held her breath while pleasure washed through her body, a moan resonated as she exhaled.

Nix's tongue traced her upper lip. She shook head and smiled. "You're very persuasive."

Torrance put palm against Nix's breastbone, then slid her hand down, clutched her breast, then curled her fingers upward until she felt her nipple, passed over it twice more until it was deadly sharp. "I can't change your mind?"

Nix reached up and pressed Torrance's hand into her breast, held it still. "Best lunch I've had in years." She lifted Torrance's hand and kissed it, then gave her a nod, indicating it was time to summon the crew.

When the crew had gathered in the clay studio, Nix stood and said, "Thank you all for your patience. I hope this will deliver you safely home." She bowed her head slightly, held the part in both hands, and offered it to Jansee.

Jansee stood quickly from her stone stool and mimicked whatever custom Nix was performing by accepting the part with both hands and bowing her head slightly. She sat down and set the part onto the small round table in the center of the gathering. She stared at it for a long while, taking in the ornamented presentation. She felt the etched corners, savored the detailed texture with her fingertips before carefully removing the feather and unwrapping the leather to reveal a white and gold major transducer that looked more like a piece of fine jewelry.

Everyone huffed and whispered words that Nix could not understand. While they sat forward to admire the part, Jansee opened a case on the floor beside her, which she had brought in anticipation of this event. She tested the part with calipers, then scanned it with a red laser that projected from the pupil of her eye. On her retina screen the laser image overlaid the schematic, and two columns of data flowed as the comparison analysis ran. "The new part is 99.999 percent accurate to spec." She sat back, stunned by Nix's accuracy, as accurate as any machined part. Her hands trembled. She took several deep breaths, steadied her hands before she picked up the part. She set the part into the case and it submerged into a yellow gel, appeared suspended. She closed and secured the lid, then turned to Nix and started clapping. The crew joined her, filled the room with staccato applause, then they all stood up and gathered around Nix, covered her in layers of arms as they all hugged her, kissed her face and head, and said their thanks. The crush of their young bodies left her excited, and regretful that she hadn't invited them all into her bed at once.

When they settled back onto their seats, Nix uncorked a large bottle of wine. "I've been saving this for something special. And this promising young artist..." she extended her hand holding the cork toward Jansee and smiled, "I'm really proud of what she's created. So it's my pleasure to invite you to explore the work of Jansee Yim, which is displayed on the far tables."

They all stood up, wine glasses in hand, and moved to the other side of the room. The tables, once dusty and worn, were now restored and varnished, overhead lighting accentuated the pieces, and the walls around the tables had been recently painted white. The work was laid out chronologically, her growth evident as each clay piece became more detailed and ideally proportioned, but the crew was most astonished to see pieces carved in marble at the farthest table. Gantu bent close, rubbed her fingertips over one of the marble pieces, then caressed the rounded shape with the palm of her hand, trying to deduce what it was, something abstract, the perfect sloped curve of a breast, a ripe piece of fruit, but there was no cleave as would be found on a peach, and no nipple, but it suggested both. Fazeef applauded, and was joined by howls from Nix, Torrance, and Derthan.

In the rarified moment, Jansee was higher than she'd ever been — filled with soaring hope from Nix's accomplishment, with Nix's praise layered upon that, and crowned by this admiration from her crew. She smiled broadly, displaying her deep dimples. Her habit, when complimented, was to look down, be humble, but this time she looked at each of their faces, wanting to remember the moment for the rest of her life.

The air in the small space was humid and tart from talking and drinking. Nix left to get more wine. She opened the cellar door, ducked her head and shoulders in to grab another bottle of wine, but stopped for a moment to savor the damp stone-scented air of the bedrock walls, freshly wetted from seeping rainwater. Ah, she loved that smell. She smiled. There was so much to be happy about. With the replacement part out of the way, knowing she had done everything she could do to help the visitors, she could finish her own piece with a clear mind, a satisfied heart. And, it was very possible that by this time tomorrow, she could pronounce her sculpture done.

As she walked back to the clay studio, she noted how unusually dry the air was after having rained just two days ago. Far off on the horizon, there was a gray line of smoke like a stray hair hanging from the head of a bent-over giant. She remembered thunder last night, though she had mostly slept through it wrapped in Torrance's arms. Who knew how many lightning strikes there might have been? She couldn't worry about it now. It was miles and miles away.

They spent the rest of the day drinking and talking, fell into telling stories from the early days of their arrival. They touched so easily — held hands, put arms over shoulders, kissed each other's faces. Nix mostly listened, content to be an observer. She studied them in preparation to say goodbye. Already, they looked so different from the people on the sculpture in the open space. *How can I go back to living a secluded life again?* But before Nix could get any deeper into her thoughts, Jansee came and sat on her lap, kissed her cheek, and whispered into her ear, "Come to the ship and have sex with me."

"Channel that energy into your art," Nix winked, then reached under and patted the cheek of her ass.

"Aw, Nix...this is your chance to sleep with the future-famous sculptor of Kepler-442B. Aren't you supposed to seduce your student? I want it." She pushed Nix's hair back and kissed her mouth, slipped her tongue inside until she felt the softness of Nix's tongue.

"I'm flattered, but you'll have to enjoy the company of your companions." Nix started to push her off, but Jansee got the hint and sprang to her feet in a flash. Nix stood up and kissed Jansee on the forehead. "You've got talent, keep pushing yourself." Jansee grabbed Nix's hand, but Nix pulled away, went to a window and looked toward the horizon, but in the darkness she couldn't see the smoke. The moon had shed its golden veil and was ghostly white, already risen hours ago. With a booming voice Nix said, "It appears we've drank right through dinner tonight. I'm hungry, but don't worry about making anything for me. I'll find something in the kitchen. I'll see you all tomorrow."

The crew was disappointed and tried to persuade Nix to stay.

"No, there's plenty of wine here, and a fresh jug of water. Stay and enjoy yourselves. Talk about the art. Nothing would make me happier." As she walked by them, their hands reached for her, held her arms, her shoulders, her hands, only for a second before letting her pass. The needful warmth of their gesture would stay with her always. When she reached the door, she stopped and turned around, went back and took each of their faces in her hands and kissed them on the lips, then turned and left. They applauded her until she was half way to the house.

First thing in the morning, Nix checked the smoke on the horizon. It had not changed in size or proximity. She squinted her eyes, wondering if it really was smoke at all, or maybe some fallen old trees, or a stone avalanche, or some other trick of the eyes.

She gathered her tools and three rolls of sandpaper and went to the sculpture to start her final inspection. Her pace was good, she was full of energy, and her mind was remarkably sharp after so much wine. She started looking from a far distance, then slowly circled, getting closer and closer. She examined, stopped to touch, to sand, to wet a few suspicious spots, and completed five trips around the sculpture by midday.

Torrance brought her lunch, but only quietly set it down by her tools and left. As Nix came around to that side of the rock, she grabbed all the food that wasn't juicy and filled a cloth napkin, stuffed it into her pocket and ate as it was convenient, continuing her inspection.

Throughout the day she had spent a total of 30 minutes sanding, sometimes with as little as one or two passes of her finest sandpaper. It looked perfect, all of it. The changes she made were so minor, she wondered if she was just doing it because she didn't want it to be done, because she wasn't ready to let go of another precious thing so soon. She made several more rounds, without making any changes, until it was too dark to see.

Gantu arrived as the cherry red sun was setting. She gathered up Nix's tools and said, "I'll take care of these. Go clean up. Dinner will be ready just after sunset."

Jansee spent the entire day testing the part. Three hours for testing had been a gross underestimate, because she had based it on test procedures for the standard part. While the installation was only slightly more complicated than normal, she had created an extensive list of edge-case tests that she felt were necessary to run considering the materials used. The extra tests were precautions and very time-consuming, but with the entire launch, crew, and cargo at stake, she wouldn't be satisfied with anything less. She started the tests with the lowest possible voltage, then worked up in increments to an expected launch load. Between each test she rechecked the integrity of the part for cracks, or any other damages, but found none. She gave her acceptance sign-off to the commander and crew only minutes before dinner was served.

The visitors had spent the better part of the day preparing a beautiful feast for Nix. The smiles never left their faces. She couldn't remember them ever being so elated as a group. During dinner they laughed, told stories, but drank only water. The skillfully prepared small proportions were so delicious she had a hard time denying her mouth such pleasures, so she ate until she was past full. When she was done eating, they cleaned up immediately and said good night. She was confused by their rush to leave.

Torrance smiled at her across the table, leaned her head toward the bedroom, where Nix soon found the room lit with tiny flickering LEDs that resembled candle flames. Torrance heard her say "Oh!" when she saw them.

Nix turned to Torrance, "You keep surprising me." Nix quickly started to undress. Torrance did the same, and it became a race. They jumped into bed, pulled the covers over their naked bodies, laughed and quivered from the pure bliss that was surging inside them. Nix gave Torrance a deep, wet kiss, then popped her head out to look at the lights again. Beneath the blanket, Torrance took Nix's nipple with her mouth. Nix laughed and sank her head deeply into the pillow.

When Torrance came out for air, Nix said, "Your candles are beautiful. Why did you wait until now?"

"No reason," Torrance said. She slid close to Nix, until their skin touched down the entire length of their bodies. She moved her hand over the curves of her hips and stomach.

Nix rolled on top of her and kissed her until they were out of breath. She pushed herself up onto her straightened arms and looked down into Torrance's eyes, "I hope you know how much I love you."

"I do."

"And how much I'll miss you."

Torrance reached up and placed her index finger against Nix's lips to silence her. "Not tonight. Tonight is 'Tiger, tiger, burning bright... .' Let's make memories instead."

Nix woke before dawn as usual. She felt a strange anxiety, a pressure on her chest, a thrumming sadness in her bones. She looked for Torrance in the bed beside her, but she was alone. How easily she had become accustomed to having her there. She laid still, rubbed her hand over her breastbone, watched the light gradually intensify by degrees through the curtains, until the tightness in her chest faded.

She showered and dressed, then opened the front door and ate her breakfast standing, her left arm leaning against the doorframe. For a long while she looked at the stone. No, she wouldn't be spending another day refining. It was done. Done. Really done. She would talk to the visitors tonight at dinner about disassembling the scaffolding, and express her plans of how she would be spending her days — mornings riding horses with them into the hills or hunting, middays in the clay studio teaching Jansee (and anyone else who was interested), and evenings cooking for them. It sounded like retirement, but when was another stone like this one going to fall from the sky? She still had ideas, yes, but she would work them out on a smaller scale.

Then Nix saw that the smoke had grown tenfold wider over the past 24 hours. She expected that it would have been extinguished by now. Had no one living nearby noticed or taken the time to put it out? She knew the women who lived in that area. She was suddenly worried that something had happened to them.

Nix ran full speed across the open space to the ship, and banged on the door. "Torrance. Help. I need your help."

For agonizing minutes, Nix waited in silence, stared up at the height of the ship, then down at the ragged grass beneath her feet. She pounded on the door again.

The door slid open and Torrance greeted her. "Come in."

"There's smoke. I can't tell if there are flames. Can you use your instrumentation to get more information on the fire?"

They scrambled up the ladders. "Yes, we've been watching it for two days."

Nix said, "And you're only telling me this now?"

As they came through the final floor and emerged onto the bridge, Nix saw that the crew was all present, dressed in uniform, and standing over various displays, their faces serious.

"It had been completely stable until about two hours ago," Gantu said.

Nix rushed to a window to make the most of the high vantage point. She could see a wide blackened area that the fire had already consumed.

"Nix, I'm about to activate the screens, unless you want to continue using the windows."

"No, show me what you've got," Nix said.

Several views of the fire appeared — infrared heat signatures on a topographical map of the ridge, a zoomed view of white-hot trees at the leading edge of the fire, radar images on the largest screen of a high-pressure system that was crowding out a moisture-carrying low, forcing it to remain out over the ocean.

Nix went from one screen to the next, absorbing the information. "No rain will save us this time," she muttered. She moved back to the infrared images. "Torrance, do you know the growth rate and how fast it's moving in our direction?"

"Yes. Pulling it up now." She moved her fingers through the air and tapped on her forearm. "Several models project it will be here by nightfall. Two other models show a sharp northward shift as the high moves ten degrees north."

Nix exited the ship as quickly as she could. *Too dry. Too dry. Everything will burn.*

Torrance ordered. "All of you, go help her. Whatever she needs with the house and the animals. *Do not* let her stay. Bring her back here by force if necessary."

They used water from the storage tanks to drench the wooden buildings and the roof of her house. They cleared every wood chip and leaf from the already liberal safety zones. Furniture and valuables were moved from the house to underground storage areas in the hillside. The crew was impressed by Nix's ingenuity and the multilayered backup systems she had put in place.

By midafternoon, the crew had done a full day of hard labor, and they were exhausted. With everything as prepared as they could make it, Nix and the crew returned to the ship to watch and wait.

Nix took a window on the bridge. The smoke from the west began to obscure the sun, great orange ribbons of fire reached into the sky like sun flares, fueled by a westerly wind that would put a vengeful, descending dragon to shame.

Torrance handed out food and water pouches to the crew. When she held out two pouches to Nix, Nix shook her head and said, "How can you eat at a time like this?"

Torrance pressed the pouches into her hands until she felt Nix take hold of them.

"We need to replenish. We're unsure what will be required of us next," Fazeef said.

Nix looked at his strong physique, restored to its original shape beneath his uniform. She pierced the water pouch with her teeth and began sucking the water out as she turned back to the window.

"We're safe in here, Nix," Derthan said.

"That's little comfort," Nix replied.

Gantu wrapped her arm around Nix's shoulder.

"The stones have been scanned," Fazeef said.

"To what purpose?" Nix asked, feeling betrayed on some level.

"For historical records, for reproduction, for whatever anyone needs them for," Torrance said.

"The stones can't be destroyed. Fires have come through before, left some spalling, uh…flaking, nothing more than superficial damage. Of course they were black with soot, but they cleaned up well after a week of scrubbing. The house has stone walls, and the roof has survived through a combination of wide safety zones and some luck with sudden rain showers that…" Nix trailed off as she saw a human figure riding a horse through the swirls of smoke in the open space. She was sure it was Zephyr.

Nix flew down the ladders and rails and arrived at the entry door with a jammed thumb. She went through the first red-light chamber with no problem, but after entering the blue-light second chamber, the main entry door did not open. She looked desperately around the room, knowing there was a video monitor somewhere. "Open this door, Torrance. I won't let her be burned alive."

First she heard Torrance's voice say "Nix," then the entire wall beside her displayed Torrance's face. "You'll die if you go out there. The winds are gusting to 40 miles per hour, they could intensify or shift direction at any moment."

"Let me out now!" Nix pounded the door with her fists, kicked it with her feet; it was only metal, surely she could bring it down. She pounded until her arms were spent, and her hands throbbed with a dull pain. She would only get out if they decided to let her out. She leaned her arms and forehead against the door to catch her breath. The door opened and she fell forward onto the grass, landing on her hands and knees. She sprang up and ran across the open space toward Zephyr.

The wind was furious, whipping and bursting in jets. The smoke stung her nose and eyes. She could hear crackling, and saw orange fiery bits surfing in the air around her. She covered her mouth with her hand, squinted her eyes and charged forward. She took hold of the horse's reins and shouted "Fire!" to the rider whose face, pointed down toward her armpit, couldn't be seen.

The crew watched the rider dismount. The rider and Nix worked together to strip the bridle and saddle off the horse, then Nix slapped its rump with the reins, prompting it to run in the opposite direction of the approaching fire.

Black, choking smoke rushed into the open space. Nix grabbed Zephyr's hand, thought to shelter in the wine cellar, were it would be cool, damp, protected by the hillside, but flames had already advanced down the hill and covered the door. She looked back toward the ship, but there was no time to cover that distance. The women ran, hand in hand, toward the house.

The crew watched on the monitors, shouted for them to run.

"Full launch readiness report," Torrance said loudly, to break through the hysteria that was building.

"Major transducer tested and verified. All system checklists are green. End report," Jansee said.

"All crew on board. Barrage jamming radar fully powered and ready for activation. End report," Derthan said.

"Inventories complete, all required and supplemental specimens stowed and secured. End report," Fazeef said.

Gantu stared out the window with her hand over her mouth, unable to speak.

"Pilot and navigator, your report!" Torrance ordered.

"Weather window is compromised. High wind and thermals from the fire could cause extreme and highly risky navigation conditions. Launch not recommended at this time. End report."

Nix and Zephyr entered the house. There was a great series of snapping as the roof's boards shrunk under the approaching heat. Nix activated the sprinkler system. Emergency lights pulsed, as a loud shhhh of water came down. With each step their clothes became soaked and heavier. They plodded into the bathroom, turned on the shower and stood under it. The women held each other close, put their heads on each other's shoulders.

"I don't think we're going to walk away from this, my love," Nix said.

"We're together. That's what matters," Zephyr said.

In the view from the ship, the house disappeared under an orange blanket of horizontal flames that blew over and around.

"What is the probability that this fire might change direction?" Gantu asked.

Fazeef said, "I only found very old wildfire data from the late 21st century, but the parameters are magnitudes smaller than this."

"Current wind speed?" Torrance said.

"West at 80.46 kph. Barometer is falling," Fazeef said.

"Recheck Doppler pressure," Torrance said.

Gantu said, "The high pressure area has shifted 15 degrees to the North in the last three minutes."

"But look out there, it must be too late," Derthan said.

Gantu covered her tear-filled eyes, "Why aren't we helping them?"

"Ignite the ship," Torrance ordered.

"There's a 60 percent chance that our ignition will draw the flames into the output ports and cause a catastrophic explosion," Jansee said.

"On my mark, 3...2...1," Torrance said.

The popping and hissing of contracting wood grew louder. The wind or roar of the fire was as loud as a passing train. The air was getting thinner. Nix felt close to passing out. She ratcheted the shower flow up and the temperature down to its coldest setting. Flames sizzled in the wooden roof above her. To think that she would die like Joan of Arc. She held Zephyr tighter in her arms. "Let's lie down." And they did, the air easier to breathe near the stone floor. They spooned against each other, as Nix tried to protect Zephyr's body with her own. She closed her eyes. Dreadful memories of the mummified Pompeians huddled on the ground against the firestorm of the volcano. Then she began to dream — Torrance was a colossal hawk, her talons plunged through the roof to grab Nix, painfully gripped her ribs, crushed her chest, gouged out her breath, but still she held Zephyr in her arms, as she was lifted up into the cold blue sky.